ε

UNDEAD

This special signed edition is limited to 750 copies.

John Rowe

UNDEAD

UNDEAD

JOHN RUSSO

UNDEAD

JOHN RUSSO

CEMETERY DANCE PUBLICATIONS

Baltimore
❖ 2012 ❖

FIRST EDITION
ISBN: 978-1-58767-255-2
Cemetery Dance Publications Edition 2012

Cemetery Dance Publications
132-B Industry Lane, Unit 7
Forest Hill, MD 21050
Email: info@cemeterydance.com
www.cemeterydance.com

CONTENTS

Introduction:
The Birth of the Dead

In developing the concepts and writing the screenplays and novels for *Night of the Living Dead* and *Return of the Living Dead,* our overriding concern and aim was to give true horror fans the kind of payoff they always hoped for, but seldom got, when they shelled out their hard-earned money at the ticket booth or the bookstore. This was the guiding principle that we were determined not to violate. When I say "we" I am referring to Russ Streiner, George Romero, Rudy Ricci, and others in our group who contributed to the development of the scripts and the movies.

As a teenager, I went to see just about every movie that came to my hometown of Clairton, Pennsylvania. It was a booming iron-and-coke town in those days. There were three movie theaters, and the movies changed twice a week. Often there were double features—and the price of admission was only fifty cents! I loved the *Dracula, Frankenstein,* and *Wolf Man* movies—enduring classics, sophisticated and literate explorations of supernatural horror and dread.

But I also went to see dozens of "B" horror films, always hoping, against the odds, that one of them would turn out to be surprisingly good. This almost never happened. The plots were trite, formulaic, uninspiring. Decidedly unscary.

In the fifties, because of the vaporization of Hiroshima and Nagasaki during World War II, everyone was scared of nuclear bombs and nuclear energy—especially nuclear energy gone awry. This pervasive psychology of fear was ripe for exploitation, and it gave rise to the "mutant monster" genre of horror films. We were treated to *The Attack of the Giant Grasshopper, The Attack of the Giant Ant...the Giant Squid...the Giant Caterpillar...*and so on.

Did I say that the "plots" were trite? I should've said "plot" (singular) because the same plot was used over and over with each of the different mutated creatures. The giant whatever would be hinted at, but not shown in its entirety, somewhere within the first twenty or so very dull minutes. The audience at first would be teased with just a fleeting glimpse of some aspect of the monster. Then a bigger piece of it would appear to the town drunk, who was never believed by the authorities. He would usually be killed or devoured—but in such a way that nobody important ever got wise. Eventually the male and female "B" actors in the lead roles would start to catch on, but at first nobody would believe them, either. Then, during the last twenty minutes or so of the movie, our hero, who was conveniently a scientist, would figure out that the giant whatever's saliva was identical to the saliva of a commonplace caterpillar or ant or octopus or grasshopper or whatever other kind of giant mutant that had to be dealt with—and this would culminate in a "grand finale" with National Guard troops arriving in the nick of time to destroy the horrible creature with flamethrowers and grenades.

Well, we didn't want our first movie to be like that. As I said, we really wanted moviegoers to get their money's worth.

In order to do this, we had to be true to both our concept and to reality. Granted, we were working with the outlandish premise that dead people could come back to life and attack the living. But, that being the case, we realized that our characters should think and act the way real folks, ordinary folks, would think and act if they actually found themselves in that kind of situation.

As the whole world knows by now, we didn't have much money to make our first movie, and we were groping for ideas that we might be able to pull off, on an excruciatingly limited budget. We made several false starts—one of these was actually a horror comedy that involved teenagers from outer space hooking up with Earth kids to play pranks and befuddle a small town full of unsuspecting adults. But we soon found out that we couldn't afford sci-fi-type special effects and we had better settle upon something that was less FX-dependent.

George Romero and I were the two writers at The Latent Image, our movie production company at that time, and we would each go to work at separate typewriters whenever we could make time; in other words, whenever we weren't making TV spots about ketchup, pickles, or beer. I said to George that whatever kind of script we came up with ought to start in a cemetery, because people were scared of cemeteries and found them spooky. I started writing a screenplay about aliens who were prowling Earth in search of human flesh. Meantime, over a Christmas break in 1967, George came up with forty pages of a story that did actually start in a cemetery and in essence was the first half of what eventually became *Night of the Living Dead,* although we didn't give it that title till after we were done shooting.

I said to George that I really liked his story. It had the right pace and feel to it, and I was hooked by the action and suspense and the twists and turns. But I was also puzzled because, "You have these people being attacked, but you never say who the attackers are, so who are they?" George said he didn't know. I said, "Seems to me they could be dead people."

He said, "That's good." And then I said, "But you never say what they're after. They attack, but they don't bite, so why are they attacking?"

He said he didn't know, and I suggested, "Why don't we use my flesh-eating idea?"

So that's how the attackers in our movie became flesh-eating zombies. In our persistent striving for a good, fresh premise, we succeeded in combining some of the best elements of the vampire, werewolf, and zombie myths into one hellacious ball of wax.

Zombies weren't heavyweight fright material until we made them into flesh-eaters. In all the zombie flicks I had seen up till then—most notably Val Lewton movies like *I Walked with a Zombie*—the "walking dead" would stumble around and occasionally choke somebody or throw somebody against a wall, or maybe, in the extreme, carry off a heroine to some sort of lurid fate—but they were never as awe-inspiring as vampires or werewolves. They were meant to be scary, but they were always a little disappointing.

Night of the Living Dead struck an atavistic chord in people. It was the fear of death magnified exponentially. Not only were you afraid to die, you were afraid to become "undead." Afraid to be attacked by a dead loved one. And afraid of what you might do to your loved one if you, by being bitten, became one of the flesh-hungry undead that you feared.

Soon after our discussions, George Romero got tied up by an important commercial client and I took over screenwriting chores. That was the way we worked in those days. We spelled each other when necessary. And we all felt it was necessary to keep the ball rolling in these early stages so that our dream of making our first feature movie would not die.

In refining our concept, ideas were bandied about by me, George Romero, Russ Streiner, and others in our immediate group. Then I rewrote George's first forty pages, putting them into screenplay format, and went on to complete the second half of the script. I wanted our story to be honest, relentless, and uncompromising. I wanted to live up to the standard set by two of my favorite genre movies—the original *Invasion of the Body Snatchers* and *Forbidden Planet* (with its "monsters from the id")—and I hoped we could cause audiences to walk out of the theater with the same stunned looks on their faces that had been produced by those two classics. That is why I suggested that our indomitable hero, Ben (played by Duane Jones), should be killed by the posse that should have saved him. I said, "Pennsylvania is a big deer-hunting state, and every year three or four hundred thousand deer are shot—and ten or twelve hunters. With all these posse guys running around in the woods, gunning down ghouls, somebody is gonna be shot by accident, and wouldn't it be ironic if it's our hero?"

This idea got incorporated into the original screenplay as did other ideas, which were implemented during filming. For instance, the "Barbara" character, played by Judith O'Dea, survives in the screenplay as written—but we decided it would be better if her brother "Johnny" came back and dragged her out of the house to be devoured.

It wasn't until 1973, after the movie had enjoyed six-plus years of phenomenal success, that I wrote the novel that was initially published by Warner Books. In the intervening years, Russ Streiner, Rudy Ricci, and I developed a screenplay for a sequel, *Return of the Living Dead,* which I later novelized. You are right now holding both original novels in your hands, appearing together for the first time, in this beautiful trade limited edition hardcover.

I also wrote the novelization of Dan O'Bannon's movie version of *Return of the Living Dead,* a hit in its own right. But the totally different novel you will read now is our very first conception—of stark horror. Not a horror comedy, but stark horror in the vein of *Night of the Living Dead.*

If the dead really did arise, and if they became flesh-eaters, they might be temporarily vanquished—but like a disease that is hard to stamp out, the possibility of a renewed "plague" would always be with us. Religious cults would spring up in the wake of the undead. Maybe they would believe that the dead still needed to be burned or "spiked." And then what would happen? Would the cult's grisly expectations be realized? Would the flesh-eaters come back? This was the question that we sought to answer in a powerfully dramatic way in our follow-up story. Which is decidedly unfunny. In other words, unlike the movie, it is not a horror comedy.

If you like good, strong horror—horror that you can believe in—I welcome you to the deliciously terrifying, no-holds-barred, gloves-off world of the original *Night of the Living Dead* and *Return of the Living Dead.*

John Russo
Pittsburgh, PA

Night
of the
Living Dead

1

Think of all the people who have lived and died and will never see the trees or the grass or the sun any more.

It all seems so brief, so worth...nothing. Doesn't it? To live for a while and then die? It all seems to add up to so very little.

Yet in a way, it is easy to envy the dead ones.

They are beyond living, and beyond dying.

They are lucky to be dead, to be done with dying and not have to live any more. To be under the ground, oblivious...oblivious of hurting, oblivious of the fear of dying.

They do not have to live any more. Or die any more. Or feel pain. Or accomplish anything. Or wonder what to do next. Or wonder what it is going to be like to have to go through dying.

Why does life seem so ugly and beautiful and sad and important while you are living it, and so trivial when it is over?

Life smolders a while and then dies and the graves wait patiently to be filled, and the end of all life is death, and the new life sings happily in the breeze and neither knows nor cares anything about the old life, and then it in turn dies also.

Life is a constant turning over into graves. Things live and then die, and sometimes they live well and sometimes poorly, but they always die, and death is the one thing that reduces all things to the least common denominator.

What is it that makes people afraid of dying?

Not the pain.

Not always.

Death can be instantaneous and almost painless.

Death itself is an end to pain.

Then why are people afraid to die?

What things might we learn from those who are dead, if they find the means to return to us?

If they come back from the dead?

Will they be our friends? Or our enemies?

Will we be able to deal with them? We...who have never conquered our fear of confronting death.

At dusk, they finally spotted the tiny church. It was way back off the road, nearly hidden in a clump of maple trees, and if they had not found it before dark they probably would not have found it at all.

It was the cemetery behind the church that was the objective of their journey. And they had hunted for it for nearly two hours, down one long, winding, rural back road after another—with ruts so deep that the bottom of the car scraped and they had to crawl along at less than fifteen miles per hour, listening to a nerve-wracking staccato spray of gravel against the fenders and sweltering in a swirl of hot, yellow dust.

They had to come to place a wreath on their father's grave.

Johnny parked the car just off the road at the foot of a grassy terrace while his sister, Barbara, looked over at him and breathed a sigh intended to convey a mixture of both tiredness and relief.

Johnny said nothing. He merely tugged angrily at the knot of his already loosened tie and stared straight ahead at the windshield, which was nearly opaque with dust.

He had not turned off the engine yet, and Barbara immediately guessed why. He wanted her to suffer a while longer in the heat of the car, to impress upon her the fact that he had not wanted to make this trip in the first place and he held her responsible for all their discomfort. He was tired and disgusted and in a mood of frozen silence now, though during the two hours that they were lost he had taken his anger and resentment out on her by snapping at her continuously and refusing to be at all cheerful, while the car bounced over the ruts and he worked hard to restrain himself from ramming the gas pedal to the floor.

He was twenty-six years old and Barbara only nineteen, but she was in many ways more mature than he was—and through their growing-up years she had pretty much learned how to deal with his moods.

She merely got out of the car without a word, and left him staring at the windshield.

"There's nobody around here," Johnny said, purposely emphasizing their aloneness. Then, he added, "If it wasn't so dark, we could find it without any trouble."

"Well, if you'd gotten up earlier..." Barbara said, and she let her voice trail off as she began moving down another row of graves.

"This is the last time I blow a Sunday on a gig like this," Johnny said. "We're either gonna have to move Mother out here or move the grave closer to home."

"Sometimes I think you complain just to hear yourself talk," Barbara told him. "Besides, you're just being silly. You know darned well Mother's too sick to make a drive like this all by herself."

Suddenly a familiar tombstone caught Johnny's eye. He scrutinized it, recognized that it was their father's, and considered not telling Barbara so she would have to hunt a while longer; but his drive to get started toward home won out over his urge to torment her.

"I think that's it over there," he said, in a flat, detached tone, and he watched while Barbara crossed over to check it out, taking care not to step on any graves as she did so.

"Yes, this is it," Barbara called out. "You ought to be glad, Johnny—now we'll soon be on our way."

He came over to their father's grave and stared at the inscription briefly before taking the wreath out of the brown paper bag.

"I don't even remember what Dad looked like," he said. "Twenty-five bucks for this thing, and I don't even remember the guy very much."

"Well, I remember him," Barbara said, chastisingly, "and I was a lot younger than you were when he died."

They both looked at the wreath, which was made out of plastic and adorned with plastic flowers. At the bottom, on a piece of red plastic shaped like a ribbon tied in a large bow, the following words were inscribed in gold: "We Still Remember."

Johnny snickered.

"Mother wants to remember—so we have to drive two hundred miles to plant a wreath on a grave. As if he's staring up through the ground to check out the decorations and make sure they're satisfactory."

"Johnny, it takes you five minutes," Barbara said angrily, and she knelt at the grave and began to pray while Johnny took the wreath and, stepping close to the headstone, squatted and pushed hard to embed its wire-pronged base into the packed earth.

He stood up and brushed off his clothes, as if he had dirtied them, and continued grumbling, "It doesn't take five minutes at all. It takes three hours and five minutes. No, six hours and five minutes. Three hours up and three hours back. Plus the two hours we wasted hunting for the damned place."

She looked up from her prayer and glowered at him, and he stopped talking.

He stared down at the ground, bored. And he began to fidget, rocking nervously back and forth with his hands in his pockets. Barbara continued to pray, taking unnecessarily long it seemed to him. And his eyes began to wander, looking all around, staring into the darkness at the shapes and shadows in the cemetery. Because of the darkness, fewer of the tombstones were visible and there seemed to be not so many of them; only the larger ones could be seen clearly. And the sounds of the night seemed louder, because of the absence of human voices. Johnny stared into the darkness.

In the distance, a strange moving shadow appeared almost as a huddled figure moving among the graves.

Probably the caretaker or a late mourner, Johnny thought, and he glanced nervously at his watch. "C'mon, Barb, church was this morning," he said, in an annoyed tone. But Barbara ignored him and continued her prayer, as if she was determined to drag it out as long as possible just to aggravate him.

Johnny lit a cigarette, idly exhaled the first puff of smoke, and looked around again.

There was definitely someone in the distance, moving among the graves. Johnny squinted, but it was too dark to make out anything but an indistinct shape that more often than not blurred and merged with the shape of trees and tombstones as it advanced slowly through the graveyard.

Johnny turned to his sister and started to say something but she made the sign of the cross and stood up, ready to leave. She turned from the grave in silence, and they both started to walk slowly away, Johnny smoking and kicking at small stones as he ambled along.

"Praying is for church," he said flatly.

"Church would do you some good," Barbara told him. "You're turning into a heathen."

"Well, Grandpa told me I was damned to hell. Remember? Right here—I jumped out at you from behind that tree. Grandpa got all shook up and told me I 'gone be demn to yell! '"

Johnny laughed.

"You used to be so scared here," he said, devilishly. "Remember? Right here I jumped out from behind that tree at you."

"Johnny!" Barbara said, with annoyance. And she smiled to show him he was not frightening her, but she knew it was too dark for him to see the smile anyway.

"I think you're still afraid," he persisted. "I think you're afraid of the people in their graves. The dead people. What if they came out of their graves after you Barbara? What would you do? Run? Pray?"

He turned around and leered at her, as though he was about to pounce.

"Johnny, stop!"

"You're still afraid."

"No!"

"You're afraid of the dead people!"

"Stop, Johnny!"

"They're coming out of their graves, Barbara! Look! Here comes one of them now!"

He pointed toward the huddled figure which had been moving among the graves. The caretaker, or whoever it was, stopped and appeared to be looking in their direction, but it was too dark to really tell.

"He's coming to get you, Barbara! He's dead! And he's going to get you."

"Johnny, stop—he'll hear you—you're ignorant."

But Johnny ran away from her and hid behind a tree.

"Johnny, you—" she began, but in her embarrassment she cut herself short and looked down at the ground as the moving figure in the distance slowly approached her and it became obvious that their paths were going to intersect.

It seemed strange to her that someone other than she or her brother would be in the cemetery at such an odd hour.

Probably either a mourner or a caretaker.

She looked up and smiled to say hello.

And Johnny, laughing, looked out from behind his tree.

And suddenly the man grabbed Barbara around the throat and was choking her and ripping at her clothes. She tried to run or scream or fight back. But his tight fingers choked off her breath and the attack was so sudden and so vicious that she was nearly paralyzed with fear.

Johnny came running and dived at the man and tackled him— and all three fell down, Johnny pounding at the man with his fists and Barbara kicking and beating with her purse. Soon Johnny and the man were rolling and pounding at each other, while Barbara— screaming and fighting for her life—was able to wrench free.

In her panic and fear, she almost bolted.

The attacker was thrashing, pounding, seemingly clawing at all parts of Johnny's body. Johnny did all he could do to hold on. The two of them struggled to their feet, each maintaining a death grip on the other—but at the same time the attacker was like a wild animal fighting much more viciously than most men fight—beating, thrashing—even biting Johnny's hands and neck. Desperately, Johnny clutched at him and they fell in a heap.

In the total darkness, the blurred form of the two seemed to Barbara like one thrashing thing, and she feared for the outcome and she had no way of telling which one had the advantage or who was going to win or lose. She was nearly overcome with the desire to run and save herself, and yet she wanted to save her brother—but she didn't know how.

She began to scream wildly for help. And her fear became even more intense through her screaming, because part of her mind knew there was no one around and no one to hear her screams.

The two men on the ground were rolling and tumbling and slashing at each other and making animal sounds—one figure gained the advantage, and in a brief outline against the dark sky Barbara saw him slam his fists down onto the other's head.

She found a tree limb and snatched it into her hands, and took a step or two toward the fighting men.

Again, the fists came down, with a heavy dull thud and the sound of cracking bone. Barbara stopped in her tracks. The figure on top had a rock and was using it to smash his enemy's brains. Moonlight fell across the face of the victor, and Barbara saw with a shudder of doom that it was not Johnny.

Again the heavy rock thudded into Johnny's head, as Barbara remained paralyzed with shock and fear. And then the rock fell to the earth and rolled and Barbara braced herself with her tree branch ready to use as a club, but the attacker did not rise. He continued to kneel over the vanquished body.

And Barbara heard strange ripping sounds, and she could not see clearly what the attacker was doing—but the ripping sounds continued in the night...ripping...ripping...as if something was being torn from Johnny's dead body.

The attacker did not seem to be concerned with Barbara...as her heart pounded wildly and she remained rooted with fear and the ripping sounds enveloped her and blotted out her sanity and her reason, and she was in such a state of extreme shock that she was near death and all she could hear was ripping...ripping...as the attacker wrenched and pulled at her brother's dead body and—yes!!—she saw in a fresh shaft of moonlight through a passing cloud that the attacker was sinking his teeth into Johnny's dead face.

Slowly, wide-eyed, like a woman paralyzed in a nightmare, Barbara began moving toward her brother's attacker. Her lips fell apart and involuntarily emitted a loud sob.

The attacker looked at her. And she was startled by the sound of his breath—an unearthly rasping sound. He stepped over Johnny's body and moved toward her in a half-standing position, like an animal hunched to spring.

Barbara let loose an ear-shattering scream of sheer horror, and she dropped her club and ran—the man coming after her slowly, with seeming difficulty in moving, almost as though he were crippled or maimed.

He advanced toward Barbara, making his way between the tombstones, while she ran stumbling and gasping for breath, and tumbled and rolled down the muddy, grassy terrace to the car. She yanked open the door. And she could hear the slow, muffled footsteps of her pursuer drawing nearer as she scrambled into the front seat and slammed the door shut.

No keys. The keys were in Johnny's pocket.

The attacker was moving closer, faster, more desperate to reach the girl.

Barbara clutched at the steering wheel, as though it alone might move the car. She sobbed. And almost too late she realized the windows were open—and she rolled them up frantically and locked the doors.

The attacker ripped at the door handles and pounded violently at the car.

Barbara began screaming again, but the man seemed impervious to screams and totally without fear of being caught or surprised.

He grabbed up a large stone from the road and shattered the window on the passenger side into a thousand little cracks. Another pounding blow, and the stone crashed through the window, and the man's hands were clawing at Barbara, trying to grab her by the hair, the face or the arms—anywhere.

She caught a glimpse of his face. It was death-white—and awfully contorted—as if by insanity or agonizing pain.

She smashed her fist into his face. And at the same instant she tugged at the emergency brake and pulled it loose and the car began to drift downhill, the attacker following after, pounding and ripping at the door handles and trying to hang on.

As the grade got steeper the car managed to pick up speed, and the man was shaken loose and forced to trot after it. The car went still faster and the man lost his footing and clutched at the fender, then the bumper, as he tumbled and fell heavily into the road. The car gained momentum, with Barbara's pursuer no longer hanging on. But he regained his footing and kept pursuing, resolutely, stolidly, in a slow, staggering shuffle.

The car was now plummeting down a steep, winding hill, Barbara frozen in the driver's seat, clenching the wheel, frightened by the darkness and the speed, yet too scared to slow down.

The light switch! She yanked it, and the headlights danced beams of light among the trees. She swerved to avoid crashing as the beams revealed the grade in the road and the car bounced and lurched over it and she saw that it was narrowing to one car width; and, about two hundred feet ahead, the downhill grade was going to end and an uphill grade begin.

On the uphill grade, the car slowed...and slowed...as its momentum carried it some distance up the upgrade. Barbara glanced backward, but could see nothing—then, in the dim outline of the road, the pursuing figure of her attacker rounded a bend and she knew he was moving fast after her.

On the upgrade, the car reached a full stop. Then, with a bolt of panic, Barbara realized it was starting to drift backward, carrying her toward her attacker...as he continued to draw nearer. The car picked up momentum as she sat paralyzed with fear.

Then she grabbed at the emergency brake and yanked it tight, the lurch of the car throwing her against the seat. She struggled with the door handle—but it would not budge until she remembered to pull the button up—and as the attacker drew nearer she yanked the door open and bolted from the car.

She ran.

The man behind her kept coming, desperately trying to move faster in his shuffling, staggering gait—as Barbara ran as fast as her legs could carry her up the steep grade of the gravel road. She fell. Skinned her knees. Picked herself up and kept running and the man kept coming after her.

She reached the main highway, at the top of the hill. And she kicked her shoes off and began to run faster—on hard blacktop rather than gravel—and she hoped to spot a car or truck or any kind of vehicle she could flag down. But there was nothing in sight. Then she came to a low stone wall, on the side of the road—and she knew there must be a house somewhere beyond the wall. She struggled over it and considered hiding behind it, but she could hear the rasping breath and plodding footsteps of her pursuer not too far behind her and he would be sure to look for her behind the wall—it was too obvious a hiding place.

Then, looking ahead for a moment to get her bearings, she thought she could make out a soft glow of a window in the distance, across a field and through the leafy overhanging branches of scattered trees.

In the dark, stumbling over boulders and dead branches and gnarled roots, she ran toward the lighted window across the field.

She came to a shed first, at the edge of a dirt road leading to the house. Beside the shed, illuminated in the glow of a naked light bulb swarming with gnats, stood two gasoline pumps of the type that farmers keep to supply their tractors and other vehicles. Barbara stopped and hid for a moment behind one of the pumps—until she realized that she was too vulnerable under the light from the shed.

As she turned, the light revealed her attacker coming closer, shuffling toward her across the dark field with its shrubs and trees and overhanging foliage.

She ran toward the house and began calling for help as loudly as she could yell. But no one came outside. No one came out onto the porch. The house remained silent and dark, except for the glow of light from one solitary window.

She pressed herself against the side of the house, in a darkened corner, and tried to look into the window, but she could see no signs of life, and apparently no one had heard her screams and no one was coming out to help her.

Silhouetted in the glow of light from the shed, the man who killed her brother was drawing nearer.

In panic, she ran to the rear of the house and into the shadows of a small back porch. Her first impulse was to cry again for help, but she silenced herself in favor of trying to stay hidden. She gasped, realized how loud her breathing was, and tried to hold her breath. Silence. Night sounds...and the sound of the wild beating of her heart...did not stop her from hearing her attacker's running footsteps slowing to a trot...then a slow walk. And finally the footsteps stopped.

Barbara glanced quickly about. She spied a rear window and peered through it, but inside everything was dark. The pursuing footsteps resumed again, louder and more ominous. She pressed herself back against the door of the house, and her hand fell on the doorknob. She looked down at it, sure that it was locked, but grabbed it with a turn, and the door opened.

2

She entered quickly, as quietly as possible, and closed the door softly behind her, bolting it and feeling in the darkness for a key. Her hand found a skeleton key and she turned it, making a barely audible rasp and click. She leaned against the door, listening, and could still hear the distant footfalls of the man approaching and trying to seek her out.

A tremble shot through her as she groped in the darkness and her hand touched the cold burner of an electric stove. The kitchen. She was in the kitchen of the old house. She pressed a button and the stove light came on, giving her enough illumination to scrutinize her surroundings without, she hoped, alerting her pursuer to where she was. For several seconds, she maintained a controlled silence and did not move a muscle. Then she got the nerve to move.

She crossed the kitchen into a large living room, unlighted and devoid of any signs of life. Her impulse was to call for help again, but she stopped herself for fear of being heard by the man outside. She darted back to the kitchen, rummaged through drawers in a kitchen cabinet, and found the silverware. She chose a large steak knife and, grasping it tightly, went to listen at the door again. All was quiet. She crept back into the living room. Beyond it she could dimly make out an alcove that contained the front entrance to the house. Seized with panic, she bolted to the front door and made sure it was locked. Then, cautiously, she peeled back a corner of the curtain to see outside. The view revealed the expansive lawn and grassy field she had run across earlier, with its large shadowy trees and shrubs and the shed and gasoline pumps lit up in the distance. Barbara could neither see nor hear any sign of her attacker.

Suddenly there was a noise from outside: the pounding and rattling of a door. Barbara dropped the curtain edge and stiffened. More sounds. She hurried to a side window. Across the lawn, she saw that the man was pounding at the door to the garage. She watched, her eyes wide with fear. The man continued to pound savagely at the door, then looked about and picked up something and smashed at it. In panic, Barbara pulled away from the window and flattened herself against the wall.

Her eyes fell on a telephone, across the room on a wooden shelf. She rushed to it and picked up the receiver. Dial tone. Thank God. She frantically dialed the operator. But the dial tone stopped and there was dead silence. Barbara depressed the buttons of the phone again and again, but she could not get the dial tone to resume. Just dead silence. For some reason, the phone was out of order. The radio. The phone. Out of order.

She slammed the receiver down and rushed to another window. A figure was crossing the lawn, coming toward the house. It seemed to be a different figure, a different man. Her heart leapt with both fear and hope—because she did not know who the new man could be, and she dared not cry out to him for help.

She ran to the door and peered out through the curtains again, anxious for a clue as to whether this new person in the yard might be friend or foe. Whoever he was, he was still walking toward the house. A shadow fell suddenly across a strip of window to the left of the door, and Barbara started and jumped back because of its abruptness.

She peeled back a corner of the window curtain and saw the back of the first attacker not ten feet away, facing the other man who was fast approaching. The attacker moved toward the new man, and Barbara did not know what to expect next. She froze against the door and glanced down at her knife—then looked back out at the two men. They joined each other, seemingly without exchange of words, under the dark, hanging trees, and stood quietly, looking back toward the cemetery. From inside the house, Barbara squinted, trying to see. Finally, the attacker moved back across the road, in the direction of the cemetery. The other man approached the house and stopped in the shadow of a tree, stolidly watching.

Barbara peered into the darkness, but could see little. She lunged toward the phone again, picked up the receiver, and heard dead silence. She barely stopped herself from slamming down the receiver.

Then suddenly came a distant sound—an approaching car. She scampered to the window and looked out, holding her breath. The road seemed empty. But after a moment a faint light appeared, bouncing and rapidly approaching—a car coming up the road. Barbara reached for the doorknob and edged the door open ever so slightly, allowing a little light to spill out over the lawn. There, under a large old tree, was the unmistakable silhouette of the second man. Barbara shuddered, choked with fear at the thought of making a break for the approaching car. The man under the tree appeared to be sitting quite still, his head and shoulders slumped over, though his gaze seemed to be directed right at the house.

Barbara allowed the car to speed by, while she just stared at the hated figure in the lawn. Her chance to run was gone. She closed the door and backed into the shadows of the house. It dawned on her that perhaps the first attacker had gone for reinforcements, and they would return en masse to batter the door down and rape her and kill her.

She glanced frantically all around her. The large, dreary room was very quiet, cast in shadow. Between the living room and the kitchen, there was a hallway and a staircase; she moved toward it stealthily and her fingers found a light switch. The light at the top of the stairs came on, and she ascended the staircase, clinging to the banister for support and hoping desperately to be able to find a place to hide. She tiptoed...tiptoed...keeping a firm grip on the handle of her knife, and then, as she reached the top of the landing, she screamed—an ear-shattering scream that ripped through her lungs and echoed through the old house—because, there, on the floor at the top of the landing, under the glow of the naked light bulb in the hall, was a corpse with the flesh ripped from its bones and its eyes missing from their sockets and the white teeth and cheekbones bared and no longer covered by skin, as if the corpse had been eaten by rats, as it lay there in its pool of dried blood.

Screaming in absolute horror, Barbara dropped her knife and ran and tumbled down the stairs. In full flight now, gagging and almost vomiting, with her brain leaping at the edge of sheer madness, she wanted to get out of that house—and she broke for the door and unlocked it and flung herself out into the night, completely unmindful of the consequences.

Suddenly she was bathed in light that almost blinded her—and as she threw her arms up to protect herself, there was a loud screeching sound, and as she struggled to run, a man jumped in front of her.

"Are you one of them?" the man shouted.

She stared, frozen.

The man standing in front of her had leaped out of a pick-up truck that he had driven onto the lawn and stopped with a screech of brakes and a jounce of glaring headlights.

Barbara stared at him, but no words would come to her lips.

"Are you one of them?" he yelled again. "I seen 'em to look like you!"

Barbara shuddered. He had his arm raised, about to strike her, and she could not make out his features because he was silhouetted against the bright headlights of the truck.

Behind the truck driver, the man under the tree took a few steps forward. Barbara screamed and stepped back, and the truck driver turned to face the advancing man—who stopped and watched and did not resume his advance.

Finally the truck driver grabbed Barbara and shoved her back into the living room so forcefully that she fell down with his body on top of her, and she closed her eyes and prepared to accept her death.

But he got off of her and slammed the door shut and locked it. And he lifted the curtains and peered out. He did not seem to be very much concerned about her, so she finally opened her eyes and stared at him.

He was carrying a tire iron in his hand. He was a black man, perhaps thirty years old, dressed in slacks and a sweater. He did not at all resemble her attacker. In fact, though his face bore an intense look, it was friendly and handsome. He appeared to be a strong man, well over six feet tall.

Barbara got to her feet and continued to stare at him.

"It's all right," he said, soothingly. "It's all right. I ain't one of those creeps. My name is Ben. I ain't going to hurt you."

She sank into a chair and began to cry softly, while he concerned himself with his surroundings. He moved into the next room and checked the locks on the windows. He turned on a lamp; it worked; and he turned it back off.

He called to Barbara from the kitchen.

"Don't you be afraid of that creep outside! I can handle him all right. There's probably gonna be lots more of them, though, soon as they find out we're here. I'm out of gas, and the gasoline pumps out back are locked. Do you have the key?"

Barbara did not reply.

"Do you have the key?" Ben repeated, trying to control his anger.

Again, Barbara said nothing. Her experiences of the past couple of hours had brought her to a state of near-catatonia.

Ben thought maybe she did not hear, so he came into the living room and addressed her directly.

"I said the gas pumps out back are locked. Is there food around here? I'll get us some food, then we can beat off that creep out there and try to make it somewhere where there is gas."

Barbara merely held her face in her hands and continued to cry.

"I guess you tried the phone," Ben said, no longer expecting an answer. And he picked it up and fiddled with it but could not get anything but dead silence, so he slammed it down into its cradle. He looked at Barbara and saw she was shivering.

"Phone's no good," he said. "We might as well have two tin cans and a string. You live here?"

She remained silent, her gaze directed toward the top of the stairs. Ben followed her stare and started toward the stairs, but half-way up he saw the corpse—and stared for a moment and slowly backed down into the living room.

His eyes fell on Barbara, and he knew she was shivering with shock, but there was nothing for him to do but force himself back into action.

"We've got to bust out of here," he said. "We've got to find some other people—somebody with guns or something."

He went into the kitchen and started rummaging, flinging open the refrigerator and the cupboards. He began filling a shopping bag with things from the refrigerator, and because he was in a hurry he literally hurled the things into the bag.

Suddenly, to his surprise, he looked up and Barbara was standing beside him.

"What's happening?" she said, in a weak whisper, so weak that Ben almost did not hear. And she stood there wide-eyed, like a child waiting for an answer.

Amazed, he stared at her.

"What's happening?" she repeated, weakly, shaking her head in fright and bewilderment.

Suddenly they were both startled by a shattering crash. Ben dropped the groceries, seized his jack-handle, and ran to the front door and looked out through the curtained window. Another shattering sound. The first attacker had joined the second man at the old pick-up truck, and with rocks the two had smashed out the headlights.

"Two of them," Ben muttered to himself, and as he watched, the two men outside started to beat with their rocks at the body of the truck—but their beating seemed to have no purpose; it seemed to be just mindless destruction. In fact, outside of smashing the headlights, they were not harming the old truck very much.

But Ben spun around with a worried look on his face.

"They're liable to wreck the engine," he said to Barbara. "How many of them are out there? Do you know?"

She backed away from him, and he lunged at her and grabbed her by the wrists and shook her, in an effort to make her understand.

"How many? Come on, now—I know you're scared. But I can handle the two that are out there now. Now, how many are there? That truck is our only chance to get out of here. How many? How many?"

"I don't know! I don't know!" she screamed. "What's happening? I don't know what's happening!"

As she struggled to break his hold on her wrists, she burst into hysterical sobbing.

Ben turned away from her and moved for the door. He lifted the curtain and looked out for a moment. The attackers were still beating at the truck, wildly trying to tear it apart.

Ben flung open the door, and leaped off of the porch, and began cautiously advancing toward the two men. As they turned to face him, he was revolted by what he saw in the glow of the light from the living room of the old house.

The faces of the attackers were the faces of humans who were dead. The flesh on their faces was rotting and oozing in places. Their eyes bulged from deep sockets. Their flesh was bloodless and pasty white. They moved with an effort, as though whatever force had brought them to life had not done a complete job. But they were horrible, ghoulish beings, and they frightened Ben to the depths of his ability to be frightened, as he moved toward them brandishing his jack-handle.

"Come and get it, now. Come and get it," Ben muttered to himself, as he concentrated on his attack, moving forward stolidly at first, then breaking almost into a run.

But the two, instead of backing off, moved toward the man, as though drawn by some deep-seated urge. Ben pounded into them, swinging his jack-handle again and again with all his might. But his blows, powerful though they were, seemed to have little effect. He couldn't stop the things, or hurt them. It was like beating a rug; every time he flung them back they advanced again, in a violent, brutal struggle. But Ben finally managed to beat them to the ground, and for a long while, he continued to pound at their heads, at their limp forms lying there on the lawn, until he was almost sobbing with each of his blows, beating and beating at them, while Barbara stood on the porch and watched in a state of shock. Over and over, he drove the jack-handle smashing into the skulls of the prostrate creatures—humanoids, or whatever they were—until the sheer violence of it set Barbara off on a rampage of screaming—screaming and holding her head and trying to cover her eyes. Again and again her screams pierced the night, mingled with Ben's sobs and the sounds of the jack-handle hammering into the skulls of the dead things.

Ben finally got hold of himself, and stopped. Breathing heavily, he stood, enveloped in the quiet of the night.

Silent now, the girl stood in the doorway and looked at him—or through him—he could not be sure which. He turned to face her and say something to comfort her, but he could not get his breath.

Suddenly, he heard a noise behind the girl, from inside the house. He leaped up onto the porch, and walking toward her from the kitchen was another of the horrible dead things. Somehow it must have broken the bolt on the kitchen door.

"Lock that door!" Ben yelled and Barbara summoned the presence of mind to shut the living-room door and lock it, as still another brutal struggle ensued in the living room.

The dead thing that Ben began struggling with this time was more horrible-looking than the other two, as if it had been dead longer, or had died a more terrible death. Patches of hair and flesh had been torn from its head and face, and the bones of its arms showed through the skin like a jacket with the elbows worn through. And one dead eye was hanging halfway out of its socket, and its mouth was twisted and caked with blood and dirt.

Ben tried to hit it, but the thing grabbed onto Ben's arm, and the jack-handle dropped to the floor. Ben groped and struggled with the thing, and finally twisted it around and wrestled it down onto the carpet. The thing was emitting strange rasping sounds from its dead throat, like the sounds that had been made by whoever had killed Barbara's brother...and it raked its hands in the direction of Ben's throat—but it did not make contact, because Ben had seized the jack-handle and he drove it point first into the thing's skull.

Ben stood up. He had to use his foot against the dead thing's head to gain leverage to pull the jack-handle out—and the dead skull flopped back with a thud against the living-room floor. And just the tiniest bit of fluid, white and not the color of blood, oozed from the wound made by the jack-handle in the dead creature's skull.

But Ben had no time to think of what it might mean, because a sound in the kitchen told him that still another of the things had gotten in. He met it in the hall and with powerful jack-handle blows drove it out beyond the kitchen door so that he could fall against it, shutting it and leaning against it to keep it shut while he tried to get his breath.

After a long silence, Ben said, "They know we're in here now. It's no secret any longer, if it ever was. And they're going to kill us if we don't protect ourselves."

He spoke directly to Barbara, as though looking for a sign that she understood and would cooperate in their struggle to survive. But she did not hear him. Her face was twitching in fright, and her eyes remained wide open in a non-blinking stare.

She was staring toward the floor, at the spot where the dead humanoid lay. It was askew on its back, in the hallway between the living room and the kitchen, its right arm jutting at a crazy angle toward the girl with fingers twisted as though to grab. Horrified, Barbara thought she saw a slight movement in the thing's hand. It twitched. The whole body twitched slightly—the bent, broken neck keeping the being's head twisted upward, in an open-mouthed, one-eyed glassy stare.

As if in a trance, Barbara took a few steps toward the thing, the fear in her face contorting into a sick frown. And the hand twitched again. The girl moved toward it, drawn toward it, staring down at it with overpowering curiosity.

The dead thing lay there twitching and staring, with the one eye hanging out and the beginnings of decay on its face and neck.

But Barbara moved closer, and the thing continued to twitch, its one eye still staring upward, glassy and pale, like the eye of a stuffed animal.

Adrenaline coursed through Barbara's body, as she felt an overpowering drive to run or scream, even though she remained rooted, fixatedly staring into the eye of the dead thing. And suddenly it moved, with a rustling sound. And Barbara jumped and screamed, jolted out of her trance, before the realization came to her that Ben had a hold on the thing's legs and was dragging it across the floor.

"Shut your eyes, girl, I'm getting this dead thing out of here," Ben said in a stern voice, and his face showed his anguish and revulsion as he dragged the dead body across the floor.

The one eye continued to twitch. And Barbara just stood there, her hands still at her mouth, watching, listening to the sounds of Ben's breathing and his struggling with the dead being. Finally, he got the body to the kitchen door, and he let the legs drop with a thud as he paused to rest and think.

Even in the dim illumination provided by the stove light, Barbara could see the shiny perspiration on Ben's face, and the rasp of his heavy breathing seemed to fill the room. His eyes were alert, and afraid. He turned quickly to see through the small window pane in the door. The dead thing still lay twitching slightly at his feet.

And outside, lurking in the shadow from the huge trees, Ben's probing eyes discerned three more beings watching and waiting, their arms dangling and eyes bulging, as they maintained a dumb, fixated stare in the direction of the house.

With a swift move, the big man flung open the kitchen door and bent to pick up the dead thing at his feet. The three ghoulish creatures outside under the trees began to take slow, shuffling, threatening steps toward the house. And, with one great heave, Ben flopped the dead, twitching form outside the door, just beyond the threshold.

The things on the lawn continued to advance, as the rasp of crickets mingled with the agonized, bellows-like rasping of their dead lungs, nearly obliterating all the other night sounds.

With another great effort, Ben heaved the dead but twitching body over the edge of the porch.

From inside the house, the big man's efforts could not be clearly discerned by Barbara, and she backed away from the door and trembled uncontrollably while she waited for Ben to finish whatever he was going to do and come back inside.

He shuddered and fumbled in his breast pocket, as the ghoulish beings on the lawn continued to move toward him with their arms extended, reaching out as though to seize him and tear him apart. Ben's fumbling fingers closed on a book of matches, and he managed to strike one and touch the burning tip to the ragged, filthy clothing of the dead thing, and with almost a popping sound the clothing caught fire.

The things in the yard stopped in their tracks. The fire blazed slowly at first. Shaking, Ben touched the match to other aspects of the thing's clothing and, intent on the advancing ghouls, he burned his fingers and snapped them, tossing the match into the heaped form. Standing, and breathing hard, he kicked the burning thing off the edge of the porch and watched it roll down three small steps onto the grass, where it lay still, the flames licking around it.

Ben watched the three beings in the yard as they stepped back slightly, trying to cover their faces with their stiff arms, as though they were afraid of fire—and his fists clenched the banister of the little porch as his face glowed in the heat of the flames.

"I'm going to get you," Ben said to himself, his voice quivering. And then he raised his voice and shouted into the deadness of the night, "I'm going to get you! All of you! You damned things!"

Ben stood defiantly on the little porch, the flaming corpse burning with an overpowering stench. Yet, the things on the lawn had stopped backing away, and they were keeping their distance now—watching and waiting.

Hearing a sudden noise, Ben spun to see Barbara standing inside the kitchen door. As his eyes met hers, he took in the blank, frozen expression on her face, and she backed away from him into the room. The big man, in great strides, re-entered the kitchen and slammed the door and reflexively went to bolt it, but the bolt had been broken loose by the things that had gotten in.

Ben seized hold of a heavy kitchen table, and dragged it and slammed it against the door. His breathing, still loud, was even more rapid than before. And his eyes continually darted about the room in search of something—but Barbara did not know what.

He rushed to the cabinets and threw them open and began rummaging through them. They were full of standard kitchen utensils and supplies. For a long time, Ben did not speak—and Barbara's staring eyes followed him about as he continued to ransack the room.

"See if you can find the light switch," he shouted suddenly—so suddenly that the sound of his voice startled Barbara and she fell back against a wall and her hand groped to a switch. The light from an overhead fixture came on, providing bright illumination. The big man continued to clatter about frantically, while the light coming on hurt Barbara's eyes and caused her to blink and squint. She remained against the wall, her hand still touching the switch, as though she did not dare to move. She watched silently, while Ben continued flinging open drawers and spilling contents onto the shelving and onto the floor.

He grabbed the silverware drawer, still open from when Barbara first discovered it, and pulled it open until it stopped itself with a crash. He rooted through it, pulled out a large bread knife and, sucking his breath in, stuffed it under his belt. Then he reached into the drawer again and produced another knife. Taking Barbara by surprise, he strode toward her and shoved the knife at her, handle first, but she backed away from him—and her action stayed his franticness and, breathing heavily through his words, he calmed himself and spoke softly but commandingly to her.

"Now...you hang on...to this."

She hesitated, but finally took the knife, and he breathed a sigh of relief. She seemed weak, almost apathetic, as though she was losing control of herself—or had given up already. She stared at the weapon in her hand, then her eyes came up to meet the man's intense face.

"All right," he said. "All right. You just listen to me, and we're gonna be okay. We have to protect ourselves—keep those things away from us, until we can find a way to get out of this damned place."

He did not know if his words penetrated through to Barbara or not, but hopefully they did.

He pulled away from her and continued to rummage, speaking only occasionally and to no one in particular between great breaths and between the brief times when his interest was totally wrapped in something found in his rummaging—something useful or potentially useful for survival.

His search was not without control; it had a coordinated purpose; it was selective, although frantic and desperate. He was looking for nails and strips of wood or planks that he might nail around doors and windows. He had made up his mind that they were going to have to fortify the old farmhouse as strongly as possible, against the impending and gathering threat of an all-out attack by the ghouls, which were increasing in number. Ben's actions were hurried, and intent after these defensive ends; at first, his search occupied his full attention and was driven by anxiety. But gradually, as he moved about and began to come up with several key items, his efforts paced down into a more deliberate flow.

He started bracing heavy tables and other articles of furniture against the most vulnerable parts of the old house.

His mood relaxed in intensity and became calmer, more analytical, as the barricading instilled a feeling of greater security. And the knowledge of the efforts toward some safety and some protection began to overtake Barbara, bringing her out of her shock and passivity.

"We'll be okay!" Ben called out, in an effort at bravery.

And Barbara watched, as he clattered about the room, spilling his findings out of drawers and off of shelves. He still had not apparently found at least one important item that he was really impatient for. Spools of thread, buttons, manicure implements, shoeshine materials...continued to spill out of drawers. And Ben got once more a little violent and urgent as he continued to rummage and bang around the room.

Finally, in a wooden box under the sink, he found what he was looking for—and he leaped suddenly and let out an exclamation of triumph as he dumped the contents of the box onto the kitchen floor. A big claw hammer thudded out. And an axe. And an old pipe tobacco tin, which Ben seized and in one gesture spilled its contents onto a shelf. Nails and screws and washers and tacks tumbled out. A few rolled too far and clattered onto the floor, but Ben dived and his fingers scooped them up. He fumbled through the little pile of things and selected the longest nails in the batch, and stuffed them into the pocket of his sweater. And even as he stuffed the nails into his pocket, he was already moving, his eyes seeking for his next need.

His eyes fell on Barbara.

"See if there's any big pieces of wood around the fireplace out there!" he yelled at her, and he turned to explore the contents of a cardboard box on top of the refrigerator. The box came up too easily, telling him it was empty, and he flung it down with a glance inside to make sure, as his impetus carried him toward a metal cabinet in the corner of the room which he was betting would contain nothing but foodstuffs—but in turning he noticed Barbara, still motionless, and his anger leaped to the surface suddenly and he shouted at her.

"Look, you—"

But he stopped himself, then spoke still frantically, but with less harshness.

"Look...I know you're scared. I'm scared, too. I'm scared just like you. But we're not gonna survive...if we don't do something to help ourselves. I'm going to board up these doors and windows. But you've got to pitch in. We've got to help ourselves, because there ain't nobody around to help us...and we're gonna be all right. Okay?

Now, I want you to get out there and see if there's any wood in that fireplace..."

He stopped, still breathing hard. Barbara merely stared at him. Then, after several seconds, she started to move, very slowly, away from the wall.

"Okay?" Ben asked, looking into her eyes.

She was still for a long moment, before nodding her head weakly.

"Okay," Ben repeated, reassuringly, in a half-whisper, and he stared after the girl momentarily as she left the kitchen—and he continued his search.

She moved into the living room area, where the darkness stopped her for an instant, slowing her pace. From the kitchen, she could still hear the clattering sounds of Ben's search. She looked ahead, into the room, and clutched the handle of her knife as the white curtains on the windows seemed to glow, and every shadow seemed suspect. Anything could be lurking in that room, behind the furniture, or in the closets.

Barbara shuddered.

On the dining table in the far corner of the room, she could see the silhouette of a bowl of large rounded flowers—and they stirred suddenly, in the breeze from an opened window. In a panic, Barbara raced for the window and slammed it shut and bolted it, and stood, breathing heavily and noticing that she had pinned part of the white curtain under the window frame when it came crashing down. But she was not going to raise it back up again, for anything. A shiver shot through her, and she turned to see Ben, who had come as far as the doorway to find out the cause of the noise—and she hoped he would stay, but he turned and resumed his banging around in the kitchen.

Alone in the room again, Barbara reached for a lamp on an end table, clicked it on and dull illumination filled the immediate area. The room felt empty. She started slowly toward the fireplace. Near it was a stack of logwood, and a few planks that might be large enough to nail across the windows. Still clutching her knife, she bent over the pile and gathered up the planking—but a spider ran across her hand, and she shrieked and dropped the wood with a clatter.

She waited, hoping Ben would not come, and this time he did not come to see what was the matter. Loud continuous noises of his activity in the kitchen told her why he had not heard her own racket with the firewood. She knelt and picked the planks up again, and steeled her mind not to be frightened by spiders.

Staggering with her awkward load, she hurried toward the kitchen and, bursting through the doorway, she found Ben pounding with the claw hammer at the hinges on a tall broom-closet door. One final swipe and a great yank freed the door, with the sound of screws ripping from torn wood, and the man stood it against the wall next to the broom closet. In the recesses of the closet, he spotted other useful items and pulled them out—an ironing board, three center boards from the dining table, and some old scrap lumber.

He smiled at Barbara when he looked up and saw her own supply of wood, which she leaned against the wall in a corner, and motioning for her to follow he grabbed the closet door and carried it across the kitchen to the back door of the house, which was the door with the broken bolt. He slapped the closet door up against the panel portion of the kitchen door and with an appraising glance he realized that he could use this same piece to cover the kitchen window, which was of modest dimensions and not placed too far from the kitchen door. He leaned against the piece of wood and groped in his sweater pocket for nails. The door started to slip slightly. It was not going to completely cover the kitchen window, but it would leave slats of glass at top and bottom; however, it would cover the glass part of the entrance door and would help make the door secure. Again, the heavy closet door slipped and he nudged it back into position, as he continued to grope for nails. Suddenly springing forward, Barbara helped out, by taking hold of the piece of lumber and holding it in position. Ben accepted her help automatically, without recognition, and gave the barricade a cursory inspection as he determined where to sink the nails; then, pulling several long nails from his pocket, he placed them and drove them in with swift, powerful blows from the claw hammer. He drove two on his side through the door and molding, then moved swiftly to her side and drove two more. Then, with the weight of the piece supported, he pounded the nails until they were completely sunken and stood back and began to add more. He wanted to use the nails sparingly but wisely, where they would do the most good, because he did not have an unlimited supply.

He tugged at the kitchen door, and it now seemed secure enough, and with the first defensive measures undertaken and accomplished, Ben began to take on confidence and assurance. He was still scared, and he continued to work quickly and, he hoped, wisely—and the fact that he had tools to work with and a plan to put into effect to maintain survival gave him the feeling that he was not entirely helpless and there were strong, positive things he could do to bring his and the girl's destiny under control.

"There! By God!" he said, finally, in a burst of self confidence. "That ought to hold those damn things and stop them from getting in here. They ain't that strong—there!"

And he drove two more nails into the molding around the kitchen window. And when he tugged at the barricade, it again seemed plenty secure.

"They ain't coming through that," Ben said, and he gave the nails a few final blows, until the heads sunk into the wood.

His eyes scrutinized the parts of the glass that remained uncovered, but they were not sufficiently wide for a human body to pass through. "I don't have too many nails," Ben said. "I'll leave that for now. It's more important to fix up some of the other places where they can get in."

Barbara did not respond to any of his talking, neither to add encouragement nor advice, and he turned from the barricade with an exasperated glance in her direction before standing back and once more surveying the room. There were no other doors or windows except the door leading to the living room.

"Well...this place is fairly secure," Ben said, tentatively, and he looked to Barbara for some sign of approval, but she remained silent, so Ben continued, raising the volume of his voice in an attempt to hammer home the meaning of what he was saying. "Now...if we have to..."

The girl just stood and watched him.

"If we have to...we just run in here—and no dragging now, or I'm gonna leave you out there to fend for yourself. If they get into any other part of the house, we run in here and board up this door."

He meant the door between the kitchen and the living room, which had been open all along. Barbara watched while he closed it, tested it, then shut it tight.

He opened it again, then quickly chose several of the lumber strips and stood them against the wall where he intended to leave them in case it became an emergency to board up the living-room door.

He groped in his pocket and realized his supply of nails was dwindling and he moved to the shelf to check the pile of stuff he had spilled from the tobacco can; he emptied the can completely and dug into the contents for all of the longest nails and tossed just those ones back into the can. Then he handed the can to Barbara.

"You take these," he said, and his voice left no room for argument or hesitation.

She reacted quickly, as though she had been jolted out of a reverie, and took the tobacco tin from Ben's big hand. She watched as he gathered as much of the lumber as he could carry into his arms and started out of the room. She did not want to be left alone, and he had not told her to remain in the kitchen, so she followed silently after him, carrying the tobacco tin in front of her as though she was not sure why she was doing it.

They entered the living room.

"It ain't gonna be too long," Ben said, breathing heavily. "They're gonna be trying to pound their way in here. They're afraid now...I think...or maybe they just ain't hungry..."

He dropped his load of wood in the middle of the floor and walked over to the large front windows, talking as he moved. His tone of voice was suddenly intense, and his speech rapid.

"They're scared of fire, too—I found that out."

Still standing dumbly in the center of the room holding her knife in one hand and the tobacco tin in the other, Barbara watched as Ben stepped forward and his eye measured the size of the big windows. He looked all around the room—and finally his eyes fixed on the large dining table and he moved quickly toward it, talking as he moved, resuming his train of thought.

"There must've been fifty, maybe a hundred of those things down in Cambria when the news broke."

Barbara watched, almost transfixed. At his mention of the number of the things, her eyes reflected amazement and frightened curiosity. Ben dragged the heavy table away from the wall, then walked around it studying its size, and hoisted one end and turned it onto its side. Bracing it against himself, he heaved on one of the legs and tried to break it free. With a great ripping sound, the table leg came loose, after a tremendous effort on Ben's part, and he dropped it onto the rug—with a loud, heavy thud. He continued talking, breathing heavily and perspiring as he worked, punctuating his remarks with vengeance on the table as he ripped all the legs off, one by one.

"I saw a big gasoline truck, you know...down at Beekman's? Beekman's diner. And I heard the radio—there's a radio in the truck..."

He wrenched at the second table leg. It cracked loudly but did not come free. He moved to where the claw hammer lay, in the middle of the floor.

"This gasoline truck came screaming out of the diner lot onto the road—must've been ten...fifteen...of those things chasing it—but I didn't see them right away—they were on the other side of the truck. And it looked strange, the way the truck was moving so fast... instead of taking its time pulling out of the diner and onto the road."

POW! POW!

With two powerful swats of the claw hammer, he freed the second table leg, and it clattered to the floor. Ben tossed it into the corner, and moved to the third leg.

"I just saw this big truck at first—and it looks funny how fast it's coming out onto the road. And then I saw those things—and the truck was moving slower, and they were catching up...and grabbing... and jumping on. They had their arms around the driver's neck..."

Another table leg fell loose and thudded to the rug. Ben was breathing very hard. And Barbara was listening, both horrified and fascinated by his story.

"And that truck just cut right across the road—through the guard rail, you know. And I had to hit my brakes, and I went screeching all over the place, and the truck smashed into a big sign and into the pumps of the Sunoco station down there. I heard the crash. And that big thing started burning—and yet it was still moving, right through the pumps and on into the station—and I'm stopped, dead in my tracks. And I saw those things... and they all started to back off... some of them running...or trying to run...but they run kind of like they're crippled. But they keep backing off. And it's like...it's like they gotta get away from the fire—and the guy driving the truck couldn't get out nohow—the cab of the truck was plowed halfway into the wall of the Sunoco station—and he's being burned alive in there and he's screaming—screaming like hell..."

Barbara's eyes deepened, and her face wrinkled in anxiety. The continuing nightmare, for her, was growing more and more complex.

Ben swatted the last table leg from the table, and the table top started to drop. It was heavy. He regained control of it and struggled, trying to drag it across the room. Barbara moved toward him and took hold of an end of the table, but did not really help much, as it was really too heavy for her to pitch in.

"I don't know what's gonna happen," Ben said. "I mean, I didn't know if the gas station was going to explode...or fly to pieces...or what's gonna happen. I just started driving down the road, trying to get far away in case there was an explosion...and the guy in the truck is screaming and screaming...and after a while he just stops."

He set down the table, and wiped beads of perspiration from his forehead. His breathing was still heavy from the previous exertion. He wiped his hand on his shirt. His eyes were wide and angry with the remembrance of the events he was describing for Barbara, and it almost seemed as though he might weep.

"And there those things were...standing back...across the road... standing looking like...looking like...like they just came back from the grave or something. And they were over by the diner, and there was cars and buses in the diner lot, with lots of windows smashed. And I knew those things must've finished off all the people in the diner, and more were outside, all over the place just biding their time for a chance to move in. So I went barreling right across the road in my truck—and I drove it right at some of those things—and I got a good look at them, I saw them for the first time in my lights—and then...I just run right down on them—and I grind down as hard as I can—and I knock a couple of them about fifty feet, flailin' into the air. And I just wanted to crush them—smash them filthy things. And they're just standing there. They don't bother to run. They don't even bother to get out of the road. Some of them keep reaching out, as if they could grab me. But they're just standing there...and the truck is running them down...as if...as if they were a bunch of bugs..." Seeing the fear in Barbara's eyes, Ben stopped himself. She was wide-eyed, staring in disgust, her hands still resting on the table top.

He refocused his attention on the table top, and started to lift it again. Barbara was practically motionless. As he tugged on the table, her hands fell away and she slowly pulled them against herself. He dragged the table, unassisted, toward the window he intended to board up with it.

He looked at Barbara. She stared back, practically expressionless.

"I'm just...I...I got kids," Ben said rubbing his perspiring forehead with his sleeve. "And...I guess they'll do all right. They can take care of themselves...but they're still only kids...and I'm being away and all...and..."

His voice trailed off, as he had gotten no response from Barbara and didn't know what to say next. He tugged at the table, and allowed it to lean against the wall.

"I'm just gonna do what I can," he said, making an effort to sound positive. "I'm going to do what I can, and I'm gonna get back...and I'm gonna see my people. And things are gonna be all right...and...I'm gonna get back."

His talk had begun to repeat itself, and he realized he had started to babble, and he saw the girl intently watching him, and he stopped. He composed himself with some effort, and started to speak a little more slowly. His voice became almost a monotone, with enforced calm, but beneath his anger and his fear he was a brave man, and he was bound and determined not to lose his confidence. He knew the girl was in need of bolstering, if she was going to be able to cope with the situation. Like it or not, his survival was to some measure dependent on hers, and on how well he could get her to cooperate and overcome her fear.

"Now, you and me are gonna be all right, too," he told her. "We can hold those things off. I mean...you can just...smash them. All you have to do is just keep your head and don't be too afraid. We can move faster than they can, and they're awfully weak compared to a grown man...and if you don't run and just keep swinging at them...

you can smash them. We're smarter than they are. And we're stronger than they are. We're gonna stop them. Okay?"

The girl stared.

"All we have to do is just keep our heads," Ben added.

They looked at each other for a moment, until Ben turned and picked up the table top again. As he started hoisting it up to the window, the girl spoke, quietly and weakly.

"Who are they?"

Ben stopped in his tracks, still supporting the heavy table top, and looked with amazement at Barbara's anxious face. Slowly, it dawned on him that the girl had never been really aware of the thing that had been happening. She had no idea of the extent of the danger, or the reason for it. She had not heard the radio announcements, the bulletins. She had been existing in a state of uninformed shock.

Incredulously, Ben shouted, "You haven't heard anything?"

She stared blankly, silently, her eyes fastened on his. Her reply was in her silence.

"You mean you don't have any idea what's going on?"

Barbara started to nod her answer, but instead she was seized with a fit of trembling. "I...I..."

Her trembling increased, she began to shake violently, and suddenly she flung her arms up and flailed them about, sobbing wildly. She began to walk in panic, wildly and aimlessly, in circles about the room.

"No...no...no...I...can't...what's happening...what's happening to us...why...what's happening...tell me...tell...me..."

Unnerved by her hysteria, Ben grabbed her, and shook her hard to bring her out of it—and her sobbing jerked to a halt, but she remained staring right through him—her eyes seemingly focused beyond him, at some far distant point. Her speech, still detached and rambling, became a little more coherent.

"We were in the cemetery...me...and Johnny...my brother, Johnny...we brought flowers for...this...man...came after me...and Johnny...he...he fought...and now he...he's..."

"All right! All right!" Ben shouted, directly into the girl's face— he had a feeling that if he couldn't bring her out of her present state of mind, she was going to go right off the deep end; she might kill

herself or do something which would result in destruction for both
of them. He tightened his grip on her wrists, and she wrenched
against him.

"Get your hands off me!"

She flung herself away from him, beating him across the chest,
taking him by surprise. But in her momentum, she stumbled over
one of the table legs, barely regained her balance, and threw her body
against the front door and stood there, poised as if to run out into
the night.

She rambled, losing any semblance of rationality.

"We've got to help him...got to get Johnny...we've got to go out
and find him...bring him..."

She advanced toward Ben, pleading with tears, the desperate
tears of a frightened child.

"Bring him here...we'll be safe...we can help him...we..."

The man stepped toward her. She backed away, suddenly frightened, holding one hand toward him defensively, and the other toward her mouth. "No...no...please...please...we've got to...we..."

He took one deliberate stride toward her. "Now...you calm
down," he said softly. "You're safe here. We can't take no chances..."

She pouted, and tears rolled down her cheeks.

"We've got to get Johnny," she said, weakly. And she put her
fingers in her mouth and stared wide-eyed at Ben, like a small child.

"Now...come on, now...you settle down," he told her. "You don't
know what these things are. It ain't no Sunday-school picnic out
there..."

She began sobbing hysterically, violently—it was clear she had
gone totally to pieces.

"Please...pleeeeese...No...no...no...Johnny...Johnny...pleeeese..."

Ben struggled to calm her, to hold her still, as she writhed and
squirmed to get away from him. Despite his strength, she wrenched
free—because he was trying hard not to hurt her. She stared at him,
their eyes met in an instant of calm—and then she screamed and
started beating at him and kicking him—kicking him again and
again, while he struggled to pin her arms at her sides and hold her
immobile against a wall. With brute force, he shoved her backwards
finally, propelling her into a soft chair—but she sprung up again,

screaming and slapping at his face. He was forced to grab her again, in a bear hug, practically slamming her into a corner. Then—he hated to do it—he brought up one powerful fist and punched her—but she jerked her head and the blow was misplaced, and did not put her out of commission. But it shocked her into dumb, wounded silence—long enough for him to hit her again, squarely. And her eyes fell sorrowfully on his and she began to crumple—she fell limp against him, as he supported her weight, easing her into his arms.

Holding her, he looked dumbly about the room. His eyes fell on the sofa. He did not carry, but almost walked her to the sofa, permitting her dead weight to fold onto it, and easing her head onto a cushion.

He stepped back and looked at her, and felt sorry for what he had to do. Still, she looked so peaceful lying there, as though she were not in any kind of danger at all. Her blonde hair was in disarray, though. And her face was wet with tears. And she was going to have a bruise where he had punched her on the chin.

Ben trembled. He hoped for both their sakes that he could find a way to pull them through. It was not going to be easy.

It was not going to be easy at all.

3

Next to the couch where Barbara lay unconscious, there was a cabinet radio of the type people used to buy in the 1930's. Ben stabbed at a button, and a glow came to the yellowed dial indicator of the radio, behind its plate of old glass, and while he waited for it to warm up he looked around for the tin of nails he had given to Barbara some time ago. He found it on the floor where Barbara had dropped it, and he selected some nails and slid them into his pocket. The radio began hissing and crackling with static. He returned to it, and played with the tuning dial. At first, he could get nothing but static—then it spun past what sounded like a voice, and Ben adjusted it carefully, trying to find the spot. Finally, the tuner brought in a metallic monotone voice...

"...ERGENCY RADIO NETWORK. NORMAL BROADCAST FACILITIES HAVE BEEN TEMPORARILY DISCONTINUED. STAY TUNED TO THIS NETWORK FOR EMERGENCY INFORMATION. YOUR LAW ENFORCEMENT AGENCIES URGE YOU TO REMAIN IN YOUR HOMES. KEEP ALL DOORS AND WINDOWS LOCKED OR BOARDED SHUT. USE ALL FOOD, WATER, AND MEDICAL SUPPLIES SPARINGLY. CIVIL DEFENSE FORCES ARE ATTEMPTING TO GAIN CONTROL OF THE SITUATION. STAY NEAR YOUR RADIO, AND REMAIN TUNED TO THIS FREQUENCY. DO NOT USE YOUR AUTOMOBILE. REMAIN IN YOUR HOMES. KEEP ALL DOORS AND WINDOWS LOCKED."

A long pause. A crackle. Then the message began repeating. It was a recording.

"OUR LIVE BROADCASTERS WILL CONVEY INFORMATION AS RECEIVED FROM CIVIL DEFENSE HEADQUARTERS. THIS IS YOUR CIVIL DEFENSE EMERGENCY RADIO NETWORK. NORMAL BROADCAST

FACILITIES HAVE BEEN TEMPORARILY DISCONTINUED. STAY TUNED TO THIS NETWORK..."

Ben waved his hand in disgust—at the repetition of the radio—and moved away as it continued its announcement. He returned to the heavy wooden tabletop still leaning against the wall beneath the living room window. Keeping his own body back in the shadows of the room, Ben peeled back the window curtain just enough to peer outside into the darkness of the lawn.

He saw there were now four ominous figures standing in the yard.

The metallic voice of the radio recording continued to repeat itself.

And the figures stood very still, their arms dangling, aspects of their silhouettes revealing tattered clothing or shaggy hair. They were cold, dead things.

Something in the distance suddenly startled Ben. From across the road, a figure was moving toward the house. The ghoulish beings were increasing in number, hour by hour. It was nothing that Ben had not expected, had not taken into account; still, the actuality of it caused his heart to leap with fear each time he saw new evidence of it.

If the things increased sufficiently in number, it was only a matter of time before they would start to attack the house, hammering and pounding, trying to force their way in.

Ben spun away from the door and rushed to the fireplace. He reached for his matches. In a little stand by the couch where Barbara lay unconscious, there was a bunch of old magazines. Grabbing them, Ben ripped pages loose and crumpled them into the fireplace. He piled kindling wood and a few larger logs, then touched the paper with a match and watched a small fire take hold.

On the mantel was a can of charcoal-lighter. Ben grabbed it gratefully and sprayed it into the fire and it whooshed into a larger blaze, almost singeing the big man's face as he worked. The larger logs began to burn. He returned to the window.

The recorded message continued to repeat itself.

"...FORCEMENT AGENCIES URGE YOU TO REMAIN IN YOUR HOMES. KEEP ALL DOORS AND WINDOWS LOCKED OR BOARDED SHUT. USE ALL FOOD, WATER

AND MEDICAL SUPPLIES SPARINGLY. CIVIL DEFENSE FORCES ARE ATTEMPTING TO..."

Ben hoisted the tabletop to the windowsill and struggled to brace it there while he placed a nail into position. He pounded hard with the claw hammer...driven by desperation...another nail...and another. With the table secure, he checked it hastily and rushed to another window and lifted the edge of its curtains and peered out.

Now there were five figures on the lawn.

Ben pivoted, letting the edge of the curtain drop, and rushed to the fire, where the biggest logs had now begun to blaze. He seized two of the discarded table legs, ripped curtains from the boarded-up window and used strips of the cloth to wrap around the ends of the table legs, then drenched the cloth with charcoal-lighter and plunged the table legs into the fire making two good flaming torches. A torch in each hand, he moved toward the door.

He nudged a big padded armchair ahead of him to the door and, taking both torches in one hand, pulled the curtain aside for another look at the yard.

The figures out there still stood silently, watching the house.

With charcoal-lighter, Ben drenched the padded armchair and touched it with a torch. It caught fire instantly, and the flames licked and climbed, casting flickering light throughout the house. The heat on Ben's face was severe, but he had to fight it as he lunged for the door, unbolting it and flinging it wide open.

From the doorway, the flaming chair cast eerie, irregular illumination out onto the lawn, and the waiting figures stepped back slightly, as though they were afraid.

Ben shoved the chair through the doorway and slid it across the front porch. He toppled it over the edge, and the flaming bulk tumbled down the steps onto the front lawn. In the rolling motion, flames leapt and sparks flew, and small particles of the chair's stuffing leapt and glowed in the night wind.

The bonfire raged in the tall grass.

Ben watched for a moment, as the waiting figures backed farther away.

Inside the house again, Ben banged the front door shut and fastened the bolt.

"...ORCES ARE ATTEMPTING TO GAIN CONTROL OF THE SITUATION. STAY NEAR YOUR RADIO, AND REMAIN TUNED TO THIS FREQUENCY. DO NOT USE YOUR AUTOMOBILE. REMAIN IN..."

Hurrying to the window, Ben put more nails into the tabletop, fastening it securely, then he stood back and surveyed the room, his glance lingering on areas of possible vulnerability. There was the second large window, still unboarded, to the left of the door; a smaller side window; a window in the dining area on the other side of the house; and the front door, which had been bolted but not boarded up.

Ben turned, still inspecting, and his eyes suddenly grew wide.

The girl was sitting up on the couch; and it was her demeanor that had startled Ben more than the fact that she had regained consciousness. Her face was bruised, and she sat in silence staring at the floor. The radio droned on, enveloping her in its metallic repetitious tone, and the fire played on her face and reflected in her eyes...staring...and blinking very seldom.

Ben took off his sweater and moved toward her. He fixed the sweater over her shoulders and looked sympathetically into her face. She just stared at the floor. Ben felt dumb and helpless, and he was both ashamed and embarrassed by what he had done to her to end their struggle earlier, even though at the time it had been a necessary thing. For a long time, he waited for a response from the girl—perhaps an outburst of anger or resentment—but no response came. Forlornly, he moved to the pile of lumber in the center of the floor, chose a table-board, and went to the front window, which was still unboarded.

"...BROADCASTERS WILL CONVEY INFORMATION AS RECEIVED FROM CIVIL DEFENSE HEADQUARTERS. THIS IS YOUR CIVIL DEFENSE EMERGENCY RADIO NETWORK. NORMAL BROADCAST FACILITIES HAVE BEEN..."

Ben succeeded in boarding up the other two windows in the living room, then moved to the front door. He got the ironing board and placed it across the door horizontally, drove nails through the board into the molding and tested it for strength; it seemed to be sufficiently strong to help keep the things out. Ben moved on in his urgency to make the house secure against attack.

In the dining area, there were two closed doors. Trying one, he found it locked, examined it, and found no latch; apparently, someone had locked it with a key. It seemed to be a closet door. Ben yanked and tugged at it several times, but it would not yield, so he concluded it was secure enough and left it alone...concluding that it had obviously been locked by the owner of the house, who lay dead in the hallway upstairs.

Ben found the other door unlocked, and it led into a den with several windows. Disappointed at the added vulnerability, Ben let out a long sigh, then thought for a moment, staring around the room. Finally, he exited briskly, slamming the door to the den and locking it behind him with the skeleton key protruding from its keyhole. His intention was to board the den up instead of attempting to secure the bay windows.

But the skeleton key gave him an idea, and he snatched it out of its keyhole and went to the dining room which would not open before. He jammed the key in the keyhole of the dining room door, tried to turn it, jiggled and played with it for a while, but the door would not open. He put the key in his pocket and gave up on the door.

The supply of lumber in the center of the living room was dwindling. Ben's eyes fell momentarily on the motionless, sad figure of Barbara as he moved to check it out. She did not look back at him at all, and he bent over the pile of wood and selected another of the table-boards, for the purpose of boarding the den door. About to start hammering, a thought struck him—and he unlocked the door again and entered the room. There were chairs, a desk, a bureau...he stepped to the desk and started to rummage through the drawers. He pulled out papers, a stack of pencils and pens, a compass—a hundred little odds and ends. Another drawer, a hundred more virtually useless items...he left it hanging open. The bureau contained mostly clothing; he ripped open the big drawers, tumbling the clothing out, and hurled them through the doorway and into the dining area, with a scrape and a crash. One drawer—two—their contents spilling out onto the floor. He looked back at the bureau, and suddenly realizing a use for it, he grabbed hold of it and shoved the huge heavy piece of furniture through the doorway, walking it through the tight opening until it cleared, scraping grooves of paint out of the door-jambs. The same for the large, old-fashioned desk—which warranted another struggle, as the man attempted to secure all things of possible value before finally nailing the den door shut.

In the closet, there was a lot of old clothing; Ben found a good warm coat and jacket and flung them over his shoulder. High on the closet shelves were piles of old boxes, suitcases, hatboxes, and an old umbrella. He paused for an instant, debating their worth, or the possible worth of what they might contain. At his feet his eyes fell on still more clutter: boxes, umbrellas, dust shoes and slippers. He picked up a pair of ladies' flats and examined them, thinking of the barefoot girl out on the couch, and tucked them under his arm. As he pulled away, something caught his eye—within the dark recesses of the closet, something shiny: the sheen of a finished piece of wood, a familiar shape lying under a pile of dirty clothing. He reached out eagerly, and his hand found what he had hoped: a rifle. He set everything down and rummaged even more eagerly all over the floor of the closet—through shoe boxes, under things—items came flying out of the closet. A shoe box contained old letters and postcards. But in a cigar box, clattering around with pipe cleaners and cleaning fluid, there was a maintenance manual and a box of ammunition.

He flipped open the box, found it better than half full, and counted the cartridges—twenty-seven of them.

The rifle was a lever-action Winchester, .32 caliber. A good, powerful weapon, with plenty of impact. Ben worked the lever to clear the load—and, one after the other, seven more cartridges ejected and clattered onto the floor. He scooped them up, put them in the box with the others, and stuffed the manual into his back pocket; then, deciding to take the whole cigar box full of material, he tucked it under his arm, gathered jackets and shoes, and left the room.

In the dining room, he dropped the load of supplies on top of the drawerless bureau, and the sight of the girl in the living room stopped him short. She remained sitting as before, not moving.

Ben called out.

"We're all right, now. This place is good and solid. And I found a gun—a gun and some bullets."

He looked at Barbara from across the room. She seemed to take no note of his talking. He turned and picked up the table-board and the hammer, to begin boarding the den, and continued talking, as if he could luck onto some words that would cause her to respond.

"So, we have a radio...and sooner or later somebody will come to get us out of here. And we have plenty of food...for a few days, at least—oh!—and I got you some shoes—we'll see in a minute if they fit—and I got some warm clothes for us..."

He got the table-board in place across the center of the den door, above the knob, and he began driving nails. His pounding and the repetition of the radio message were the only sounds. The last nail in, the check for sturdiness, and the big man turned to the girl again.

"...AGENCIES URGE YOU TO REMAIN IN YOUR HOMES. KEEP ALL DOORS AND WINDOWS..."

Other than her upright position, the girl showed no signs of life. Her wide eyes just stared at the floor, or through it, as though at some point beyond.

"...LOCKED OR BOARDED SHUT..."

"Hey, that's us—" Ben said. "Our windows are boarded up. We're doing all right—"

He managed a smile, but with the girl not looking at him his attempt was half hearted. He took up the rifle, the cigar box, a coat and the shoes he had gotten for her in one clumsy armful and knelt with his bundle in front of the girl and dropped it at her feet. Taking in his hands the shoes he had found for her, he reached out toward her and said, "These aren't the prettiest things in the world, I guess—but they ought to keep your feet warm..."

Looking up at her, he again found it hard to go on talking in the face of her catatonia. He did not really know how to cope with it. Her stillness caused him to be as gentle toward her as he could be, but she did not react, and that both puzzled and frustrated Ben.

He held one of the shoes near her foot, waiting for her to lift her leg and slip into it. Finally, taking hold of one of her ankles, he lifted it and fumbled to put the shoe on her foot. It did not go on easily, partly because it was too small, but mostly because of her limpness.

But he did succeed in getting it on and he set her foot down gently and took hold of the other one.

After completing the task of putting on both her shoes for her, he leaned back on his haunches and looked into her face. She seemed to be staring at her feet.

"That's a real Cinderella story," he said, in an attempt at a joke.

No response. The man reached reflexively for his sweater pocket—but he had given Barbara his sweater.

"Hey—you know you got my cigarettes?"

He tried to smile again, but still got no reaction. He reached toward her and his hand entered the pocket of the sweater he had draped over her shoulders. His action made the girl appear to be looking directly at him, and her stare made him uncomfortable.

"You got my cigarettes," he said again, in a gentler tone, as one would try to explain some concept to a child, and as he spoke he pulled the pack of cigarettes from the pocket and leaned back on his haunches, as if he should not have ventured to touch her. He fumbled for a cigarette, put it in his mouth and lit it, trying not to look at the girl.

Her gaze still seemed to be fixed on his face.

The radio continued to drone, making her silence somehow more eerie for Ben. He would have been glad to have the metallic tones of the radio overridden by the sounds of another human voice.

"...TUNED TO THIS NETWORK FOR EMERGENCY INFORMATION. YOUR LAW ENFORCEMENT AGENCIES URGE YOU TO REMAIN IN YOUR HOMES. KEEP ALL DOORS AND WINDOWS LOCKED OR BOARDED SHUT..."

Ben inhaled his first puff of smoke and blew it through his nose. "We're doing okay," he repeated. "All our doors and windows are secure. Now...maybe you ought to lie down, you...Do you smoke?" Hopefully, he held up the burning cigarette. Her stare dropped from him back to the floor. He took another drag and blew the smoke out quickly.

"Maybe you—"

He cut himself short. He was getting nowhere. His time had better be spent in securing the old house against attack.

He scooped up the rifle and ammunition and sat in a chair across from Barbara and began methodically loading the shells into the chamber.

"Now, I don't know if you're hearing me or not—or if you're out cold or something. But I'm going upstairs now. Okay? Now we're safe down here. Nothing can get in here—at least not easy. I mean, they might be able to bust in, but it's gonna take some sweat, and I could hear them and I think I could keep them out. Later on, I'm gonna fix things good, so they can't get in nohow, but it's good for the time being. You're okay here."

He continued to load the rifle as he spoke, his cigarette dangling from his lip, causing him to squint from the smoke curling around his eyes.

"Now the upstairs is the only other way something can get in here, so I'm gonna go up and fix that."

He finished loading the last shell and was about to stand up when his glance fell on the girl again, and he tried to get through one last time.

"Okay? You gonna be all right?"

She remained silent. The man stood, tucked the rifle under his arm, grabbed up as much lumber as he could carry, and started for the stairs.

The girl looked up at him as he turned his back and he was aware of it, but he kept moving and her stare followed him.

"I'm gonna be upstairs. You're all right now. I'll be close by—upstairs. I'll come running if I hear anything."

He started up the stairs.

At the top of the landing, with a quick sucking in of his breath, he was confronted once again with the body that lay there torn and defaced. It was the corpse of a woman, probably an elderly woman, judging from the style of the remaining clothing that lay ripped into tatters and crusted in dried blood. Most of the flesh had been gnawed from the bones. The head was nearly severed from the body, the spinal column chewed through.

Ben set down his supplies and almost gagged at the sight of the corpse and tried not to look at it. The body was lying half across a blood-soaked throw rug, and a few feet away was another throw rug, with oriental patterns and a fringe sewn around its edge. The man grabbed the second rug and ripped away part of the fringe. Once the initial tear was made, the rest of the fringe peeled off easily. He freed it and, taking the rifle, tied one end of the fringe around the barrel and the other around the narrow part of the stock. This done, he slung the rifle over his shoulder, feeling more confident now that he could carry the weapon with him at all times, while he continued to work.

Then he leaned over the corpse and took hold of one end of the rug on which it lay, and began dragging it across the floor, holding his breath and gagging once or twice because of the stench of rotting flesh and the grisly appearance of the mutilated thing he had to struggle to pull down the darkened hallway, which contained several closed doors.

He deposited his ugly load at one of the doorways and threw open the door and jumped back with the rifle cocked, as if something might leap out at him. The door banged against the wall and squeaked as it settled down and stopped moving.

Nothing came out of the room.

Ben entered cautiously, with the rifle on the ready.

The room was vacant. Apparently it had been vacant for a long time. There were old yellowed newspapers on the floor, and a spider web in one corner.

There was a closet. Ben opened it slowly, pointing the rifle, ready to fire if necessary.

The closet contained nothing but dust, which rolled across the shelves in little balls and made Ben cough.

He stepped over to the windows and looked outside and down to the front lawn. Through the leafy overhang of the surrounding maple trees, he could make out the threatening forms of the dead things that stood there, watching and waiting, moving ever so slightly under the thick foliage. There appeared to be about six of them now, standing on the front lawn.

They moved around the truck, but they did not beat on it any more. Apparently they no longer felt threatened by it, now that the headlights had been smashed out. They took no more notice of it than if it had been a tree, or a pile of bricks. It seemed to have no meaning for them.

With a shudder, Ben realized that nothing human had any meaning for the dead things. Only the human beings themselves. The dead things were interested in human beings only to kill. Only to rip the flesh from their bodies. Only to make the human beings dead...like the dead things themselves.

Ben had a sudden impulse to smash the barrel of his rifle through the window and begin firing down on the ugly things on the lawn. But he controlled himself...calmed himself down. There was no sense in expending ammunition foolishly; all too well he knew how important it would be in the event of an all-out attack.

He withdrew from the window and returned to the corpse that lay at the threshold of the vacant room. Taking hold of the carpet and holding his breath once again, he dragged the corpse inside. And he left the room and shut the door, intending to board it up later. He thought of the closet door, which he could have removed and used to accomplish his boarding; but he did not think he would return for it; he did not want to enter that room ever again.

There were three more doors in the bloodstained hallway; one down at the end and two more opposite the vacant room with the corpse. The one down at the end was probably a bathroom; Ben tried it and found that it was. That left two more doors. They were probably bedrooms.

With his rifle cocked and ready to fire, Ben eased open the nearest of the two remaining doors. He jumped back, startled by his own reflection in a full-length mirror screwed onto the back of the door. His fingers groped and found the light switch. It turned out to be a child's bedroom. The bed sheets were rumpled and stained with blood, as if they had been clawed loose by someone struggling to hang on while he (or she) was being dragged from the bed. But there was no body in the room. Anxiously, afraid of what he might find, Ben searched around the bed and under it—and in the closet, which contained the clothing of a boy perhaps eleven or twelve years old. There were a couple of baseball bats, and an old skinned up baseball with the cover half off, lying on the floor of the closet.

Ben guessed that the boy was dead. Probably he had been dragged out of the house by some of those things that now stood watching and waiting outside. Probably the dead lady in the hall had been the boy's grandmother.

The thought of it renewed in Ben the terror of what was happening, which he had been able to suppress while his mind was occupied with working hard and taking defensive measures and concentrating on his own survival.

He thought of his own children—two boys, one nine and one thirteen. He did not have a wife any longer; she was dead; she had died several years ago and left him to raise the children alone. It was not easy. He loved the boys, but his job took him out of town often and much of the time he had to leave them in the care of their grandmother while he traveled and tried to earn enough money to support them all. He had been on his way home to them, but in the breakdown of communications during the present emergency his train had not arrived and he had started to hitchhike, desperate to get home. Nobody would pick him up and, walking at the outskirts of the town he had been in, he began encountering signs of destruction and murder. It puzzled him at first. He became scared. Then, in a restaurant he heard a newscast and he knew he had to get back to his family right away. He could not get a bus or cab. He even tried renting a car or just paying someone to take him where he wanted to go. Finally, hitchhiking again, a farmer picked him up and drove him a long way, but dropped him off out in the country, in the middle of nowhere it seemed. Ben got the truck on the front lawn from a dead man—a man who had been dragged from it and killed at the edge of a dirt road. He had continued listening to broadcasts on the truck radio, and he knew as much about what was happening as anyone else—which was very little. But he knew he wanted to survive and get back to his boys and their grandmother—although his reason told him that they were probably much better off in this emergency than he was himself. At least they were in a town, with other people and police protection and food and medical care if they required it. And their grandmother was a capable person. The boys would probably be all right. Ben tried to convince himself of that, but it was not easy, while he was confronted with the bloodstained sheets and mattress of the young boy who had probably been killed not so very long ago. And the old farmhouse was more a prison than it was a refuge for him and Barbara—although he did not even know her name and he could not help her, it seemed, and she was unwilling or unable to help herself.

Ben retreated from the child's room and tried the other closed door. The old lady's bedroom. He did not turn the light on at first. His eyes fell on the edge of the bed, with its white sheets, and he could see well enough to know that there were several large pieces of furniture in there. He flicked a switch, and the lights revealed nothing out of the ordinary—a bed and a couple of dressers. A quilt was folded and lying on top of the sheets, but the bed had not been slept in. Probably the old lady had gotten the boy to sleep and was preparing for bed herself when they were both attacked.

Ben entered the room and began to drag furniture out into the hallway. His plan was to get all the things of any possible use out of the boy's room and the old lady's room, and then board up the doors.

He did not know if the dead things could climb or not, or if they could think or not, or if they had any way of getting into the house through the upstairs windows. But he was not going to take any chances. Besides, when he was working, it gave him a feeling of accomplishing something and he did not worry too much or feel sorry for himself.

The noise of his work filled the old house.

4

Downstairs, Barbara still sat dazed on the couch.

The fire flickered on her face, and the burning wood popped loudly now and again, but she did not seem to take notice of these things. Objects in the room were silhouetted and the atmosphere was stark; if earlier Barbara would have expressed some fear of such surroundings, now she did not care. Her capacity to react had been bludgeoned out of her. She was already a victim of the dead things, because they had driven her into shock—she had lost her ability to think or feel.

"...BROADCAST FACILITIES HAVE BEEN TEMPORARILY DISCONTINUED. STAY TUNED TO THIS..."

From the radio, there was suddenly a buzzing sound and crackling static. Then, a hodgepodge of newsroom sounds (as heard earlier by Barbara's brother, Johnny, on their car radio); but this time the sounds were coming in clearer: typewriters, ticker-tape machine, low voices talking in the background.

Barbara did not stir, as if she had failed to discern any difference in the broadcast, even though the repetitious Civil Defense message had ceased and something obviously was about to happen.

"...ER...LADIES AND GENTLEMEN...WHAT?... YEAH, YEAH...LA...YEAH, I GOT THAT ONE... WHAT?...ANOTHER ONE?...PUT IT THROUGH CENTRAL...OKAY, CHARLIE, I'M ON THE AIR NOW...YEAH. LADIES AND GENTLEMEN, LISTEN CAREFULLY, PLEASE. WE NOW HAVE THE LATEST BULLETINS FROM EMERGENCY CENTRAL..."

The voice of the newscaster sounded tired, but he began reading his report factually and unemotionally, with the air of a professional commentator who has been covering a major event for forty-eight hours and is no longer impressed with the latest developments.

"...UP-TO-THE-MINUTE REPORTS INFORM US THAT THE...SIEGE...FIRST DOCUMENTED IN THE MIDWEST-ERN SECTION OF THE COUNTRY IS INDEED SPREAD ACROSS THE COUNTRY, AND IS IN FACT WORLDWIDE. MEDICAL AND SCIENTIFIC ADVISORS HAVE BEEN SUM-MONED TO THE WHITE HOUSE, AND REPORTERS ON THE SCENE IN WASHINGTON INFORM US THAT THE PRESIDENT IS PLANNING TO MAKE PUBLIC THE RE-SULTS OF THAT CONFERENCE IN AN ADDRESS TO THE NATION OVER YOUR CIVIL DEFENSE EMERGENCY NET-WORK..."

None of the preceding brought any response from Barbara. She did not move. She did not get up to call Ben, in case he might hear something of value in his efforts to protect them both.

"...THE STRANGE...BEINGS...THAT HAVE APPEARED IN MOST PARTS OF THE NATION SEEM TO HAVE CER-TAIN PREDICTABLE PATTERNS OF BEHAVIOR. IN THE FEW HOURS FOLLOWING INITIAL REPORTS OF VIO-LENCE AND DEATH, AND APPARENTLY DERANGED AT-TACKS ON THE LIVES OF PEOPLE TAKEN COMPLETELY OFF GUARD, IT HAS BEEN ESTABLISHED THAT THE ALIEN BEINGS ARE HUMAN IN MANY PHYSICAL AND BE-HAVIORAL ASPECTS. HYPOTHESES AS TO THEIR ORIGIN AND THEIR AIMS HAVE TO THIS POINT BEEN SO VAR-IED AND SO DIVERSE THAT WE MUST ONLY REPORT THESE FACTORS TO BE UNKNOWN. TEAMS OF SCIEN-TISTS AND PHYSICIANS PRESENTLY HAVE THE CORPSES OF SEVERAL OF THE AGGRESSORS, AND THESE CORPS-ES ARE BEING STUDIED FOR CLUES THAT MIGHT NE-GATE OR CONFIRM EXISTING THEORIES. THE MOST... OVERWHELMING FACT...IS THAT THESE...BEINGS ARE INFILTRATING THROUGH URBAN AND RURAL AREAS THROUGHOUT THE NATION, IN FORCES OF VARYING NUMBER, AND IF THEY HAVE NOT AS YET EVIDENCED THEMSELVES IN YOUR AREA, PLEASE...TAKE EVERY AVAILABLE PRECAUTION. ATTACK MAY COME AT ANY TIME, IN ANY PLACE, WITHOUT WARNING. REPEAT-

ING THE IMPORTANT FACTS FROM OUR PREVIOUS REPORTS: THERE IS AN AGGRESSIVE FORCE...ARMY... OF UNEXPLAINED, UNIDENTIFIED...HUMANOID BE-INGS...THAT HAS APPEARED...IN WORLDWIDE PRO-PORTIONS...AND THESE BEINGS ARE TOTALLY AGGRES-SIVE...IRRATIONAL IN THEIR VIOLENCE. CIVIL DEFENSE EFFORTS ARE UNDERWAY, AND INVESTIGATIONS AS TO THE ORIGIN AND PURPOSE OF THE AGGRESSORS ARE BEING CONDUCTED. ALL CITIZENS ARE URGED TO TAKE UTMOST PRECAUTIONARY MEASURES TO DE-FEND AGAINST THE...INSIDIOUS...ALIEN...FORCE. THEY ARE WEAK IN PHYSICAL STRENGTH, AND ARE EAS-ILY DISTINGUISHABLE FROM HUMANS BY THEIR DE-FORMED APPEARANCE. THEY ARE USUALLY UNARMED BUT APPEAR CAPABLE OF HANDLING WEAPONS. THEY HAVE APPEARED, NOT LIKE AN ORGANIZED ARMY. NOT WITH ANY APPARENT REASON OR PLAN...INDEED, THEY SEEMED TO BE DRIVEN BY THE URGES OF EN-TRANCED...OR...OR OBSESSED MINDS. THEY APPEAR TO BE TOTALLY UNTHINKING. THEY CAN...I REPEAT: THEY CAN BE STOPPED BY IMMOBILIZATION; THAT IS, BY BLINDING OR DISMEMBERING. THEY ARE, ON THE AVERAGE, WEAKER IN STRENGTH THAN AN ADULT HUMAN, BUT THEIR STRENGTH IS IN NUMBERS, IN SURPRISE, AND IN THE FACT THAT THEY ARE BEYOND OUR NORMAL REALM OF UNDERSTANDING. THEY AP-PEAR TO BE IRRATIONAL, NON-COMMUNICATIVE BE-INGS...AND THEY ARE DEFINITELY TO BE CONSIDERED OUR ENEMIES IN WHAT WE MUST CALL A STATE OF... NATIONAL EMERGENCY. IF ENCOUNTERED, THEY ARE TO BE AVOIDED OR DESTROYED. UNDER NO CIRCUM-STANCES SHOULD YOU ALLOW YOURSELVES OR YOUR FAMILIES TO BE ALONE OR UNGUARDED WHILE THIS MENACE PREVAILS. THESE BEINGS ARE FLESH-EATERS. THEY ARE EATING THE FLESH OF THE PEOPLE THEY KILL. THE PRINCIPAL CHARACTERISTIC OF THEIR ON-SLAUGHT IS THEIR DEPRAVED, INSANE QUEST FOR HU-

MAN FLESH. I REPEAT: THESE ALIEN BEINGS ARE EAT-
ING THE FLESH OF THEIR VICTIMS..."

At this Barbara bolted from the couch in wild, screaming hysteria, as though the words of the commentator had finally penetrated
her numbed state and forced upon her brain a realization of what
exactly had happened to her brother. She could hear the ripping
sounds of his flesh and could see the specter of the thing that had
killed him, and her screams struggled to obliterate these things as she
hurtled across the room and crashed her body against the front door.

Startled, unslinging his gun, Ben leaped down the stairs. The
girl was clawing at the barricades, trying to break out of the house,
sobbing in wild desperation. Ben rushed toward her, but she writhed
out of his reach, ran across the room—toward the maze of heaped-
up furniture in front of the door in the dining area which Ben had
found locked.

Suddenly that door flew open and—from out of the maze of
furniture—strong hands grabbed Barbara. She screamed in terror, as
Ben leaped and began swinging the butt of his rifle.

Whoever it was who had gotten hold of Barbara, he let go of the
girl and ducked, and the rifle butt missed him and crashed against a
piece of furniture. Quickly, Ben brought it up, and almost squeezed
the trigger.

"No! Don't shoot!" a voice yelled, and Ben narrowly stopped
himself from firing.

"We're from town—we're not—" the man said.

"We're not some of those things!" a second voice said, and Ben
saw another man step out from behind the partially opened door,
which he had thought to be locked.

The man hiding behind the furniture stood up, slowly as though
he thought Ben might still shoot him. He was not a full-grown man.
He was a boy, maybe sixteen years old, in blue jeans and denim jacket. The man behind him was about forty years old, bald, wearing a
white shirt and loosened tie—and carrying a heavy pipe in his hand.

"We're not some of those things," the bald man repeated. "We're
in the same fix you're in."

Barbara had flung herself onto the couch, and was sobbing sporadically. All three men glanced at her, as though she were an object of common concern that would convince each of them of the other's good intentions. The boy finally went over to her and looked at her sympathetically.

Ben stared, dumbfounded at the presence of the strangers.

The radio voice continued with its information about the emergency.

The bald man backed away from Ben nervously, not taking his eyes off of Ben's rifle, and crouched beside the radio to listen, still holding his length of pipe.

"...PERIODIC REPORTS, AS INFORMATION REACHES THIS NEWSROOM, AS WELL AS SURVIVAL INFORMATION AND A LISTING OF RED CROSS RESCUE POINTS, WHERE PICK-UPS WILL BE MADE AS OFTEN AS POSSIBLE WITH THE EQUIPMENT AND STAFF PRESENTLY AVAILABLE..."

Ben still stood staring at the two new people. He exuded, despite himself, an air of resentment, as though they had intruded on his private little fortress. He did not resent their presence as much as he resented the fact that they had obviously been in the house all this time without coming up to help him or Barbara. He was not sure of their motive in revealing themselves now, and he did not know how completely he should trust them.

The bald man looked up from the radio. "There's no need to stare at us that way," he said to Ben.

"We're not dead, like those things out there. My name is Harry Cooper. The boy's name is Tom. We've been holed up in the cellar."

"Man, I could've used some help," Ben said, barely controlling his anger. "How long you guys been down there?"

"That's the cellar. It's the safest place," Harry Cooper said, with a tone in his voice to convey the idea that anybody who wouldn't hole up in the cellar in such an emergency must be an idiot.

The boy, Tom, got up from beside the couch, where he had been trying to think of a way to comfort Barbara, and came over to join in the ensuing discussion.

"Looks like you got things pretty secure up here," Tom said to Ben, in a friendly way.

Ben pounced on him.

"Man, you mean you couldn't hear the racket we were making up here?"

Cooper pulled himself to his feet. "How were we supposed to know what was going on?" he said, defensively. "It could have been those things trying to get in here, for all we knew."

"That girl was screaming," Ben said, angrily. "Surely you must know what a girl's screaming sounds like. Those things don't make that kind of noise. Anybody decent would know somebody was up here that could use some help."

Tom said, "You can't really tell what's going on from down there. The walls are thick. You can't hear."

"We thought we could hear screams," Cooper added. "But that might have meant those things were in the house after her."

"And you wouldn't come up and help?" Ben turned his back on them, contemptuously.

The boy seemed to be ashamed of himself, but Cooper remained undaunted by Ben's contempt, probably accustomed to a lifetime of rationalizing his cowardice.

"Well...I...if...there was more of us..." the boy said. But he turned away, and did not have the gumption to continue his excuses.

Cooper persisted.

"That racket sounded like the place was being ripped apart. How were we supposed—"

But Ben cut him off.

"You just said it was hard to hear down there. Now you say it sounded like the place was being ripped apart. You'd better get your story straight, mister."

Cooper exploded.

"Bullshit! I don't have to take any crap from you. Or any insults. We've got a safe place in that cellar. And you or nobody else is going to tell me to risk my life when I've got a safe place."

"All right... why don't we settle—" Tom began. But Cooper did not allow him to continue. He went on talking, but in a calmer voice, espousing his own point of view.

"All right. We came up. Okay? We're here. Now I suggest we all go back downstairs before any of these things find out we're in here."

"They can't get in here," Ben said, as though it were a certainty. He had plenty of doubts in his own mind, but he did not feel like discussing them for the benefit of those two strangers who were, as far as he could see, one boy and one coward.

"You got the whole place boarded up?" Tom asked. He was a bit skeptical, but he was willing to submerge his skepticism in favor of group harmony.

"Most of it," Ben replied, keeping his voice in an even, analytical tone. "All but the upstairs. It's weak in places, but it won't be hard to fix it up good. I got the stuff and I—"

Cooper broke in, his voice at a high pitch again.

"You're insane! You can't make it secure up here. The cellar's the safest place in the damned house!"

"I'm tellin' you they can't get in here." Ben shouted at him.

"And I'm telling you those things turned over our car! We were damned lucky to get away in one piece—now you're trying to tell me they can't get through a lousy pile of wood?"

Ben stared for a moment, and did not know what to say. He knew the cellar had certain advantages, but he could not abide being told about it by someone like Cooper, who was obviously a coward. Ben knew he had managed to do pretty well so far, and he did not want to throw in his lot entirely with someone who might panic or run, in an emergency.

Tom took advantage of the lull to throw in an additional fact, which he thought might soften Ben and stop the argument between him and Cooper:

"Harry's wife and kid are downstairs. The kid's been hurt, pretty badly. Harry doesn't want to leave them anywhere where they might be threatened, or subjected to any more attacks by those things."

The statement took Ben by surprise. He softened, and exhaled a deep breath. Nobody said anything for a long moment, until finally he swallowed, and made his point again.

"Well...I...I think we're better off up here." Glancing around at the barricades, Tom said, "We could strengthen all this stuff up, Mr. Cooper." And he eyed the bald man hopefully, looking to him to cooperate with Ben at least a little, so that they might be safer and make the best of the circumstances.

Ben continued, emphasizing the strong points of his argument. "With all of us working, we can fix this place up so nothing can get in here. And we have food. The stove. The refrigerator. A warm fire. And we have the radio."

Cooper merely glowered, in a new burst of anger. "Man, you're crazy. Everything that's up here, we can bring downstairs with us. You've got a million windows up here. All these windows—you're gonna make them strong enough to keep those things out?"

"Those things don't have any strength," Ben said, with controlled anger. "I smashed three of them and pushed another one out the door."

"I'm telling you they turned our car over on its roof!" Cooper spat.

"Oh, hell, any good five men can do that," Ben said.

"That's my point! Only there's not going to be five—there's going to be twenty...thirty...maybe a hundred of those things! Once they all know we're in here, this place will be crawling with them!"

Calmly, Ben said, "Well, if there's that many, they're gonna get us no matter where we are."

"We fixed the cellar door so it locks and boards from the inside," Tom said. "It's really strong. I don't think anything could get in there."

"It'd be the only door we'd have to protect," Cooper added, in a slightly less hysterical tone. "But all these doors and windows—why, we'd never know where they were going to hit us next."

"But the cellar has one big disadvantage," Tom pointed out. "There's no place to run—I mean, if they ever did get in—there's no back exit. We'd be done for." The bald man stared, his mouth wide open. He could not believe Tom would desert the sanctity of the basement, for any reason, because he himself felt so driven to remain there, as if nothing could touch him—like a rat in his hole.

"I think we should fortify the entire house as good as we can—and keep the basement for a stronghold, a last resort," Ben said, decisively. "That way we can run to the cellar when everything else falls through. We can maintain contact with what's going on out there for as long as possible."

"That makes sense," Tom said. "I don't know, Mr. Cooper. I think he's right. I think we should stay up here."

"The upstairs is just as much of a trap as the basement," Ben said, analytically. "There are three rooms up there and they have to be boarded up. But those things are weak. We can keep them out. I have this gun now, and I didn't have it before and I still managed to beat three of them off. Now...we might have to try and get out of here on our own, because there's no guarantee anyone is going to send help—and maybe nobody even knows we're in here. If someone does come to help—and this house gets full of those things—we'd be scared to open the cellar door and let the rescue party know we're in here."

"How many of the things are outside now?" Tom asked.

"I think six or seven," Ben replied. "I can't get an accurate count because of the darkness and the trees."

"Look, you two can do whatever you like," Cooper said, morosely. "I'm going back down to the cellar, and you'd better decide—because I'm gonna board up that door and I'm not gonna be crazy enough to unlock it again, no matter what happens."

"Wait a minute!" Tom exclaimed. "Let's think about this for a minute, Mr. Cooper—all our lives depend on what we decide."

"Nope. I've made my decision. You make yours. And you can stew in your own juice if you decide to stay up here."

Alarmed, Tom began to urge desperately. "Now wait a minute, damn it, let's think about this a while—we can make it to the cellar if we have to—and if we do decide to stay down there, we'll need some things from up here. Now, let's at least consider this a while—"

Ben added: "Man, if you box yourself into that cellar, and if there's a lot of those things that get into the house—you've had it. At least up here you can make a break for it—you outran them once, or you wouldn't even be here."

Flustered and still not quite decided, Tom went to one of the front windows and peered out through the barricade.

"Yeah, looks like six—or maybe eight of them out there now," he said, his voice showing his increased alarm after attempting a headcount.

"That's more than there were," Ben admitted. "There are quite a few out back, too—unless they're the same ones that are out here now."

He burst into the kitchen, as the fringed rifle sling snapped and the weapon started to fall; he twisted to keep it on his back and tried to grab it, reaching behind. His attention on the gun, he did not see the window as he moved toward it; but regaining control of the gun he looked up—and stopped cold. Hands were reaching through broken glass behind the barricades—graying, rotting hands, scratching, reaching, trying to grab—and through aspects of the glass could be seen the inhuman faces behind the hands. The barrier was being strained, no doubt about that, but it seemed to be holding well enough.

The man smashed with the rifle butt against the ugly extremities. Once. Twice. The rifle butt stamped down on the decaying hands... driving one of them back with a shattering of the already broken glass it had been reaching through. The rifle butt smashed another of the hands against the window molding solidly—but the hand, unfeeling of any pain, continued to claw after a hold.

Ben slid his finger to the trigger and turned the rifle, smashing the barrel through some unbroken glass, and two of the gray hands seized the protruding metal. A dead face appeared behind the hands...ugly...expressionless...rotting flesh hanging from the bones. Ben's face looked directly through the opening in the barricade into the dead eyes beyond, the man struggling desperately to control the weapon and the zombie thing outside trying to pull it away by the barrel. For a brief instant, the muzzle pointed directly at the hideous face; then...BLAM! The report shattered the air and the lifeless thing was thrown back, propelled by the blast, its head torn partially away, its still outstretched hands falling back with the crumpling body.

The other hands continued to clutch and grab.

Tom rushed into the kitchen behind Ben, and Harry was standing cautiously a few feet from the doorway. A distant voice, that of Harry's wife, Helen, suddenly began to cry out from the cellar.

"Harry! Harry! Harry! Are you all right?!"

"It's all right, Helen. We're all right!" Cooper called out in a quavering voice which betrayed his fear and anxiety and was not likely to calm Helen very much.

Tom immediately rushed to Ben's aid. The big man was pounding at a dead hand that was trying to work at the barricade from the bottom. The blows from the rifle butt seemed ineffectual as the hand, oblivious except for the physical jouncing from the impact, continued to claw and grab. Tom leaped against the barricaded window and seized the rotting wrist with both his hands and tried to bend the wrist back in an effort to break it, but it seemed limp and almost totally pliable. Disgust crept over Tom's face. He tried to scrape the cold thing against the edge of the broken glass, and the absence of blood was immediately evident in an appalling way, as the sharp edge of broken glass ripped into what looked like rotting flesh. Another hand suddenly grabbed at Tom's hand and tried to pull it through the glass. Tom yelled, and Ben tried to swing the barrel of his rifle toward the thing struggling with Tom; but another hand clutched at him even while he was trying to help the boy—a hand was clawing and ripping Ben's shirt, but he managed to free himself and step back long enough to aim the gun. Another loud blast, and the hands Tom was fighting jerked back and fell into darkness. Badly shaken, Tom just stared through an opening in the broken glass behind the barricade. Ben took careful aim and pulled the trigger again; the blast ripped through the thing's chest, leaving a big gaping hole—but it remained on its feet, backing slowly away.

"Oh, good God!" Tom exclaimed, panicked at the failure of the rifle, as the dead thing recovered and stepped forward again, oblivious to the fact that half of its upper torso had been blown away.

Ben cocked his weapon and fired again—another loud report. This time the shell ripped through the thing's thigh, just below the pelvis. The thing backed away, but as it tried to put weight on its right leg it fell to a heap. Tom and Ben just stared, in disbelief. The thing was still moving away, dragging itself with its arms and pushing against the ground with its remaining useful leg.

"Mother of God! What are these things?"

Tom fell back against the wall. His eyes fell on Harry, and he saw the unmistakable cowardly fear in the bald man's face.

Ben wet his lips, took a deep breath and held it, carefully sighting down the barrel of the rifle again. He pulled the trigger. The shell seemed to blow open the skull of the crawling form, and it fell backwards.

"Damn...damn thing from hell!"

Ben's voice trembled as he let out his held breath.

Outside, the thing that had fallen limply, without the use of its eyes, moved its arms in groping, clutching motions, seemingly still trying to drag itself away.

From the cellar:

"Harry! Harry!"

After a moment of silence, Ben turned from the barricaded window with its shattered glass. "We have to board up this place a lot stronger," he said and, out of breath, he made a move to start to work when Harry spoke: "You're crazy! Those things are gonna be at every door and window in this place! We've got to get into the cellar!"

Ben turned to Harry and faced him, with absolute fury in his eyes. In his rage, his voice bellowed, deeper and more commanding.

"Get into your goddamned cellar! Get the hell out of here!"

The shouting stopped Harry for an instant, then his adamancy returned. His mind made up, he knew he would have to go into the cellar without the others if need be, and he had better gather whatever supplies they would let him keep without interference. Perhaps in the confusion of the moment, he thought, he could snatch up a lot of things without an argument. He moved toward the refrigerator, but Ben stopped him.

"Don't you touch any of that food," Ben warned.

He tightened his grip on the rifle, and though he did not point it at Harry, Harry was well aware of the power it implied.

Harry allowed his fingers to fall away from the handle of the refrigerator.

"Now, if I stay up here," Ben said, "I'm gonna be fighting for what's up here—and that food and that radio and anything else that's up here is part of what I'm fighting for. And you are dead wrong— you understand? But if you're going to the cellar, get your ass moving—go down there and get out of here, man, and don't mess with me anymore."

Harry turned to Tom.

"This man is crazy, Tom! He's crazy! We've got to have food down there! We've got a right!"

Ben confronted Tom also. "You going down there with him?"

"No beating around the bush. You going, or ain't you? This is your last chance."

After a long moment of silence, Tom turned and faced Harry Cooper apologetically, for he had decided in favor of Ben.

"Harry...I think he's right..."

"You're crazy."

"I really think we're better off up here."

"You're crazy. I have a kid down there. She couldn't possibly take all the racket up here, and those things reaching through the glass. We'll be lucky if she lives, as it is now."

"Okay," Ben said. "You're the kid's father. If you're dumb enough to go die in that trap, it's your business. But I'm not dumb enough to go with you. It's just bad luck for the kid that her old man's so dumb. Now, you get the hell down the cellar. You can be boss down there. And I'm boss up here. And you ain't taking any of this food, and you ain't touching anything that's up here."

"Harry, we can get food to you," Tom said, "if you want to stay down there and..."

"You bastards!" Harry said. From the cellar, his wife was still crying out:

"Harry! Harry! What's going on, Harry?"

He moved toward the cellar, but Tom stopped him.

"Send Judy up here," Tom said. "She'll want to stay up here with me."

Ben glanced at Tom, with a surprised expression on his face. No one had told him there was anybody in the cellar except for Harry's wife and daughter.

"My girlfriend," Tom explained. "Judy's my girlfriend."

"You should've told me she was down there," Ben said.

In the meantime, Harry had pivoted and stomped down the cellar stairs, and the sound of lighter footsteps told them the girl was on her way up.

She hugged Tom and looked sheepishly at Ben. She was about Tom's age, dressed similarly to him, in blue jeans and denim jacket. She was a pretty girl, blond, scared, and probably—Ben thought—going to be about as much of a problem as Barbara. With Tom, she moved to the closed cellar door, behind which could be heard the sounds of Harry boarding it up.

"You know I won't open this door again!" Harry shouted, through it. "I mean it!"

"We can fix it up here!" Tom shouted back, not giving up. "With your help we could—"

"Let him go," Ben said. "His mind is made up. You'd be better off to just forget about him."

"We're better off up here!" Tom shouted. "There are good places we can run to up here!"

From behind the cellar door, there was no reply. Just the sound of Harry's footsteps going down the stairs.

Ben tied the broken fringe back onto the rifle, then began reloading it, replacing the spent shells. When it was loaded, he strapped it to his shoulder again, then turned and moved toward the upstairs. In passing, his glance fell on Barbara; he stepped backwards off the stairs and looked at her.

The radio had taken up again with its monotonous recorded message.

Tom had not given up and was still pleading with Harry, shouting against the closed cellar door.

"Harry, we'd be better off if we was all working together! We'll let you have food when you need it—" He glanced warily at Ben, half-expecting reprisal for making his offer of food, contrary to Ben's wishes. "And if we pound on the door, those things might be chasing us, and you can let us in."

Still no answer from Harry.

Tom listened a while longer, then retreated, disappointed and worried about the fractionalization that had occurred and the realization that each of them could be heavily dependent on any of the others if worse came to worst.

Judy was sitting quietly in a chair, and she gave Tom a worried look as he stood beside her and brushed her cheek with his hand.

Ben was with Barbara, stooping beside her as she lay on the couch. She stared into an unseeing void. Ben felt sorry for her, and just as helpless as ever where she was concerned.

"Hey...hey, honey?"

She made no response. He brushed her hair back from her eyes. She trembled; it almost seemed for a moment that she might acknowledge his tenderness, but she did not. Ben felt very sorrowful, almost as he would feel for one of his children at a time of illness. He massaged his forehead and eyes, tired from the fear and exertion of the past hours. He bent finally to cover the girl with a coat that he had brought from the den, then stepped away and heaved a log onto the fire and stirred it to keep the blaze good and warm; his primary concern in this effort was for the girl. Behind him, Tom stepped forward, and Ben sensed his presence and his worries concerning Harry Cooper.

"He's wrong, man," Ben said, positively.

Tom remained silent.

"I'm not boxing myself in down there," Ben added. "We might be here several days. We'll get it good and strong up here, and he'll come up and join us. He won't stay down there very long. He'll want to see what's going on—or maybe if we get a chance to get out, he'll come up and help us. I have a truck outside...but I need gas. If I could get to those pumps out back...maybe we'd have a chance to save ourselves."

With that, Ben turned and mounted the stairs to continue his work up there, taking it for granted that Tom would be willing and able to man the downstairs.

5

The cellar, with its stark gray walls and dusty clutter, was cold and damp. Cardboard cartons tied with cord and a hanging grid of pipe-work all looked dirty in the heavy shadows cast by bare light bulbs. The cartons took up much of the space; they varied in size from grocery boxes with faded brand names to large packing crates that might have contained furniture. The washing machine, an old roller type, sat off in a corner of the cellar near a makeshift shower stall. Lines for drying clothes were strung over the pipe work so low that Harry was forced to duck under them as he walked from the stairs to the other side of the confining quarters.

A pair of stationary tubs and an old metallic cabinet stood against one of the walls, where Harry's wife, Helen, leaned over the faucet of one of the tubs, wetting a cloth with cold water. She looked up as Harry entered, but remained more interested in what she was doing at the moment; she wrung out the cloth, feeling it to ascertain that it retained the correct amount of dampness, and took it to where a young girl, their daughter, lay motionless atop a homemade worktable. On a pegboard above the table there were hanging tools and cables, and built into the table itself were drawers for smaller tools—screws and bolts, washers, and so forth.

Helen's movements were a little stiff in the coolness of the cellar; she was wearing a dress and sweater while a warmer coat was spread on the table under the little girl, its sides flopped up and over her, covering her legs and chest. The woman bent over her daughter and wiped her head with the cool cloth.

Harry quietly walked up behind Helen as she concentrated on caring for the girl, pulling the coat more securely around her. Without bothering to look up at Harry, she said, "Karen has a bad fever now."

Harry sighed, with concern for his daughter. Then he said, "There's two more people upstairs."

"Two?"

"Yeah," Harry acknowledged. Then, half-defensively: "I wasn't about to take any unnecessary chances."

Helen remained silent, while Harry awaited some sign that she approved of his decision. "How did we know what was going on up there?" he said finally, flinging his arms into the air with a shrug. Then he reached nervously to his breast pocket for a cigarette, produced a pack that turned out to be empty, and crumpled it in his hand and pitched it to the floor. He stepped over to the worktable where there was another pack, snatched it up, and it, too, was empty—and with the same crumpling action Harry discarded the pack, violently this time, the action spinning him into a position facing his wife and daughter. Helen continued to quietly swab the girl's forehead, while Harry stared at them for a moment.

"Does she seem to be all right?" Harry asked, anxiously.

Helen was silent. The daughter, Karen, motionless.

Harry was sweating to the point where beads of sweat had formed all over his face. He waited and, seeing no answer forthcoming, changed the subject.

"They're all staying upstairs...idiots! We should stick together. It's the safest down here."

He went to his wife's purse and rummaged through the contents long enough to find a pack of cigarettes. He tore the pack open, yanked a cigarette out, lit it, and dragged in the first puff deeply; it made him cough slightly.

"They don't stand a chance up there. They can't hold those things off forever. There's too many ways they can get into the house up there."

Helen remained silent, as if her respect and tolerance of her husband's ideas had long ago been dissipated.

On the floor, next to the workbench, was a small transistor radio. Harry's glance fell on it and he stabbed at it, scooped it up, and clicked it on.

"They had a radio on upstairs. Must've been Civil Defense or...I think it's not just us, this thing is happening all over."

The tiny radio would pick up nothing but static, try as Harry might. He spun the tuning dial back and forth, listening anxiously, but across the receiving band the transistor just continued to hiss.

Harry held it up and turned it into various positions, trying for reception, spinning the tuner constantly. Still, nothing but hissing. He began pacing the room, holding the radio up and down and sideways, with no results.

"This damned thing—"

Still just static.

Helen stopped wiping her daughter's forehead, neatly folded the cloth, and draped it over the prostrate girl's brow. Gently placing her hand on her daughter's chest, she looked over toward her husband, who was still pacing around the cellar, his cigarette dangling from his lip, waving the little radio around in the air.

The radio continued to emit nothing but static at varying volumes.

"Harry—"

He continued his fidgeting with the radio, as though it had become an obsession. He moved near the wall at the foot of the stairs, holding it high and still spinning the dial. He was breathing and perspiring heavily.

"Harry—that thing can't pick up anything in this stinking dungeon!"

Her rising tone of voice stopped him; he turned and looked at her; about to cry, she brought her hands up to her face. Then, shaking her head, she bit her lip and just stared at the floor.

Looking at her, Harry's anger rose and swept over him, putting him momentarily at a loss for words; his face began twitching, his emotion searching for some vehicle of expression, until he pivoted violently and flung the radio across the room, smashing it against the wall, and launched into an orgy of shouting.

"I hate you—right? I hate the kid? I wanna see you die here, right? In this stinking place? My God, Helen, do you realize what's happening? Those things are all over the place—they'll kill us all! I enjoy watching my kid suffer like this? I enjoy seeing all this happen?"

Helen's head jerked toward him. She looked at him with an expression that was half anguish and half pleading.

"Karen needs help, Harry...she needs a doctor. She's...she's going to maybe die here. We have to get out of here, Harry. We have to."

"Oh, yeah—let's just walk out. We can pack up right now and get ready to go, and I'll just say to those things—excuse me, my wife and kid are uncomfortable here, we're going into town. For God's sake...there's maybe twenty of those things out there. And there's more every minute."

Harry's sarcasm did not help him to make his point with Helen; rather, it increased her disgust with him and made her more bitter. But she knew shouting back at him would do no good. Attempting to reason with him was the only thing that ever stood a chance of changing his mind, once he had convinced himself of something— provided you could convince him that he had thought up the new idea himself, giving him the opportunity of backing off from his previous position gracefully.

"There's people upstairs," Helen said. "We should stick together, you said it yourself. Those people aren't our enemies, are they? Up-stairs, downstairs—what's the difference? Maybe they can help us. Let's get out of here..."

A pounding sound interrupted her.

Both she and Harry held their breath and listened. The sound repeated itself—coming from the door at the top of the stairs. They glanced anxiously at their helpless daughter. For a long moment, they were half convinced they were being attacked. But then they heard Tom's voice.

"Harry!"

More pounding. Harry just stared up at the door and did not answer the call. He was sticking to his decision not to open the door again or have anything to do with the people upstairs. Tears welled in Helen's eyes as her frustration and disappointment in her hus-band increased and swept over her. More pounding. Helen looked at Harry. She knew he was a coward. More pounding; then a pause; maybe Tom was going to give up. Helen leaped up and ran to the foot of the stairs.

"Yes...yes, Tom!"

Harry, running after her, grabbed her shoulders from behind and stopped her. She squirmed and struggled to free herself.

"Harry! Let me go! Let me go!"

She struggled violently, and the force of her determination rather than her physical strength shocked Harry and cowed him, and he stepped away from her and just stared—his wife had never defied him openly like this before.

Tom's voice again sounded through the barricaded door:

"Harry...Helen...we have food, and some medicine and other things up here..."

Harry stared up at the door, speechlessly.

"There's gonna be a thing on the radio in ten minutes, Harry—a Civil Defense thing—to tell us what to do!"

Looking up at the door, Helen shouted, "We're coming up Tom! We'll be up in a minute!"

Harry spun and glowered at her.

"You're out of your mind, Helen. All it takes is a minute for those things to grab a hold of you and kill you. If they get in up there, it'll be too late to change your mind, don't you see that? Can't you see that we're safe as long as we keep that door sealed up?"

"I don't give a damn!" she spat at him. "I don't care Harry—I don't care any more; I want to get out of here—go upstairs—see if someone will help us. Maybe Karen will be okay."

Calming suddenly, she stopped shouting, got control of herself, and stepped toward Harry and spoke in a softer tone.

"Harry...please...for just a minute, we'll go up and see what's up there. We'll hear the radio, and maybe we can figure some way to get out of here. Maybe with all of us we can make it, Harry."

Harry, his adamancy weakening somewhat, took the cigarette from his mouth, exhaling the last puff, and dropped it to the floor. He stepped on it to snuff it out; the smoke came in a long stream through his pursed lips.

Startlingly, Tom's voice penetrated again.

"Harry! Hey, Harry! Ben found a television upstairs! Come on up—we'll see the Civil Defense broadcast on TV."

Harry wavered. Helen spoke soothingly to him, her tone an attempt to relieve the distress she thought he must feel in going against his original decision. "Come on...let's go up. There'll be something on TV that tells us what to do. You can tell them it was me that wanted to go up."

"All right," Harry said. "All right. This is your decision. We'll go up—but don't blame me if we all get killed."

Her eyes fell away from him, and she began mounting the stairs, taking the lead as he fell in behind, so the people upstairs would know their coming up was her doing.

Together, she and Harry began unboarding the cellar door.

6

Harry lifted the last heavy timber away, and the door came away from the jamb with a creaking noise. Helen peered out into the dining area, and beyond that into the semi-darkened living room. Harry, standing behind his wife, felt tense and hostile—and angry with himself because he had reneged on his decision about the cellar. Helen, too, was overwrought, because of the emotional strain of her argument with Harry and the fact that she was about to meet strange people in an anxious circumstance.

But only Tom and Barbara were in the living room. Barbara, overcome with nervous exhaustion and shock, was sleeping fitfully on the couch, in front of the fire.

In an effort to be friendly, Tom said, "We can see the broadcast, I think—if the TV works. I have to go help Ben carry it downstairs. Judy is in the kitchen, I'll get her, and she can take care of Karen for you while you're up here watching the television."

Helen managed a smile to express her thanks, and Tom immediately turned on his heels and went into the kitchen to get his girl-friend.

Helen moved over to the fire, seeking its warmth, and looked down at Barbara sympathetically and brushed back her hair and pulled the overcoat around her shoulders.

"Poor thing...she must have been through a lot," Helen said, to no one in particular.

Harry, during these moments, had been flitting all over the house, from door to window to kitchen to living room, checking out the actual degree of security, which he felt was practically non-existent, and worrying about the imminence of attack at any second.

Tom and Judy came out of the kitchen, and Tom said to Helen, "I think her brother was killed out there." And he nodded his head toward Barbara, who moaned softly in her fitful sleep, as though she had heard his comment.

Ben came to the top of the stairs, and began shouting.

"Tom! Hey, Tom! Are you gonna give me a hand with this thing, or ain't you?"

Tom, startled, aware of his procrastination, bolted for the upstairs to help Ben while Judy opened the cellar door and went down to watch Karen.

Harry, still pacing around in his anxiety, strode briskly over to where his wife was looking after Barbara.

"Her brother was killed," Helen said, as if telling that to Harry might soften him and jolt him out of his self-interest.

"This place is ridiculous," Harry said. "There's a million weak spots up here."

Frightened suddenly by a noise, Harry paused in his pacing long enough to listen and ascertain to his satisfaction that it was only Tom and Ben, struggling with the television, making their way down the steps.

Helen glowered at Harry. "You're a pain in the ass," she told him. "Why can't you make the best of things and do something to help somebody—instead of complaining all the time?"

Harry, not really hearing her, was staring through a slat in the barricaded front window into the gloom outside.

"I can't see a damn thing out there!" he exclaimed. "There could be fifty million of those things. I can't see a thing—that's how much good these windows do us!"

Ben, who with Tom had reached the landing with the heavy television set, arrived in time to hear the last part of Harry's remark; he glowered even as he moved with his end of the burden, but said nothing, as he and Tom dragged two chairs together and gingerly deposited the TV on them, in the center of the room. They hunted for an outlet, found it, then slid and walked the set on the two chairs until the cord was close enough to be plugged in.

As Ben knelt behind the set to plug in the cord, Harry said, "Wake that girl up. If there's going to be a thing on the tube, she might as well know where she stands. I don't want to be responsible for her."

Shocked, Helen blurted, "Harry, stop acting like a child!"

Ben got to his feet, his eyes flashing anger. "I don't want to hear any more from you, mister. If you stay up here, you'll take your orders from me—and that includes leaving that girl alone. She needs rest—she's just about out of her head as it is now. Now, we're just going to let her sleep it off. And nobody's going to touch her unless I say so."

Ben stared Harry down for a moment, to ascertain that he had been at least temporarily squelched; then his hand plunged immediately to the television set. As he snapped it on, the occupants of the room jockeyed for vantage points in front of it, and there were a few seconds of dead silence as they all waited to see if the set would actually warm up. All eyes were on the tube. A hiss began, and increased in volume. Ben twisted the volume all the way. A glowing band appeared and spread, filling the screen.

"It's on! It's on!" Helen shouted.

There were murmurs of excitement and anticipation—but the tube showed nothing. No picture, no sound. Just the glow and hiss of the tube. Ben's hand raced the tuning dial through the clicks of the various stations.

Harry jumped up, fidgeting. "Play with the rabbit ears. We should be able to get something—"

Ben fussed with horizontal and vertical, with brightness and contrast. On one station, he finally got sound: he adjusted the volume. The picture tumbled; he played with it and finally brought it in. Full-screen was a commentator, in the middle of a news report.

Hushed, the people in the room settled back to watch and listen.

"...ASSIGN LITTLE CREDIBILITY TO THE THEORY THAT THIS ONSLAUGHT IS A PRODUCT OF MASS HYSTERIA..."

"Mass hysteria!" Harry snarled. "What do they think—we're imagining all this?"

"Shut up!" Ben bellowed. "I want to hear what's going on!"

"...AUTHORITIES ADVISE UTMOST CAUTION UNTIL THE MENACE CAN BE BROUGHT UNDER ABSOLUTE CONTROL. EYEWITNESS ACCOUNTS HAVE BEEN INVESTIGATED AND DOCUMENTED. CORPSES OF VANQUISHED AGGRESSORS ARE PRESENTLY BEING EXAMINED BY MEDICAL PATHOLOGISTS, BUT AUTOPSY

EFFORTS HAVE BEEN HAMPERED BY THE MUTILATED CONDITION OF THESE CORPSES. SECURITY MEASURES INSTITUTED IN METROPOLITAN AREAS INCLUDE EN-FORCED CURFEWS AND SAFETY PATROLS BY ARMED PERSONNEL. CITIZENS ARE URGED TO REMAIN IN THEIR HOMES. THOSE WHO IGNORE THIS WARNING EXPOSE THEMSELVES TO INTENSE DANGER—FROM THE AG-GRESSORS THEMSELVES, AND FROM ARMED CITIZEN-RY WHOSE IMPULSE MAY BE TO SHOOT FIRST AND ASK QUESTIONS LATER. RURAL OR OTHERWISE ISOLATED DWELLINGS HAVE MOST FREQUENTLY BEEN THE OB-JECTIVE OF FRENZIED, CONCERTED ATTACK. ISOLAT-ED FAMILIES ARE IN EXTREME DANGER. ESCAPE AT-TEMPTS SHOULD BE MADE IN HEAVILY ARMED GROUPS, AND BY MOTOR VEHICLE IF POSSIBLE. APPRAISE YOUR SITUATION CAREFULLY BEFORE DECIDING ON AN ES-CAPE TACTIC. FIRE IS AN EFFECTIVE WEAPON. THESE BEINGS ARE HIGHLY FLAMMABLE. ESCAPE GROUPS SHOULD STRIKE OUT FOR THE NEAREST URBAN COM-MUNITY. MANNED DEFENSE OUTPOSTS HAVE BEEN ESTABLISHED ON MAJOR ARTERIES LEADING INTO ALL COMMUNITIES. THESE OUTPOSTS ARE EQUIPPED TO DEFEND REFUGEES AND TO OFFER MEDICAL AND SUR-GICAL ASSISTANCE. POLICE AND VIGILANTE PATROLS ARE IN THE PROCESS OF COMBING REMOTE AREAS IN SEARCH AND DESTROY MISSIONS AGAINST ALL AGGRES-SORS. THESE PATROLS ARE ATTEMPTING TO EVACUATE ISOLATED FAMILIES. BUT RESCUE EFFORTS ARE PRO-CEEDING SLOWLY, DUE TO THE INCREASED DANGER OF NIGHT AND THE SHEER ENORMITY OF THE TASK. RESCUE, FOR THOSE IN ISOLATED CIRCUMSTANCES, IS HIGHLY UNDEPENDABLE. YOU SHOULD NOT WAIT FOR A RESCUE PARTY UNLESS THERE IS NO POSSIBILITY OF ESCAPE. IF YOU ARE FEW AGAINST MANY, YOU WILL ALMOST CERTAINLY BE OVERCOME IF YOU REMAIN IN ONE SPOT. THE AGGRESSORS ARE IRRATIONAL AND DE-MENTED. THEIR SOLE URGE IS THEIR QUEST FOR HU-

MAN FLESH. SHERIFF CONAN W. MCCLELLAN, OF THE COUNTY DEPARTMENT OF PUBLIC PROTECTION, WAS INTERVIEWED MINUTES AFTER HE AND HIS VIGILANTE PATROL HAD VANQUISHED SEVERAL OF THE AGGRESSORS. WE BRING YOU NOW THE RESULTS OF THAT INTERVIEW..."

On the TV screen, the image of the commentator was replaced by newsreel footage, taken earlier that night. The footage showed dense woods, a dirt road, searchlights dancing among the trees, while men moved around peering into the darkness and shouting at one another. Sporadic distant gunfire could be heard over all this. Then the news camera showed footage of posted guards maintaining the periphery of a small clearing. Still, gunfire could be heard in the distance. Some of the men were smoking, others drinking coffee from paper containers or talking in small groups. The area was illuminated by a large bonfire. A closer shot revealed Sheriff McClellan, the central figure of the scene, shouting commands, supervising defensive measures, and at the same time trying to answer the reporter's questions as he paced around not straying too far—because of the cord and microphone hanging around his neck.

McClellan was a big man, gruff and used to commanding men and making them do what they were told in some semblance of order. He was dressed in civilian clothes, but carried a big rifle with scope and a belt of ammunition of heavy caliber.

At the moment, he had some of his men engaged in dragging bodies to the bonfire and throwing them on it to burn. The crackle of the bonfire, the shouts and bustle of activity, formed a constant background for McClellan's commentary as he did his best to answer what he was asked—while his primary concerns were his efforts in dealing with the aggressors and controlling his search party.

"Things ain't going too badly," McClellan said. "The men are taking it pretty well. We killed nineteen of those things today, right around this general area. These last three we found trying to claw their way into an abandoned mine shed—nobody was in there—but these things just pounding and clawing, trying to bust their way in. They must've thought there was people in there. We heard the racket and sneaked up on them and blasted them down."

"What's your opinion, then, Sheriff? Can we defeat these things?"

"There ain't no problem—except just getting to them in time, before they kill off all the people that are trapped. But me and my men can handle them okay. We ain't lost nobody or suffered any casualties. All you gotta do is shoot for the brain. You can tell any-body out there—all you gotta do is draw a sharp bead and shoot for the brain—or beat 'em down and lop their heads off. They don't go anywhere once you chop their heads off. Then you gotta burn 'em."

"Then I'd have a decent chance, even if I was surrounded by two or three of them?"

"If you had yourself a club, or a good torch, you could hold 'em off or burn 'em to death. They catch fire like nothin'—go up like wax paper. But the best thing is to shoot for the brain. You don't want to get too close, unless you have to. Don't wait for us to rescue you, because if they get you too far outnumbered, you've had it. Their strength is in numbers. We're doin' our best—but we only got so many men and a whole lot of open country to comb."

"But you think you can bring the situation under control?"

"At least in our county. We got things in our favor now. It's only a question of time. We don't know for certain how many of them there are...but we know when we find 'em we're able to kill 'em. So it's a matter of time. They are weak—but there's pretty many of 'em. Don't wait for no rescue party. Arm yourself to the teeth, get together in a group, and try to make it to a rescue station—that's the best way. But if you're alone, you have to sit still and wait for help...and we'll try like hell to get you before they do."

"What are these things, Sheriff? In your opinion, what are they?"

"They're...they're dead. They're dead humans. That's all they are. Whatever brought 'em back and made 'em this way, I wish to God I knew—"

The television coverage had switched back to the live announcer, who resumed speaking in his matter-of-fact tone.

"...YOU HAVE HEARD SHERIFF CONAN W. MCCLEL-LAN, OF THE COUNTY DEPARTMENT OF PUBLIC PRO-TECTION. THIS IS YOUR CIVIL DEFENSE EMERGENCY NETWORK, WITH REPORTS EVERY HOUR ON THE HOUR, FOR THE DURATION OF THIS EMERGENCY. RE-

MAIN IN YOUR HOMES. KEEP ALL DOORS AND WIN-
DOWS LOCKED. DO NOT UNDER ANY CIRC—"

Ben reached over and clicked off the television

Excited, Tom said, "Why'd you shut it off for?"

Ben shrugged. "The man said the reports only come on every hour. We heard all we need to know. We have to try and get out of here."

Helen agreed. "He said the rescue stations have doctors and medical supplies...if we could get there, they could help my daughter."

Harry laughed, scornfully. "How are we gonna bust out of here? We have a sick girl, a woman out of her head—and this place is crawling with those things."

"Willard is the nearest town," Tom said, ignoring Harry's objections. "They'd have a checkpoint there—about seventeen miles from here."

"You from here? You know the area?" Ben asked, excitedly.

"Sure," Tom replied, confidently. "Judy and I were going swimming up the road. We heard the news on her portable radio, and we came in here and found the lady dead upstairs. Not too long after, Harry and his wife and kid fought their way in here—I was scared, but I opened the basement door and let them in."

"Well, I think we ought to stick right here and wait for a rescue party," Harry said. "That fellow on the TV said if you're few against many, you don't have a chance—we can't hike seventeen miles cross-country through that army of things out there..."

"We don't have to tramp," Ben said. "My truck's right outside the door."

This stopped Harry. There was a long moment of silence while the fact of the truck sank into everybody's head.

"But I'm just about out of gas," Ben added. "There's a couple of gas pumps by the shed out back, but they're both locked up."

"The key ought to be around somewhere," Tom said. "There's a big key ring in the basement. I'll go look."

In his enthusiasm, now that escape seemed to be a possibility, he bolted for the cellar door and scampered down the stairs.

Ben turned to Harry. "Is there a fruit cellar down there?"

"Yeah. Why?"

"We're gonna need lots of jars. We can make Molotov cocktails...
scare those things back...then fight our way to the pump and gas up
the truck."

"We're gonna need kerosene, then," Harry said. "There's a jug of
that in the basement, too."

Helen said, "Judy and I can help. We can rip up sheets and
things." Then she added, in a hushed tone, "I don't think Barbara's
going to be much help at all."

"How do you know her name?" Ben asked, startled.

"She was mumbling it in her sleep—something about her brother telling her over and over—'Barbara, you're afraid.' It must have
happened just before he died."

There was a sudden clatter, and Tom came up out of the cellar.
"Here's the key ring," he said. "The pump key is marked with a piece
of tape. I talked with Judy. She's in favor of trying to escape."

"Good," Ben said. "Then nothing's holding us back. Anybody
who's got any second thoughts better decide now. If that's the key for
sure, we're in good shape—but we should take a crowbar anyway, in
case the key doesn't work. The crowbar can double as a weapon for
whoever goes with me. But I don't want to get all the way out there
and find out we can't get the pump open."

"I'll go," Tom said. "You and me can fight our way to the pump.
The women can stay in the cellar and take care of the kid. We should
have a stretcher—Helen and Judy maybe can make one."

Ben turned to Harry and spoke sternly, emphasizing his words.

"Harry, you're gonna have to guard the upstairs. Once we unboard the front door, those things can get in here easily. But it has
to stay unlocked, so me and Tom can get back in after we get back
here with the truck. You've got to guard the door, and unlock it for
us right away, 'cause we'll probably come flying on the run with a
bunch of those things coming right behind us. We'll board the door
up again as fast as we can once we're safe inside the house. If we don't
get back, well, then you'll be able to see from upstairs, and you can
barricade the door again and go to the basement—you and the rest
can sit tight and hope for a rescue party."

Facing Ben, Harry said, "I want the gun, then. It's the best thing for me to use. You're not going to have time to stop and aim—"

Ben cut him off, in no uncertain terms.

"I'm keeping this gun. Nobody else lays a hand on it. I found it, and it's mine."

Harry said, "How do we know you and Tom won't just get the truck gassed up and cut out?"

Ben glowered, trying to control his anger. "That's the chance you have to take," he said evenly and forcefully. "If we cut out, you'll have your goddamn basement—like you've been crying about all along."

"We're going to die here," Helen said, pleadingly, "if we don't all work together."

Ben looked at her, sizing her up. He had pretty much decided she was not a coward like her husband. He'd almost rather have her guarding the front door—but she was not nearly as strong as Harry, provided he did not chicken out.

Ben addressed all of them, in commanding tones.

"Let's get busy. More of those things are coming to surround us all the time. And we've got a lot to do if we're gonna bust out of here. If everything goes right, two or three hours from now we'll be taking a hot shower in the Willard Hotel."

Nobody laughed.

They separated, each to begin his or her assigned task.

Ben turned the radio back on. It began repeating its recorded message. The time was approximately 11:30. One half-hour to go until midnight, when there would be another regular broadcast.

It would come in the middle of their escape preparations. They could take time out to watch it on the television, in case it contained current information that might prove helpful.

In the meantime, there was nothing to do...but to work hard... and to hope.

7

Helen and Harry Cooper came down into the basement and found Judy watching over the sick girl, Karen, who now seemed a little delirious. She tossed and turned, and moaned softly now and then, as she lay on the makeshift worktable.

"Has she asked for me?" Helen asked, intently. "Has she spoken at all?"

Harry reached down and covered his daughter, where she had shaken off the coat that was covering her, in her delirium.

"She's been moaning and crying out constantly," Judy said, her face showing her worry and concern for the child.

"Poor baby!" Helen sighed, and she touched her hand to Karen's forehead and felt the increase of fever.

"Get another damp cloth," Harry said. "I'm going to start making a stretcher. Judy, I'll give you the box of fruit jars over there, and you take them up to Tom. He'll have to come down here for the kerosene. We're going to make Molotov cocktails."

The idea of making something like that seemed weird to Judy, like something she had seen but only vaguely understood, from the movies. She knew a Molotov cocktail was something that caught fire when you threw it at a tank, but she had no idea how to make one. But she stood waiting patiently while Harry dug out the old, dusty box of fruit jars and loaded it into her arms. It wasn't heavy, but she was too loaded down to carry anything else.

"You'll have to send Tom back down for the kerosene," Harry repeated. "Helen and I will take care of Karen and start making the stretcher. Tell Tom to bring us some old sheets or blankets."

Harry watched after her, as she climbed the stairs out of the cellar, as though she would be likely not to do it right if he didn't watch her. "We'll be damned lucky if we make it," he said, turning to Helen. "It would be tough enough for half a dozen men to beat their way through those things."

Helen looked up from where she had been applying her dampened cloth to Karen's forehead. She didn't say anything to combat Harry's pessimism; she merely trembled. As her eyes looked into the fever-tossed, agonized face of her young daughter, she caught her breath and almost did not dare to hope that they would make it.

"Lord help us," she mumbled, when her breath came to her again.

Over by the workbench, Harry had begun pounding on something, in his effort to fashion a crude stretcher.

8

Ben had returned to the vacant room, which contained the mutilated corpse of the old lady who had once lived there. The vacant room was the one that looked out onto the front lawn, and Harry would have to station himself there to toss Molotov cocktails from the window.

Ben held his breath and tried not to look at the corpse, but he knew he had to get it out of the room. Seeing a thing like that was the very thing which was likely to spook Harry and bring his cowardice trembling to the surface—and then he would panic and run, and fail to do the job that was expected of him.

The entire room smelled of the rotting corpse, which had been closed in there for a couple of hours. Ben had to step into the hall for a while, to allow the room to air out. He went into the bathroom and lifted the window an inch or two, and sucked cold night air into his nostrils—but the scent of the dead things outside came to him faintly, mingled with the normal odors of dampness and freshly cut grass and plowed fields. The man closed the bathroom window and returned to the room which he hated to enter.

He began dragging the corpse out into the hallway and toward the child's room across the hall. On its blood-crusted carpet, it slid along fairly easily on the bare floor, but when it reached the rug in the child's room, it balked and was harder to drag. Ben grunted, gagged with the stench of a lungful of the dead woman's odor, and with a desperate heave got it into the room, near the bunk bed, stepped over it quickly to get out of there, and slammed the door.

Again, he went to the bathroom and opened the window enough to suck in "fresh" air.

When he returned to the vacant room, it still smelled bad, but not as bad as before. He went to the window, taking pains to keep his body pressed close against the wall, where he could not be seen very easily. With his hand, he rubbed a clean spot on the dirty, uncurtained window.

There were now at least thirty of the things standing down there on the front lawn. And, in the fields beyond, several more could be seen, making their way toward the house.

9

Barbara was sitting up, by the fire. She had a morose, almost vacant, expression on her face, as though she no longer cared whether she lived or died.

In the corner of the room that had once been the dining area, Tom and Judy were making Molotov cocktails. Judy was using a pair of scissors to cut up an old bed sheet into strips, while Tom was filling the fruit jars with kerosene from a can. Then, together, they began soaking the cloth strips in kerosene in the bottom of a dish and forcing these makeshift fuses through holes which Tom had cut in the caps of the jars.

They worked silently for a long time, but when Judy looked over at Barbara, sitting so inert and morbid on the sofa, with the fire flickering in her face, she felt a need to make conversation—to relieve the silence.

"Tom...do you think we're doing the right thing?" she asked suddenly, looking up from her task with the fuses. She stared at her hands, with the odor of kerosene coming off them.

Tom looked at her and smiled, tensely but reassuringly. "Sure, honey. I don't think we have a chance if we stay here. There are more and more of those things all the time. The television broadcast advised anyone who was in a situation like ours to try to escape."

"But—what about the rescue parties?"

"We can't take a chance on waiting. Nobody might ever come to help us. Think how many people must be trapped, like we are."

Judy fell silent as she returned to her task with the fuses.

"I think we're going to make it," Tom said. "We're not all that far from the gas pumps. And Ben said he beat down three of those things before. And now we have the gun."

He looked at her intently, noticing the worried look on her face, which he had never before seen in the short time they had been going together.

"But...why do you have to be the one to go out there?" she said finally.

"Honey, you're talking like Harry Cooper now. Somebody has to go. We can't just sit here and wait for those things to kill us. Besides, we're gonna be all right—you wait and see. We're gonna make it."

She leaned forward and put her arms around him, awkwardly, trying to touch him with her kerosened hands.

About to kiss, they were startled by the loud sound of Harry's footsteps, coming up out of the basement. A tense look on his face, he entered the room and said angrily, "What's the matter? Doesn't anybody keep their head around here? It's almost time for another broadcast."

"Five more minutes," Tom said, looking at his wristwatch.

"Well, we've got to get the damned thing warmed up," Harry said, and he stepped over to the television and turned it on just as Ben came down from the upstairs.

"What's going on?" Ben said.

"Another broadcast," Tom answered, and to show Ben he had not been loafing he continued working with the fuses, dipping them and forcing them into the jars.

Ben moved over to Barbara and looked at her, shaking his head sadly.

"Goddamn this television," Harry said. "It takes half a century to warm up. We could all die waiting for it."

He nervously struck a match and lit a cigarette, while the picture tube began to glow and the sound came on.

"We've got to get that girl down into the basement," Harry added, with a glance in Barbara's direction. "She's no good to herself or anyone else up here."

Nobody made a reply to Harry's comment, and they all fell silent as the news broadcast came on. It was a different commentator, but the newsroom was the same, with its multitude of clocks on the wall showing what time it was in various parts of the nation, and its background of ticker-tape sounds and blurred human voices.

"GOOD EVENING, LADIES AND GENTLEMEN. IT IS NOW MIDNIGHT, EASTERN TIME. THIS IS YOUR CIVIL DEFENSE NETWORK, WITH REPORTS EVERY HOUR ON

THE HOUR FOR THE DURATION OF THIS...EMERGENCY.
STAY TUNED TO THIS WAVELENGTH FOR SURVIVAL IN-
FORMATION.

"LADIES AND GENTLEMEN...INCREDIBLE AS IT MAY
SEEM...THE LATEST REPORT FROM THE PRESIDENT'S
RESEARCH TEAM AT WALTER READE HOSPITAL CON-
FIRMS WHAT MANY OF US HAVE ACCEPTED AS FACT
WITHOUT BOTHERING TO WAIT FOR OFFICIAL CON-
FIRMATION. THE ARMY OF AGGRESSORS WHICH HAS
BESIEGED MANY OF THE EASTERN AND MIDWESTERN
SECTIONS OF OUR COUNTRY IS MADE UP OF DEAD HU-
MAN BEINGS."

Judy shuddered as the announcer paused, allowing time for his
statement to sink in. The expression on his face showed that he hardly believed it himself.

"I didn't need him to tell me that," Ben said.

"Quiet!" Harry yelled.

"THE RECENTLY DEAD HAVE BEEN RETURNING TO
LIFE AND FEASTING ON HUMAN FLESH. DEAD PEOPLE
FROM MORGUES, HOSPITALS, FUNERAL PARLORS...
AS WELL AS MANY OF THOSE KILLED DURING OR AS
A RESULT OF THE CHAOS CREATED DURING THIS
EMERGENCY...HAVE BEEN RETURNED TO LIFE IN A DE-
PRAVED, INCOMPLETE FORM...WITH AN URGE TO KILL
OTHER HUMANS AND DEVOUR THEIR FLESH.

"EXPLANATIONS FOR THE CAUSES OF THIS INCRED-
IBLE PHENOMENON HAVE NOT BEEN FORTHCOM-
ING FROM THE WHITE HOUSE OR FROM POSITIONS
OF AUTHORITY, BUT SPECULATION CENTERS ON THE
RECENT VENUS PROBE, WHICH WAS UNSUCCESSFUL.
THAT ROCKET SHIP, YOU REMEMBER, STARTED FOR
VENUS MORE THAN A WEEK AGO—BUT NEVER GOT
THERE. INSTEAD, IT RETURNED TO EARTH, CARRYING A
MYSTERIOUS HIGH-LEVEL RADIATION WITH IT. COULD
THAT RADIATION HAVE BEEN RESPONSIBLE FOR THE
WHOLESALE MURDER WE ARE NOW WITNESSING?
SPECULATION ON THE ANSWER TO THAT QUESTION

HAS RUN RAMPANT HERE IN WASHINGTON AND ELSE-
WHERE, WHILE THE WHITE HOUSE HAS MAINTAINED
A CURTAIN OF SILENCE AND HAS ATTEMPTED TO DEAL
WITH THIS EMERGENCY BY PHYSICAL MEANS—THAT
IS, BY ORGANIZING RESISTANCE AND SEARCH AND DE-
STROY MISSIONS AGAINST THE...AGGRESSORS. MEET-
INGS AT THE PENTAGON AND THE WHITE HOUSE
HAVE REMAINED CLOSED TO REPORTERS, AND MEM-
BERS OF THE MILITARY AND CIVILIAN ADVISORS HAVE
REFUSED TO CONDUCT INTERVIEWS OR TO ANSWER
QUESTIONS THRUST AT THEM BY REPORTERS, ON THE
WAY TO OR FROM SUCH MEETINGS.

"HOWEVER, THE LATEST OFFICIAL COMMUNIQUÉ
FROM THE PENTAGON HAS CONFIRMED THAT THE AG-
GRESSORS ARE DEAD. THEY ARE NOT INVADERS FROM
ANOTHER PLANET. THEY ARE THE RECENTLY DEAD
FROM RIGHT HERE ON EARTH. NOT ALL OF THE RE-
CENTLY DEAD HAVE RETURNED TO LIFE—BUT IN CER-
TAIN AREAS OF THE COUNTRY, THE EAST AND MID-
WEST IN PARTICULAR, THE PHENOMENON IS MORE
WIDESPREAD THAN ELSEWHERE. WHY THE MIDWEST
SHOULD BE AN AREA SO GREATLY AFFLICTED IS NOT
EASILY EXPLAINED, EVEN BY THE MOST CALCULATED
SPECULATION. THE VENUS PROBE, YOU REMEMBER,
CRASHED IN THE ATLANTIC OCEAN, JUST OFF THE
EASTERN SEABOARD.

"PERHAPS WE SHALL NEVER KNOW THE EXACT REA-
SONS FOR THE TERRIBLE PHENOMENON WE ARE NOW
WITNESSING.

"THERE IS SOME HOPE, HOWEVER, THAT THE MEN-
ACE WILL BE BROUGHT UNDER CONTROL...PERHAPS IN
A MATTER OF SEVERAL DAYS OR WEEKS. THE...AGGRES-
SORS...CAN BE KILLED BY GUNSHOT OR A HEAVY BLOW
TO THE HEAD. THEY ARE AFRAID OF FIRE, AND THEY
BURN EASILY. THEY HAVE ALL THE CHARACTERISTICS
OF DEAD PEOPLE...EXCEPT THEY ARE NOT DEAD—FOR
REASONS WE DO NOT AS YET UNDERSTAND, THEIR

BRAINS HAVE BEEN ACTIVATED AND THEY ARE CAN-
NIBALS.

"IN ADDITION, ANYONE WHO DIES FROM A WOUND
INFLICTED BY THE FLESH-EATERS MAY HIMSELF COME
BACK TO LIFE IN THE SAME FORM AS THE AGGRES-
SORS THEMSELVES. THE DISEASE THAT THESE THINGS
CARRY IS COMMUNICABLE THROUGH OPEN FLESH
WOUNDS OR SCRATCHES, AND TAKES EFFECT MIN-
UTES AFTER THE APPARENT DEATH OF THE WOUND-
ED PERSON. ANYONE WHO DIES DURING THIS EMER-
GENCY SHOULD BE IMMEDIATELY DECAPITATED OR
CREMATED. SURVIVORS WILL FIND THESE MEASURES
DIFFICULT TO UNDERTAKE, BUT THEY MUST BE UN-
DERTAKEN ANYWAY, OR ELSE THE AUTHORITIES MUST
BE ALERTED TO UNDERTAKE IT FOR YOU. THOSE WHO
DIE DURING THIS EMERGENCY ARE NOT CORPSES IN
THE USUAL SENSE, THEY ARE DEAD FLESH—BUT HIGH-
LY DANGEROUS AND A THREAT TO ALL LIFE ON OUR
PLANET. I REPEAT, THEY MUST BE BURNED OR DECAPI-
TATED..."

A shudder went through Harry, and all the eyes in the room
turned on him.

"How did your kid get hurt?" Ben asked.

"One of those things grabbed her, while we were all trying to
run. I'm not sure—but I think she was bitten on the arm."

They all stared at Harry, feeling sorry for him, but realizing at the
same time the threat Karen would be to them, if she died.

"You or Helen had better stay with her at all times," Ben warned.
"If she doesn't pull through...well..."

His voice trailed off.

Harry covered his face with his hands, as he tried to accept the
thought of what he would have to do. Knowing his daughter might
die had been bad enough but now—

Another shudder went through him.

The people in the living room had their eyes glued to the tube
and were avoiding looking in Harry's direction.

"You'll have to tell Helen what to expect," Ben said. "Otherwise, she won't know how to deal with it if it happens."

Ben thought of his own children, and trembled with anguish and homesickness for them. Then he forced his attention back to the television, in case he might learn something that would be of value in trying to escape.

But the tube faded to a glow.

The broadcast was over.

Clattering his chair, Tom got to his feet. "We'd better get started," he said. "There's nothing more we can do here."

Ben slung his gun over his shoulder, as he bent to pick up a claw hammer and crowbar. Facing Harry, he said, "You've got to station yourself in the empty room upstairs. All women will stay in the cellar. Soon as Tom and I have the front door unboarded, you start tossing the Molotov cocktails. Make sure they catch fire good—throw every one of them—but don't hit the truck. If you can catch a couple of those things on fire, so much the better. When we hear your footsteps on the stairs, me and Tom'll be gone. It'll be up to you Harry—you've got to guard the front door. Got yourself a good length of pipe?"

"I have a pitchfork."

"Good...okay."

While Ben delivered his instructions, Tom knelt near the fire and soaked a table-leg in kerosene so it would make a good torch.

With a little coaxing, Judy got Barbara to her feet and ushered her down into the basement. But Tom turned, as he had heard only one pair of feet descending the stairs. Judy stood looking at him from behind the half-opened cellar door—an anguished look on her face as Harry left the room with his box of Molotov cocktails and Tom began to help Ben unboard the front door.

Judy worried and watched in silence, while the man and the boy engaged in the painstaking work of very quietly undoing the barricade, so as not to give alarm to the lurking things outside. With crowbar and claw hammer, slowly and carefully, both Tom and Ben worked on each piece of lumber. Each nail-creak was a menace. They were alert to the constant danger—until the barricade was finally undone.

Tom lit the torch and handed it to Ben, and they posted themselves by the door, waiting for the Molotov shower to begin.

Ben shifted the curtain and peered outside, sizing up the situation they were about to plunge themselves into. On the lawn, under the trees, many shadowy figures were lurking, silent and threatening in the darkness; several of the dead things were standing near the truck—it was going to be a hard fight for Tom and Ben to get into it. And across the field, along the route that the truck would have to take to the gas pumps, many more of the flesh-eaters were watching and waiting.

If anything went wrong, they would never get back to the house alive.

Judy still had not gone down into the cellar. Her eyes were fastened on Tom, as if she wanted to continue seeing him until the last possible moment—because once he was gone out into the night she might never see him again.

Suddenly—a cry from upstairs. A window flew open, and the first fiery blaze lit the yard.

Ben flung the front door open, and in the glow of the blazing kerosene fire he watched as the creatures moaned with their hideous rasping sounds and began clutching at themselves dumbly and backing slowly away. More cocktails followed, crashing in the yard with a splintering sound as the flames leaped up and illuminated the old truck and the eerie dead things that had been stationed around it.

Several of the things caught fire and walked and staggered with the flames—their dead flesh popping and crackling and burning with a terrible stench—until they were consumed by the fire and brought down by it, not killed but immobilized, still moving and making rasping sounds until there was not sufficient body left to continue to move any longer...

Still, the bombs showered from upstairs. The field beyond the house was now lit up dimly, the shadows of trees and bushes moving eerily and changing complexion as each new puddle of fire took hold and the flames rose and fell.

Ben and Tom stood on the porch, watching the dead things burning and backing away, while they kept their weapons ready to use on any of the beings who might attack before they were to make their break for the truck.

"That's all Ben—run for it!" Harry shouted from upstairs, slamming the door to the vacant room and scurrying for the stairs.

His voice echoed, as Tom and Ben burst into the yard, surrounded by puddles of flame and threatened by the dead ghouls, some of which were starting to move forward, their fear of fire not as strong as their urge for human flesh.

Tom clubbed at one of the attackers with the crowbar and it went down, but it was still struggling on the ground. Ben stabbed at it with the torch, and it caught fire and burst into a blaze as it began to die, clutching at itself.

Harry had gotten to the front door—too late to stop Judy from running out onto the lawn. "I'm going with them!" she screamed, and Harry clutched at her, but she ran right by him and stopped, caught short, when he slammed the front door.

Two of the ghouls were coming for her; she could not get back inside, and her way to the truck was blocked.

She screamed, and Ben turned and saw her while Tom leaped into the driver's seat of the truck. One of the things was clutching at him, and he had to drive it back by kicking it hard in the chest.

Ben wheeled and clubbed at the two ghouls in front of Judy. The stock of the rifle thudded against their dead skulls and brought them to the earth, each with a sickening crunch and a splintering of bone that was already dead.

Ben grabbed the frightened girl and pushed her into the truck, then leaped into the bed of it as Tom's eyes fell on Judy and the truck lurched out. It careened and skidded in a U-turn for the old shed and the gas pumps across the field. Several ghouls, clawing and pounding at the humans inside, fell away from the truck as it moved—and Ben set still another one on fire with his torch and beat at it as it continued to try to hang on even while it was burning—until it was shaken loose finally and fell with its head under the tire of the truck.

Temporarily in the clear, Tom raced the truck across the field, while many of the ghouls followed after, staggering slowly but in relentless pursuit of their objective. Ben aimed and fired several shots cocking and firing in rapid succession—and wasting ammunition, actually—as most of his shots missed as the truck jounced over the ruts in the grassy field, but one creature went down, with half its skull blown completely away.

The others continued to follow after the old truck, as it screeched to a halt in front of the gas pumps and the shed, and Tom and Ben leaped out. Still more attackers were approaching, several parties of them now making their way across the field. Tom fumbled with the key to the locked pumps. Ben shoved him back, hurriedly aimed the gun and fired, blowing the lock to pieces. Gas spurted all over the place, as Ben handed the torch to Tom so he would have some means of protecting himself—he had left his crowbar in the truck.

Her eyes wide with fear, Judy stared through the windshield, first at Tom, then out into the field, as the creatures continued to advance. Several of them were less than thirty yards away.

Gas still spurting, Tom crammed the nozzle into the mouth of the gas tank and his torch fell from his hands onto the gasoline-soaked ground. Tongues of flame leaped up—and set fire to the truck.

The rear fender was burning. Ben saw it out of the corner of his eye as he crouched and leveled off with his weapon and fired. An approaching attacker went down but got back up again, a gaping hole in its chest, just below the neck.

In force of numbers, the attackers continued to advance.

Tom stared at the truck as the flames began to lick and spread. Ben stared, too, momentarily—he did not know what to do. Then he wheeled and yelled, as Tom leaped into the flaming truck and it lurched and skidded across the field, plowing down some of the attackers in its way. Tom wanted to get the truck away from the gas pumps, to prevent them from exploding. Ben yelled again, but to no avail, as the flaming truck sped away, driven by the panicked Tom—Judy scared speechless beside him in the front seat.

Several of the things were upon Ben. He thrashed and pounded at them with the torch and gun. Figuring that Tom was lost, he knew he had to try and fight his own way back to the house.

Ben succeeded in setting fire to two of the ghouls that were attacking him and beating a third one to the ground.

He ran, swinging the torch and gun, spinning in all directions so as not to be brought down from behind. The stench of the ghouls alone was almost overpowering as mobs of them threatened to close in and tear him apart.

From inside the house, Harry had been able to see only pieces of the action, although he kept darting back and forth from door to window, squinting through the barricades, trying to make sure of what was going on outside. From his point of view the escape attempt seemed to have met with total doom—and if so, he wanted to lock the front door and run into the basement and barricade it.

Harry saw the truck catch fire—and saw Tom drive it away. As for Ben, he appeared to be overwhelmed. Harry ran to another window.

The truck, almost completely in flames, was speeding away from the house, toward a small rise. Eerily, it was lighting up its own path as it lurched and bounced along in the otherwise pitch-black field. Suddenly it screeched to a halt. Harry could see a figure, that of Tom, crawling out of the driver's side and trying to help Judy get out, too. Then—an overpowering blast. The truck exploded violently, the noise and flames shattering the night.

In the midst of his struggles with the ghouls, Ben looked up and shuddered as he realized what had happened to Judy and Tom. The flames from the exploded truck helped him to see his way clear to fight a little nearer to the house. With powerful, desperate blows from his torch and gun, Ben continued to beat back his attackers in a life-or-death attempt to gain safety.

Several ghouls were at the front door, trying to beat their way into the house. From inside, Harry was in complete terror. Finally, heedless of anybody's plight but his own, he panicked and bolted for the cellar.

But Ben had slugged his way through the attackers on the porch—and now he was pounding for admission at the front door. Spinning, with a powerful lunge he kicked the last attacker off the porch; in the rebound he ploughed his shoulder against the door; it crashed open and Ben burst through in time to catch Harry at the cellar door.

But there was no time to redress Harry. Ben turned frantically to re-boarding the door as his eyes met Harry's for an instant and they both fell to work—as if Harry thought he could maintain some vestige of respect in Ben's eyes by pitching in and helping now.

They managed to get the door boarded up. The house was temporarily safe.

They turned and looked at each other, Harry shaking with fear, sweat streaming from his face. Both men knew what was coming—and Ben's fist crashed against Harry's face even as he was attempting to back away.

Harry was driven back, one punch after another, until Ben cornered him and slammed him against the wall and held him there, staring into his face. Ben spat his words out, each word punctuated by an additional slam of Harry against the wall.

"You...rotten...goddamn...next...time...you do something...like that...I'll drag you outside and feed...you...to those things!"

Ben slammed him one final time, and he slid down the wall and crumpled on the floor, his face bruised and his nose streaming with blood.

Ben moved to the cellar door.

"Come on up! It's us...It's all over...Tom and Judy are dead!"

He pivoted, hurled himself across the room to a window, and saw the ghouls moving closer to the house. Despite his exhaustion, he shuddered.

What on earth were they going to do now?

10

By midnight, Sheriff McClellan and his men had established the camp where they intended to bed down for the night. They had kept on the march until the sun sank low enough to make it impossible to go any farther, then on McClellan's command they had pitched camp in an open field where any approaching aggressors would be easy to spot because of the absence of concealing foliage; to make doubly sure the place was secure from attack, they had posted guards and established a periphery of defense.

Luckily, the night was warm and without any threat of rain. Most of the men had blankets and sleeping bags but there were very few tents. The posse had been organized in too big a hurry, and a lot of its members were inexperienced and did not have the proper gear for living in the woods; in addition to the normally difficult problems of feeding and supplying a posse of forty or fifty men, there had been a myriad of pesky complaints common to novices—like poison ivy and blistered feet.

Through it all, McClellan had alternately bullied and pampered the men, to keep them on the move in a disciplined fashion, combing the rural areas in search of those who might require aid or rescue—until nightfall made it unwise to try to proceed any further. Then, reluctantly, the gruff sheriff had given the order to pitch camp and had supervised the establishment of it and the maintenance of proper defenses.

The men were tired. But the warmth of the campfires and smell of hot coffee went a long way toward reviving their flagging spirits; and, not too long after midnight a van arrived loaded down with box lunches for all the men so they would not have to bed down hungry. Candles and Coleman lanterns burned in various parts of the camp, giving it from a distance a rustic but cheerful look, and here and there a card game got started despite the fact that they all knew they'd have to break camp and be on the move without any breakfast, come dawn.

McClellan sat by himself just outside his tent, listening to the murmur of surrounding voices and the occasional rattle of a fork or spoon or a heavier piece of equipment. His maps were spread out on a field table in front of him, lighted by an overhanging lantern with a buzzing circle of gnats and other insects that intermittently annoyed McClellan by flying into his face. He was impatient to finish with the maps so he could extinguish the lantern and turn in for the night.

With his red pencil, he made a mark on the spot he knew to be his position—fifteen miles north of a little town called Willard. Still farther north, for a stretch of several miles, there were scattered farmhouses and a tiny village or two where the inhabitants were relatively isolated and presumed to be in dire need of help, although the status of any of the families in the area still to be combed by McClellan's posse was largely a matter of speculation, because of the communications breakdown that had occurred in the early stages of the emergency.

The county had been divided into sectors, each sector to be patrolled by a combination of posse volunteers and National Guard troops. The objectives were to reestablish communications in areas where lines were down or power stations were out of commission; to bring safety and law and order to villages and larger communities, where order was threatened not only by marauding ghouls but by looters and rapists taking advantage of the chaos created by the emergency; and to send rescue parties out into rural or remote areas, where people could be trapped in their homes with no way of defending themselves adequately or calling for help.

McClellan's sector happened to be a particularly dangerous one. In addition to the normal number of recently dead from hospitals, morgues and funeral homes, a bus full of people—the driver frightened by several of the dead things suddenly appearing in front of him as he rounded a curve—had crashed through a guard rail and over an embankment, killing everyone on board, presumably, but when McClellan's posse found the bus there were only a few ghouls wandering around aimlessly, and these were gunned down and burned. One of them, with several shattered rib bones protruding through the front of its chest, was wearing a bus driver's uniform; and from that McClellan was pretty certain of what had happened to the other people. Long before the official announcement was made public, McClellan and his men, working hard out in the endangered areas, knew that the aggressors were dead humans and that anyone who died was likely to become an aggressor. Although many of the men carried knives and machetes to protect themselves against wounds and contamination, their procedure was to avoid tangling with the flesh-eaters at close range, by gunning them down at a distance; then, by making use of meat hooks, they would drag the dead things to a pile, soak them with gasoline, and set fire to them. Anyone who had touched a meat hook, or anything suspected of having been in contact with a ghoul, would wash his hands with plenty of soap and water and afterward in a solution of alcohol. It was not known whether or not these measures would be totally effective, but they had seemed to be so far—and nobody could think of what else to do, under the circumstances.

As McClellan had stated earlier in his news interview, his posse had suffered no losses and no casualties in the eight hours or so that it had been in the field.

By splitting up into squads at times, they had managed to cover quite a number of isolated farmhouses during the hard day's trek, and had rescued some and had found some dead—with the flesh picked from their bodies. They had also gunned down quite a few, when it could be seen that they were no longer dead—or human.

Now, with a day's experience behind him, the sheriff had the means to gauge and evaluate the task that lay before him; and looking on the map at the territory that remained to be combed, he figured he could do it in three or four more days, by pushing the men hard. He hated to push men—but he was good at it, and there were situations, like this one, where it was absolutely necessary; a lot of lives might depend on just how quickly the posse was able to get to them.

As McClellan slapped at a gnat that had lighted on his forehead, a heavy shadow fell across his map table and he looked up to see his deputy, George Henderson.

George was a strong, wiry man of medium height, wearing hunting clothes that looked well-worn and fitted his body the way that clothes will do when they are used to the body that is wearing them. He unslung his rifle and scratched the stubble of beard on his chin.

"You're standing in my light," McClellan said gruffly, his head tilted downward as though to continue scrutinizing his map.

George gave a snort, which was intended to pass as a laugh, and stepped aside, disappointed that he could not think of a wisecrack to hurl back at McClellan. Instead, he said, "I checked the guards. Five of the bastards were asleep."

"You're kidding," McClellan said, shoving himself away from his map table as though he would stomp out and crucify the five men.

"Yep," George said.

He meant, yep, he was kidding. He chuckled, and this time McClellan was the one who merely snorted.

"All the guards are posted," George said. "I made them take black coffee to stay awake."

"If any of those things get into this camp with these men in sleeping bags—"

"A lot of them are keeping pistols in their sleeping bags with them. And the ones that don't have pistols are keeping their rifles or machetes close by."

"We ought to keep the fires going," McClellan said. "Tell the next change of guards to keep feeding the fires all night."

"Okay," George said. "But I already thought of it. I was going to tell them anyway."

McClellan snorted, as though George couldn't possibly think of such a concept on his own.

"You're just pissed off because you didn't think of it first," George said, and he pulled up a field chair and sat down a few feet from the table. "Am I sitting in your light?" he asked, with a tone of mock sarcasm.

"Why don't you go get yourself a cup of coffee?" was McClellan's only reply—as though he was suggesting it merely to get rid of George.

"Did you get any?" George asked.

"Nope. I don't want it to keep me awake."

"You're gonna be snoozing like a big panda bear, while these men are standing watch and I'm out half the night checking the guards."

"If you were capable of the brain work, I'd hand it over to you," McClellan said, kidding. "Then you'd be the one to sleep. As it is, I've got to keep my mind fresh so this organization doesn't fall to pieces."

"Hah! That's a good one!" George exclaimed. "If it wasn't for me doin' the shit-work, these men would all be playin' cards or shootin' marbles—"

"I want everybody out of their sacks at four-thirty," McClellan broke in, in a serious tone.

"What?"

"Four-thirty. We've got to break camp and be on the move soon as we can see to navigate. Any time we spend screwin' around could mean somebody else dead."

"How much you figure on doin' tomorrow?"

"I got ten farmhouses I'd like to cover before noon. You can take a look at the map and see which ones. If we get that far, we'll break for lunch. We can radio ahead and let them know where we're gonna be."

George bent over the map and peered at it. The farmhouses that the sheriff intended to cover, marked in red, were back off a road shown on the map as a two-lane blacktop. The field where the posse was presently camped lay about two or three miles south of the blacktop road, and they had been marching in its direction all the previous day, advancing generally toward it with digressions as squads of men branched out in flanking movements to cover scattered dwellings before returning to the main body of the posse.

McClellan lit a cigarette and dragged on it, while George scrutinized their previous route and sized up the one that lay ahead.

The last house in their anticipated line of march was the old Miller farm, where Mrs. Miller—if she was still alive—lived with her grandson, Jimmy, a boy eleven years old.

"We ought to send out a separate patrol to get to this place," George said, pointing to the red X that marked the Miller farm on McClellan's map. "I know Mrs. Miller. She'd be pretty helpless. She and her grandson are all alone out there."

"We should be there before noon," McClellan said. "If they ain't dead already, they should be all right."

"I'm going to get me some coffee," George said. "Then I'm gonna rustle the second round of guards out of their sacks."

11

Surprisingly, considering the violence of the explosion, the truck stopped burning rather quickly. It had not had much gasoline in it, and when that was gone there was very little about the truck that was combustible. Just the seats and the upholstery. And the human bodies inside.

The metal, with its paint charred and blistered, cooled rapidly in the night air.

And the ghouls came forward, slowly at first, and clustered around the truck. The smell of burning flesh drew them closer. But the hot metal at first prevented them from attaining what enticed them and was so near to their grasp.

When the metal was cold as death and smoke no longer curled from the ruins of the truck, the flesh-eaters moved in like vultures.

Tom and Judy could not feel their limbs being torn from their dead bodies. They could not hear bones and cartilage being twisted and broken and separated at the joints. They could not cry out when the ravenous ghouls ripped out their hearts and lungs and kidneys and intestines.

The ghouls fought among themselves, clawed and struggled with each other for possession of the once living organs; then, when possession was asserted, they went off—each to hover alone in near-privacy, except for other hungry ghouls looking on—to devour whatever organ or piece of a human body the lucky ones had managed to claim. They were like dogs, dragging their bones off to a corner to chew and gnaw, while other dogs looked on.

Several of the ghouls, in search of a comfortable place to eat where they would not have to defend their meals from one another, found refuge in the darkened front lawn of the old farmhouse, under the big silent trees.

There they waited patiently and watched the house—and ate, while the sound of teeth biting and ripping into dead human flesh and bone filled the night air. And, constantly, there was the rasp of crickets and the rasp of the heavy breathing of dead lungs mingling with the other night sounds.

12

Inside the house, the mood was one of hopelessness and despair. Barbara was once again sitting on the sofa, her vacant eyes staring into space. Harry was sulking in a corner, his head slung back in a rocking chair that creaked every time he moved, which was not very often; his face was swollen; he was holding an ice-pack against his eye. His other eye, like a wandering sentinel, followed Ben who was pacing about the room; when Ben's pacing took him to the kitchen, or to some area out of Harry's sight, the good eye nervously relaxed a little. Ben's movements made virtually the only sound in the room, other than the occasional creaking of Harry's rocking chair.

Ben was checking the defenses, by force of habit rather than hope, while his rifle remained slung on his back. With the failure of the escape attempt, he had allowed himself to become almost totally dejected; he felt as powerless as the others who were imprisoned in the house with him. He could not think of what to try next in order to escape, yet he knew that in time they would all be doomed if they stayed put. Harry continued to watch with his good eye, while Ben paced from door to kitchen to window; he started to go upstairs, stopped, checked himself, and went to the door again.

Suddenly, there was a noise on the cellar stairs and Helen entered the living room. "It's ten minutes to three," she said, to no one in particular. "There'll be another broadcast in ten more minutes."

Nobody said anything.

"Maybe the situation has improved somehow," Helen said, without feeling much of a basis for it.

"You or Harry had better get downstairs and maintain a watch over your kid," Ben said.

"In a little while," Helen said, after a long pause. "I want to watch the broadcast first."

Ben looked at her, as though to give her an argument, but he held his tongue; he was too tired and depressed to haggle with anybody. He only hoped the little girl didn't die while they were all watching the television.

Turning his back on the people in the room, he peeled back the curtain and peered through the window of the barricaded front door. Suddenly his eyes widened with fear and revulsion, but he continued to watch for a long time. There were many ghouls lurking in the shadows of the trees. Some of the things were out in the open, much nearer the house than they had dared come before. The remains of the charred bodies of several ghouls felled during the escape attempt were dimly apparent on various parts of the lawn; for some as yet unaccountable reason, the flesh-eaters never bothered to devour one of their own; they preferred fresh human meat.

And some of the ghouls had what they wanted, for Ben's eyes were fastened on a truly grisly scene; at the edge of the lawn, in the moonlight, several ghouls were devouring what had once been Tom...and Judy. They were ripping and tearing into pieces of human bodies...ghoulish teeth...biting into human arms and hands and fingers...sucking and chewing on human hearts and lungs. Ben stared... fascinated...and repulsed...

With a convulsive movement, his fingers released the curtain as he spun around, badly shaken, and faced the others, beads of perspiration on his forehead.

"Don't...don't...none of you look out there," Ben said, holding his stomach to keep from gagging. "You won't like what you see."

Harry's good eye fastened on Ben and watched him, satisfied and contemptuous to see the big man weaken. Ben moved for the television and clicked it on.

Barbara's scream pierced the room. Ben jumped back from the television. She was on her feet, screaming uncontrollably.

"We'll never get out of here...None of us! We'll never get out of here alive Johneeee! Johneee!...Oh! Oh...GOD...None of us...None of us...Help...Oh God...God...!"

Before anyone could move to her, she choked up as suddenly as she had begun and slumped, sobbing violently, to the couch, her face buried in her hands. Helen tried to soothe her, but great sobs came wracking from deep within. As she grew gradually quiet, the sobs diminished and stopped, but she remained slumped on the couch, her face covered with her hands. Helen pulled the overcoat over her, but the action seemed so futile—Barbara made no reaction whatsoever.

Ben allowed himself to sink very slowly into a chair in front of the TV. Harry's good eye went from Barbara to Ben; his eye fastened on the gun, which Ben lowered butt first to the floor and leaned across his legs. His arm through the fringed sling, Ben maintained his grip on the forepiece. Harry watched.

Helen bent over and placed her hand tenderly on Barbara. "Come on, honey...come and talk to me. It'll make you feel better."

But Barbara made no response. Helen sat down on the other end of the sofa.

Ben remained transfixed before the TV; he was lost in thought, his mind trying to come up with a solution to their dilemma—there was no more kerosene, no vehicle to escape in, and very little ammunition for the rifle. There was nothing on the TV screen; just a dull glow and low hiss of scanning lines and static—he had turned the set on too early.

Harry's good eye was fastened on the gun, the sling wound around Ben's arm.

"Where's your car?" Ben asked, the sound of his voice startling, breaking the virtual silence.

Harry shifted his eye, trying to make it look as though he had not been looking in Ben's direction.

"We were trying to get to a motel before dark," Helen said. "We pulled off the road to look at a map, and those...things...attacked us. We ran...and ran..."

"It has to be at least a mile and a half away," Harry said bitterly, as though it satisfied him to see one of Ben's ideas thwarted, even at the cost of his own survival.

"It was all we could do to save Karen," Helen added.

"Do you think we could get to the car?" Ben said. "Is there any chance it would be in the clear, if we could break away from this house?"

"Not a chance," Harry said, flatly.

Ben shouted, angrily, "You give up too easy, man! You want to die in this house?"

"I told you those things turned over our car!" Harry spat.

"It's lying in a gully with its wheels up in the air," Helen said.

"Well...if we could get to it, maybe we could do something..." Ben conjectured.

"You gonna turn it over by yourself?" Harry said.

"Johnny has the keys...keys..." Barbara mumbled under her breath.

But nobody heard her—because suddenly there was a loud crackle from the television and the picture and sound faded in.

"GOOD MORNING, LADIES AND GENTLEMEN. THIS IS YOUR CIVIL DEFENSE EMERGENCY NETWORK. EASTERN STANDARD TIME IS NOW THREE A.M.

"IN MOST AREAS AFFLICTED BY THIS...TRAGIC PHENOMENON...WE ARE SEEING THE FIRST SIGNS THAT IT WILL BE POSSIBLE TO BRING THINGS UNDER CONTROL. CIVILIAN AUTHORITIES WORKING HAND IN HAND WITH THE NATIONAL GUARD HAVE ESTABLISHED ORDER IN MOST OF THE AFFECTED COMMUNITIES, AND WHILE CURFEWS ARE STILL IN EFFECT, THE INTENSITY OF THE ONSLAUGHT DOES SEEM TO BE RELENTING, AND LAW ENFORCEMENT AGENCIES ARE PREDICTING A RETURN TO NORMALITY WITHIN THE NEAR FUTURE—PERHAPS—WITHIN THE NEXT WEEK.

"DESPITE THIS WORD OF ENCOURAGEMENT, HOWEVER, THE AUTHORITIES WARN THAT A STATE OF VIGILANCE MUST BE MAINTAINED. NO ONE IS CERTAIN HOW LONG THE DEAD WILL CONTINUE TO RISE, OR WHAT WERE THE EXACT REASONS FOR THIS PHENOMENON. ANYONE KILLED OR WOUNDED BY ONE OF THE... AGGRESSORS...IS A POTENTIAL ENEMY OF LIVE HUMAN BEINGS. WE MUST CONTINUE TO BURN OR DECAPITATE ALL CORPSES. GRISLY AS THIS ADVICE SOUNDS, IT IS AN ABSOLUTE NECESSITY. DOCTOR LEWIS STANFORD, OF THE COUNTY HEALTH DEPARTMENT, REPEATEDLY EMPHASIZED THIS POINT IN AN INTERVIEW TAPED EARLIER TODAY IN THIS TELEVISION STUDIO..."

The narrator faded out, as the taped interview faded in Doctor Lewis Stanford, seated behind his desk, was being interviewed by a reporter holding a microphone and wearing a headset.

"DOCTOR, CAN YOU OR YOUR COLLEAGUES SHED ANY LIGHT ON THE CAUSES OF THIS PHENOMENON?"

(The doctor fidgeted in his chair and shook his head.)

"WELL...NO...IT'S NOTHING THAT WE CAN READILY EXPLAIN. I'M NOT GOING TO SAY THAT WE WON'T HAVE AN ANSWER FOR YOU IN THE NEAR FUTURE, BUT SO FAR OUR RESEARCH HAS YIELDED NO CONCLUSIVE ANSWERS..."

"WHAT ABOUT THE VENUS PROBE?"

"THE VENUS PROBE?"

"YES, SIR."

"UH...I'M...NOT QUALIFIED TO COMMENT ON THAT."

"BUT THAT IS WHERE MOST OF THE SPECULATION HAS BEEN DIRECTED, SIR."

"STILL AND ALL, I AM NOT AN AEROSPACE EXPERT. I AM UNACQUAINTED WITH THAT PARTICULAR EXPLORATION ATTEMPT. I AM A MEDICAL PATHOLOGIST—"

"WHAT LIGHT CAN YOU SHED ON THIS, DOCTOR?"

"WELL...I FEEL THAT OUR EFFORTS HAVE BEEN DIRECTED PROPERLY. WE'RE DOING WHAT WE'VE BEEN TRAINED TO DO...THAT IS, WE ARE TRYING TO DISCOVER A MEDICAL OR PATHOLOGICAL REASON FOR A PHENOMENON THAT IS WITHOUT PRECEDENT IN OUR MEDICAL HISTORY. WE ARE TREATING WHAT HAPPENED TO THESE...DEAD...PEOPLE AS A DISEASE WHICH VERY PROBABLY HAS A BIOLOGICAL EXPLANATION FOR IT; IN OTHER WORDS, IT IS MOST LIKELY CAUSED BY MICROBES OR VIRUSES PREVIOUSLY UNKNOWN TO US OR PREVIOUSLY NOT A THREAT TO US, UNTIL SOMETHING HAPPENED TO ACTIVATE THEM. WHETHER OR NOT THE VENUS PROBE HAD ANYTHING TO DO WITH THIS IS SOMETHING WE COULDN'T DETERMINE FOR CERTAIN UNTIL WE ISOLATE THE VIRUS OR MICROBE

AND GO TO VENUS AND FIND THAT THEY ACTUALLY
EXIST THERE."

"IS THERE A CHANCE THAT WHATEVER IS CAUSING
THIS WILL SPREAD—WILL BE WITH US PERMANENTLY
NOW? WILL WE HAVE TO GO ON BURNING OUR CORPS-
ES?"

"I DON'T KNOW...I DON'T KNOW. IT IS POSSIBLE,
HOWEVER, THAT THE DISEASED ORGANISMS WHICH
ARE RESPONSIBLE FOR THIS PHENOMENON ARE
SHORT-LIVED—THAT IS, THEY MAY ALL DIE OFF IN A
SHORT TIME; THEY MAY BE A MUTANT BREED THAT IS
NOT CAPABLE OF REPRODUCTION. WE ARE VERY HOPE-
FUL THAT THIS WILL TURN OUT TO BE THE CASE."

"WHAT CLUES HAVE YOU DISCOVERED SO FAR,
DOCTOR STANFORD?"

"OUR RESEARCH IS JUST BEGINNING. EARLIER TO-
DAY, IN THE COLD ROOM AT THE UNIVERSITY, WE
HAD A CADAVER—A CADAVER FROM WHICH ALL FOUR
LIMBS HAD BEEN AMPUTATED. IN A SHORT TIME AFTER
BEING REMOVED FROM THE COLD ROOM, IT OPENED
ITS EYES. IT WAS DEAD, BUT IT OPENED ITS EYES AND
BEGAN TO MOVE. OUR PROBLEM NOW IS TO OBTAIN
MORE SUCH CADAVERS FOR EXAMINATION AND EX-
PERIMENTATION—WE HAVE TO ASK THE MILITARY
PERSONNEL AND THE CIVILIAN PATROLS THAT ARE
OUT IN THE FIELD TO STOP BURNING ALL OF THESE
THINGS—TO DEACTIVATE SOME AND BRING THEM TO
US STILL ALIVE, SO WE CAN STUDY THEM. SO FAR, WE
HAVE NOT BEEN SUCCESSFUL IN OBTAINING MANY OF
SUCH CADAVERS..."

"THEN HOW DOES THIS FIT IN WITH YOUR TELL-
ING PEOPLE THEY SHOULD BURN OR DECAPITATE ANY-
BODY, EVEN RELATIVES OR NEXT OF KIN, WHO DIES
DURING THIS EMERGENCY?"

"THAT ADVICE STILL HOLDS TRUE FOR THE GEN-
ERAL PUBLIC. IF WE ARE TO OBTAIN CADAVERS FOR
EXAMINATION, WE WANT TO DO IT IN AN ORGANIZED

WAY SO THEY CAN BE HANDLED UNDER STERILE CON-
DITIONS AND WITH AS LITTLE RISK AS POSSIBLE—BOTH
AS TO THE PARTIES INVOLVED AND AS TO THE DANGER
OF PROLONGING THIS EMERGENCY. THE PUBLIC IN
GENERAL SHOULD CONTINUE TO BURN ALL CORPSES.
JUST DRAG THEM OUTSIDE AND BURN THEM. THEY'RE
JUST DEAD FLESH, AND DANGEROUS—"

With this final word from Doctor Stanford, the TV report faded
back to the live announcer.

"THAT REPORT, WHICH YOU JUST SAW, WAS TAPED
EARLIER TODAY IN OUR STUDIO. RECAPPING DOCTOR
STANFORD'S ADVICE IT IS STILL MANDATORY FOR CI-
VILIANS TO BURN OR DECAPITATE ANYONE WHO DIES
DURING THIS EMERGENCY. IT IS A DIFFICULT THING TO
DO, BUT THE AUTHORITIES ADVISE THAT YOU MUST
DO IT. IF YOU CANNOT BRING YOURSELF TO DO IT, YOU
MUST CONTACT YOUR LOCAL POLICE OR PROTECTION
AGENCY, AND THEY WILL DO IT FOR YOU.

"NOW OUR TV CAMERAS TAKE YOU TO WASHING-
TON, WHERE LATE EVENING REPORTERS SUCCEEDED
IN INTERVIEWING GENERAL OSGOOD AND HIS STAFF,
AS HE WAS RETURNING FROM A HIGH-LEVEL CONFER-
ENCE AT THE PENTAGON..."

Again the commentator faded out and newsreel footage faded
in—

But, suddenly there was a crash from outside and the lights went
out. The screen went blank. The house was submerged in darkness.

Ben's voice rang out:

"Is there a fuse box in the cellar?"

"It's...it's not the fuse," Harry stammered. "The power lines must
be down!"

Ben squirted charcoal-lighter into the embers of the fire, and
with a loud whoosh the flames leapt up. He threw a bundle of rolled-
up newspapers onto the fire. Then, in the half-light, he opened the
cellar door wide and began to work his way downstairs.

Harry seized Helen by the arm and pulled her face close to his so he could whisper. "Helen...I've got to get that gun. We can go to the cellar. You have to help me!"

He had let the ice pack come away from his eye, and in the flickering light from the fire Helen saw its blackened, swollen condition—and the desperation in his face.

"I'm not going to help you," she whispered hoarsely. "Haven't you had enough? He'd kill us both."

"That man is crazy!" Harry argued, fighting to hold his voice to a whisper. "He's already responsible for two people being dead—I've got to get that gun—"

Harry was cut short by the sound of Ben's footsteps at the top of the stairs, and Ben entered the room. "It's not the fuse box," he announced, with an air of hopelessness. "I had to feel my way to it—but I found a flashlight down there. All the fuses are okay. I left the flashlight at the head of the stairs, so we can see to go down. You'd better go down there and see to your daughter. She'll be—"

Crash! From the kitchen, the sound of splintering glass. Then more racket. Moans and loud crashes. The walls of the house began to shake. The dead things outside were attacking it en masse. Some of them had gotten into the den and were hammering at the barricaded door.

Ben was on his feet immediately, trying to reinforce the barricades. With hammer and crowbar, he swung through the broken glass at the dead things and tried to shore up the pieces of lumber that were threatening to give way under the onslaught.

"Harry! Harry! Give me a hand over here!"

Harry came over behind Ben, and instead of helping ripped the gun from Ben's back. Holding the gun on Ben, Harry backed toward the cellar. Ben turned around, panicked; the things were breaking into the house.

"What are you up to, man? We've got to keep those things out!"

"Now we'll see who's going to shoot who," Harry said, backing away and waving the gun in Ben's direction. "I'm going to the cellar, and I'm taking the two women with me—and you can rot up here, you crazy bastard!"

Ignoring Harry, Ben threw his body against the window, where the barricades were starting to come apart. At least a half-dozen ghouls were outside the window, pounding at it, forcing the nails loose.

Harry froze for a moment, transfixed by the fury of the attack and by Ben's indifference to the fact that he no longer had possession of the rifle; Harry had expected Ben to beg to be allowed to come with the others to the cellar.

Purposely, Ben let the ghouls pry loose one of the largest pieces of lumber that had been nailed across the living room window; then, when it was loose, he spun and hurled it in Harry's direction. The gun was hit and knocked aside, and it fired its shot harmlessly into the floor. Ben leaped upon Harry and, after a brief violent struggle, succeeded in wrenching the gun away.

Helen watched, frozen in place, with the noise of the ghouls pounding in her ears.

Harry backed away from Ben, toward the cellar.

Ben cocked and fired. Harry screamed. A great clot of blood appeared at his chest. Clutching the wound, he began to sink; he fell through the entranceway to the cellar stairs, then reeled and grabbed the banister, staggered, and fell head first down the stairs.

Some ghouls had broken through the window, and they had Helen by the hair and by the neck, ripping and clawing at her. Ben pounded and smashed at them with the butt of the rifle; then he leveled off and shot two of them in the face. Freed, Helen ran screaming to the cellar and, in the absence of light, she too fell and tumbled down the stairs. Her screams grew louder, as she realized she had fallen onto something large and soft—the dead body of her husband; her hand was wet and slippery with his blood. Then, out of the darkness something stumbled toward her, and moaned softly, and clutched at her.

"Karen?"

It was Karen. But she was dead. Her eyes flickered in the dark.

She let go of her dead father's wrist, which she had been holding to her lips; she had been chewing the tender flesh on the underside of his forearm.

Helen struggled to see in the darkness.

"Karen? Baby?"

The dead little girl had a garden trowel. Silently, staring without a word, she plunged the trowel into her mother's chest. Helen fell back, screaming and clutching while the life-blood gushed from her and her daughter began stabbing her again and again. Helen's screams mingled with the other sounds of destruction echoing through the old house.

Then the screams stopped. But the garden trowel continued to stab downward, again and again, hacking Helen's body to bits, rending and tearing the bloody flesh. When the trowel fell from her dead blood-stained hands, Karen bent over her mother, drooling, and bared her teeth...She dug her hands into the gaping wounds...

Upstairs, Ben was continuing to fight as hard as he could, hoping to drive the things back.

With the hysteria of revenge, Barbara too had flung herself into the attack. She smashed a chair against one aggressor, and it went down, and she threw herself upon it and beat her fists into its face—then the thing grabbed her and they rolled and struggled, the dead creature clawing at Barbara and sinking its teeth into her neck. Ben stepped up and pointed his gun directly in the thing's face and fired, and the force of the explosion hurled the thing back, splattering Barbara with blood and bits of bone as the back of her attacker's head was blown off. She jumped to her feet screaming and screaming—and ran straight into a cluster of ghouls that had smashed through the living room door.

The ghouls seized Barbara, ripping and tearing at her and dragging her outside the house. She looked up, as more attackers moved in for the kill, and began to struggle for possession of her soon-to-be-dead body. One of the attackers was her brother, Johnny, back from the dead. He stared evilly, his teeth smashed and his face caked with dried blood and dirt, as he moved toward Barbara and dug his fingers into her throat. She screamed, and passed out, dead of shock. The ghouls dragged her out into the night, ripping her apart and digging their hands and teeth into the soft parts of her body—while groups of two or three of the flesh-eaters pulled and twisted at her limbs, trying to break and tear bone and cartilage to dismember her body.

Inside the house, Ben was nearly overwhelmed. At least twenty or thirty ghouls were now in the house, the barricades broken through. There was no way that Ben could continue to stand and fight.

For a moment, there was a stand-off as the ghouls stood and stared, confronting the man that they had trapped, like a rat in a corner of a room.

Ben backed toward the cellar door. Then, from behind, the little girl, Karen, seized him, clawing and tearing at him—and he wheeled and grabbed her by the throat and hurled her against the wall—but she got to her feet and advanced toward him, her face smeared with her mother's blood—and the other ghouls, too, had started to advance.

Ben stepped onto the cellar stairs, slamming the door behind him and frantically barricading it as the ghouls pounded and smashed at the door and the walls. The sounds of their rasping breath and their insane pounding and smashing filled Ben's ears as he trembled and hoped that the barricade would hold. Though the pounding continued for a long time, the door seemed to be strong. The ghouls seemed unable to break it down. Ben sat there in the dark—overwhelmed by the hopelessness of his situation and the fact that everybody was dead who had tried to hold out in the old house, everybody but him.

Then his fingers closed around the flashlight that he had left there earlier when he had come to check out the fuse box, and, turning it on and pointing its beam of light ahead of him, he began to descend into the basement.

In the peripheral illumination from the beam of the flashlight, Ben looked at his arm and—with a shock—saw that he was bleeding. The girl, Karen—she had bitten him in their struggle.

Frozen on the stairs, Ben stared at the teeth marks in his arm. If he died, he was going to become—

—unless a cure could be found—

He did not allow his mind to complete the horrible thought of what might happen to him.

The pounding of the ghouls at the cellar door was growing weaker, and more half-hearted.

The flesh-eaters, content to devour and fight over the remains of the slaughtered Barbara, were wandering out of the house, out into the yard—where groups of ghouls were already sinking their teeth into warm human flesh and organs—and gnawing at human bone.

At the foot of the stairs, the beam of Ben's flashlight fell on the ash-white dead face of Harry Cooper, with his arm half chewed through at the elbow.

And slowly in a little while Harry's eyelids began to flutter...and come open...

13

The sounds of men breaking camp disturbed the normal hush and silence of the woods in the gray dawn. A damp mist hung over the field where the men had slept, and as they straggled to assemble in the clearing which McClellan had designated, white breath hissed from their mouths and nostrils and hovered around them as they walked. They did not talk much, but they stuck close together in little groups, in case one of the dead things should attack them out of the fog.

George Henderson spat on the ground and said to the sheriff, "It's a wonder how it could be so warm last night and so cold this morning. Maybe we got some rain movin' in."

"Naw," McClellan said. "I checked the weather report. The sun'll come up and burn this fog in a few hours."

"It'll be hell if it rains, and these men have to slog through mud," George said. "There'll be some people that won't get rescued."

As the two men talked, a white jeep station wagon, its engine growling, nosed its way in circles through the tall, damp grass—as two posse men, fully armed, followed along behind the jeep—stopping here and there to pick up bed rolls and packed-up tents and throw them on board.

The campfires had all been doused; there were beds of wet, black coals scattered throughout the field, in proximity to the tents and bed rolls.

"Hurry it up, men!" McClellan yelled. "How'd you like it if your wife or daughter was waitin' for you to haul ass and save her from those things?"

The men stepped it up a little bit.

Soon they were all assembled in the clearing under the trees, where McClellan's tent had been pitched.

14

The circle of light on Harry Cooper's face grew larger as Ben descended the staircase. Ben moved the flashlight quickly to take in the whole picture. Harry lay dead in a pool of blood, his arm chewed halfway through. Helen lay dead too, not far away, a garden trowel protruding from her hacked-up chest.

With an additional flutter of his eyelids, Harry opened his eyes wide. Then he began to sit up. Holding the flashlight and the gun at the same time, Ben stepped as close as he dared, and took careful aim. He quivered but pulled the trigger—and was jolted by recoil as the top of Harry's head was blown off and the loud report of the rifle echoed in the dank basement.

Ben looked down, moving the flashlight and pointing it. He shuddered as he thought he could see splatters of blood on the bottoms of his trouser legs.

Then, he remembered Helen—and he pointed the flashlight in her direction. Her face and hair were caked with blood; blood had come in a stream from her mouth and nostrils, and several of her teeth were broken and twisted; her ribs, where some flesh had been eaten away, showed glistening white in the beam of the flashlight. In a little while, she opened her eyes—and Ben fired. Her body heaved and twitched with an abrupt convulsion, as the bullet smacked into her brain.

Ben threw the rifle down and covered his eyes with his hands. Tears rolled down his cheeks as he stepped over the dead bodies. Moving the flashlight around, he was overcome by the loneliness and the dismalness of the dark cellar—and his eyes fell on the table that had been Karen's makeshift sick bed. In a fit of rage, he overturned the table and hurled it to the floor, with a crash. Then he staggered about aimlessly in his grief, stumbling over objects in the dark as though they weren't there if the flashlight failed to show them.

Tom. Judy. Barbara. Harry. Helen.

All dead.

If only the truck hadn't caught fire.

If only...

If only...

Gathering his senses together somewhat, Ben picked up the rifle and cocked it. He looked all around, pointing the gun and the flashlight. His eyes scanned his surroundings for possible areas of threat or vulnerability. Moving around slowly and quietly, holding his breath though it wanted to come gasping out of him, he probed behind the packing crates and in the dark corners of the cellar.

There was nobody around. Nobody in hiding. Just the dead bodies of Harry and Helen Cooper.

Ben sat in a corner, leaning against a wall of concrete block, and cried softly.

He looked down at the wound on his arm. And at the blood splattered on his trousers.

Upstairs, the noise of the ghouls had stopped. Perhaps a few were still in the house, lurking silently.

From exhaustion, finally, Ben's head nodded and he yielded to an agonized, nervous sleep.

His last thoughts were of his children.

15

Sunrise.

Bird sounds. Then the sounds of dogs, and human voices.

The rising sun, bright and warm. Dew on the high grass of a meadow.

More sounds, in the distance.

The whir of a helicopter.

Men with dogs and guns, working their way up from the woods that surrounded the meadow. Shouts...muffled talk...panting and straining of dogs against leashes...Sheriff McClellan's posse.

16

Ben nodded and snapped awake—startled, unsure of his surroundings.

He thought he heard a helicopter. Or maybe he was dreaming.

He listened.

Nothing.

Then, in the distance, a beating of metal wings.

A helicopter. Definitely.

Ben clutched the rifle and listened and looked all around. The basement was not dark any longer; but it was not bright, either; it was dusky and dank, illuminated in varying shades of gray by whatever sunlight could filter through the high, tiny windows. The helicopter sounds continued to fade in...and recede. Ben strained his ears, but could hear no other signs of human activity.

Finally, stepping gingerly and trying not to look, he got past the corpses of Helen and Harry Cooper and began to sneak up the cellar stairs.

The stairs creaked, startling him, but he paused only momentarily, then continued his ascent toward the barricaded door.

17

A few men, some German shepherds on leashes, came up out of the woods and onto the edge of the sunlit, dewy meadow. They stopped and looked all around, as if they were scrutinizing the meadow for possible danger. The boots and trouser legs of the men were damp, from plodding through the wet grass.

Sheriff McClellan was the next man up from the surrounding thicket—he was breathing hard because of his weight and the difficult job of leading the men through the woods, when none of them had had any rest or any breakfast. He was armed with his rifle and pistol, with a belt of ammunition slung over his shoulder. He paused, looked back over his shoulder into the woods, and mopped perspiration from his brow with a balled-up dirty handkerchief.

More men were still working their way out of the woods, into the clearing. McClellan shouted at them.

"Come on—let's step it up, now! Never can tell what we'll run into up here—"

His voice broke off as his deputy, George Henderson, came over to him and opened his mouth to say something.

But McClellan spoke first.

"You keeping in touch with the squad cars, George?"

George was wearing a sweatband and carrying a rifle and a sidearm—and he also had a walkie-talkie strapped on his back. Breathing hard, he hunched and adjusted the straps of his burden. "Yeah... they know where we are. They should be intercepting us at the Miller farmhouse."

"Good," McClellan said. "These men is dog tired. They can use some rest and hot coffee..." Then, looking back toward the men moving up from behind, he shouted, "Let's push along, now—the squad cars'll be waiting with coffee and sandwiches at the house!"

The men continued to push on, across the meadow. And soon they began to work their way cautiously into the strip of woods on the other side.

18

At the top of the cellar stairs, Ben was listening as intently as he could, behind the barricade.

For a long time, he had not been able to hear any helicopter sounds; perhaps it had landed somewhere, or flown away. Ben wished he could have been upstairs, so he could wave to it from the lawn.

Then—from far off—he heard the distinct sound of a dog— barking. He listened for a long time, but heard nothing more. He was tempted to undo the barricade and take his chances on going out there to look around.

19

When the men worked their way through the narrow belt of trees on the far side of the meadow, they came out into a cemetery, the one Barbara and Johnny had come to with the wreath for their father. The posse continued its advance, threading its way among the grave markers.

Down a dirt road, and up a short grade, the men found Barbara's car, with the smashed window. The headlight switch was on, but the battery was dead. There were no signs of blood, and the men could not find any corpses anywhere near the car.

"Maybe whoever was in here escaped and got away," McClellan said, hopefully. "Move on, men! We can't do any good here!"

The men passed through the cemetery and out onto the two-lane blacktop road, where several squad cars were parked, waiting. There were also one or two motorcycle patrolmen, and one of them dismounted and hailed McClellan.

"Hi, Sheriff! How's things goin'?"

McClellan advanced, mopping his brow, and stopped to shake hands with the motorcycle patrolman. Meanwhile, the men in the posse began to catch up and regroup.

McClellan said, "Sure glad to see you fellas, Charlie. We been at it damn near all night—but I don't want to break till we get to the Miller house over there. We might be screwin' around while somebody needs our help—we'll see, first, then stop and get some coffee."

"Sure, Sheriff."

The two men looked around at the gathering posse, which was beginning to fill up the neck in the blacktop road.

"Get started over that wall and through that field!" George Henderson shouted, with the walkie-talkie on his back. "The Miller farmhouse is over there!"

He took the time to unsling the walkie-talkie and hand it to one of the cops in a squad car. Then, leading a squad of men, he began to move toward the field in front of the Miller house.

Gunshots rang out almost immediately.

"Ghouls! Ghouls—all over the place!" a voice yelled. A bevy of gunshots split the air. More men moved up, running and firing from behind trees.

The police dogs growled and strained at their leashes, hating the scent of the dead things.

The posse advanced in squads, across the field and toward the shed with the gasoline pumps—where several of the flesh-eaters were lurking and trying to get away, but they were gunned down.

Nearer the house, there were still more ghouls, and firing repeatedly, the squads of men moved forward, felling the dead things with a trail of bullets.

There were more of the creatures, trying to hide in and around a burned-out truck—but they were unsuccessful; they tried to run, but the posse gunned them down.

Each time a ghoul fell, one of the men moved forward and hacked at it with a machete, until the head was severed from the body. That way, they knew the ghoul would not get to its feet again.

For better than half an hour, the echo of gunshots was constant in the fields surrounding the old Miller farmhouse.

20

Still at the top of the cellar stairs, Ben knew for sure now that there were men outside. The gunshots were undeniable. And he even thought he had heard a car engine. But he was afraid to open the door, because some of the creatures might still be in the house. Yet... he knew he was going to have to open the door...Slowly, quietly, he began undoing the heavy barricades...

21

McClellan fired, and the dead thing fifty feet in front of him clutched at its face with a convulsive movement and toppled to the earth, like a sack of potatoes, with a dull thud.

More gunshots rang out. And two more of the ghouls fell heavily to the ground.

"Get up here, boys!" McClellan yelled. "There's three more for the fire!"

The men with machetes moved up and hacking quickly and furiously, severed the heads from the dead ghouls.

The sheriff and his men had advanced to the lawn of the old farmhouse and were crouching and firing repeatedly, blasting down the dead creatures that surrounded the place.

"Shoot for the eyes, boys!" McClellan cried out. "Like I told you before...always aim right for the eyes!"

The flurry of gunfire was constant—crack! crack! crack!—as the posse surrounded the house.

Then there was silence, as all the ghouls had apparently been felled, and the men's eyes scanned the old place and its environs, looking for a new target to gun down.

Suddenly, from the house—a loud noise. George Henderson had moved up beside McClellan, and the two of them watched and listened, frozen in their tracks.

"There's something in there," Henderson said, unnecessarily. "I heard a noise."

Inside, ready to shoot or swing, Ben had slammed open the cellar door. The force of his shoulder against the door had carried him into the living room, which was empty—there were no ghouls lurking there; there was only the ramshackle destruction from the recent siege. Ben edged his way through the twisted wreckage and overturned furniture toward the front door. There was no light in the place; despite the early morning sunlight, it remained dark under the heavy foliage of the surrounding trees. Some of the barricades partially remained, although weakened and widened for entry by the marauding ghouls. Ben's hands crept to what was left of a curtain; he pulled it back and started to peek out...but...a shot rang out—and Ben reeled, driven back—a circle of blood on his forehead, right between his eyes.

Simultaneously, McClellan shouted:

"Damn it, what'd you shoot for? I told you to be careful—there might be people in there!"

The posse member who had fired the shot said, "Naw, you can see this place is demolished. Anybody in there'd be dead. And if they're dead—"

Several men, led by George Henderson, advanced to kick in the front door. They stepped back and peered cautiously inside. Their faces searched the room. A patch of sunlight from the opened door fell partially on Ben. He was dead. The men looked down at him without pity, as they stepped past him to the cellar. They did not know he was a man.

Squads of men began to enter the house, moving cautiously through the rooms in military fashion, checking for possible aggressors lurking inside.

Two men with machetes came forward and began hacking at Ben, severing his head from his body.

"Somebody put up a good fight here," McClellan said to George Henderson later, when they were sipping black coffee on the front lawn, near a squad car. "It's a damn shame they couldn't hold out a while longer."

"I wonder who it was," Henderson replied, taking a bite of his sandwich. "It wasn't Mrs. Miller. We found what was left of her—upstairs in her room. But we didn't find any trace of her grandson."

"I guess we ain't never going to know," said the sheriff, "but then again there's lots of things we ain't going to know about this damned business."

22

Ben's head and body were heaved onto the bonfire with the rest. And the meat hook was yanked out of his chest, with a hard tug on the part of the gloved hand that was yanking it.

Then the lumber and the dead bodies were drenched in gasoline by still another pair of gloved hands.

And the touch of a flaming torch set the whole thing ablaze.

The men stared into the broiling hot fire, and watched flesh curling and melting from dead bone, much as the paint curls and melts from a burning blackening page of newsprint. They backed away from the heat finally and went to where they could discard their meat hooks and gloves and wash their hands in sterile alcohol.

But they could not escape the stench of burning flesh.

Return
of the
Living Dead

PROLOGUE

Think of all the people who have lived and died and will never again see the trees or the grass or the sun.

It all seems so brief, so worth...nothing. To live for a short while and then die. It all seems to add up to so very little. Why do we fight so hard to stay alive, to preserve life, to hang on to that fleeting flicker of something which nobody has been able to define?

It is easy to envy the dead ones.

They are beyond living, and beyond dying.

They are lucky to be dead, to be done with dying and to not have to fear the inevitable. To not have to struggle for life that is threatened. To be under the ground, oblivious. To be oblivious of hurting, oblivious of the fear of dying.

They do not have to live any more. Or feel pain. Or accomplish anything. Or wonder what to do next. Or wonder what it is going to be like to have to go through dying.

Why does life seem so ugly and beautiful and sad and important while you are living it, and so trivial when it is over?

The fire of life smoulders a while and then is extinguished, and the graves wait patiently to be filled. The end of all life is death, and the new life sings happily in the breeze and neither knows nor cares anything about the old life, and then it in turn also dies.

Life is a constant, endless creation of graves. Things live and then die, and sometimes they live well and sometimes poorly, but they always die, and death is the common denominator of all things living; the one thing that sends all things to oblivion.

What is it that makes people afraid of dying?

Not pain. Not always.

Death can be instantaneous and almost painless.

Death itself is an end to pain.

Death can be like falling asleep.

Then why are people afraid to die?

And which of us, once dead, would wish to forsake the peace of death to return to life again?

1

Dawn is a time of rebirth.

All life senses this, the rising again to face new beginnings. Our story begins at dawn. Or should we say, our story begins again.

Orange light fired the morning, accenting the colors of a green, wooded landscape.

A pick-up truck shuddered through the woods, raising a cloud of dust as it bounced over the ruts in the dusty road between the trees. The people in the truck were in a hurry to get somewhere, and they were late.

Bert Miller, an angry-looking man wearing an old-fashioned suit that looked new because it was worn so seldom, tended to the business of keeping his truck under control, a task he performed with a combination of anger and skill—anger that caused him to drive too fast and would make an accident seem inevitable, and skill that prevented that accident from happening. Bert was about forty years old, with the weathered face and calloused hands of a farmer. He had a shock of straight black hair that refused to stay down, no matter how it had been wetted and parted and combed, although Bert did not wet and comb it too often. A farmer is what he was, and he wanted to be nothing else, even if his farm was not a rich one and he had to work excessively hard every day of his life to scratch out a meager living for himself and his three daughters. His wife was dead. She had died giving birth to their youngest daughter, Karen, who was pregnant herself and was sitting with Bert on the seat of the pick-up truck.

Karen was very tense and scared, clutching her armrest, hoping her father would not see her being frightened and use it as an excuse to yell at her while he continued to drive as fast as possible, negotiating tight, twisting curves and sharp upgrades by what seemed to Karen to be a combination of luck and bullheadedness.

In the back of the truck, bouncing and sliding, were Karen's two sisters, Ann and Sue Ellen. They were more scared than Karen, and had reason to be. Their seat in the back of the careening truck was a low wooden bench on which they had to sit to keep their dresses clean. Sitting in the bed of the truck would doubtless have been safer, for the bench was unanchored and bounced and vibrated terribly with each lurch of the truck. They had known what sort of ride they were in for, and were not at all surprised by it, considering how angry their father was that morning after the argument at home.

It was Karen's fault that they were late. In her eighth month of pregnancy, she had gotten up that morning complaining of nausea and weakness. That had been enough to set Bert to yelling. He accused Karen of faking morning sickness to get out of doing her Christian duty with the rest of the family, and had gone on shouting that it wasn't enough she had to disgrace him by giving birth to a child without being married, but she also didn't have any respect for anybody dead or living and had lost her religion, and it was enough to cause her poor dead mother to turn over in her grave.

Bert had insisted Karen get dressed and come along with the rest of the family, ignoring her protests that she was sick. But, in deference to her pregnancy, he had made her climb into the front seat of the truck while his other two daughters sat in the back.

Then, because they were going to be late and because Bert needed very little provocation to bring his anger over Karen's illegitimate pregnancy bursting to the surface, Bert had gunned the truck out, grinding gears and spewing gravel, and they had lurched toward their destination.

"It's going to be *our* funeral if he doesn't slow down," Sue Ellen said, as she and Ann hung onto the sides of the bench as if it would offer them any stability and protection during the bone-shaking ride. Ann did not reply. Even though the noise of the truck on the dirt and gravel road was deafening, she was afraid her father would hear them talking.

"He can't hear from up there," Sue Ellen said, reading her sister's thoughts. But still Ann said nothing. The dirt road straightened out a bit and became smoother for a stretch of about half a mile that was relatively safe to take at high speed, as long as there wasn't any oncoming traffic. But at least the wooden bench stopped bouncing and the two girls relaxed ever so slightly. There was only one more set of curves and another straightaway, where they would come up on the Dorsey farmhouse.

Bert Miller gunned the truck a little, braked it for the curves, scaring his daughters, and slowed when he got into the straightaway and saw it lined, as expected, with all the cars and trucks of the farmers who lived in the valley. Some people had been able to park in a field near the side of the Dorsey house, and when the field had filled up, the rest had just squeezed their vehicles over to one side, as far off the narrow dirt road as possible. Bert Miller did the same, slamming his pick-up truck to a halt and getting out and banging the door shut without so much as a glance over his shoulder at any of his daughters. He would have treated them that way even if he had not been angry. He expected them to fend for themselves.

Ann and Sue Ellen climbed down from the bed of the truck, being careful not to soil their clean print dresses, and came around to help Karen get down from the cab. Bert Miller had already advanced twenty or thirty paces toward the Dorsey farmhouse. Nobody was standing on the porch, and he assumed that meant the services were in progress. Bert pulled at the knot of his tie and made an attempt to flatten a stubborn cowlick with the palm of his hand, as he continued walking.

Karen stepped tentatively and awkwardly off the running board, helped by her two sisters, then straightened up and tugged her maternity blouse down over her belly. She felt embarrassed and undignified, and was aware that all the people inside the Dorsey house would know she was pregnant without being married.

"I didn't want to come," she said. "They're all going to gossip."

"You're gonna have to face it sooner or later," Ann said. "If not now, after the baby's—"

She cut herself off, having seen their father staring at them angrily, waiting for them to come along. He was on the porch, having halted there so they could enter together as a family.

As they approached the house, the girls could hear people crying inside. Bert Miller opened the screen door and entered, with his daughters behind him.

The living room was jammed with people, some filling all the sofas and chairs, the rest standing. The coffin was against a wall on the far side of the room, resting on what looked like a low table or some sawhorses and boards which had been draped with a white sheet and then surmounted with flowers. In the coffin was the body of a child, a nine-year-old girl, the youngest Dorsey daughter. She had died of rheumatic fever.

There was a stirring among the congregation as the Miller family entered the room, a self-conscious stirring because a prayer had been about to begin and nobody knew whether to interrupt the prayer to greet the latecomers. Also, there was the sight of Karen's obvious pregnancy.

Over by the coffin, Reverend Michaels continued to thumb through his prayer book, seemingly unaware of any interruption. The parents of the dead child were standing next to the Reverend, staring into the small coffin with faces full of helpless, dumb-stricken grief. Having found the appropriate prayer, Reverend Michaels turned toward his congregation and saw that Bert Miller and his three daughters had arrived.

"Please be seated or stand quietly," the Reverend admonished them. "The service is about to begin." He stared at Bert Miller, letting the man know that his tardiness was noticed, then allowed his disapproving eyes to fasten on Karen and linger there, staring into her eyes until she averted them by bowing her head in shame and embarrassment. Mr. and Mrs. Dorsey continued to stare at the coffin all the while, not sure how to act or what to say, and almost beyond caring about the formalities of the service in their anguish over the death of their young daughter.

"I ask each and all of you to join me in prayer," Reverend Michaels said, and after a short pause he began the funeral prayer that each member of the congregation was expected to know by heart:

"May the soul rest in peace.

May the soul leave her body.

May the body remain.

May the body turn to dust as the Lord has spoken.

May the body never rise again.

Release the soul unto Heaven and all else turn to dust."

During the prayer, several of the mourners readjusted their seating to make room for Karen, while her father and sisters remained standing in the rear of the room.

The prayer finished, Reverend Michaels closed his prayer book. The congregation remained very still and silent, not shuffling and stirring as often happens at the conclusion of group prayer. There was no sound in the room except for quiet weeping.

Reverend Michaels looked toward the rear of the room, as if expecting something for which he did not have to ask. The service was clearly not over. The parents of the dead child, the mother sobbing quietly, the father silently showing the strain of his grief in his eyes, continued to stand arm in arm by the open casket.

The grief and sadness in the room was suddenly accompanied by an undercurrent of tension. The Reverend continued to look to the back of the room. Pairs of eyes, previously focused on the faces of the distraught parents, began to turn in the direction of the door. After a few moments, the mother, too, stopped sobbing and looked up, joining her husband's gaze as he looked over the heads of the congregants. Now, all weeping had ceased, and no one seemed to be breathing. All was still, as if the dozens of eyes were willing something to happen. A man in the far corner of the room stood up and all the eyes stared at what he held in his hands.

The man was tall, lean, and wearing a worn brown suit. He walked across the rear of the room, and came down a path cleared for him by the mourners. All eyes stared at the large wooden mallet he carried. He walked slowly through the room, looking hard at the father of the dead child. He approached the coffin and gave the mallet to Mr. Dorsey. At the same time, placing his left hand sympathetically on the grieved father's shoulder, Reverend Michaels produced in his right hand a large metal spike similar to the kind that are used in the construction of railroads.

The Reverend handed the spike to Mr. Dorsey.

The faces of the assembled mourners were tense and expectant as they all looked in the direction of the coffin. There was no sound now but a few shuffling footsteps. The dim light in the room seemed to accentuate the silence.

As most of the congregation watched, Mr. Dorsey placed the spike to his dead child's forehead, and then, with the reverberating sound of wood against metal, the father pounded the spike deep into the skull of his daughter.

Tears streamed down the man's stolid, silent face.

Mrs. Dorsey screamed, unable to control herself, and continued to sob in anguish in the arms of several of the women who rushed forward to comfort her.

Suddenly the screen door burst open and slammed against the farmhouse wall with a crash. A small boy stood in the doorway, excited and out of breath, his eyes on Reverend Michaels as the symbol of authority. "It fell!" he cried. "The bus! It rolled over and over! I was right there! It went right over the hill...everybody...a-all of them dead, I think!"

Everyone in the congregation began shouting questions at once. A man in the back of the room near the door began shaking the boy to get more information out of him. "Where did it happen? When?" he demanded.

"At the crossroads. A few minutes ago. The bus wrecked and fell," the boy repeated, trying to catch his breath.

Reverend Michaels became stern. He shouted for the attention of his congregation. They faced him, waiting for his instructions. They needed the authority of his voice, though they all could have predicted what he would say. If there were dead people on the bus and if some would die later as the result of injuries, the spikes needed to be driven into their skulls to ensure that the peace of death would be final and complete as the Lord had intended.

"You all know what needs to be done," Reverend Michaels intoned solemnly. "But, we must hurry. There is not much time."

The congregation began to move, people scrambling, hurrying out of the room. Several men had bags of spikes, and mallets, which had become symbols of death and were often brought to funerals. Others always carried these items with them in their cars.

Bert Miller turned to face his daughters. Ann, terribly frightened, had buried her face in her hands. She backed against the wall as her father moved toward her. "I don't want to go!" she yelled desperately, cringing from her father.

Bert seized Ann by the wrists and shook her to bring her face up so he could stare into her eyes. "You're *going!* And so's Sue Ellen. The only one who ain't goin' is Karen, because she's pregnant. She can stay here and wait for us till we get back."

The rest of the people had already piled out of the room as Ann and Sue Ellen were shoved out ahead of their father. Karen watched, scared and shaking.

2

Excerpt from a Civil Defense broadcast made during the emergency which beset the eastern half of the United States ten years ago:

"...UP-TO-THE-MINUTE REPORTS INFORM US THAT THE SIEGE FIRST DOCUMENTED TWENTY-FOUR HOURS AGO HAS INDEED SPREAD OVER MOST OF THE EASTERN UNITED STATES. MEDICAL AND SCENTIFIC ADVISORS HAVE BEEN SUMMONED TO THE WHITE HOUSE, AND REPORTERS ON THE SCENE IN WASHINGTON INFORM US THAT THE PRESIDENT IS PLANNING TO MAKE PUBLIC THE RESULTS OF THAT CONFERENCE IN AN ADDRESS TO THE NATION OVER YOUR CIVIL DEFENSE EMERGENCY NETWORK...

"...THE STRANGE BEINGS THAT HAVE APPEARED IN ALARMING NUMBERS SEEM TO HAVE CERTAIN PREDICTABLE PATTERNS OF BEHAVIOR. IN THE FEW HOURS FOLLOWING INITIAL REPORTS OF VIOLENCE AND DEATH, AND APPARENTLY DERANGED ATTACKS ON THE LIVES OF PEOPLE TAKEN COMPLETELY OFF GUARD, IT HAS BEEN ESTABLISHED THAT THE ALIEN BEINGS HAVE MANY HUMAN PHYSICAL AND BEHAVIORAL CHARACTERISTICS. HYPOTHESES AS TO THEIR ORIGIN AND THEIR AIMS HAVE TO THIS POINT BEEN SO VARIED AND SO DIVERSE THAT WE MUST ONLY REPORT THESE FACTORS TO BE UNKNOWN. TEAMS OF SCIENTISTS AND PHYSICIANS HAVE THE CORPSES OF SEVERAL OF THE AGGRESSORS, AND THESE CORPSES ARE BEING STUDIED AT THIS MOMENT FOR CLUES THAT MIGHT NEGATE OR CONFIRM EXISTING THEORIES. THE MOST OVERWHELMING FACT IS THAT THESE BEINGS ARE INFILTRATING THROUGH URBAN AND RURAL AREAS THROUGHOUT THE EASTERN HALF OF THE NATION IN FORCES OF VARYING NUMBER, AND

IF THEY HAVE NOT YET EVIDENCED THEMSELVES IN YOUR AREA, PLEASE—*TAKE EVERY AVAILABLE PRECAU-TION!* ATTACK MAY COME AT ANY TIME, IN ANY PLACE, WITHOUT WARNING. REPEATING THE IMPORTANT FACTS FROM OUR PREVIOUS REPORTS: THERE IS AN AGGRESSIVE FORCE—AN ARMY—OF UNEXPLAINED, UNIDENTIFIED, HUMANOID BEINGS. THEY HAVE AP-PEARED, AT RANDOM, AT VARIOUS URBAN AND RU-RAL LOCATIONS THROUGHOUT THE EASTERN STATES. THESE BEINGS ARE TOTALLY AGGRESSIVE AND IRRA-TIONAL IN THEIR VIOLENCE. CIVIL DEFENSE EFFORTS ARE UNDERWAY, AND INVESTIGATIONS AS TO THE ORI-GIN AND PURPOSE OF THE AGGRESSORS ARE BEING CONDUCTED. ALL CITIZENS ARE URGED TO TAKE UT-MOST PRECAUTIONARY MEASURES TO DEFEND THEM-SELVES AGAINST THIS INSIDIOUS ALIEN FORCE. THESE BEINGS ARE WEAK IN PHYSICAL STRENGTH, HOWEVER, AND ARE EASILY DISTINGUISHABLE FROM HUMANS BY THEIR DEFORMED APPEARANCE. THEY ARE USUALLY UNARMED BUT APPEAR CAPABLE OF HANDLING WEA-PONS. THEY HAVE APPEARED WITHOUT ANY REASON OR PLAN, UNLIKE ORGANIZED ARMIES AS WE KNOW THEM. THEY SEEM TO BE DRIVEN BY THE URGES OF ENTRANCED OR OBSESSED MINDS. THEY APPEAR TO BE TOTALLY UNTHINKING. THEY CAN—I REPEAT—*THEY CAN BE STOPPED BY IMMOBILIZATION*; THEY CAN BE STOPPED BY BLINDING OR DISMEMBERMENT. THEY ARE, REMEMBER, WEAKER IN STRENGTH THAN THE AVERAGE ADULT HUMAN—BUT THEIR STRENGTH IS IN NUMBERS, IN SURPRISE, AND IN THE FACT THAT THEIR EXISTENCE IS BEYOND OUR NORMAL REALM OF UNDERSTANDING. THEY APPEAR TO BE IRRATIO-NAL, NON-COMMUNICATIVE BEINGS, AND THEY ARE DEFINITELY TO BE CONSIDERED OUR ENEMIES IN WHAT WE MUST CALL A STATE OF DIRE EMERGENCY. IF ENCOUNTERED, THEY ARE TO BE AVOIDED OR DE-STROYED. UNDER NO CIRCUMSTANCES SHOULD YOU

ALLOW YOURSELVES OR YOUR FAMILIES TO BE ALONE OR UNGUARDED WHILE THIS MENACE PREVAILS.

"...*THESE BEINGS ARE FLESH-EATERS.* THEY ARE *EATING THE FLESH* OF THE PEOPLE THEY KILL. THE PRINCIPAL CHARACTERISTIC OF THEIR ONSLAUGHT IS THEIR DEPRAVED, INSANE QUEST FOR HUMAN FLESH. I REPEAT: THESE ALIEN BEINGS ARE *EATING THE FLESH OF THEIR VICTIMS...*"

3

Sheriff Conan McClellan was sipping a cup of morning coffee in his office when the report of the wrecked bus came over the police band. He knew the crossroads and the embankment where the bus had reportedly gone over. The initial report did not mention any fire, and it was not a steep drop. Depending on how fast the bus was going when it had gone over the edge, and if it had managed to avoid the big trees before bringing itself to a halt, there could be survivors.

McClellan made sure that a call had gone out for extra ambulances and emergency medical supplies from all the nearby communities. He alerted the emergency rooms of the nearest hospitals. He also phoned the morgue. Then he got into a squad car driven by one of his men, Deputy Greene, a rookie, and told Greene to head out toward the scene of the accident. Greene was nervous but trying not to show it; he had not yet had occasion to encounter any dead men on the job as a policeman and from what he had heard from the report and knowing the preparations his superior had made, he was pretty sure he was going to encounter his first bodies that day.

Sheriff McClellan was a good man, with the upsetting but perhaps necessary habit of practically *hunting* for ways to baptize his men by fire. Once they had been through a crisis without buckling, he knew he could depend on them. And, he felt, they knew they could then depend on themselves. Greene was about to become *very* dependable, McClellan mused.

The Sheriff, himself, was more nervous on this call than he usually was, and he knew why. The bus wreck they were fast approaching reminded him too much of the first accident that he had covered as a rookie policeman. A bus carrying grade-school children had been struck head-on by a truck overloaded with steel reinforcement rods, the kind that are used to reinforce concrete. The rods had been torn loose on impact and had hurtled like spears through the interior of the school bus, impaling many of the children and tearing off heads and arms. McClellan had almost resigned from the force as the result of that one accident, deciding his six-month career as a policeman was enough. Now, after twenty-six years, he felt he could face whatever the world could throw at him, no matter how terrible. He never showed his emotions, but he never forgot anything—or anyone—that touched him deeply. His men respected him, but thought he was a bit too thick-skinned to be human. McClellan knew it was the only way to survive his job.

Deputy Greene knew what he was headed for. He was thinking about the reports he'd heard on the car radio. If he had been alone he might have driven more slowly, in hopes of getting there after some of the disaster had been cleaned up. But with Sheriff McClellan sitting in the front seat, he could not dawdle. If he wished McClellan had picked someone else to drive him to the scene of the accident, he had the wisdom not to mention it.

With the lights flashing and the siren screaming they were rapidly approaching the scene, and would be there in about ten minutes from the time they had departed police headquarters.

The bus had gone over the embankment after negotiating a steep climb in the highway and starting down the other side. A police barricade had been put up along the side of the road, and a patrolman was directing the emergency vehicles to the crash scene while directing other traffic to continue ahead. Luckily, there was rarely much traffic on this rural road, and if there were any survivors, they could be transferred quickly to a hospital. The patrolman waved McClellan's car on, and Greene eased it up over the hill slowly to where they could see the bent and twisted guard rail about two hundred yards above the crossroads formed by a bridge over the river and the junction of three highways. There was no evidence of why the bus had gone out of control. Possibly it had been forced over by a car or truck which had kept going after the bus went over.

Greene pulled the car over, leaving the lights flashing, and he and the Sheriff got out. Far from being late on the scene, they seemed to be among the first to arrive which did not give Greene any comfort. There was one other patrol car, parked to one side, as much on the shoulder as possible, its lights still flashing. McClellan figured that the patrolman directing traffic had come from that car.

McClellan looked down along the path of the wrecked bus, but saw nobody moving toward it. In the distance, the bus was not clearly discernible; its fatal path had taken it into a thick growth of trees which now concealed the extent of the catastrophe.

McClellan motioned to Greene and told him to come along, as he began to work his way down toward the wrecked bus. They could see smoke rising out of the trees, but it was certainly not enough smoke for a big fire. Still, this did not give McClellan cause to expect large numbers of survivors; if there had been any, he reasoned, their first impulse would have been to go for help by climbing out of the woods and onto the road. Since nobody was climbing up, there was probably nobody able to climb. But he noticed that the weeds were tramped down and there were muddy footprints in places, as though, for some reason, a considerable number of people had made their way down *toward* the wreckage. McClellan did not understand that. If a group of people had gone down there, who were they and where could they be?

4

Ann and Sue Ellen were spattered with blood, their carefully washed and ironed dresses now muddy and torn. Sue Ellen slipped and fell, losing her grip on the legs of the dead man she was helping to carry, and struck her face against the dead man's shoe. A sob came from her throat. Bert Miller offered no word of sympathy or encouragement, but by his stern, angry looks bade his daughter get up and keep going. Sue Ellen dragged herself to her feet, picked up the legs of the corpse and kept going. Her father had the body by its arms, and he himself was out of breath. But he had to keep going. And so did she. Bert wanted his daughters to learn that life was hard, there were tasks to be done, and those with the proper moral fiber did what had to be done without complaining or expecting any reward for it on this earth. He had given Ann and Sue Ellen the choice of either helping to carry the dead or driving the spikes. They elected to carry the bodies of their own free will. So they must do that job. And they must get it done quickly. Before the authorities got to the scene to stop them. The authorities did not like to admit the necessity of spiking the dead, though it had clearly been necessary once before.

Sue Ellen and her father got the dead man to a clearing in the woods where other dead bodies were laid out. They dropped the man down, and the girl turned away as his head lolled crazily to one side, exposing the gash that had almost severed the head from its neck. Sue Ellen covered her eyes with her hands, then remembered too late that her hands were bloody. She pulled them away, but left a fresh smear of blood on each cheek. She began to cry. She could hear her father's hoarse breathing as he rested for a moment and watched as Ann struggled while dragging the body of a three-year-old child through the weeds and into the clearing. A large wooden splinter, part of a sheared-off tree branch, was stuck in the child's chest; the child's mouth was open and its teeth were caked with blood. Bert Miller had made Ann drag the child's body alone, while he and Sue Ellen carried the dead man, a much heavier burden. The man and the child were the last of the bodies to be carried from the wreckage of the bus. Others in the clearing had already begun to drive the spikes.

Ann and Sue Ellen collapsed on the ground, panting, near shock, not looking at each other, because each reminded the other of the horrible experience they had both been through. Each felt alone, frightened beyond comprehension, wanting to run and hide out of sight of the activity in the clearing, which filled them with such revulsion that they both shut their eyes against it. But they could hear it, the cacophony of wood against metal, the splitting of dead skulls, accompanied by the hoarse breathing and cries and comments of those who were using the spikes and mallets. The bus wreck had left no survivors. Reverend Michaels strode among the dead bodies, most of them horribly mangled, and over each one he stopped and hurriedly said the prayer designed to help ensure the eternal peace of death. Now and then, in his feverish work, he took time to encourage his parishioners and to praise them for having the strength to carry out God's work.

"Hurry! Hurry!" Michaels shouted. "We must spike as many as possible before the police come!"

When they heard the sound of police sirens, the people became afraid and knew they must leave at once, even if they had not finished their work. Thirteen corpses had been spiked out of a total of thirty-four dead. Reverend Michaels shook his head, hoping his prayers would be sufficient for the unspiked bodies. Then he led his congregation out of the clearing and away from the woods, toward the valley from which they had come. They went quietly and furtively by a back way by which they would encounter no police or other intruders who might disapprove of what they had done, of how the dead had been treated. The Reverend prayed as he made his way through the woods, asking the Lord's help for the twenty-one corpses that had not been spiked, asking Him to grant them Eternal Peace. He knew that they were easy prey to forces unbelievable in their horror.

At about the time that the last several bodies were being spiked, Sheriff McClellan and Deputy Greene were working their way down to where the bus lay broken and shattered. In the distance, they heard the rhythmic sounds of wood striking against metal and wondered what they were.

They searched the weeds with their eyes as they walked, half-expecting to find broken bodies thrown clear of the wreckage, but they saw nothing and there was no evidence of survivors.

When they reached the bus, it was empty.

There were some thin plumes of smoke rising from the body of the bus, but there seemed to be no danger of explosion. The inside appeared to be a bloody mess. There was evidence of carnage on a dreadful scale, but no dead or wounded remained. All the passengers, dead or living, had disappeared. Amid the twisted metal and shards of broken glass, Greene's eyes fell on a bloody severed hand, and it made him gag. He gulped and pointed, showing it to McClellan, who looked but said nothing. He himself had noticed what looked like a finger, or a piece of a finger, lying partially under a brand new powder-blue lady's suitcase, but he did not feel it necessary to tell Greene. If they had wanted to sift through the debris, they would doubtless have found more bits and pieces of human bodies, along with broken teeth and eyeglasses, but at this point they were far more interested in what happened to the people who survived—or did not survive—this disaster. McClellan knew then that the tramped down weeds leading from the road to the clearing must have been caused by a large group of people going to the site of the wrecked bus. They had carried off the dead bodies. Or the survivors, if there were any. But why? Perhaps they had felt it a necessary thing to do, fearing the bus might explode before the survivors could be rescued and the dead identified—except to McClellan there did not seem to be any real danger of an explosion. Whatever small fire had caused the smoke—perhaps a lit cigarette had fallen amongst some spilled luggage—had burned itself out quickly and had not been burning in the vicinity of any fuel lines likely to ignite.

"Somebody dragged the people out of here," McClellan said. "Look for trampled-down places through the woods. We can probably figure out which way they went."

Greene stared, dumbfounded. Both he and McClellan had stepped down out of the bus, and Greene was glad to be out of there.

He had really hoped they would be heading back up the hill toward the patrol car.

"Get *moving!*" McClellan snapped at his rookie. "You can't quit a job in the middle of it. Those people didn't sprout wings and fly into heaven, like angels. If they're all dead, somebody moved them. We have to find out *where*—in case some of them *ain't* dead and need help."

"Looters?" Greene suggested, anxious to show he was thinking, though he was embarrassed by McClellan's bawling-out.

"Possibly," the Sheriff conceded. "But if they was scavengers, why didn't they take all the luggage?" He let his question hang in the air as his eyes searched out a place where it looked as though the woods had been penetrated.

Greene stepped up beside McClellan, and they both drew their pistols. If there was a chance they might actually surprise a gang of looters, they wanted to be ready. They proceeded cautiously, not wishing to be surprised. If there *were* looters, they might have a look-out lying in ambush.

The two men made their way through some crushed-down weeds toward the surrounding woods. Greene, the young deputy, was alert and strong-looking, if a little unnerved. He was twenty-three years old, tall and handsome in his patrolman's uniform. McClellan was older by twenty-five years, paunchy but barrel-chested—a little slow and short-winded maybe, but a hard man to knock down. And if he stayed on his feet and got a chance to deliver a punch or two, who-ever he hit would be the one to go down. McClellan was wise and slow, like an old bear. Greene, a younger man, had the fine reflexes of youth but was still untried and undisciplined. The knocks and bruises and experiences of years of hard, patient work would come.

The woods had the feel of silence not tempered by man's pres-ence. When man is nearby, certain animals behave and sound dif-ferently, or make no sound at all. McClellan noticed the change in the sounds as he and Greene made their way in amongst the trees; it caused him to sense that if there had been a group of people busy somewhere back in the woods they had probably all fled. Without explaining to Greene, he began to move faster and to worry less about looters or a possible ambush.

It was not hard for the men to track down where the injured—or dead bodies—had been taken. A plainly legible trail of blood, torn clothing, footprints and smashed-down weeds led to the clearing in the woods. McClellan and Greene approached the clearing with caution, pistols ready. Concealing themselves behind trees, they saw that nobody was stirring, and they moved into the clearing. They saw irregular rows of mangled bodies lying flat on their backs, some with spikes driven into their skulls. For a long moment, neither McClellan nor Greene moved or spoke. Then, wordlessly, they moved to the edges of the clearing and skirted it rapidly, sweeping the surrounding trees and bushes with their pistols and their eyes. They saw no signs of the presence of other people, so they put their pistols away and stood silently among the torn and mutilated bodies.

"Check and see if any are alive," McClellan said finally, and he and Greene went from one bloodied body to another only to find no signs of life.

"Not the work of scavengers," McClellan said, breaking the grim silence.

"The s-spikes—" Greene managed to stammer.

"Somebody thinks it's happening again. We must've scared them off before they could finish."

Greene looked questioningly at the Sheriff. "You're not *from* here, Greene," McClellan said. "This area was one of the hardest hit, ten years ago. Remember? The dead had to be burned or decapitated. The brain had to be destroyed. I don't know if those creatures were really dead or not—not in the usual sense. *Nobody* knows. But somebody is afraid it's going to happen again. That's why there are spikes in the heads."

Greene blanched. "It *can't* happen again," he said. "It was brought under control. I remember. I was only thirteen years old. We read about it, saw it on TV, and still didn't want to believe it. There was very little of the disease in my town. But there was some... enough to convince us that it was real."

"It was real enough," McClellan said. "Something I try to forget. *Want* to forget. But it was real, all right."

"It can't happen again," Greene repeated, as though saying it again could make it true because he wanted to believe it.

"I don't know," McClellan said. "I hope so. But they never did find out for sure what caused it. Maybe it can come back, like a plague of tent worms or Japanese beetles." He tried to chuckle, having intended this last comment as an attempt to lighten the moment, but no chuckle came—and the comment just hung in the air.

Greene was still staring at the rows of bodies. He had drawn his pistol again, almost involuntarily, but it stayed at his side, useless.

"Come on," McClellan said. "You and me have got to snap out of it. There'll be people here soon—ambulance attendants and probably reporters. Nosy sons-of-bitches. I'll stand guard here. You go on back to the bus and show the ambulance people where to come."

It did not escape Greene that the Sheriff had said they must *both* snap out of it. McClellan was being kind, showing Greene that he was just as rattled as he was and that there was no shame in it. Greene experienced a flicker of closeness and respect for the Sheriff. As he made his way back toward the wrecked bus he called to mind something he had read once which had impressed him upon reading it: *the brave man and the coward are both afraid, but the coward runs and the brave man does not.*

When Greene got back to the bus, seven or eight ambulance attendants and a doctor had arrived on the scene and had probably been there several minutes. They were milling around, shocked and uncomprehending, asking each other questions none of them could answer. Like the patrolmen, they were more thrown by the absence of bodies than they would have been by a score of mangled and mutilated people. They could deal with corpses or wounded; it was what they had been trained to do. But the absence of dead and wounded in a situation where they had been anticipated stumped the ambulance people and made them feel somehow disoriented and uneasy. The situation made no sense to them and they felt vaguely uncomfortable.

As Greene approached, they looked at him hopefully, expecting that he would tell them what to do.

"This way!" Greene said, pointing back in the woods. "The bus passengers are back there!" Then, lowering his voice, he added, "You won't need anything but stretchers. No medical supplies. They're all dead."

In the distance, scrambling down over the hill from where the bus had broken through the guard rail, Greene spotted an approaching crowd. They were carrying equipment which, when they got closer, he realized were cameras and tripods. News reporters, television and newspaper people were suddenly everywhere and Greene debated for an instant whether or not he should remain by the bus to try to keep the reporters and cameramen corralled there. But he knew they wouldn't listen. When they found the bus empty, they would follow the ambulance people into the woods. When more police arrived they could cordon off the area surrounding the clearing. But by then it would be too late. The bodies would be on their way up the hill, on stretchers. The reporters would see everything and get the full story. It would make a big splash, frighten people out of their wits and recall the plague that had happened ten years ago. Greene shrugged resignedly. He knew there was no way to keep the grisly event out of the news. Turning his back on the advancing scene, he started walking toward that terrible scene hidden in the woods.

5

Excerpt from a Civil Defense broadcast, ten years earlier:
"GOOD EVENING, LADIES AND GENTLEMEN. IT IS
NOW MIDNIGHT, EASTERN STANDARD TIME. THIS IS
YOUR CIVIL DEFENSE EMERGENCY NETWORK, WITH
REPORTS EVERY HOUR ON THE HOUR FOR THE DU-
RATION OF THIS EMERGENCY. STAY TUNED TO THIS
WAVELENGTH FOR SURVIVAL INFORMATION.

"LADIES AND GENTLEMEN, INCREDIBLE AS IT MAY
SEEM, THE LATEST REPORT FROM THE PENTAGON AND
THE PRESIDENT'S RESEARCH TEAM AT WALTER READE
HOSPITAL CONFIRMS WHAT MANY OF US ALREADY
BELIEVE. THE ARMY OF AGGRESSORS WHICH HAS BE-
SIEGED MANY OF THE EASTERN AND MIDWESTERN
STATES OF OUR COUNTRY IS MADE UP OF *DEAD HU-
MAN BEINGS.*

"THE RECENTLY DEAD HAVE BEEN RETURNING TO
LIFE BY SOME UNKNOWN FORCE AND FEASTING ON
HUMAN FLESH. THE DEAD FROM MORGUES, HOSPI-
TALS, FUNERAL PARLORS, AS WELL AS MANY OF THOSE
KILLED DURING OR AS A RESULT OF THE CHAOS CREAT-
ED DURING THIS EMERGENCY, HAVE BEEN RETURNED
TO LIFE IN A DEPRAVED, INCOMPLETE FORM AND THEY
HAVE COME BACK AMONG US WITH AN URGE TO KILL
OTHER HUMANS AND DEVOUR THEIR FLESH.

"EXPLANATIONS FOR THE CAUSES OF THIS IN-
CREDIBLE PHENOMENON ARE NOT FORTHCOMING
FROM THE WALTER READE TEAM, THE WHITE HOUSE
OR FROM ANY GOVERNMENTAL AUTHORITY AT THIS
MOMENT, BUT SPECULATION CENTERS ON THE RE-
CENT VENUS MISSION, WHICH WAS UNSUCCESSFUL.
THAT SPACE PROBE STARTED FOR VENUS MORE THAN
A WEEK AGO, BUT THE SHIP SWERVED OFF COURSE

AND NEVER ENTERED THE PLANET'S ATMOSPHERE. IN-STEAD, IT RETURNED TO EARTH, CRASHING INTO THE ATLANTIC OCEAN. IT CARRIED A MYSTERIOUS HIGH-LEVEL RADIATION WITH IT, THE ORIGINS OF WHICH ARE STILL—WE ARE LED TO BELIEVE—UNKNOWN. COULD THAT RADIATION HAVE BEEN RESPONSIBLE FOR THE EPIDEMIC OF DEATH AND HORROR WE ARE NOW WITNESSING? SPECULATION ON THE ANSWER OR ANSWERS TO THAT QUESTION HAS RUN RAMPANT HERE IN WASHINGTON AND ELSEWHERE, WHILE THE WHITE HOUSE HAS MAINTAINED A CURTAIN OF SI-LENCE ON SCIENTIFIC THEORIES AND IS ATTEMPTING TO DEAL WITH THIS EMERGENCY ON A RETALIATO-RY BASIS. THE GOVERNMENT IS ORGANIZING RESIS-TANCE TEAMS IN THE FORM OF SEARCH AND DESTROY SQUADRONS AGAINST THE AGGRESSORS. THE DETAILS OF THESE MISSIONS ARE NOT KNOWN AT PRESENT. MEETINGS AT THE PENTAGON AND THE WHITE HOUSE HAVE REMAINED CLOSED TO REPORTERS, AND MEM-BERS OF THE MILITARY AND CIVILIAN ADVISORS HAVE REFUSED TO CONDUCT INTERVIEWS OR TO ANSWER QUESTIONS POSED BY REPORTERS ON THEIR WAY TO OR FROM SUCH MEETINGS.

I REPEAT: *THE LATEST OFFICIAL COMMUNIQUE FROM THE PENTAGON HAS CONFIRMED THAT THE AGGRESSORS ARE DEAD.* THEY ARE *NOT* INVADERS FROM ANOTHER PLANET. THEY ARE THE *RECENTLY DEAD* FROM RIGHT HERE ON EARTH. NOT ALL OF THE RECENTLY DEAD HAVE RETURNED TO LIFE, BUT IN CERTAIN AREAS OF THE COUNTRY, THE EASTERN SEABORD AND THE MID-WEST IN PARTICULAR, THE PHENOMENON IS MORE WIDESPREAD THAN ELSEWHERE. WHY THE MIDWEST SHOULD BE AN AREA SO GREATLY AFFLICTED CANNOT BE EXPLAINED, EVEN BY THE WILDEST SPECULATION. PERHAPS THE NEARNESS TO OUR COASTLINE OF THE VENUS PROBE'S RE-ENTRY IS A FACTOR. AT THIS MO-MENT, WE HAVE NO ANSWERS. PERHAPS WE SHALL

NEVER KNOW THE EXACT REASONS FOR THE TERRIBLE PHENOMENON WE ARE NOW WITNESSING.

"THERE IS SOME HOPE, HOWEVER, THAT THE MENACE WILL BE BROUGHT UNDER CONTROL, PERHAPS IN A MATTER OF SEVERAL DAYS OR WEEKS. IT HAS BEEN DISCOVERED THAT THE AGGRESSORS CAN BE KILLED—OR IS IT KILLED AGAIN?—BY A GUNSHOT OR A HEAVY BLOW TO THE HEAD. THEY ARE AFRAID OF FIRE, AND THEY BURN EASILY. THESE BEINGS HAVE ALL THE CHARACTERISTICS OF DEAD PEOPLE—EXCEPT THEY ARE NOT DEAD—AND FOR REASONS WE DO NOT AS YET UNDERSTAND, THEIR BRAINS HAVE BEEN ACTIVATED AND THEY ARE CANNIBALS.

"I HAVE JUST BEEN HANDED A NEW BULLETIN WHICH STATES THAT IT HAS BEEN LEARNED THAT ANYONE WHO DIES FROM A WOUND INFLICTED BY THE FLESH-EATERS MAY HIMSELF COME BACK TO LIFE IN THE SAME FORM AS THE AGGRESSORS THEMSELVES. THE DISEASE, OR WHATEVER IT IS, THAT THESE THINGS CARRY *IS COMMUNICABLE* THROUGH OPEN FLESH WOUNDS OR SCRATCHES, AND TAKES EFFECT MINUTES AFTER THE APPARENT DEATH OF THE WOUNDED PERSON. ANYONE WHO DIES DURING THIS EMERGENCY SHOULD BE DECAPITATED OR CREMATED IMMEDIATELY. SURVIVORS WILL FIND THESE MEASURES EMOTIONALLY DIFFICULT TO UNDERTAKE, BUT THEY MUST BE UNDERTAKEN ANYWAY, OR ELSE THE AUTHORITIES MUST BE ALERTED TO UNDERTAKE THEM FOR YOU. THOSE WHO DIE DURING THIS EMERGENCY ARE NOT CORPSES IN THE USUAL SENSE. THEY ARE DEAD FLESH—BUT HIGHLY DANGEROUS AND A THREAT TO ALL LIFE ON OUR PLANET. I REPEAT, BODIES OF THOSE WHO DIE DURING THIS EMERGENCY *MUST BE BURNED OR DECAPITATED...*"

6

On the screen of the television above the bar, there was coverage of the bus wreck and of the bizarre events which followed. The commentary had been long and sensational, the news cameras dwelling unnecessarily, McClellan thought, on the mangled bodies being transported on stretchers from the bloody clearing in the woods. Most of the stretchers were covered and the condition of the corpses could not be seen clearly, but the commentator's voice filled in the gory details the video was mercifully lacking.

McClellan purposely averted his eyes from the screen. He and Greene had stopped off for a drink, to try and blur some of the day's images. Both men were completely drained, both physically and emotionally, and needed a quiet place to sit and try and sort out what they had seen. They had chosen this particular place because it was seldom crowded and when they entered the barroom, it was empty of customers as they had hoped. The Sheriff had ordered a shot and a beer, and Greene had followed suit. They downed their shots without a word, neither of them feeling like talking though they were glad for each other's company and had just picked up their beers when the door to the place banged open and a man entered the dim room. He staggered a little, sizing up the place and its potential for suitable diversion, then walked over to the bar and sat down on the stool next to McClellan.

McClellan tried not to look directly at the man. He did not know him and did not wish to make his acquaintance. He particularly did not wish to be drawn into an inane conversation with a drunk after all he had recently been through. And having the day's events played back on the television put him even more on edge.

The man was dressed in blue coveralls and was carrying a metal lunch-bucket which he slammed down onto the bar while yelling at the bartender to serve him a double-header of Seagram's 7 and a bottle of Budweiser. Once served, the man quickly downed his whisky and ordered another, then turned his bloodshot eyes to the flickering screen above the bar. While the newscast was in progress, he would belch or snort at passages he found wryly amusing—or would look directly at McClellan as if he expected the Sheriff to belch or snort in agreement. When the belches and snorts got no response, the drunk began to mutter; and when the muttering got still no response, he began to throw in loud comments.

The two policemen were sitting in silence. McClellan tried to keep his head turned toward Greene, in hopes that the drunk would take the hint and keep quiet. But the Sheriff's eyes darted toward the screen when he heard his own voice, recorded earlier that day during an interview at the scene of the bus accident.

"You tell 'em, Sheriff," the drunk said, spinning around in time to catch McClellan's eyes as he glanced at the TV.

"Yeah, yeah," McClellan sighed under his breath.

Greene looked over and smiled at his partner in an attempt to be sympathetic. He knew the last thing McClellan wanted to do was talk about the afternoon's events.

The drunk went on talking, slurring his words. "Sheriff, I think them people are right. Let 'em pound the goddamn nails in. Just to make sure, know what I mean?"

McClellan slid off his stool, pulled out his wallet and slapped some bills down on the bar. "Greene, let's get out of here."

The bartender came over and counted the money, the drunk shouting after the two lawmen as they went out the door, "It happened before, it can happen again! You *seen* it, Sheriff. You seen it with your own eyes!"

McClellan and Greene stepped out into the night air and kept walking, both wishing to put some distance between themselves and the saloon. The night air seemed very clear, the black sky illuminated by countless stars. A sparse but steady stream of automobile traffic moved along the street where the two lawmen were walking, the street forming one of the outer boundaries of a small park.

"Let's get out of here," said McClellan, walking swiftly. "Will you drop me off at home? My wife has the car."

They picked their way through traffic and headed toward their patrol car, parked on the outer edge of the park. As they approached the car, Greene suddenly stopped and flung out his arm to stop Mc-

Clellan. "You hear that?" he asked, staring toward a clump of trees twenty-five yards away. His voice was barely above a whisper.

They both stood perfectly still, listening. They heard rustling leaves and what sounded like a scuffle—then a muffled female scream. Pulling out their service revolvers, they began to run. They raced into the darkened park and saw three struggling figures, two of which were silhouetted against the star-studded sky as, noticing the men running toward them, they got up to flee. Two men had been grappling with a woman; the interruption had enabled her to get to her feet, but one of the men knocked her down as he tried to make his escape.

"Halt! *Police!*" Greene yelled.

McClellan fired a warning shot into the air.

Greene, looking down and trying not to trip over the ivy ground cover as they ran deeper into the park, did not see one of the shadowy figures dive into a clump of bushes just as McClellan fired his gun. Greene blinked his eyes, trying to get used to the darkness. He continued to move forward, his revolver drawn.

The woman, still down on the ground, hurt and exhausted, had managed to grab the ankle of her assailant as he tried to escape from the scene and, with the energy that often comes to those during an emergency, she was doggedly holding on. The man was balancing himself on one leg, shaking and kicking his other leg, hoping he could get the woman to loosen her grip. He finally lashed out with a solid kick, his heavy boot heel smashing into the woman's jaw and, with a loud snapping sound, she went limp, her neck broken.

Greene reached the man at just that moment, leaped at him with a flying tackle, and they both went down heavily, rolling on the ground. The man untangled himself from Greene's hold and got to his feet, with Greene after him. Suddenly a shot exploded from the bush and Greene reeled, staggered momentarily, and fell.

McClellan immediately fired and hit the man behind the bush, a square shot right in the chest, slamming the man over backwards like a duck in a shooting gallery.

The other assailant was still on the run, going out of the park toward the street. McClellan turned his body slowly, following the running man with the barrel of his revolver, patiently timing his shot. The man began running and dodging through a burst of traffic, brakes squealing as startled drivers tried to avoid the zigzagging figure. McClellan squeezed his trigger and the running man received the blast, jerking, lunging forward, and slamming head first across the hood of a parked car on the far side of the street.

McClellan stepped over to Greene, knelt, felt Greene's chest and came away with a bloody hand. He put two fingers on Greene's wrist, but there was no pulse. Greene was dead. McClellan wiped his hand in the grass.

He checked the woman. She was dead, too. Her neck was broken, her head angled grotesquely off to one side. Her clothes were partially torn, her face, shoulders and thighs bruised. Rape sickened him. What had probably started as a mugging had ended like this. McClellan had seen it too many times.

His gun ready, the Sheriff approached the parked car where the man he had shot lay sprawled across the hood. His headlong dive had been stopped by the windshield, his head cracking against the glass and shattering it into a pattern like a spider's web. McClellan opened the door of the car, left foolishly unlocked by its owner, he noticed, and looked at the wide-open eyes of the dead man through the cracked windshield. Was a wallet or some sex worth dying this stupid way? And the deaths of the two men could not make up for the loss of Greene. Four more dead in a day of death, thought McClellan. There was nothing to do but notify Greene's family and phone the morgue.

The Sheriff stayed on hand, directing traffic and keeping curious onlookers away, until the patrol cars and the morgue's ambulance arrived. Then he went home to bed, tired, but knowing beforehand that he would be unable to sleep.

7

Several hours past midnight, two bodies were delivered to the County Morgue. Unloaded from an ambulance, they rested on wheeled stretchers, wrapped in green clinical shrouds. Two men from the coroner's office stood by while the morgue attendant and his assistant prepared the delivery papers for signature.

"These the two from the park?" the morgue attendant asked. He already knew the answer to his question, but was making conversation. The attendant appreciated any company during the night shift.

"That's them," one of the men from the coroner's office replied, more tersely than the morgue attendant would have liked.

"How about Deputy Greene and the woman?" the attendant continued, trying to prolong the conversation.

"They're at O'Neil's Funeral Parlor."

The morgue attendant, about to sign the delivery papers, lifted his pen from the form and looked up. "You know, it's a real shame about that Greene fellow."

"Yeah," one of the coroner's men said impatiently.

The morgue attendant finally completed the signing of the papers. He scratched his head, looking at the shrouded bodies. "We hardly have any room, what with that busload from this afternoon," he complained.

"I'm sure you'll manage," one of the coroner's men said, as he and his partner wearily climbed into their ambulance and drove away.

The morgue attendant and his assistant watched the ambulance go, then turned toward the shrouded forms on the stretchers. "Let's give 'em a free ride," the assistant said humorlessly.

Entering the morgue, they wheeled the stretchers into a large, cold, sterile room filled with table after sheet-draped metal table, the body of a bus accident victim lying on each one. They wheeled the new deliveries into place and turned to leave. Neither man noticed as the arm of one of the loosely covered bodies from the afternoon's disaster slid out from under its sheet and hung down. The fingers twitched almost imperceptibly.

The morgue attendant and his assistant returned to their office, and the attendant told the other man that it was his turn to make coffee. The small radio in the office was tuned to an all-night talk show. Someone had phoned in to say that ten years ago, when the dead had come back to life, the authorities should have made more of an effort to find out exactly what had caused it, instead of suppressing it as soon as the thing had seemed under control. The caller suggested that it could have been caused by spores or something, and added that if there *was* something capable of sustaining life, or at least preventing complete and total death, maybe the spores or whatever the cause was could be studied and refined and used as a medicine. Maybe it could even be used to increase everybody's life span.

The talk show host chuckled nervously and said the spores or radiation or whatever had caused the terror ten years ago, had been thought to have come from Venus, and scientists believed now that there was no life on Venus. If there was no life there, he continued, how could the planet possess a substance—or force—that could give eternal life? The man who had phoned in said that he didn't know, but it certainly ought to be studied.

The morgue attendant got up and spun the dial of the radio, hunting for music.

At O'Neil's Funeral Parlor, Mr. O'Neil wheeled a casket into place in the chapel room. O'Neil was a neat, slender, conservatively dressed, cheerful-looking man in his mid-fifties, and most people seeing him away from his place of business would have guessed him to be a bank teller or an accountant. Having maneuvered the casket to where he wanted it, he lifted the lid to reveal the embalmed body of Deputy Greene, dressed in a crisp black suit with a red carnation in the lapel.

O'Neil stepped back from the casket, satisfying himself that his work was all it should be, and stooped to move a flower stand into place to the left of the coffin. He decided to bring up the kneeler and the rest of the paraphernalia later. He wanted to do a particularly good job for Greene, as he had been acquainted with the family for some time. He had worked quickly and efficiently throughout the night to get Greene ready, so the family would not have to endure a long, agonizing wake before the man could be buried. Dawn was still a few hours away.

O'Neil bent over the flower stand, and could not see the slight tremor in Greene's face, a quivering of the jaw muscles accompanied by just a hint of flutter in the eyelids. If O'Neil had seen these things, he would doubtless have dismissed them as the workings of some of the dying nerves, or the work of his own imagination.

A loud noise from the basement shattered the silence of the chapel and O'Neil turned in alarm, heading for the staircase, muttering to himself. He descended the stairs quickly, passed through a basement storage room housing folding chairs, caskets, flower baskets, stands, boxes of funeral flags, candles—all the stock of a funerary establishment neatly arranged and ready for sale or use by clients. O'Neil continued briskly into the embalming room, where the bright light revealed a black and white cat standing on the body of the young woman who had been killed in the park. A sheet covered the still form up to the chin. The pieces of a broken bottle lay next to the body on the marble slab, the last few drips of fluid still dripping onto the floor.

What had taken place seemed obvious to O'Neil and he yelled exasperatedly at the animal, "You bad cat! Now come away from there."

He shooed the cat away with his arms, wiped up the fluid and then dried his hands. His movements were slow and deliberate; it was late and he was very tired. But he had a full day ahead of him, beginning with an early-morning burial, and he wanted to get all the embalming done during what remained of the night.

Still wiping his hands dry, he moved to the counter where his equipment was spread: scalpels, needles, tubes, bottles of fluid, makeup. There was also a half-eaten sandwich on one end of the counter, the sandwich resting on its crumpled waxed paper wrapper. O'Neil had not eaten in the presence of Greene's body, although he reasoned that there was nothing really wrong with doing so. But at one point during the long night he became hungry and had brought the sandwich with him into the basement. Spotting its remains, he wrapped up his unfinished snack and threw it into a wastebasket, sweeping the crumbs with his palm and making sure they went into the basket too. Then he reached up and flicked on a radio, found some light music and turned the volume down low.

Upstairs, in his casket, Deputy Greene's eyes were open wide. The body lay still, unmoving, its eyes fixed and staring toward the ceiling.

In another of the chapel rooms of the funeral parlor, a second body was laid out. The casket contained the remains of a middle-aged black man. Its eyes were open also.

O'Neil stood at his work table, his back to the sheet-covered body, mixing liquids with a steady hand, the soft music soothing his tiredness. He was humming quietly with the melodies. Flask in hand, he turned around to walk to the slab on which the corpse rested. The still basement vibrated with the loudness of the man's horrified scream. He backed up into the counter, his elbows knocking bottles and tools to the floor, the beaker in his hand crashing in a fountain of glass.

The dead woman had raised her shoulders off the slab, her back arching, the sheet sliding down over her breasts as she sat up further. Her head began to rise, her hair lifting from the cold marble surface, her eyes open wide. Finally she was sitting upright and, turning her head, she spied O'Neil. The man watched, his mouth open in frozen terror, no sound coming from his throat. Sluggishly, almost looking like a woman sleepily getting out of bed, she pushed herself from the table, put her bare feet on the floor, and began walking toward O'Neil.

Upstairs, Deputy Greene moved a finger, then a hand, gradually sitting up stiffly in his coffin. He blinked once or twice, moving his head slowly from side to side and up and down, as if examining his surroundings. At one point he cocked his head to one side as if he heard the scream from downstairs in the embalming laboratory.

The black man sat up in his coffin. He leaned heavily to one side, and he and the casket fell off the platform at the front of the chapel, knocking over and smashing the stands of flowers. The black man's body lay for a while amid the broken vases and mangled gladiolas, unmoving, as if it could not get up. Then, slowly, almost as if in pain, he pulled himself to his feet. He stood up and walked through the chapel door with his eyes straight ahead of him, then turned and continued down the corridor to the chapel where the body of Deputy Greene was still sitting in his coffin.

Bent backward over his worktable, O'Neil screamed from the deepest reaches of his soul. The body of the dead woman leaned over him, her hands clawing at his throat and at his face, her eyes staring wildly and insanely and hungrily at him. Then, awkwardly grabbing a handful of sharp instruments, she began stabbing at O'Neil, over and over. His agonized screams echoed and reverberated in the embalming room. Again and again she drove the scalpels into his face and chest. Finally the screams stopped. O'Neil's eyes bulged and blood gushed from what had been his face, as the creature over him continued to stab and stab long after the stabbing had accomplished its terrible purpose.

The strange, unworldly sounds of teeth tearing and chewing newly dead flesh mingled with the sounds of low, sweet music in the embalming room. The dead woman continued to sink her teeth into O'Neil's flesh, gnawing at his face and neck, until her own face was covered with warm blood.

Upstairs, Greene's body had slowly crawled out of his coffin and was staggering about, following the figure of the black man who had headed for the front door and was pounding against the glass with the ornate metal flower stand that he had taken from next to Greene's casket. The glass broke, the heavy metal dropping from the black man's hands. The door opened, and the body of what had been Deputy Greene followed the striding form of the black man out into the dark street.

The two dead men moved as though they were conscious of each other's presence but indifferent to each other. They were both pulled by the same force, had the same wants. Indeed, they both did crave the same thing. And what they craved was living human flesh.

* * *

The sky over the County Morgue was beginning to lighten. The corridors of the building were quiet except for the faint strains of an all-night country music program coming from the office of the morgue attendant and his assistant. The cold holding rooms were silent, the tables still covered with the sheet-covered bodies, thirteen covered bodies of those who had died so violently that afternoon. The thirteen who had had spikes driven into their skulls that afternoon. Twenty-three tables lay empty.

The office of the morgue employees was not quite empty. It was filled with the chewed, bloody pieces of what had once been two men. Their bones, hair and flesh lay scattered around the room in congealing puddles of blood: red, smeared handprints mute testimony to their struggle to live in a fight with the dead.

In mid-morning Sheriff McClellan was at the morgue, examining the scene of the tragedy. He had made his way inside through a cordon of eager, curious reporters and TV cameramen. The police had the entire building roped off, and were not allowing any reporters inside the morgue. Still, the reporters knew what had happened. They had talked to patrolmen, medical examiners and other officials on their way in and out of the building. It was no secret that only thirteen corpses remained in the morgue, not counting the remains of the attendant and his assistant, and the thirteen corpses that remained were the bus accident victims which had had spikes driven into their skulls immediately after the accident by persons who had thus far not been identified or apprehended by the police.

When McClellan left the morgue building he had to face the reporters and the news cameras once again. As a path was cleared to his patrol car, he was barraged with shouts and questions. He knew complete silence on his part would only fire speculation and inspire panic—possibly leading to mass hysteria—so he stopped to answer some of the reporters' questions.

Microphones were jammed into the Sheriff's face, and the shouting of questions rose to an incomprehensible babble, making it impossible for him to distinguish any particular question. McClellan shouted for quiet and order, then stood still and refused to say anything until the din subsided and the reporters calmed down.

When the shouting stopped, McClellan announced that he had decided not to answer any specific questions, but that he would make a statement if they were willing to listen quietly. On hearing that, the voices of the reporters rose to a clamor again, briefly, but subsided in favor of hearing what the Sheriff had to say rather than not hearing anything at all.

The Sheriff's speech was intended to have a calming effect, but it did not entirely succeed. He recited the events of the preceding day, toning them down, and refusing to connect them with the murder of the undertaker, O'Neil. He admitted not having a clue as to who would want to perpetrate the sort of thing that had been done at the morgue. In the face of a further barrage of questions after his statement—which had concluded without giving the reporters any real satisfaction—McClellan stuck to his guns, refusing to say that the phenomenon of ten years ago was definitely repeating itself, and insisting that bodies had disappeared and had been stolen, certainly a bizarre and unsettling state of affairs, but one which could be explained rationally. He added that an investigation was already underway.

McClellan did not believe the things he was saying. He knew he was backpedaling, trying to gain time, not wanting mounting alarm to build to a frenzy too quickly, a state of affairs that was unavoidable if the phenomena continued.

The Sheriff had one fact in mind that gave him some consolation: They had brought this...this plague...under control once before. If it was happening again, they would know how to deal with it.

Unless, maybe, this time it was going to be a whole lot worse.

8

Bert Miller had his eyes riveted to the television.

He had watched the interview with Sheriff McClellan and had scoffed at it. Now he was watching an interview with the pastor, Reverend Michaels, who, Bert thought, was speaking forcefully and intelligently. That morning, the Reverend had phoned a TV station, told them who he was, and confessed to having led a group of church members to the scene of the bus accident three days before and that it had been their intention to drive spikes into the skulls of all persons killed in the accident. He admitted that they had succeeded in spiking only thirteen of the dead before being frightened away by the arrival of police and ambulances, and it was clear, the Reverend pointed out, that those thirteen corpses must have been the ones that did not rise with the others who had risen and killed the morgue attendants.

"Yes, the dead are rising again," Michaels was saying. "This is the work of the Devil, in his battle against God's will. We live in a pagan society. We worship witchcraft and astrology and other forms of Satanism. Now we must call on the Lord to help us change our evil ways. No one wants to admit that what happened ten years ago is happening again. We try to hide the horrible events from our memory, finding them too terrible to accept. *But we cannot hide from the Devil.* Now he's forcing us to face reality again. The dead must be spiked. The body must be permitted to return to dust, as the Lord intended. Only then can we rise, when the Lord calls us, on the Last Day. Only the soul is sacred—"

Sue Ellen jumped up from her chair and turned off the television.

Angrily, Bert reached for the knobs, yelling, "Now stay away from it!"

Sue Ellen stood in front of the set and confronted her father. "No...please, *please* leave it off. I can't stand all that talk anymore. It's all crazy. What you made us do—carrying all those dead bodies—I can't stand it!"

Bert rushed toward his daughter, grabbed her by the shoulders and shook her. "Didn't you hear what the Reverend said? It's that plague comin' back and we've all got to get ready for it. It's the Devil's work—and maybe we all deserve it!"

Sue Ellen began to cry. Annoyed, Bert looked around the living room, where some of the windows had been boarded up. He had been sawing and hammering and pounding all morning, while his daughters stayed in their rooms, too scared to come downstairs. Bert resented their not coming down and helping.

In a weak and hopeless voice, Sue Ellen pleaded with her father. "Daddy...please...I can't stand all this. Why can't we just leave the dead people alone?"

"Because they won't leave us alone!" he bellowed. "That's why! You didn't see it ten years ago. I sent you away and you were lucky. But we're not running from the Devil this time—we're gonna stay and do our Christian duty!"

Still crying, Sue Ellen ran toward the kitchen as her two sisters entered the room and caught her in their arms. She squirmed free and ran up the stairs.

"Spoiled brat!" Bert yelled after her.

Ann shot a look at her father, begging him with her eyes to calm down.

In response Bert pointed an angry finger toward Karen. "Lookit your sister, knocked up by nobody knows who. If *she* knows, she sure ain't tellin'. Probably some drug-crazy punk! Sometimes I'm glad your mother didn't live to see it."

Turning, trying to hide the tears in her eyes, Karen hung her head and moved toward the stairs. She was seventeen years old, with a plain, sad face that became almost pretty when it lit up with a smile. But there was very little to smile about these days. It was obvious that her child was due very shortly.

Ann, the eldest, was the most level-headed and the prettiest of Bert Miller's daughters. Her hair was long and blond, carefully brushed and parted in the middle. She had deep blue eyes, a wide mouth and regular features. Many of the town's young men were attracted to her, but she did not have a regular boyfriend because her father had succeeded in frightening away any that she liked. They rarely—if ever—asked her for a second date. Despite this, she loved her father, knew that in his strange way he loved his girls, and tried to understand him. But she knew that she would move away from him as soon as she was able.

She went over to her father and touched his arm lightly. "Daddy, please, it's bad enough for Karen," she said quietly.

Bert looked at Ann, not knowing what to say to her. Of all his daughters, she had always been the one most successful at getting him to do what she wanted. Rather than answering her, he let out his breath, picked up his claw-hammer from where he had left it on the seat of a chair, and went over to a barricaded window and began pounding. He drove two more nails into a heavy piece of lumber that had already been nailed to the window frame. Then he stooped to select another piece of wood, walked to another window, and began to board it up.

"Do you really believe it'll happen again?" Ann asked him. The whole thing still seemed unbelievable to her. As a child, when the thing happened ten years ago, the aunt the three girls had stayed with had sheltered them from all the news about it. They had not been permitted to go outdoors or to listen to radio or TV broadcasts. Afterward there had been laws prohibiting the rehashing of the crisis; the excuses for this, whether proper or not, were that it would be morally and emotionally damaging to subject the populace to a repetition of the experience, that it was best to try to forget it, and that it was not likely to occur again.

"It's happening all right," Bert said, momentarily stopping his hammering. "It was on the television just now, before your crazy sister turned it off."

"It's hard to believe," Ann said.

"Maybe it's hard," Bert admitted ironically, "but you'll believe it by and by. If we don't get this house boarded up, the dead'll be in after us. And if there's enough of 'em, they'll get in—boarded up or not."

Bert turned back to the window and began pounding nails.

Ann ran upstairs to comfort her sisters. She found Karen in Sue Ellen's room, watching as Sue Ellen threw clothes into an opened suitcase. Karen, sitting on the bed next to the suitcase, lifted up a tear-streaked face as Ann entered. Sue Ellen did not look up but continued packing with fierce concentration.

"Sue?" Ann said tentatively.

"I'm getting out," Sue Ellen blurted. She pushed her hair back from her eyes, red and puffy from crying. She was not crying now but was on the verge of starting again. She came over to Ann and hugged her, and the tears came.

"Where will you go?" Ann said, holding her tightly and softly running her hand down her sister's hair.

Sue Ellen stepped back and blotted her contorted face with a handkerchief. "I don't know," she sobbed. "I'm scared to stay here and I'm scared to go. But I think I'd rather go. Maybe into the city somewhere."

"Aren't you afraid of what they've been saying on the TV?"

Sue Ellen sank down onto the bed wearing only her panties and bra. She had taken off her old clothes and had not yet changed into the fresh ones she wanted to wear when she left. "I'm more afraid to stay here," she said finally, and started to cry again as memories flooded her mind. "I thought I'd die—carrying those people through the woods. I wished I was one of them, so I wouldn't have to do it. And I'm not going to do anything like that ever again. Daddy won't be able to *make* me do it. In the city they have protection—I can hide somewhere and not have to face any of this till it's over." Tears streamed down her cheeks.

"Maybe we should go too," Karen said.

"No, I don't think it's right to go," Ann said to Karen. "We can't all leave Daddy now. He's boarding up the house to protect us. We'll be all right. Sue Ellen can go, but we two should stay here and help him."

"Karen," Sue Ellen said, "I know your baby will be beautiful." The two sisters hugged each other tightly while Ann watched. Her eyes were also glistening with tears.

"What about Billy?" Ann asked. "Aren't you at least going to tell him?"

Billy was Sue Ellen's boyfriend, a fellow she had dated a few times against her father's wishes but with his grudging approval. Things were not serious between her and Billy. They had known each other too short a time. They had a good time together and she was beginning to care for him, but did not feel seriously committed yet.

"I don't know what to tell Billy," Sue Ellen said. "If we had a telephone I could call him. I've got to get out. Maybe I can write to him...or something." Having finished her packing, she slammed shut her suitcase and went to her chest of drawers to begin putting on fresh clothes.

Her sisters watched Sue Ellen get ready. They did not like to lose her but both felt it would only be temporary and might even work out for the best.

9

Excerpt from a Civil Defense broadcast:

"...AUTHORITIES ADVISE UTMOST CAUTION UNTIL THE MENACE CAN BE BROUGHT UNDER ABSOLUTE CONTROL. EYEWITNESS ACCOUNTS HAVE BEEN INVESTIGATED AND DOCUMENTED. CORPSES OF VANQUISHED AGGRESSORS ARE PRESENTLY BEING EXAMINED BY MEDICAL PATHOLOGISTS, BUT AUTOPSY EFFORTS HAVE BEEN HAMPERED BY THE MUTILATED CONDITION OF THE BODIES. SECURITY MEASURES INSTITUTED IN METROPOLITAN AREAS INCLUDE ENFORCED CURFEWS AND SAFETY PATROLS BY ARMED PERSONNEL.

"CITIZENS ARE URGED TO REMAIN IN THEIR HOMES. THOSE WHO IGNORE THIS WARNING EXPOSE THEMSELVES TO INTENSE DANGER, BOTH FROM THE AGGRESSORS THEMSELVES, AND FROM ARMED CITIZENRY, WHOSE IMPULSE MAY BE TO SHOOT FIRST AND ASK QUESTIONS LATER. RURAL OR OTHERWISE ISOLATED DWELLINGS HAVE MOST FREQUENTLY BEEN THE OBJECTIVE OF FRENZIED, CONCERTED ATTACK. ISOLATED FAMILES ARE IN EXTREME DANGER. EVACUATION ATTEMPTS SHOULD BE MADE IN HEAVILY ARMED GROUPS, AND BY MOTORIZED VEHICLES IF POSSIBLE.

"APPRAISE YOUR SITUATION CAREFULLY BEFORE DECIDING UPON AN ESCAPE TACTIC. FIRE IS AN EFFECTIVE WEAPON. THESE BEINGS ARE HIGHLY FLAMMABLE. EVACUEES SHOULD STRIKE OUT FOR THE NEAREST URBAN COMMUNITY. MANNED DEFENSE OUTPOSTS HAVE BEEN ESTABLISHED ON MAJOR ARTERIES LEADING INTO ALL COMMUNITIES. THESE OUTPOSTS ARE EQUIPPED TO DEFEND REFUGEES AND TO OFFER FOOD AND MEDICAL ASSISTANCE. POLICE AND

VIGILANTE PATROLS ARE IN THE PROCESS OF COMB-
ING REMOTE AREAS IN SEARCH-AND-DESTROY MIS-
SIONS AGAINST ALL AGGRESSORS. THESE PATROLS ARE
ATTEMPTING TO EVACUATE ISOLATED FAMILIES. BUT
RESCUE EFFORTS ARE PROCEEDING SLOWLY, DUE TO
THE INCREASED DANGER AT NIGHT AND THE SHEER
ENORMITY OF THE TASK.

"RESCUE, FOR THOSE IN THE ISOLATED AREAS, IS
EXTREMELY DIFFICULT. IF EVACUATION IS IMPOSSI-
BLE, HOWEVER, STAY IN YOUR HOME AND WAIT FOR
A RESCUE TEAM. DO NOT GO OUT ALONE. IF YOU ARE
FEW AGAINST MANY, YOU WILL ALMOST CERTAINLY BE
OVERCOME. THE AGGRESSORS ARE IRRATIONAL AND
DEMENTED. THEIR SOLE URGE IS THEIR QUEST FOR
HUMAN FLESH.

"THE RANKS OF THE AGGRESSORS ARE CONSTANTLY
BEING SWELLED BY FRESH VICTIMS OF THE AGGRES-
SORS THEMSELVES AND BY THOSE WHO HAVE DIED
DURING THIS EMERGENCY, WITH ITS CATASTROPHIC
RATE OF MORTALITY DUE TO CHAOS, ACCIDENT, AND
THE TURNING OF PEOPLE AGAINST EACH OTHER OUT
OF FEAR.

"THE CURRENT RAMPAGE OF LAWLESSNESS IS IN-
CREASING THE NUMBERS OF THE AGGRESSORS AND
HAMPERING THE EFFORTS OF LAW ENFORCEMENT
PERSONNEL WHO ARE TRYING TO BRING THE MENACE
UNDER CONTROL..."

10

After a final, tearful goodbye to Karen and Ann, Sue Ellen, in stocking feet, tiptoed downstairs with her suitcase and stopped, peeking around the landing.

Bert Miller sat dozing in an armchair, his hammer, saw, and tin of nails beside him on the floor. The living-room windows, all four of them, were boarded solid and the front door was bolted shut. Bert had further secured the door by means of heavy iron brackets and wooden bars, top, bottom and center. The iron brackets were screwed into the door-frame very solidly and the wooden bars, twice as big as two-by-fours, were slotted into the brackets so they would prevent any but the most insistent force from battering down the door, but could be removed easily to permit the occupants of the house to enter or exit.

Afraid to risk tiptoeing past her father and not wanting to disturb the barred door, Sue Ellen looked toward the kitchen. Its two windows and one door had been permanently boarded shut by heavy nails driven into thick wooden planks. The kitchen offered no exit, and the house had no basement. Sue Ellen realized that her father had done much toward making the downstairs impregnable. She thought he probably figured he could defend the upstairs against the slim chance that any aggressors could find a way to get in up there, or else he planned to board the upstairs windows later.

Sue Ellen thought of going upstairs and asking one of her sisters to follow her back down and bolt the front door after she'd left. She wondered if they could do it quietly enough. Just then, Bert stirred on the chair, and Sue Ellen was afraid of losing her opportunity to escape by not taking immediate advantage of her father's being asleep. She knew she'd have to risk letting herself out, somehow, and besides, she did not want to get either of her sisters in trouble. She knew her father would be furious at her leaving, and she didn't want to make things even more difficult for Ann and Karen. She waited on the landing until her father was snoring loudly once again, then she crept softly to the door and, holding her breath and terrified of dropping the heavy beams as she lifted each one from its bracket, unbolted it. She considered it a miracle that her father did not awaken, and quickly stepped onto the porch. She pulled the door shut carefully, pulling slowly and praying with all her heart that it wouldn't creak. Finally, the metal tongue clicked into its slot and she let out her breath in relief. Still afraid that the click had awakened him, she ran down the front stairs, took her shoes from her bag, slipped them on, and ran across the front yard to the dirt road. Her father seemed to be sleeping very soundly and she hoped she would have a good head start before he woke and noticed the beams stacked on the floor next to the door if the girls hadn't replaced them. Panting, she kept running until she rounded a bend in the road and could no longer see the house.

It was near dusk. In less than an hour it would probably be dark—pitch dark—Sue figured, because the sky was overcast and the air smelled damp. She tried to remember what she had heard about the expected weather. She felt terribly alone suddenly, as the weight of the decision to leave home washed over her. For just a moment, as she walked down the dusty road, she considered changing her mind and going home. She kept thinking of Karen's expected baby. But then she had the image of her father waking up as she returned to the house with her suitcase, and that scream fest was too terrible to think about. Fighting back tears, she kept walking.

It was about a mile hike from the Miller farm to the highway, and Sue Ellen guessed she would try to flag down a bus or, if she got lucky, maybe she'd catch a ride into town with someone who knew her. The town, Willard, was six miles northeast of the intersection of the dirt road with the two-lane blacktop highway. Now that Sue Ellen considered it, her chances of getting a ride into Willard did not seem good, especially with the rapid approach of darkness. The thought of walking the six miles on the highway by herself panicked her, though she had done it several times in the daylight with her sisters. Once again, she considered going back and could not keep her thoughts from the farmhouse. But she kept going.

Stretching down the long valley away from the house was a six-acre field where Bert Miller had planted corn. Trampling and breaking the young cornstalks in their awkwardness and single-mind-edness, three humanoid forms made their way toward the house, attracted by the faint slashes of light from the boarded-up windows and—perhaps—the smell of live flesh emanating from within.

In the cornfield, the obsessed creatures stopped moving, as if they found it painful to move and difficult to sustain any rapid movement. In the pale light of dusk their skin appeared greenish-white, almost luminescent. They were ragged, disheveled, their clothing torn and caked with blood. Each had been wounded gravely enough to have caused his death. They appeared to have been victims of an automobile accident. Two had faces smashed and disfigured, foreheads gashed, bits of glass embedded in their cheeks as would be the result of having been thrown against or through an automobile windshield; the third had a large hole in his chest and a shirtfront bloody and oozing secretions from internal organs, the probable result of sudden impact against a steering column. These were dead beings, who had been human, animated now by a force beyond normal comprehension, driven by a lust for live human flesh.

As they stood silently, one of the creatures turned its body, slowly, painfully, to look behind the group.

Three more humanoids were approaching, catching up, making their way through the cornfield. They moved stiffly, awkwardly. One had an arm and part of its face missing, and seemed to be grinning through teeth stained with blood. It stumbled and fell suddenly, smashing cornstalks to the ground with a horrible crackling noise, then flailed around and made a hissing, groaning sound until it pulled itself to its feet. Its companions had gone ahead, moving with great effort and seeming concentration, toward the Bert Miller farmhouse, its lights showing in the distance.

In her upstairs bedroom, Ann was comforting Karen, trying to convince both herself and her sister that Sue Ellen would do all right on her own, that the farmhouse would be safe, that the baby would be born and everything would work out somehow.

"*I'm* the one who should have left," Karen said, crying. "Me with a baby! I should be some place close to a hospital!"

"You *are* close to a hospital," Ann insisted. "Ten minutes away. When the labor pains begin, Daddy will drive you into Willard in the pick-up truck. Maybe we'll *all* go if it's not safe here. Daddy won't want the baby to be in danger."

"I think he'd rather see the baby dead!" Karen said, and began to cry again.

"That's not true!" Ann retorted. "You'll see, Karen. When the baby is born, Daddy will be a proud grandfather."

"I hope the baby comes soon," Karen sobbed, seeing its birth as a way to escape the farmhouse.

Suddenly, there was a noise from outside, the sound of footsteps on the front porch.

The two girls listened. They heard the door open.

"Sue Ellen's back!" Karen cried happily, her face suddenly brightening through her tears.

Ann jumped up smiling, but the smile froze on her face and her eyes caught her sister's as terrible screams echoed from the downstairs.

"Karen! You stay here! Lock the door after I leave!" Ann yelled, and left her sister, almost paralyzed with fear, cowering in the bedroom as she slammed the door and ran down the stairs.

She reached the landing in time to see her father being torn apart. Three ghoulish figures were on him. His screams had stopped. The hideous things were chewing at his face, his arms, tearing and digging at the soft flesh of his stomach to get at the organs inside. One of Bert Miller's eyes stared wide at the ceiling; the socket of the other eye was empty, gushing fluid and blood.

Ann's scream stuck in her throat. A ghoul chewing a mouthful of flesh looked up at her, almost with an air of curiosity, as she staggered backward, loosing the earsplitting scream that at first had refused to come out. The ghoul got to its feet and started after Ann as she got her weak legs moving. Legs feeling like jelly, she scrambled and fell up the stairs, threw herself against the bedroom door and found it locked.

"Karen! *Karennn!*"

The blood covered creature reached the landing, its face hideous in the glare of light from a naked bulb in the hallway.

Karen got the door unbolted and Ann rushed inside. She bolted the door, stood panicked for a moment then flung herself to the other side of the room to try and move a heavy dresser against the door. She looked at Karen, almost ready to ask her to help before realizing through her terror that she could expect almost no help from the pregnant girl. The dresser refused to budge. Outside, the flesh-hungry thing had begun beating with its fists against the bedroom walls. And there were the sounds of more footsteps on the stairs.

Ann tugged and struggled even harder with the heavy dresser; it moved a few inches. Karen came over, her face numbed and contorted, and weakly took hold of a corner of the dresser, going through the motions of trying to help. Ann began tearing out the dresser drawers, throwing them on the bed, trying to lighten the task of sliding the piece of furniture across the floor.

The bedroom door was beginning to give. Strangely, horrifyingly, the heavy steel bolt was holding, but the door itself was beginning to come apart, its wood splintering under the hail of blows from the creatures outside. The increasing force of the hammering and battering of many fists was destroying the door itself.

The dresser began to slide again, moving a few more inches, then slammed into a wall. Ann could not angle it around the bed.

Karen screamed, throwing herself to the floor, trying to force her swollen body under the bed. The thought leaped into her head that the ghouls might drag Ann away and leave her alone so that she and her baby might survive—a terrible nightmarish idea that she was instantly ashamed of having thought. But all she wanted to do was survive. She could not keep her body from shaking as she crawled further and further under the bed.

Ann backed herself against the jammed dresser, trying to force herself between it and the back wall, as the incessant pounding continued against the splintered door. Through the din Ann thought she heard the loud crack of a gunshot. Then a flurry of gunshots. And the distant wailing of a police siren and the churning of tires on dirt and gravel, getting louder as the siren died. Tears streamed down her face. Perhaps they would live through this hell on earth.

11

Another gunshot rang out, followed by a heavy, dull thud from the living room and, in the distance, the triumphant shout of a human voice.

The siren cried into the night once again, wailing loudly. Brakes squealed to a halt outside on the lawn.

Ann heard more gunshots and more sounds of bodies falling downstairs. A wild laugh echoed from the front yard. She heard grinding gears and churning tires of still another vehicle, wheeling and maneuvering somewhere outside.

Neither Ann nor Karen could see what was happening from their hiding places in the bedroom. But they both had the sense that they were being rescued. The almost deafening pounding on the door had diminished and finally ceased, but they were still too terrified to leave the room and go outside to see who had arrived.

Suddenly, they heard a scramble of feet outside on the porch, then noises and shouts in the living room, and a burst of gunfire at close range.

Then silence.

"Goddamn it to hell!" said a man's voice. "That finishes the bastards, doesn't it?"

"Go through the house!"

The command had come from a second voice, more authoritative. Through the battered door the girls heard the sounds of footsteps running into the kitchen, and up the stairs.

More shots rang out, echoing in the narrow hallway outside the bedroom door, accompanied by the blood chilling sounds of bodies hitting the floor.

"Got three more up here!" a voice yelled. "The door's locked— somebody's hiding inside!"

Immediately there was the sound of someone else coming up the stairs.

"Who's in there?" the authoritative voice said. The girls thought they heard a high pitched giggle after the question.

"Come out or we'll shoot the door down."

Ann spoke up. "It's us. P-people in here. Ann and Karen Miller. Don't shoot. We'll open the door." She was still extremely frightened and was tuned into every sound from beyond the door. Outside, an engine was turned off and she heard scuffling as the doors of a vehicle opened and slammed shut.

"What a goddamn mess," said a girl's voice from down in the yard.

"So, what the hell," somebody else said. "Let's go in and see what we can find."

Ann slid back the bolt on the battered bedroom door and stepped back as the door opened inward on her. The first thing she saw was the gun, its muzzle pointed at her chest. She jumped back, and saw that the gun was being held by a policeman, a State Trooper.

The Trooper looked at Ann wordlessly for a moment, then said, "Who else is inside?"

"Just my s-sister," Ann stammered. "She's p-pregnant."

The second man, whom Ann could not see, giggled again.

"Tell her she can come out," the State Trooper said. He was a tall, well-built young man in his early thirties and not bad looking.

Karen crawled out from under the bed and came forward timidly, and the State Trooper took Ann by the arm and led both her and her sister out of the room. The second man looked at them, smiling. He did not have a uniform but was wearing a plaid shirt and jeans. He had a revolver tucked under his belt and a rifle in his hands.

"You don't have to be afraid of us. We *rescued* you, for Chrissake," the man in the plaid shirt said. Without waiting for an answer he pivoted, stepped over the body of one of the beings that had been gunned down in the hall, and disappeared down the stairs.

Karen and Ann did not look at the dead bodies. Keeping their eyes straight ahead of them, they followed the policeman down the stairs and into the living room.

They reached the landing in time to see their father's remains being dragged out of the living room and across the front porch. Karen gasped, threw herself against Ann and began to cry. Ann cried softly also. Moments later, they heard the loud report of a single bullet fired from somewhere at the edge of the lawn.

The State Trooper looked at Ann apologetically. "I'm sorry," he said in a low voice. "No way around it. If we didn't do that he'd try to get up again. They all do, 'less the brain's destroyed. You might think you'd want him to be alive again, but you wouldn't, believe me. You wouldn't want him *that* way."

"I know," Ann managed to say in a strangled voice. "It's all right. We understand. It's hard to accept, is all...but we'd like to bury him."

"Of course," the Trooper said.

The man in the plaid shirt stared at Ann from the doorway. He had been the one who fired the shot out in the yard. He holstered his revolver, more slowly than necessary, and picked up his rifle which he had left leaning against the wall. He had a gleam in his eye, and a grin which seemed perpetual but not necessarily friendly. That permanent smile gave a strange look to his face, which was not remarkable otherwise; his features were regular and his hair sandy and unkempt. He seemed to be in his early twenties. His physique was hard and wiry.

"Flack is my deputy," the Trooper explained. "Mr. Flack, please see if you can see what happened to Wade and Angel."

"Right, boss," Flack said with a smirk. "I have a hunch they're making things comfortable for our friends in the back of the truck. Want me to bring the friends in, too? And how about the girl in the car?"

"Bring them all in," the Trooper said. At the mention of the girl in the car, Ann's heart jumped.

"We found a girl in trouble down the road," he explained. "Rescued her. She seemed right out of her head. My name's Trooper Carter, by the way. *John* Carter. You can call me Mr. Carter."

Ann led Karen over to a couch and they both sat down, not knowing what to say. John Carter sat in a chair, keeping his eyes on the girls, carefully scrutinizing them, then unholstered his service revolver, flicked open the cylinder and began reloading, placing the empty cartridges in an ashtray and inserting new bullets from his belt.

The girls turned to look as Flack re-entered the living room, backing through the doorway carrying the legs and feet of a man who had been tied and gagged while another State Trooper had the man by the arms and shoulders. The man was dead weight and Flack and the Trooper struggled with their burden, bringing the tied-and-gagged man to the center of the living room, where they let him drop heavily to the floor. Ann thought they handled him roughly, like a sack of corn.

"Heavy son-of-a-bitch," the Trooper remarked to no one in particular. "Let's go get the other one."

"That's Wade," Mr. Carter explained, gesturing with the hand that had been inserting bullets into the cylinder of his revolver. "My partner, Trooper Wade Connely."

Wade stood up, drew himself tall when he saw the two girls on the couch, and made a movement to tip his hat before he and Flack went out the door again.

"Wade's a good man," Carter said. *"All* these people working with me are good people."

Just then there were footsteps on the porch and a girl came in the house, pushing Sue Ellen ahead of her. She was helping Sue Ellen, supporting her with an arm around her waist. Ann jumped up. Sue Ellen looked stunned and disheveled. Her cheek was bruised and her lip was cut and bloody.

"I guess you know her. That's Angel, by the way," Carter said, seeing Ann rush to the girl, followed by Karen. They hugged her, half-laughing, half-crying.

"She's our sister!" Karen gasped. "Sue! What's happened to you?"

"She was unconscious—" Angel began, but was interrupted by Flack and Wade dragging in another trussed and gagged prisoner whom they proceeded to dump in the center of the living room next to the first one. Both tied-and-gagged men were in civilian clothes, in their late twenties or early thirties, and looked as though they had been roughed up. They darted their eyes about the room, taking in their surroundings, their glances fastening momentarily on each face for appraisal, although they were clearly powerless to do anything about their situation.

"Tough customers," Carter remarked. And Flack nudged one of the bound men with his foot and let out that strange giggle.

Karen and Ann had stretched Sue Ellen on the couch, with Angel helping them. As soon as she hit the couch, Sue Ellen lost consciousness, and began to mumble deliriously. Neither Ann nor Karen could understand or make any sense out of what she might be muttering. Ann glanced up at Angel, trying to read the other girl's face for unspoken knowledge of whatever had befallen Sue Ellen.

Angel bit her lip. "She was unconscious in the car," she said. "We found her being attacked, trying to fight off some of those *things*. Flack saved her. She's been out of her head ever since."

"Did those things give her her wounds?" Ann demanded. "If they did, she's in terrible danger. If she dies she'll turn into one of them!"

"Yeah...I mean—I *guess* they did. Sure. There's bruises and blood on her. But she ain't gonna die. She's just out of her head is all."

"Nobody knows how to cure the disease those things got," Flack blurted out. "If she dies we'll have to make sure she don't get up again."

"There was no need for you to say that, no cause to frighten the girls," Carter admonished his deputy and fastened his eyes on Flack, staring him down.

"I'll say anything I damn well please," Flack spat. "Just 'cause you got a uniform don't make you boss over *me*. I'll turn in my deputy badge." This struck him as being very funny somehow and he laughed uproariously.

Ann and Karen were not paying any attention to the men. Karen was pressing her palm to Sue Ellen's forehead, while Ann had gone to the kitchen to make some cold compresses.

Angel came over and put her hand on Flack's shoulder, but he knocked it away. The girl's eyes spat fire for a second, but she said nothing. Flack did not give her the courtesy of looking at her, instead stepping nearer to the prisoners on the floor. He nudged one of them with the toe of his boot. This got no response on the part of the prisoners, except a turning of their eyes toward Flack.

Wade Connely laughed. "Tough customers," he remarked, as Carter had done earlier. He looked to Carter for approval but Carter refrained from responding.

A sulky look on her face, Angel had begun roaming idly and inquisitively about the room, stopping to examine various objects, pausing to look at and pick up ornaments on the mantelpiece, then setting the objects back down as though they disappointed her or weren't worth bothering with. She caught a glimpse of herself in the mirror, took out a comb and began combing her long red hair. Her face was hard. She was not a pretty girl and there was something wild and insolent about her, as if she had suffered a deep hurt at some point in her life and was looking for an opportunity to hurt someone else. Like Flack, she was dressed in blue jeans and a plaid shirt.

"When I nudge him a little he doesn't say anything," Flack was saying, still prodding one of the prisoners with the toe of his boot. "You think there's anything else I can do to get his attention?"

"Beats me," Wade Connely said, smiling, moving toward the front of the room for a look out the window.

Flack lifted his foot and moved it to a position above the crotch of one of the prisoners.

"Leave those prisoners alone!" Carter yelled, and glowered at Flack. The look on his face caused Flack to put down his foot.

The sound of an approaching vehicle could be heard in the room.

"What's that?" Carter asked, his hand tightening on his gun.

Wade Connely bobbed his head, trying to find a place to peek through the narrow spaces of the boarded-up window. "Motorcycle," he announced. "Stopping."

They all listened while the sound of the bike's engine cut off. Wade continued to watch through the window.

"Who is it?" Carter asked insistently, looking toward the three sisters.

"Probably Billy," Ann said. "Sue Ellen's boyfriend."

"Come and look," Carter told Ann. The gruffness of the request startled her.

She came over to the window. "It's Billy," she confirmed. "We'd better let him in." She didn't move to do it, however, because she had looked behind her to see Flack and Wade Connely with drawn pistols.

"Put your guns away, gentlemen," Trooper Carter said. "The young lady will let the young man in. I presume he's young," he added, ushering Ann to the door.

Ann opened the door and Billy barged into the room and stopped short when he saw all the strangers.

"Ann—what's going on?

"Billy...Sue Ellen's hurt."

Billy's eyes darted quickly from one face to another before he spotted Sue Ellen stretched out on the couch and went directly over to her. He crouched, felt Sue Ellen's forehead, and got no response. "What's the matter with her, Karen? What happened to her?" The panic in Billy's voice was obvious. He removed his motorcycle helmet and his youthfulness became more apparent. He looked not more than seventeen years old. His denim jacket was too big for his slender shoulders, and his jeans covered very long, very thin legs. He had sandy hair and freckles and a prominent Adam's apple that would have been less noticeable if he weighed more.

Karen answered Billy's questions about Sue Ellen. "We don't know what happened to her, Billy. She tried to leave home this evening, walking by herself. She got attacked by the...the things, and these men saved her."

Billy looked over at the three strange men. Flack wore his usual smirk. Wade Connely had his eyes fastened on Billy, openly, almost brazenly sizing the youth up. Carter, as if intentionally trying to convey an impression of disinterest in the boy, whistled a short burst of a tune and stopped, his eyes staring all the while into the cold fireplace. When Billy's eyes came back to Flack, the smirk was still there, hard and insolent. On impulse Billy blurted, "Are you sure they *saved* her—or did they help do this to her?"

Flack came over and glared at Billy. "Now *that* wasn't a nice thing to *say*."

"Shut *up!*" It was Carter's voice. He had jumped to his feet, staring everybody down. Having gotten everybody's attention, he altered his voice, making it calm and serene. "The girl—Sue Ellen, is that her name—was being attacked by those *things* and we saved her. We saved the other girls, too. Their father we couldn't do anything for.

He was dead when we got here. Ask the girls if you don't believe us. But I think you'll find you owe us a debt of gratitude."

"I'm sorry," Billy said.

"That's better," Carter said, ending the discussion.

Ann came over to Billy timidly and touched him on the elbow. "Billy...maybe you can help me move Sue Ellen, carry her upstairs. I think we should put her to bed and get some covers over her." Billy followed Ann to the couch and the two of them looked down at Sue Ellen, trying to figure out the best way to try to move her.

"I'll make some hot tea for her," Karen said. "I think we all can use some." She got up and went into the kitchen.

Angel went over to one of the boarded-up windows and found a place where she could see out. "There's more of those things out there," she said, jumping back involuntarily. "At least half a dozen more, moving around the lawn."

"Where the hell do they all come from?" Wade Connely exclaimed.

Flack laughed morbidly. He was standing over the two prisoners, glowering at them menacingly while their silent eyes stared back. "Damn criminals," Flack said. "Why do we bother saving their lousy skins? Hey, Wade...what do you think? Maybe we should leave them to the zombies."

Wade grinned and nodded. He reached a foot out from where he was sitting and prodded one of the prisoners with his boot, in the same manner as one man might prod another with an elbow if they were both enjoying a good joke.

Flack walked over to Billy and Ann before they could begin moving Sue Ellen. In a sincere voice Flack said, "You'd do well to keep away from those two." He gestured at the two prisoners. "They're dangerous. Don't even know why we bother with them. Maybe we'll use them for zombie feed. Times like this it's martial law, so to speak. Besides, the bastards don't deserve any human consideration. If I told you what they did, you'd want to help lynch 'em."

Billy turned away, not knowing what to say. Ann bent over Sue Ellen, waiting for Billy to help her. They sat Sue Ellen up and they each put one of her arms over their shoulders, holding on to her forearms, their other arms around her waist. Her feet dragged on the floor as they carried her to the stairway. Angel continued to stare after Ann and Billy and Sue Ellen long after the three had disappeared from view, though they could still be heard struggling up the stairs.

In the kitchen, Karen was rattling cups and saucers, making tea.

12

Flack looked at Wade Connely. "Wade, before we get too comfortable, you and I have got work to do."

Wade stood up and grinned. The bound and gagged men on the floor followed Wade and Flack with their eyes.

"It's gonna be dark for a long time now," Flack said. "We might need a bonfire to cheer things up. There's plenty of dead, dry skin outside. It ought to be put to some use."

Angel jerked her head toward Flack and stared at the man as though she didn't know whether to laugh or shudder. Wade grinned, then chuckled as he and Flack picked up their rifles and went outside into the yard. The area was bathed in the stark illumination furnished by bright lights on both the front and side porches. Keeping their rifles ready, Flack and Wade Connely stepped to the back of their pick-up truck and Wade covered him while Flack struck matches and got a kerosene lantern going. He placed the lantern atop the cab of the truck, where it would increase the light spilling out over the front lawn.

At the edge of the lighted area, several humanoid forms backed off and stood still, trying to conceal themselves in shadow as if they were frightened by the presence of men with fire. The humanoids moved with their characteristic painful slowness and did not really succeed in concealing themselves, but merely moved from the bright light into light which was murkier and must have seemed like total darkness to their dim eyesight. Flack and Wade Connely scanned the perimeter of the lit area and also peered deep into the darkness beyond. By comparing observations, they were sure they had spotted at least eleven humanoids trying to keep hidden in the overhang of trees and shrubs. A half dozen more were apparent in the shadowy light at the edges of the lawn.

"We better light some torches," Flack said. "We can use our revolvers and keep the rifles leaning against the side of the porch in case we need to get to them in a hurry."

The two men moved to the back of the truck and again Wade Connely covered Flack while he wrapped and tied cloth strips around the ends of what looked to be old table legs. Flack soaked the rags in kerosene from a five-gallon can, struck a match and lit the make-shift torches one by one.

"That'll keep the dead bastards away," Wade said. And, each with torch in hand, he and Flack stepped away from the back of the truck, leaned their rifles against the porch railing, drew their revolvers and surveyed the once-human debris in the front yard.

The area was littered with the bodies of vanquished ghouls, while others not yet conquered had gathered enough courage to move out of the partial darkness and now stood, bathed in stark light and hard shadows, looking on. An eerie, hissing sound came from the edges of the lawn and from the deeper darkness, a sick sound emanating from the dead things that made their presence more ominous. This sound was the painful rasping breaths of dead lungs, a chorus of death-rattles that sent chills up the spines of the two men carrying the torches. They observed several of the creatures step forward out of the semi-darkness and it made them uneasy.

"Bastards don't stay frightened long," Wade Connely said, whispering, as though not wanting to call the things' attention to himself.

"Get the meat hooks," Flack said, his voice as tight and strained as Wade's. Before moving, Wade shot a glance at Flack because it was so unlike Flack to let anyone see he was rattled. It made Wade feel better to know tough old Flack was as nervous as he was.

Flack stared with horrified fascination into the faces of the dead things. Their complexions, so bloodless and white, emphasized the black, swollen bruises they must have sustained prior to death. He wondered if the black, caked, dried blood was from their own wounds or from wounds of recent victims of their quest for human flesh.

One of the creatures took a step forward and Flack gritted his teeth. A loud report belched forth when Flack squeezed his trigger, and the dead thing was flung backward by the force of the bullet exploding inside its brain, blasting out the back of its skull, crumpling the thing onto the grass in a stinking heap of soiled clothing and rotting flesh and dead bones.

The rest of the creatures did not back off. They seemed uninterested in the death of one of their own kind. They did not attack and cannibalize the newly fallen one. They craved instead freshly slaughtered human flesh, warm and bleeding, still with the taste of life. Warm human flesh was the only kind that could nourish the living dead.

Wade Connely looked up, startled, when Flack's gun went off. He watched the shot humanoid reel and tumble to the earth and shuddered when its companions exhibited no reaction, no wariness or fear of a similar fate. You could not frighten these things off by killing them. The only thing they seemed to fear instinctively was fire, their dry, dead skin being exceedingly flammable.

"Gimme a meat hook. *Hurry up!*" Flack shouted, the bark of his voice setting Wade moving again, rummaging in the back of the truck. Wade pulled out two pairs of gloves, tossed one pair over toward Flack and put the other pair on. With every move the two men made, they had to juggle torches and revolvers from one hand to another.

"Only one meat hook," Flack said. "I'll do the work, you keep me covered." Figuring to rely on his flaming torch for protection, Flack holstered his revolver and took the meat hook Wade handed him.

Wade Connely covered while Flack moved over to the body of one of the vanquished humanoids and, swinging the meat hook hard, thrust it into the soft abdominal flesh of the solar plexus, where the bones of the rib cage would furnish a solid anchor for the hook so it could be used to drag the dead body over the ground. One by one, Flack moved each corpse in this way, dragging them to a chosen spot in the center of the lawn and piling them like firewood. Working fast and hard because of the undercurrent of fear the task inspired in him, Flack finished the grisly job of piling nearly a dozen dead bodies in a surprisingly short time.

The stench of the rotting flesh was overpowering, making the two men breathe in short gasps when they could no longer hold their breath. Flack was exhausted. He needed more air than this method of breathing provided, and he finally forced himself to breathe normally, fighting against gagging and the urge to vomit.

When the corpses were stacked in a pile, Flack poured kerosene over them, sloshing the fluid out of the can in great quantities, splashing it sloppily in his hurry to get finished. Wade Connely watched, his finger tightening on the trigger when he considered shooting a few more of the things for the peace of mind he thought he might get from blasting a few more. "Save your ammunition," Flack said, noticing Wade's anxiety.

"*You* shot one," Wade replied.

Flack capped the can of kerosene. The ghouls were doused, ready to be burned. The two men did not intend to immediately ignite the dead bodies, but wanted to do it later should it become necessary to make a break from the house to the vehicles. Hopefully the bonfire of dead flesh would cause any attacking humanoids to back away. With a back-up of supporting gunfire and handheld torches, an escape path could be cleared.

The two men took off their gloves and tossed them into the back of the truck along with the meat hook. They backed into the house, carrying their rifles and torches. Wade made another trip outside for the lantern and the can of kerosene. When he entered the living room again, he barred the door and bolted it.

13

Angel was dozing on the couch. John Carter was sitting in the easy chair by the cold fireplace, his eyes straying now and then to the trussed-up prisoners lying flat on their backs in the center of the floor. Beside Carter an empty teacup rested on the arm of the chair.

Flack and Wade went into the kitchen to wash their hands, found cups on the kitchen table and a steaming pot of tea on the stove. "I want more than tea, for Chrissake," Flack said, "I'm *hungry*," and opened the refrigerator to look for something to eat.

Upstairs, Billy and Ann got Sue Ellen into bed and were watching over her hoping she would regain consciousness.

Karen walked slowly to the top of the stairs, having left the kitchen upon hearing Wade and Flack enter the living room. She averted her eyes and held back tears when she passed her father's bedroom on her way down the hall. The door to that bedroom was half closed, a pale beam of light from the hall throwing murky shadows into the room. Most of the room hid in darkness. Deep in the room, seeking the blackest spot, a hulking humanoid form stood silent. This dead being had feasted on Bert Miller's flesh. Its bestial craving temporarily sated, it was content to remain motionless, biding its time, for now unmotivated and devoid of purpose.

Karen entered the room where Sue Ellen was, half-expecting to see her sister awake and doing better. Ann and Billy looked up, their faces conveying the message that there had been no change in her condition. "I'll watch her," Karen said. "You two can go downstairs and get some tea, if you want to."

As Billy and Ann started down the stairs they heard a wild squeal of laughter from the living room. Flack, stuffing a sandwich into his mouth, rushed past the landing followed by Wade Connely as Ann and Billy reached the bottom of the steps and entered the living room.

Angel was laughing, kneeling before something in the far corner of the room. Wade and Flack were hovering over her, and Flack's giggle joined Angel's excited cries. The two bound and gagged men strained to look in the direction of Angel's laughter. They saw that she had moved a set of bookshelves and discovered an old floor safe with a combination lock.

"Bet I can guess the combination," Angel said, wetting her lips with a flick of her tongue. "I had an aunt who was psychic."

"Maybe the real vultures got us after all."

Everybody looked in Billy's direction, stunned, just staring at him.

"That was an ungrateful thing to say," Angel said, her eyes flashing.

Flack and Wade turned and took a few menacing steps forward, Flack drawing a knife from a sheath on his belt. Suddenly Flack swung the knife toward Wade, handle first, the handle thrust toward Wade's lips as though it were a microphone. Wade laughed, understanding the charade to come. Angel grinned and laughed. John Carter remained silent in his chair, watching everything. Ann and Billy, beginning to be frightened, felt cold beads of sweat run down their faces.

Holding the "microphone" toward Wade, Flack said, "I understand that—just a couple of hours ago—State Troopers rescued a few country bumpkins during an attack of ghoul-like creatures."

"That's the way I got the story," Wade replied, looking serious and obviously enjoying his part. "The Troopers came out of nowhere and rescued the country-folk in the nick of time. I'd say that the Troopers were really troopers about the whole thing." He grinned broadly at his own wit.

"Indeed they were," Flack said. "And what does it feel like, Trooper Connely, to be a hero, to have saved the lives of total strangers? To have risked your neck for persons you didn't even know?"

"It feels good at first, but..."

"But what?"

"People have short memories," Wade said slowly, looking directly at Ann and Billy.

"Now you just wait a minute!" Billy blurted, but Flack cut him short, pushing him backward onto the couch. Flack leaned over the boy, holding him down with a knee on his chest, the point of the knife inches from Billy's throat.

"*You* wait a minute, pal," Flack retorted, spitting the words through clenched teeth.

"What did you do to Sue Ellen?" Ann blurted. She was so frightened the words rushed out before she could stop them, her fear giving voice to something which before had only been a subconscious suspicion.

Flack looked astonished, wounded, stunned. He left the boy on the couch, facing Ann with a hurt look in his eyes. Billy lay on the couch, rubbing his throat and chest, his flushed face contorted with anger, fear and pain.

In a serious, sincere tone Flack said, "You see those two prisoners over there? Take a good look at them. Child molesters! And we have to risk our necks to keep their filthy flesh alive just to bring them to trial." Flack paused and grinned. "We didn't really have to stop and save *your* lives. But *we* did. And since we'll be holed up here a while, we're going to need some cooperation. Now, I think it's time we had a little something to eat. A little home-cooked meal. We don't know how bad it's going to get out there. Now, which one of you is the cook?"

Ann and Billy looked at each other. Billy, his face still red, was sitting upright on the couch.

"All right. I'll do it," Ann said in a barely audible voice. She made a move toward the kitchen but stopped when she heard the sound of the TV. John Carter had flicked on the set and stood over it waiting for the tube to warm up.

Carter's eyes were fastened on the TV screen, not that he was particularly interested in the picture slowly forming; he was simply uninterested in anything else at the moment. He possessed an aura of quiet authority. Although he had not said much, his presence was always a factor in the room. He seemed to speak only when he disapproved of something or wanted a thing done a certain way. He was willing to let things happen until they needed to be stopped. Carter was clearly the boss without needing to constantly remind everyone of it.

A news program drew everybody's attention. An announcer was speaking from behind a desk in the television studio:

"Apparently the phenomena is not confined to the two-state area as was first believed. Reports have been coming in from all over. A night nurse in a New York hospital tells of her bizarre experience."

The people in the living room of the Miller farmhouse moved closer to the TV as the image dissolved from the announcer to a news film of a young woman being interviewed. Karen, drawn downstairs by the sound of the broadcast, moved quietly to a place next to Ann. The prisoners on the floor raised their heads to try and see the screen, peering between the legs standing in front of the set. On-screen, the nurse spoke into a microphone hand-held by a reporter on the scene at the New York Hospital.

"Well," she began to explain, still very shaken from the experience, "I had just wheeled a dead organ donor from the operating room downstairs into the anteroom. The heart had been removed. I wheeled him into place, turned away for a moment, and when I turned back again he was walking toward me—I still can't believe it—I ran out of the room, called for help and when we looked inside, he had broken through a window. In a second, he was gone."

The broadcast returned to the anchorman in the studio. "I repeat, terrible reports of this kind are coming in from all across the nation."

Karen suddenly moaned loudly, backed against a chair and fell into it, doubled over in pain. Billy and Ann rushed to her and tried to help her walk to the couch. She moved slowly, very stiffly, frightened at the possibility that her labor pains had begun. "It's supposed to be a month away!" Karen cried, her arms folded over her body as Ann and Billy eased her down onto the couch. "This can't be happening now!"

"How bad is it?" Ann asked.

"That pain before hurt real bad. And it feels like it's goin' to start again."

While Billy and Ann tried to comfort Karen, the TV broadcast continued, watched attentively by Flack and Angel, John Carter and Wade Connely. The face of the announcer filled the screen.

"The recently dead—people from morgues, funeral homes and hospitals—are coming back to life and feasting on human flesh. No one knows how many people have been killed by the ghouls only to rise themselves to join the ranks of the walking dead. Obviously, if this plague is not checked, it could lead to the destruction of the human race. In most areas local police, National Guard units and volunteers have begun working around the clock in order to control the problem. Needless to say, this is turning both our cities and rural areas into bloody battlefields. And the disaster has been worsened by the fact that people are turning against each other. Bands of looters and rapists are wandering the countryside—especially in remote rural areas—taking advantage of the breakdown of law and order that has come in the wake of the invasion of the ghouls. Reports of murder, rape and arson have become commonplace. Here in our own county, Sheriff Conan McClellan, who dealt efficiently with a similar emergency ten years ago, has once again taken command of an armed posse of policemen and civilian volunteers. We interviewed Sheriff McClellan earlier today."

The TV broadcast cut to newsreel footage of the McClellan interview. McClellan and a reporter stood in the foreground, while in the background there was a bustle of activity. A bivouac area could be seen behind the two men. Tents were going up, and men with dogs, guns, campfires, Jeeps and emergency vehicles were everywhere. The Sheriff had on civilian clothes—the trousers of his dark suit were tucked into scuffed hiking boots, and his tie was loosened. He looked very tired. He carried a high-powered rifle with a scope and a belt of ammunition over his shoulder.

"Sheriff...how does the present emergency compare with what happened ten years ago?" asked the reporter, holding up a mike.

The Sheriff answered decisively. "This is worse. Much worse. The *people* have turned against each other. We can control the ghouls, I think, but we have the looters and rapists to contend with."

"Do you have any explanation for what's happening?"

"None whatsoever. I just do my job. I never thought this damned business would happen all over again."

"Sheriff, what makes you think you can defeat the ghouls?"

"We did it once before. We can defeat and destroy these things. Cleaning up afterward, that's the difficult—"

John Carter stood and switched off the set. He turned and faced Ann and Billy, who had been listening to Karen's regular moaning. They were quietly asking her about the intensity of her pains, trying to keep her calm, and talking about the likelihood of the baby's premature birth.

"It hurts so bad," Karen wailed after a particularly bad spasm of pain. "And the pains are coming again and again."

"We'll have to get her to a hospital," Billy said, darting his eyes toward John Carter for approval.

Carter shook his head from side to side. "It's too dangerous to go outside." Flack smirked, jerked a cigarette out of a pack and lit it.

"Let's get Karen upstairs for now," Ann said resignedly to Billy.

Billy and Ann helped Karen from the couch and started for the stairs. Flack stepped in front of them and stopped them. Seized with another contraction, Karen bent over, moaning, clutching her abdomen.

"Where do you think you're going?" Flack demanded.

Ann tried to help Karen while Billy stared bewilderedly into the man's face. Karen stopped moaning and also looked at him curiously. Ann looked over at John Carter, a pleading look in her eyes.

"Just ask my permission," Flack said.

Angel nudged Wade in the ribs, amused by the whole thing. Wade Connely grinned. Flack made his lips into an oval and blew a chorus of smoke-rings.

"Please," Ann breathed, looking at Carter. She could not understand why he allowed one of his men to act like this, considering the situation.

"Please what?" Flack insisted, prodding, enjoying the authority.

Tears came to Ann's eyes. "Please let us take her upstairs," she whispered, looking at Flack helplessly.

"That's better," Flack said. "All right. Go ahead."

Billy and Ann hurried up the stairs with Karen, who had broken into a sweat.

"Come on you guys," Angel said. "Let's get this safe open."

Flack faced Carter and spoke angrily. "Let's get off this merry-go-round. Let's figure what we're gonna do with these people and do it."

"Relax," Carter said. "The games are just beginning."

Wade Connely chuckled and winked at Angel who was kneeling on the floor and spinning the combination of the safe, her ear to the mechanism.

"Screw the games," Flack said. "We're wasting time here. If we don't crack the Kingsley place somebody else will."

At the mention of the Kingsley place, the two men on the floor eyed each other.

"Dammit, you guys!" Angel yelled. "Shut up and help me with this safe!"

Wade Connely moved a few paces and stood looking down at Angel. "Sandpaper your fingers," he said jokingly.

"I'll crack this son-of-a-bitch," Angel said. "I can feel the clicks."

"I don't trust them upstairs," Flack said to John Carter.

Carter glanced toward the stairs, then to Flack, considering that idea. "Maybe you're right."

"How many of those things are outside?" Flack asked suddenly.

Wade moved to a boarded-up window and looked out. "Christ! The front yard is full of them!" He hurried from one window to another, sizing up the situation and not liking it. "We're surrounded on all sides! There must be thirty or more zombies out there!"

"So what?" Carter asked calmly. "We can burn our way through them like we did before."

Wade Connely stared skeptically.

Flack nudged one of the prisoners with the toe of his boot. "Zombie feed," he said quietly.

14

Upstairs, a single humanoid still lurked silently in the dark recesses of Bert Miller's bedroom. The three young people had stumbled past the half-opened door, Ann and Billy helping Karen down the hall to her own room. The humanoid had moved slightly, stirred by the awareness of nearby human flesh.

Billy left Ann tending to Karen while he peeked in on Sue Ellen. To his surprise, Sue Ellen was awake, though she lay very still and quiet in the soft glow of light from a lamp near the side of the bed. She looked up at Billy as he entered the room. She appeared dazed and weak.

Coming over to the bed, Billy said, "Sue—are you all right?"

Sue Ellen began crying softly, as though she did not have the strength to cry harder. Billy sat on the bed, not knowing what to say or do.

"That *man!*" Sue Ellen blurted through her tears. "I heard his voice downstairs—he—he *raped* me!" The girl buried her face in her hands and sobs jerked through her body.

Standing by the door, Ann had heard everything and came over and flung her arms around her younger sister, hugging her while she continued to cry.

Billy's eyes turned toward the door and widened suddenly.

Flack stood in the doorway.

"Okay, so now you know," Flack said, brandishing his revolver. "Everybody downstairs."

"You bastard!" Billy yelled, and started across the room toward Flack but Ann grabbed his arm and stopped him.

"Billy!" Ann screamed. "He'll kill you!"

"You learn fast," Flack said. "Everybody downstairs to join the party."

"My sister is going to have a baby," Ann said, hoping that somewhere in this man were some human feelings.

"She doesn't have to come down," Flack said. "She can stay here and have it." This struck him as very funny and he let out one of his giggles.

"Please, you don't mean it, Flack," Ann pleaded, out of desperation. She couldn't believe the man's cruelty.

"He means it," Sue Ellen said bitterly. She shuddered when she looked at the man, and turned her tearful face to the wall.

"Goddammit, get your asses downstairs!" Flack said, menacingly pointing his revolver. Karen's moans echoed down the hall.

Billy and Ann helped Sue Ellen out of bed and the three preceded Flack down the stairs, his gun pointing at their backs.

Angel looked up, smiling evilly. "What *are* we going to do with them?"

Wade Connely grinned. "They ought to satisfy more than a few of those things outside."

"Zombie feed," Flack said, keeping his gun trained on Ann, Billy and Sue Ellen. He liked that expression.

"Where's the other one?" John Carter demanded suddenly.

"She's still having a baby," Flack said with a snicker.

"I don't care if she's taking a crap. Angel, go get her. I want us all together down here."

Angel obediently started for the stairs.

Suddenly a clattering noise came from outside the house. John Carter gestured for Wade to take a look. Wade hurried to the window.

"Two of them are near the porch," Wade said. "The bastards must be getting hungry again."

"Tell them it ain't suppertime," Flack said. "*Yet*," he added for emphasis.

Wade poked his rifle between two pieces of wood, broke a pane of glass and fired two shots, each carefully aimed. Outside, near the truck, two ghouls went down, each hit between the eyes. "We're gonna need fire to fight our way out of here," Wade said, turning from the window and cocking his lever-action rifle.

Upstairs, Angel headed toward the bedroom where Karen lay moaning, walking quickly past the doorway of Bert Miller's darkened bedroom.

A pair of hands brutally grabbed Angel, one over her mouth and face, the other around her neck. Choking the woman, the humanoid creature dragged her quickly into the recesses of the dark bedroom. He put an end to her thrashing by slamming her head against the wall, knocking her unconscious. The sounds of the brief struggle were completely drowned by the firing of Wade's rifle downstairs.

The ghoul knelt over the unconscious girl, its dead lips drooling spittle. With a glint of lust in its eyes, it bit into the soft flesh of her neck and lingered there. Then its rough hands moved down, and pulled her blouse off her body in one brutal motion. The ghoul bent its head and sunk its teeth into the girl's firm breasts, chewing bits out of one and then the other. All the while, groans came from deep within its throat and the ghoul's body moved rhythmically.

When the being raised its head, it tore away one of her nipples. More determined than before, it ripped off the rest of her clothing and relished the soft pulpiness of her thighs and groin until it had chewed its fill.

In the living room, Wade Connely had poked his rifle through another opening and was still firing. He missed, and several ghouls backed off, disappearing behind the overhanging branches and hiding in the shadows of surrounding trees. The dead things had begun to associate the belch and roar of gunfire with the destruction or potential destruction of themselves. Or perhaps it was only that the fire spitting from the barrels frightened them, flames being the one thing that they seemed to really fear.

Wade cocked his rifle to fire again but Carter yelled, "All right! That's enough!"

"They backed off," Wade said. "I got two and missed the rest."

"Stop wasting ammo then," Carter said. Then he called upstairs. "Angel! Let's get a move on!"

"There's clothesline in the kitchen cabinet. Bring it in here, Wade," Flack ordered.

Wade did as he was told, and he and Flack used the rope to tie up Ann, Sue Ellen and Billy so they were unable to move and had to lie on the floor with their hands tied behind their backs. Carter drew his revolver and pointed it at them. "Now, which one of you knows the combination to the safe?"

Flack viciously grabbed Ann by the ropes binding her ankles and dragged her over to the safe. He stood over her, jamming the barrel of his gun up under her chin. "You don't want me to blow that pretty little chin up through the back of your head, now do you?"

"There's nothing in the safe," Ann said in a hoarse whisper.

"Don't give me that!" Flack belched.

"Sue Ellen knows the combination," Ann said. "There's nothing in it. Nothing but phonograph records and old junk."

Carter had gotten up and stood over Sue Ellen, his revolver pointed at her head. "Sixteen, twenty-three, fifty-three," Sue Ellen managed. Then, clearing her throat, she continued, "Sixteen clockwise, once around to twenty-three, then the other way to fifty-three."

"Try it," Carter said.

Wade knelt by the safe and began spinning the dial. The door opened. Flack laughed, a derisive laugh that turned very mean. Wade pulled out a stack of record albums and began throwing them around the room.

"Stupid hicks!" Flack said, and stepped over to where Billy lay tied up and helpless and fetched the boy a hard kick in the ribs. Billy screamed and writhed on the floor, tears of pain starting from his eyes.

"Keep all of them covered," Carter said. "I'm going upstairs to see what's keeping Angel."

Carter trotted up the stairs and ran into the room where Karen lay on her bed sweating and moaning in pain. She stared at him wordlessly, pupils dilated in fear. Carter looked around quickly, then pivoted and ran down the hallway until he heard sounds coming from another bedroom and stopped in his tracks. Pistol pointed into the room, he advanced until he could peer into the shadows. His hand found a wall switch near the door and he flicked it on, then flicked it off instantly. The ghoul barely flinched at the sudden brightness, engrossed in its task of devouring Angel. In the brief flash of illumination, Carter had a horrifying image burned into his brain: the grotesque remains of the cannibalized girl and the dead white face of her devourer, smeared with blood. Carter backed out of the room, shaken. He thought of shooting the dead thing but changed his mind when he decided he had a use for it. He could leave it in the house to take care of those who would be left behind.

Carter hurried down the stairs into the living room. To Flack he said, "Let's get out of here. Like you said, we have an appointment with Mr. Kingsley."

"Where's Angel?" Wade asked.

Carter gave Flack and Wade a hard, haunted look. "Ask me later. Let's get out of here! Fast. You three, on your feet!" He waved his gun at Ann, Billy and Sue Ellen, but they could not move because their ankles were tied tightly together.

"Cut their feet loose," Carter said impatiently. "Except for the boy's."

Flack unsheathed his knife and cut through the ropes around Ann's and Sue Ellen's ankles. "What about them?" Flack said, pointing at the tied-up men.

"I think we'll leave them here to satisfy our dinner guests," Carter said. "No—on second thought, I got a better idea. Untie one of them."

Flack used his knife to cut through the gag and ropes of one of the two men lying on the floor. Immediately Carter fired his revolver at the man, hitting him in the abdomen, the man writhing, screaming, his wound spurting blood through his fingers.

Flack let out his insane laugh.

The wounded man moaned and went limp, losing consciousness.

"He'll die and come back as one of the zombies," Carter said. "When he wakes up he'll want breakfast—and there it is, all trussed up and waiting for him."

Flack bent over the man still tied up and looked him in the eyes, the two pairs of eyes locking together in mutual hatred. "Zombie feed," Flack repeated, tormenting the man by nudging him in the ribs with the toe of his boot.

"Let's get movin'," Carter said, and waited while Flack lighted two torches made of old table legs and handed one to him. "Wade, you drive the cop car," Carter said. "The two girls will ride in back. Me and Flack will ride in the truck."

Wade marched the girls to the door, holding his gun on them. Flack opened the door, his torch blazing, and as they moved off the porch he tossed the torch into the pile of dead bodies doused with kerosene and the heap burst into roaring flames.

Surrounding ghouls backed away from the house, awed by the presence of fire.

Flack aimed and fired, felling a humanoid which had been lurking in the vicinity of the patrol car.

Wade moved Ann and Sue Ellen along quickly, prodding them with his rifle barrel, forcing them into the back seat of the patrol car.

Carter plunged his torch into the chest of an attacking ghoul, setting the creature on fire. The dead thing reeled and fell down, hissing, moaning, flailing and clutching at the flames which continued to devour its dry, bloodless flesh.

Carter and Flack dragged Billy along roughly by the ropes that bound his body, then lifted him by the ropes and heaved him into the back of the truck as though he were a side of beef, then Flack hopped in back while Carter climbed into the driver's seat and started the engine.

Crouched in the back of the truck, Flack fired at several ghouls lurking at the edge of the clearing, they having moved back from the blazing fire.

Wade had his car window down and was firing also, a wild and panicked look on his face as he tried to make sure none of the creatures would mob the car before he could get started out of there, following behind the truck.

The fire continued to blaze brightly, rising from the pile of bodies, and in the field stretching away from the farmhouse more ghouls were visible. Wade counted fifteen or twenty of them, moving through the cornfield, approaching the edges of the expansive lawn.

More of the dead creatures were in the road as the truck lurched out suddenly, followed by the patrol car with Wade driving and the girls getting a bumpy, terrifying ride in back. In the bed of the truck, Billy bounced and slid on his side, his body jouncing into jagged contact with a couple of gasoline-powered generators and their cables.

Bearing down on the accelerator, Carter gritted his teeth and his eyes flashed as the truck rammed the first ghoul in the road. Then another, and another. The thuds were loud, the dead things having been smacked hard, staggering in the beam of the headlights. But they stood up again, slowly as though stunned, rising one after another after the truck hit them.

Wade kept the patrol car following closely behind the truck, his knuckles clenched white on the steering wheel, Ann and Sue Ellen, arms still tied, huddled in back restraining their screams though their faces were frozen in horror.

From the bed of the truck, Flack continued to fire his rifle, bouncing and taking aim with difficulty in the glare of careening headlights of the patrol car. The truck squealed and slid around a tight curve, and Flack and Billy were both thrown against the generators, the butt of Flack's rifle inadvertently slamming into Billy's ribs. The boy screamed helplessly while Flack cursed and seized the side of the truck to pull himself up into a half-crouch.

Then they hit a straightaway and there appeared still more ghouls in the road.

Having slowed for the curve which the truck had taken so dangerously, the patrol car had fallen about a hundred feet behind.

The truck slammed into one of the humanoids, knocking it forward and into the air, and running it over with a heavy *thump-thump* as two sets of tires went over the fallen body. From the car, Wade saw the dead thing lying in the road, its head crushed flat, and he ran over it, too, because there was no way to get around it. But he had braked, putting even more distance between the car and the truck.

In his rear-view mirror, Carter saw the car lagging behind and hit his brakes, put the truck in reverse, and ran the truck backward toward the approaching car. Several more ghouls were bowled over in the process, some of them still rising from having been hit before. His eyes wide with fear, Wade screeched the car to a halt, and now both vehicles were stopped in the road with nine or ten ghouls closing in.

Carter wound down his window and fired at an approaching humanoid, hitting him between the eyes and blowing out the back of his skull, the force of the blast knocking the dead thing over an embankment at the edge of the road. Sticking his head out the truck window, Carter yelled, "Feed the bastards!"

From the back of the car, Ann and Sue Ellen screamed as they saw Flack lower the tailgate, lean against the cab and shove Billy away with his feet. Billy slid from the truck, the ropes around his body making it impossible for him to grab on to the truck bed and save himself. His foot managed to hook itself around the corner of one of the generators and for a split second it seemed that he wouldn't go over. Flack saw what happened and gave Billy another kick. The girls saw the generator go over the bed of the truck along with Billy's trussed-up body.

Hearing the thud in the road, Carter hit the accelerator and lurched out, almost throwing Flack into the road head first. Hanging onto the side of the truck, Flack yelled, "The generator! Hold it! The generator! We lost it!"

Flack's voice was lost in the roar of the truck and Carter kept going. And Wade wasn't about to stop. He ran the car way off the road onto the shoulder to get around Billy and the generator, as the ghouls started to close in.

Five or six humanoids converged upon Billy's limp form as he lay unconscious in the dirt road. Several of these creatures, having been hit or run over by the truck, were grotesquely mangled and deformed, much bloodier than they had been earlier and even more hideous. One had a chest crushed and flattened on one side, splintered ribs jutting through pierced skin and torn clothing. Another had the flesh abraded from its face by rough, sliding contact with the dirt and gravel road; its nose was almost gone, and the white of its cheekbones showed where they were no longer covered by dead skin. Still another had suffered the loss of a leg, and had to drag itself along slowly, its body oozing toward the place where Billy lay helpless in the middle of the road.

Mercifully, Billy did not feel any pain as the first ghoul to reach him stumbled and lunged, falling upon the boy and sinking dead teeth into the soft flesh of his throat. The blood began to flow. Lured by the smell of blood, the rest of the dead things came to satisfy their hunger. Billy was soon dead and being ripped apart.

The truck and the patrol car sped away safely. In the back of the car, Ann and Sue Ellen cried and cried, terrified and helpless in the anguish of grief for which there was no comfort. They did not care if they lived or died, and they knew they would probably not live.

When they reached the highway, both vehicles stopped. Wade took strips of cloth from the trunk of the car and gagged the two sobbing girls. Flack hopped off the bed of the truck, raised the tailgate and secured it, then climbed into the cab next to John Carter.

"The Kingsley estate," Carter said, and made a right turn onto the highway.

Flack grinned, showing his approval.

The truck ground through its gear-changes and hit a cruising speed. The patrol car followed.

15

In the living room of the Miller farmhouse, two State Troopers lay on the floor, one tied and gagged, the other wounded in the upper right side of his abdomen, just below the rib cage. The wounded one lay very still, as blood continued to trickle from the hole in his side. Officers Carl Martinelli and Dave Benton had been overpowered and captured by John Carter and his gang of looters after being lured to an ambush by the girl, Angel. She had put on a good act, pretending that her brother had been attacked and badly wounded by several of the humanoid creatures. Fearing that the brother would die and the girl would need assistance in disposing of the body, Troopers Benton and Martinelli had driven with Angel in their patrol car to an isolated farmhouse where Carter, Flack and Wade Connely took them by surprise and captured them. They were forced to exchange clothes with Connely and Carter, and were tied and gagged while two of the outlaws disguised themselves as State Troopers. The gang had killed the occupants of the farmhouse and robbed whatever was of value.

Without taking his eyes off his partner's inert body, Dave Benton was struggling to free himself. His efforts took the form of trying to stretch and loosen the ropes which bound his wrists, in hopes that he could slip his hands through, but the ropes were so tight that his wrists hurt, and trying to free himself in that way seemed impossible. He ceased his struggles abruptly and, forcing himself to be calm and rational, moved his eyes appraisingly about the room in search of something which could be of help.

The living room door was shut, but not barred. John Carter had wanted the door closed in hopes of delaying the creatures outside and saving the victims inside for a more ironic fate. Through cracks between the planks of the boarded-up windows, Dave Benton could see that fire still blazed in the front yard; he supposed that because of the fire the flesh-eaters had so far not mounted a concerted attack against the house. Dave knew the attack would come; it was merely a matter of time—time for the dead things to get hungry enough, for the fire to die down, for the things to lose their fear. Dave did not know that some of the creatures had temporarily satisfied themselves on the flesh of the boy, Billy, who had been tossed from the bed of the truck to appease the ghouls while Carter's gang made good their escape.

Dave had to free himself somehow so he could replace the beams in the brackets on the door and tend to his partner's wound before the worst happened. He had hope that his partner would not die. He'd had experience with gunshot wounds and the loss of blood did not seem too great and he knew if no vital organs were damaged, first aid could accomplish a lot and Carl could be gotten to a hospital. A shudder went through Dave when he thought of what would happen if he could not get free and Carl did die and came back as one of the flesh-hungry ghouls. Dave did not know of the danger upstairs, in what had been Bert Miller's bedroom; he knew something had happened to Angel but he didn't know what.

There did not seem to be anything in the living room sharp enough to cut rope. There was a mirror over the fireplace, and Dave tried to think of a way to break it. Maybe he could get to his feet and manage to hit the mirror with something heavy. No, this did not seem workable; the mirror was too high, and Dave's movements were very limited because of the way he was tied. He figured he could crawl to the kitchen and try to get a knife out of a drawer.

At that moment, Carl Martinelli moaned and raised his head off the floor.

Dave stared at his partner, wishing he could say something to his friend.

Carl moaned again, clutched at his wound, and allowed his head to fall back onto the floor.

Dave was very relieved that his partner was still alive and had regained consciousness. Carl's eyes were open, and he was breathing heavily, obviously in pain. Dave could do nothing but watch; he could not talk because his gag was too tight; but he knew that if Carl did not die yet and if he kept his wits about him there was hope.

After lying still for a few seconds, Carl pulled his hand away from his wound and looked at the hand stained with blood, staring as if it could somehow tell him how bad his wound was. Dave squirmed around and made sounds in his throat, trying to gain Carl's attention and help him reorient himself. Carl got an elbow under himself and sat up painfully, staring with glazed eyes at Dave as he rolled around on the floor.

Dave jerked his head a couple of times, and made still more sounds, indicating the unboarded door. Carl looked, understood, and struggled to his feet. He took a few tentative steps, found he could move without keeling over, and slowly went to the door and, after what seemed to be an eternity to Dave, boarded it. Dave watched, assessing his partner's movements, and feeling a large measure of relief.

Carl turned from the door and felt his wound, unbuttoning his shirt to look. Dave made his deep, throaty sounds again, and Carl realized he had to get his partner untied. The wounded man felt as if he were working in slow motion.

"Slug's still rattling around inside there," Carl said. "Hurts like hell. I think it nicked a rib." His voice sounded weak and unsure at first but got better as he knelt carefully and began to untie Dave and kept on talking. "My head hurts. I fell pretty hard I guess. I think I'll be okay." His talking seemed to reassure him that he really was alive.

Carl got Dave's hands untied and waited while Dave unfastened his own gag and untied his ankles. Dave stood up and rubbed his numbed wrists.

"Sit down," Dave said. "Lie down, on the couch. We've got to find something to get you bandaged up. Boy, am I glad you're here."

Carl did as he was told, with Dave helping him to lie down. Carl moaned, his forehead beaded with sweat. "Rotten bastards," he said. "Heavier slugs would've finished me for sure. I'll get the sons-of-bitches if it's the last thing I do."

"I think he shot you with a .32," Dave said, and his voice trailed off as he rounded the corner and disappeared into the kitchen. He was uneasy about the upper floor and his idea was to arm himself before going upstairs. He rummaged through a drawer in the kitchen cabinet, and found a heavy cleaver and a couple of long knives. He took them out and put them on the kitchen table. Then, under the cabinet, he spotted a tool box and a burlap sack. The sack was filled with heavy iron spikes. Dave opened the tool box and took out a large claw hammer which he felt would make a handy weapon.

Carl propped himself up on his elbow when Dave entered the living room. Dave handed Carl one of the knives so he would not be without protection. Then, holding the cleaver in one hand and the claw hammer in the other, Dave started for the upstairs. He ascended the steps slowly and quietly, not sure of what he would encounter.

At the top of the stairs, standing in the glare of a naked light-bulb, Dave paused. The door to a darkened bedroom was half open. Dave pushed open the door further with his foot, his weapons ready, as light from the hallway spilled into the room. Dave's heart jumped to his throat. He caught a glimpse of Angel's remains as the dead thing which had devoured her turned, its face smeared with blood, and started for the door. Dave held his ground, swung as hard as he could with his claw hammer, hitting the ghoul in the forehead and knocking it back. Dave came at the thing, swinging at it with the hammer and slashing with the cleaver too. The cleaver opened a gash in the dead thing's throat, the hammer hit its chest, then its head again, and the creature went down. It did not move. But Dave bent over it and smashed its head again and again until it was a bloody pulp.

Dave flicked the light on in the room, and ran downstairs for the bag of spikes.

Once back in the room, he drove a spike into the ghoul's shattered skull. Then he looked at Angel, wondering if there was enough left of her to rise again. Not daring to take a chance, he bent over her and hammered a spike into her skull. Then he backed out of the room, turned the light off and shut the door. In the hallway, he shuddered, leaning against the wall.

From downstairs came Carl Martinelli's voice, pained but surprisingly strong. "Dave! *Dave!* What's going on up there?"

Shaken and breathing heavily, Dave walked to the top of the stairs to reply. "It's okay!" he yelled. "One of those things was up here! I finished it off!" He lowered his voice. "It's what got Angel."

Carl heard. He stared speechlessly at the stairway, sitting up on the couch. The horror of what their fate could have been swept over him. He clenched his knife, finding that his hand was strong enough to hold it and make it useful for defense. He had not lost so much blood that he was helpless. He could defend himself and survive.

Upstairs, Dave had heard the steady moaning of the girl, Karen. He entered her bedroom which was at the end of the hall. Bathed in perspiration, she was lying flat on her back on the drenched sheets. She seemed delirious, but she looked at Dave. He saw the tears running down her cheeks. "The pains are coming every few minutes," she said. "My baby is going to be born. Help me, please, whoever you are. *Please!*" Her voice had a weak, futile sound. Dave let his breath out slowly, pitying her, despairing of his ability to handle the situation. All he knew about the delivery of babies had been learned in a handful of brief childbirth classes he and his wife had attended in preparation for the birth of their son. The son was now two years old. Dave had had a few years to forget the little that he had ever known. "I'm a policeman. A real one—don't worry. I'll help you," he said, trying to sound reassuring. "Can you help, too?" Karen nodded her head and looked at Dave hopefully before he ran down the stairs.

In the kitchen he rummaged in a closet where he found clean white towels and washcloths and a stack of clean sheets. He also found a bottle of antiseptic solution. And a revolver. And a box of ammunition. Excitedly, he snatched the gun into his hand, checked to see that it was loaded, found that it was, and tucked it under his belt. He spotted a denim jacket hanging on a hook, tried it on and found that it fit, kept it on and spilled the ammunition into the jacket pockets. Then he began tearing one of the bed sheets into strips for bandages. This done, he brought the cloth strips and the bottle of antiseptic solution into the living room and looked at Carl Martinelli, who struggled to sit up and began removing his torn and bloody shirt. "I'm going to get you cleaned up and bandaged," Dave said. "Then you're going to help me deliver a baby."

"You're kidding," Carl said, wincing as Dave poured the antiseptic onto his wound.

"No, I'm not. The girl's in labor up there. And her baby's going to be born."

Outside, the flames rising from the pile of dead bodies were beginning to die down.

16

The once-human bodies continued to burn in front of the farm-house. In the eerie fire-lit darkness, the ghouls began to converge on the house, approaching by way of the side porch. The humanoids tried to stay as far as possible from the bonfire and concentrated their assault on the boarded-up door and window on that side of the kitchen. Every so often, one of the creatures squinted at the light from the upstairs bedroom. Karen's screams floated out over the lawn above the grotesque faces of the living dead.

Some of the ghouls had rocks, and held pieces of tree branches which they used awkwardly as clubs. Very quickly the porch light was bashed out and the window pane was shattered. Dead hands reached through shards of glass, beating and pounding on the wooden bar-ricades which had been nailed in place by Bert Miller. When the glass cut into the dead flesh of the attackers, they did not bleed and did not seem to mind their new wounds, though nerves and blood vessels were slashed and severed. Under the onslaught, the barricades were beginning to give.

As frightened as the girl, Carl and Dave worked feverishly trying to assist in a totally unfamiliar task. They mopped her face with cool cloths, let her dig her fingers into their arms as hard as she wanted to in her agony, and sincerely hoped Mother Nature wouldn't throw them any curves and that it would happen just the way it was sup-posed to happen. Every few moments, the men's eyes would leave her face and they would look at each other, both hearing the sounds of the kitchen being ripped apart, yet not daring to leave the bedroom. When it seemed as though the writhing body could stand the pain no longer, Karen gave one mighty cry and her son entered a world of nightmares.

Dave, in a trance, it seemed to Carl, cut the umbilical cord, wiped the tiny crying boy with a clean towel, and the men wrapped the baby gently in another. From what they could tell, the child was healthy. But when they looked over at the bed to attend to Karen, who had been breathing heavily but steadily after the delivery, her eyes stared at the ceiling, her mouth slightly open as if surprised.

Placing the baby on the foot of the bed, Dave passed his palm over her face, and her expression became one of sleep. "Poor kid, I really thought she was going to make it," he whispered.

"We did our best," Carl said. "*Now* what're we gonna do?" He looked at the baby and looked at Karen. She seemed rather peaceful in death, as though the giving of life made the passing sweeter.

The pounding of the ghouls at the kitchen door downstairs seemed more frenzied, and more frightening. The moans and hammering of the creatures could be heard throughout the house.

"We've gotta get out of here!" Dave said. "Those things are breaking in!"

Carl looked at Karen. "Don't we have to take care of her?"

Dave handed Carl the baby. "I'll do it," he said. "But take the baby downstairs."

Carl left the room, and Dave stood over the dead mother with the hammer and a spike. Resignedly, he lifted the hammer; then, his face tight with emotion, he heavily swung the hammer. The sounds of metal striking metal filled the room. The spike cracked its way into Karen's skull and was hammered in deeper. The hammer dropped from Dave's hand and he sagged against the wall, sickened and weak-kneed. When he gathered himself together, he ran from the room.

He half-stumbled down the stairs, caught himself and turned the corner at the landing. He stopped in his tracks. With a splintering sound, the kitchen door broke down and ghouls stepped into the house.

Dave fired once, twice, with the revolver. Loud reports echoed in the room. One ghoul went down. The second one reeled, hit in the chest, then stumbled and fell over the first one's body. The acrid smell of gunpowder mingled with the foul smell of rotting flesh, as the wounded ghoul thrashed and struggled to get up. Dave dived for the tool box and came up with a flashlight.

Carl had unboarded the living room door and was poised there with a cleaver—and the baby. Dave took the baby and handed Carl the flashlight. "Can you make it?" Dave asked, as the two men steeled themselves to make a break from the besieged house, despite the burden of the newborn baby and the uncertain condition of Carl's wound. Carl gritted his teeth and nodded his head to show Dave he was ready to give it a good try.

They opened the door cautiously and saw that the front yard was relatively clear. Dave and Carl burst through the doorway and out onto the lawn. Shining the flashlight, they crossed the lawn with its debris of burned and fallen bodies and reached the dirt road. They chose a direction and kept running, finding the road clear for the moment since the ghouls had massed themselves for the attack on the house.

Carl moved the beam of the flashlight in the road and spotted a tangle of machinery and wires. He ran, flashing his light on his discovery, then halted in his tracks, breathing heavily and painfully because of his wound. "The generator!" Dave yelled. "It must've fallen from the truck!"

"I think I can carry one end of it," Carl said. "Those trees—near the top of the hill. Let's try and get it up there!"

They began dragging the generator and its cables, at the same time hanging onto the baby and their weapons. Carl found the going difficult; his wound hurt terribly, but he summoned the strength to go on, and his fear of what might happen if they stopped made him stronger.

Two ghouls appeared suddenly in the bouncing beam of the flashlight. Dave dropped his end of the generator and moved toward the ghouls while Carl kept the flashlight trained on them. The ghouls started to approach, but the light served to blind and confuse them while their heads made easy targets, trapped in the beam of light. Dave blasted each of them down with well-placed shots and watched them crumple to the earth and roll, clutching their faces.

The two men continued climbing the steep hill, struggling and stumbling through brush and tall grass. Carl kept going, but when they reached the top he collapsed. They had taken refuge in a clump of trees, some seventy-five yards from the road. Carl lay weak and exhausted, breathing heavily, half-sprawled against the trunk of a tree. Dave laid the baby on some soft grass next to Carl and handed Carl the revolver.

With Carl aiming the beam from the flashlight, Dave set to work. He began to stretch and hang the generator wires through the low branches of trees, so that the wires would encircle an area of about a hundred square feet. When the generator was running the wires would be electrically charged, and within the encircled area Carl, Dave and the baby would be relatively safe. While Dave continued to work frantically, Carl got his breath back, stopped hurting so much, and picked up the baby and rocked it, making sure it was warm and protected inside the folds of its makeshift blanket.

Carl kept moving the beam of the flashlight, dancing it through the foliage, keeping a lookout for danger. Twice while Dave was stringing the generator wires, the horrid white faces of humanoids were revealed in the beam of light and the work had to stop while the two men watched and waited for the dead things to approach close enough for Carl to shoot them down.

Carl reloaded the revolver while Dave kept watch with the cleaver and a knife. Then Dave started the generator, pulling a cord similar to the cord on a lawn mower, until the gasoline-powered engine turned over. The engine revved up and purred, running smoothly. Dave took the flashlight and uncapped the gasoline tank and peered in, and was gratified to discover a full tank. The two men and the baby huddled together in the center of the small electrified area.

"How are you doing?" Dave asked, breathing deeply and resting a little—but keeping his eyes moving through the dark surrounding foliage.

"Okay," Carl said. "I'll make it. My bandage has soaked through a little...but I didn't bleed too much, considering. This kid's probably scared to death."

"I'll bet he's *starving* to death. Listen, the wire's about five feet away on each side, so stay put."

Suddenly there was a flash and a loud crackling burst of flame as the body of a ghoul touching the electrified wire became silhouetted for an instant in the intense light and then ran off, burning and groaning into the night. The ghoul stumbled and rolled, its breath hissing from dead lungs, flames and sparks leaping from its burning clothing.

For a short while the woods were silent, except for the rasp of crickets.

"We can stay here overnight," Dave said. "But the baby's got to be taken care of and fed. In the morning we'll try to find some people. Maybe we can get you and the baby to the hospital in Willard. It's not too far."

"I'll be okay," Carl said. "If the slug had hit anything vital I'd be dead by now. I just hope it doesn't get infected."

"I sure wish we could see," Dave said. "We should've ransacked the house for some candles."

"We've got to save the flashlight," Carl said, but he switched it on anyway and shined it on the baby, taking care to aim the beam off to one side.

"Still sleeping," Dave said. "Amazing after all he's been through."

"Maybe he's sick," Carl speculated. "Is it natural for newborn babies to sleep this deeply?"

Just then there was a rustling sound of something moving through the underbrush and Carl pointed the flashlight and moved it around, searching. The beam located two ghouls, their dead white faces starkly illuminated against the background of shadows and dark green foliage. One of the dead things had been a woman and must have died of natural causes, as there was no visible evidence of wounds, but her dress was ripped away in places, revealing a dead white leg and a hard, flattened bloodless breast. Carl moved the circle of light away from the two creatures and allowed them to approach. He heard the rustling sound of their movements and the painful wheezing of their dead lungs. Then they touched the wires and burst into flames, their skin much drier and deader than the ghoul who had burned on the wires earlier, because with a crackle of electricity and a mad dance of sparks these two were consumed in flames. The woman made a frightening fiery image, running with a burning mass of hair until falling and rolling down the grassy hill. Her companion had fallen among the trees and continued to burn there, the flames rising from dead flesh, making a low orange glow, casting flickering shadows among the trees.

Dave and Carl looked at each other, their faces illuminated weirdly. Carl switched the flashlight off. "How long will the generator run?" he asked. "We got enough gas to get through the night?"

Dave considered the question a while and realized he didn't know the answer. He took the flashlight from Carl and went over to the generator, scanned the motor and fuel tank in the beam of light, looking for instructions. There were none. He sized up the tank as compared to the one on his power mower at home and also tried to compare the two engines; the generator was much larger, in both respects. Dave clicked the flashlight off and rejoined Carl and the baby. "It should last until morning," he pronounced. But he didn't feel confident.

Carl looked toward Dave, although he could not see his face in the dark. Then he looked at the baby, patted it and said softly, "Hang on, pal."

The generator motor continued to hum.

In a little while, despite their attempts to keep scanning the surrounding foliage for signs of danger, both men dozed off in total exhaustion.

17

In the first light of dawn, the generator continued to run, its lawn mower sound filling the surrounding woods.

Dave, Carl and the baby were asleep, the baby cradled against Dave's inert body. They were protected within the circle of generator wires strung through the branches of trees.

A few yards from the circle of wire lay the charred unmoving corpse of a vanquished ghoul, wisps of smoke still rising from its blackened remains. On the grassy hill, sprawled where they had fallen, were the charred remains of two more of the vanquished humanoids.

The generator motor sputtered.

Carl moaned feverishly in his sleep.

The motor continued to run smoothly again, as if a bubble in the fuel line had caused it to miss a beat.

The baby stirred slightly, still cuddled against Dave's body. The revolver remained weakly clutched in Dave's right hand. Carl had dropped his cleaver onto the dewy grass.

The morning air was damp with a faint mist that had not yet been burned off by the rising sun.

The generator sputtered again, and stopped. The chirping of birds and the quieter sounds of the woods stood out in the shocking silence of the stopped engine.

The two men and the baby continued to sleep. In their sleep they were now defenseless, and were being approached by soft footsteps moving cautiously through the tall grass of the hill and entering the clump of trees. Whoever was approaching had been lured by the sound of the generator, now silent.

Dave slumbered, tiredness and anxiety etched on his face as he slept the deep sleep of exhaustion, his mind wracked with dreams of his wife and child. He was not a handsome man, but his face possessed strength and character; his short sandy hair was rumpled and matted, there was a bruise on his forehead and a smudge of dirt on his cheek. He was dressed in the jeans and flannel shirt which had formerly belonged to John Carter, while Carl was wearing similar clothes once belonging to Wade Connely.

Carl was deeply asleep, but was not sleeping well. He moaned and stirred frequently in the throes of fever brought on by his wound. Though the morning was damp and cool, Carl's brow ran with perspiration, his dark, wavy hair hanging down and plastered against his forehead. His complexion, normally ruddy, was pale. His wound radiated a soreness and stiffness that had spread through the muscles of his side, so that he was aware of it even in sleep though it did not rouse him to consciousness. The tiredness of his body helped numb the pain.

The approaching footsteps continued to move as softly as possible, picking their way carefully amidst foliage and dead branches in the clump of trees.

Quietly, a hand parted a low-hanging branch, revealing the face of a boy peering between the leaves. The boy's face was dirty and tanned, his eyes alert, the eyes of one who is used to living in the woods. The boy's eyes surveyed the dead generator and the circle of wires, and the two men and the baby sleeping within the circle. Then the boy took a quiet and decisive step forward, his arm raised in a gesture of silence. He was carrying a bow and a quiver of arrows, a hunting knife tucked under his belt.

Other boys stepped forward, all of them armed. Some carried bows and arrows, others had knives and guns. They moved silently out of the woods, surrounding Dave and Carl and the baby.

The first boy, the leader, ducked under the useless cable from the dead generator, advanced quickly and quietly and stepped on Dave's wrist, preventing him from using the revolver. Other boys moved forward, pointing their weapons.

Startled, Carl jerked awake and tried to raise himself up, but his bewilderment and the pain in his side caused him to fall back to the ground. The stiffness of his muscles had gotten worse during the night, and he sat there staring at the newcomers and realizing at the same time that he had a fever and that his wound was probably infected.

"Who are you?" Dave demanded of the leader, after he came to his senses and realized that they were surrounded. He was not sure of the exact nature of the predicament they were in, and he retained some hope that it would turn out for the better somehow, if he played his cards right. The hope came from the fact that they were, after all, surrounded by *boys*, their ages seeming to range from about thirteen up to perhaps eighteen. There were about a dozen boys in the pack.

One of the boys reached down and gingerly picked up Dave's revolver and fondled it in his hand, pleased with the acquisition. The boy flipped out the cylinder and noted that the revolver was loaded.

"That's *my* gun," Dave said, "and we need it to protect ourselves and the baby. Put it down on the ground."

"Shut up," the leader said with soft-spoken authority and power.

"I'd like to get some more ammunition for this," the boy with the revolver said, gloating.

"Frisk them," the leader ordered to the troops behind him.

Carl stood up painfully, not wanting to be rolled around on the ground. Obligingly, he raised his hands over his head and stood with his legs apart. The boys frisked him, quickly and professionally, taking from him one long knife and the heavy cleaver, which had been next to him on the ground. He did not have any wallet, watch or money; anything of value had already been taken the previous day by John Carter's gang.

Dave laid the baby on the ground gently, and rose to his feet also. He raised his hands over his head and allowed his pockets to be turned inside out. From him the boys got only the flashlight and the revolver, and the ammunition for the revolver which was inside his jacket pockets. Dave stooped and picked up the baby, and the baby woke up and started crying.

The tribe of boys began grumbling, disappointed not to have found any money.

"We don't have anything," Carl said, speaking with effort. "We've already been plucked clean." He debated the advisability of telling the boys they were State Troopers, finally deciding the revelation would not improve their chances. He was certain it would most probably have the reverse effect if the boys had committed any crimes during these lawless days.

The baby continued to cry. Dave held it tightly and rocked it and looked to the boys' leader hoping the gang's hostility was based on fear and that there might be a chance to get out of this together, helping each other. "The baby's hungry," Dave said at last, seeing nothing but hatred in the boy's eyes.

"Shut up," the leader said again, as though it was his response to everything.

"We've got to get this baby to a doctor," Dave said. "His mother is dead. And my partner is wounded."

"We're State Troopers," Carl said, taking a chance.

"Yeah. I'm the mayor," the boy with the revolver said. He seemed to be the second in command.

"Where did you come from?" the leader asked.

"The Miller farmhouse up the road," Dave said, pointing down the hill, then patted the baby and tried to comfort it while it continued to cry terribly. "Everybody else was killed. The baby's mother died. Why don't you go down there and see?"

One of the boys snickered. "Sure...and get torn apart by all those monsters down there."

Dave had decided the boys weren't going to give him and Carl any help, so it was best to channel their energy somewhere before they got more dangerous. Maybe he and Carl and the baby would be lucky enough to escape with their weapons. His mind formulated an argument. "You can see we don't have any money or anything valuable. Why don't you just give us back our gun so we can protect ourselves and try to find some food for this baby?" He looked to the leader for an answer.

"Good try," the leader said. "But we're keeping the gun. We need it, too. It's dog eat dog now—you should know that." He laughed cruelly. "Now *get moving*." He raised his bow, an arrow pointed at Dave's chest.

Dave and Carl hesitated. The other boys also pointed their weapons. The boy with the revolver squeezed the trigger, so that the hammer moved back; a further squeeze and a round would fire. "I said *move!*" the leader shouted. The force behind his voice made the threatening arrow quiver slightly.

Reluctantly, Dave and Carl began to walk down the grassy hill toward the dirt road, the baby still crying.

The leader called after them, using his right arm—the arm that still held the bow—to point up the road, away from the Miller house. "There's another farm about three miles up that way! You might be able to get some help there!"

"To hell with them, let them fend for themselves," the second in command said, fondling the revolver. "'Specially if they're State Troopers. They could put in a call and get someone on our ass."

"Phone lines are dead," the leader said. "Besides, we'll be long gone before they can do us any damage. What say we try that farmhouse, like they said? If they're all dead, it should be easy pickins."

The leader gave the command to move forward and, whooping and yelling, the tribe of boys began to run down the hill, toward the scene of desolation and death.

18

It took Dave and Carl the better part of an hour to cover the three miles to the next farm. During the trek, which was exceedingly painful for Carl, the baby cried itself to exhaustion and fell asleep, weak from hunger. Dave continued to carry the baby, keeping a lookout for possible attack. The two men had to move slowly, keeping to the cover of foliage at the side of the road wherever possible. The surrounding terrain, above and below the road, was so hilly and thick with undergrowth that it would have been impossible to travel through it, especially for Carl in his condition.

Carl's fever was much worse. His shirt, soaked with perspiration, his body becoming weaker with each step. For the last mile or so, he moved in a dogged half-stumble, refusing to give up, fighting a lapse into delirium or unconsciousness. They were terrified to stop, but they did anyway, a couple of times, to give Carl a chance to rest. The rest periods did not seem to help; he seemed to do better when he could keep moving, and for the last half mile Dave tried to support his partner and help carry him along. If they could get to the farmhouse, he reasoned, there was a good chance they could obtain some kind of help. If there *was* a farmhouse. If the boys had not lied.

They rounded a bend in the road and spotted a small shed through the trees. At the same time they came upon a dead chicken in the road. They kept moving, not commenting, and when they had advanced a few more yards, past the clump of trees which obscured the chicken shed, they saw a white frame farmhouse about forty yards back from the road. Instinctively, both men stepped behind the protection of a huge tree. They peeked out, looking toward the house across its yards of tree-dotted lawn. There were dead, inert forms on the lawn—the remains of dead animals and some humanoid forms, ghouls which had obviously been conquered. The windows of the house had been boarded up; the place had evidently withstood an assault.

Looking at each other and making a wordless decision, Carl and Dave stepped from behind their tree.

A shot rang out and Carl was blasted back and fell dead.

For an instant Dave did not move, seeing the frozen expression on Carl's face and the blood soaking through the front of his shirt. Then a flurry of shots rang out and Dave dived and rolled for cover, ending up in a gully behind some low shrubs. In his rolling he had tried to protect the baby with his body and had apparently succeeded—the infant was badly shaken up, but unhurt. He was crying violently, the tiny body wracked with sobs that seemed too terrible for it to sustain. Dave was afraid the baby was going to die. Keeping as flat as he could in the gully, he peeked over the edge, back at Carl's body near the tree. He saw what he had not seen earlier; in addition to the chest wound, the top of Carl's head had been blown off, probably struck by a second bullet in the flurry which had followed the first lone shot. Guilty relief swept over Dave as he realized that at least Carl would not get up again. He would not become one of *them*. Then he shuddered at the deeper realization of the sorrow he felt at his partner's death. All these feelings were mixed with the knowledge that he and the baby were trapped and had to find a way to survive. The people in the farmhouse had mistaken Carl and Dave for attacking humanoids, and had fired without asking any questions.

The baby continued to cry loudly, so loudly that Dave felt sure it could be heard from the house. "Help me! Please! I have a baby! Help me, please!" he shouted across the lawn.

Another shot rang out, disturbing leaves. Then came a moment of silence. Dave tried again, cupping his hand around his mouth. "I've got a newborn infant with me who's starving. *Please!* You don't need to help *me*—but take the baby!"

He waited. There was only silence. He waited for a long time. A voice came, muffled behind the barricades of the boarded-up house. "You, out there! Show yourself!"

Dave hesitated. The voice came again. "Show yourself, by God! We've got to be sure you're not one of those things!"

Anger grew inside Dave. He wanted to inform whoever it was that they had already killed his partner because of their itchy trigger fingers, but he figured he had better keep quiet about that for the moment. If they knew they had killed a man, they might decide not to leave any witnesses. Dave cupped his hand and yelled as loud as he could, "I'm going to get to my feet! Don't shoot, for God's sake! I'm a *man*—and I have a *baby!*"

Unaccountably, the baby suddenly stopped crying. Dave looked at it, ascertaining that it was still alive and realizing that even if it were not he would still use it to gain admittance to the farmhouse. He got up, holding the baby in plain view above his head, then he scrambled awkwardly up out of the gully and stepped from the shelter of an overhanging tree so that anybody in the house could clearly see what he was. Walking slowly, holding the baby carefully, he approached the house. He saw the glint of gun barrels in the boarded-up windows and he tried to be ready to dive for cover in case a shot rang out.

A dead goat lay in the yard close to the house, some of its bones picked as clean as if buzzards had feasted on it. Dave saw that the goat had been shot almost exactly in the right eye; the socket of that eye was caked with blood, while the partially visible pupil stared out.

Twenty feet from the front porch of the farmhouse, Dave stopped, still holding the baby above his head. He spoke in the direction of a window with a cracked glass and protruding rifle barrel. "This baby was born last night. The mother died. Her name was Karen Miller. She was your neighbor, up the road. The baby hasn't had anything to eat. Would you be kind enough to give it a little milk?"

Dave lowered the baby, hugged it to his chest, feeling its weak breathing against his ribs. He figured if the people inside didn't know he was human by now and needed help, they would never figure it out.

A man's voice came from behind the cracked pane. "We have no milk. Our goat is dead. Can't you see?"

Before Dave could reply, the man's voice boomed again. "How do we know you ain't one of the looters or rapists that have been loose around here? We knew Karen—knew her whole family. They came to our daughter's funeral. Maybe you robbed them and did them in."

"My name is Dave Benton and I'm a State Trooper," Dave said. He jiggled the baby and it began to cry as if on cue, and Dave hoped it would win him some sympathy.

It did. A woman's voice came from behind the cracked pane of glass, "Henry! The *baby*. For goodness sakes, *let the man in!*"

The protruding rifle barrel withdrew through the broken place in the window and shortly after it was gone, Dave heard the sounds of the door being undone; he listened as three bolts were unlatched. The door opened and Dave stared apprehensively, the baby continuing to cry. Two middle-aged people stood in the doorway, a man and a woman. The man continued to point his rifle at Dave and to look him over very suspiciously. The woman seemed more kindly; she had gray hair done up in a bun and wore a faded print dress. The man wore overalls and a flannel shirt, his face creased and hard, his complexion sunburned and his head bald. The couple were Mr. and Mrs. Dorsey, parents of the dead child to whose funeral Bert Miller had come with his three daughters. Mrs. Dorsey brightened when she saw the baby, eyed her husband and pushed the barrel of his rifle aside so it was not pointing at Dave or the baby any longer. "Well, hurry up inside now," she said, noticing Dave's hesitancy and stepping back to allow him to enter.

Dave followed the retreating farm couple inside and watched while Henry Dorsey secured the door. Mrs. Dorsey took the baby and held it up, looking at it with love and concern. "We've got to get milk or the baby will starve to death," Dave said. "He hasn't eaten since he was born."

Mr. Dorsey spun from the door. "Can't help ya there, I told you. Our goat's dead." He jerked a thumb in the direction of a big hulking young man, whom Dave had not noticed, sitting in a rocking chair in a dark corner of the room. "My son shot the goat. Thought it was one of them dead things. When it comes to brains, my boy didn't quite get his share. He don't take after his old man noways. Trouble is—" He caught himself. "You say you're a State Trooper?"

"That's right. My partner and I were captured by a gang of looters. They took our uniforms. Now he's dead."

When Dave stopped talking, the only sound in the room was the pat-pat of Mrs. Dorsey's hand as she patted the baby, hugging it to her. Nobody knew what to say. The baby had stopped crying. Mr. Dorsey gave a long stare in the direction of his feeble-minded son, who let his head hang and cringed in his chair as it stopped rocking. Dave got the idea that it was the son whose thoughtless bullet had killed Carl, with the old man joining in the shooting spree afterward.

"We'll see to it he has a decent burial, if we can," Mrs. Dorsey said. "It's not much, but it's the best we can do." Her words hung in the air and did not comfort anybody.

The idiot son wrung his hands and sulked in a scared sort of way, and began rocking back and forth involuntarily, the chair squeaking.

"Don't you have some powdered milk? Canned evaporated milk?" Dave asked.

Mrs. Dorsey shook her head. "We been livin' off canned stuff I put up last fall," she explained, her eyes downcast, "but if we stay holed up here much longer it's gonna run out."

"Is there anywhere else around here where we can find milk?" Dave looked from husband to wife and back again.

Mr. Dorsey spoke, his voice harsh and grating without his meaning it to be. "Ain't no other homes around for miles except the Kingsley estate. And the Miller farm."

"Kingsley?" Dave brightened at the recognition of the name.

"Kingsley Country Club's five miles north on the highway, over the hill. Least that's where the golf course begins. Three miles further's the club and then the mansion's a mile or so beyond that. Kingsley owns practically the whole area. But I'd say yer best bet'd be the gas station."

"Gas station?"

"Log Cabin Gas Station, seven miles south down to the main road. They sell bread and milk—least they used to."

Dave mulled the information over in his mind. If he could get some form of transportation and a rifle, he could try to make it to the gas station for milk and food. Then he could set out after John Carter and his gang, and the captive Miller girls.

Mr. Dorsey watched Dave thinking, and read his mind. "I got two trucks and a car. I kin let ya take the car if ya wanna chance it. I'll even give ya a rifle to take with ya. We'll keep the baby here—for collateral."

"If you'll do what you say, I'll take the chance," Dave said, looking Mr. Dorsey in the eyes. "We can't let the baby die from hunger—not after all he's been through. With your help, maybe he'll make it."

"I'll do the best I can while you're gone," Mrs. Dorsey said. "I'll make some weak tea and feed him that, for a stimulant. Doctor told me to do that for my first born, when he was allergic to milk and couldn't eat much else. I won't give him much tea, just enough to see if it helps."

Dave did not say anything. He found it impossible to thank the couple, considering either the man or his son had killed Carl. But they were trying to be kind now, perhaps as an atonement. Dave was not unappreciative. But nothing could bring Carl back.

The feeble-minded son kept rocking back and forth, back and forth, in his squeaking chair.

19

Overcome by mental and physical exhaustion, Ann and Sue El-len fell asleep in the patrol car driven by Wade Connely. He was still following behind the truck. Both truck and car were traveling at about fifty miles an hour, with less than three car lengths separating the two vehicles. Wade wanted to stay close. He felt the truck could knock anything out of its way without going out of control, but he didn't trust the car to do the same. If one of the dead creatures appeared in the road, Wade wanted the truck to hit it first.

John Carter glanced in his rear-view mirror, and didn't like the way he was being tailgated. He made a move for his blinker-lights to warn Wade off. Flack yelled, "Look out!" and ducked, covering his eyes, and Carter saw three humanoid creatures standing in the beam of his headlights in the middle of the road. Carter hit his brakes, which was a bad move. The truck squealed and swerved, hitting two of the dead things and knocking them aside. Wade had to hit his brakes hard to avoid crashing into the truck, and with a loud screech of burning rubber the car careened to one side of the truck to get more braking distance and hit the third humanoid, up-ending it, causing its flailing body to flip up over the hood of the patrol car and through the windshield. Wade screamed and the car went out of control. It crashed through a guard rail and smashed into a tree.

All this happened in split-seconds, and Carter and Flack had a partial view of the accident through rear-view mirrors. Carter brought the truck to a halt on the edge of the road. Drawing their revolvers and grabbing a couple of flashlights, Carter and Flack ran back to the scene of the wrecked car.

The ghoul that had been flipped against the windshield had, on impact, been hurled against the tree. It lay broken like a rag doll, its breath rasping weakly and painfully while it moved one arm feebly, like an insect half-crushed but refusing to die. Flack walked over, shining his light on the ghoul, and fired a carefully placed shot between its eyes. Its movements ceased, part of its skull having been blown away.

Wade Connely was dead, his cracked head and lacerated face protruding through the windshield, his neck practically severed clean through. Though the engine was not running, having been totaled on impact, the headlights were still on, running on battery power, and one of the rear doors had sprung open, lighting the interior. The girls in back were still alive and appeared to be in good condition. They were sitting close together, tied and gagged and unable to move, their eyes wide with fright and their faces frozen in shock. Carter and Flack helped Ann and Sue Ellen out of the car and herded them toward the truck. Before doing so, Carter yanked loose the battery cable of the car, so the lights would go off and not attract attention. Then, knowing what would happen if he didn't do it, he shined his light in Wade's face and fired a shot into his skull.

Flack lowered the tailgate and forced the girls to climb onto the bed of the truck. He made them lie on their sides so he could tie them that way, using lengths of rope to secure them to the heavy generator. He did not want them to be able to get up and signal to passersby. When this work was done and the tailgate raised again and locked in place, Flack climbed into the cab with Carter and they nosed out onto the highway, heading for the Kingsley estate. There was less than an hour remaining of darkness, and they wanted to be in position to attack the estate at dawn. The loss of the patrol car was going to be a handicap; it had been an immense aid to their disguise as State Troopers. Carter would have to pull it off somehow, using just the uniform. He and Flack discussed the matter as they rode, and figured out a way to take the Kingsleys by surprise.

In the bed of the truck, Ann and Sue Ellen lay on their sides, getting another bumpy and frightening ride. Their minds were a jumble of fearful, disjointed thoughts. Ann had a bruise on her head, which hurt—not badly enough to make her think it was serious, but just badly enough to add to the pain and discomfort and panic that were coursing through her system. Her gag was soaked with saliva and tasted sour and rotten. She felt nauseous, on the verge of vomiting—and had to fight to keep it down lest it cause her to suffocate. Sue Ellen simply lay as still as possible, her mind too tired for tears, her cheek vibrating against the roughened metal bed of the truck. She had no idea of where she was being taken, and for the moment she didn't care. In the back of her mind she felt both she and Ann would soon be dead. If they had not been asleep in the back seat, their bodies completely relaxed, perhaps they would not have survived the car accident. And perhaps that would have been the best thing—to go out suddenly, unaware it was happening, oblivious to fear. Doubtless, Flack and Carter would have fired bullets into their dead brains, completing their deaths and making their rest peaceful and permanent.

20

Dave drove as fast as he could in Mr. Dorsey's car, keeping a sharp lookout for danger in the road. The car was a 1956 Chevy, rusty and filthy dirty, hard to start and still harder to navigate, with loose steering and almost nonexistent brakes. It rattled and vibrated on the dirt and gravel road, never making a speed over forty.

The road was surprisingly clear of ghouls. In one place Dave spotted some, way back in a field on the left side of the road. They appeared to be just standing very still, not engaging in any activity for the moment, as if they did not know what to do. Dave speculated that maybe the dead things experienced a certain inertia that they had to overcome with the beginning of each new day—as if each dawn was a surprise to them, rousing them from death. Or maybe they had simply done all the ravaging they could do in this particular rural area of few farms, and were going to move on toward other areas with a more plentiful supply of human flesh.

Dave shuddered.

He did not want to think the humanoids could reason and would have been more terrified of them if he thought they could.

He thought of his wife and son, who did not know if he was alive or dead. He maintained a hope of getting back to them. They were probably relatively safe, in the protection of the high-rise apartment building where they lived in the center of the city. The cities had been well-protected ten years earlier during the first emergency of this type, with their centralized police forces and their ability to maintain communications. It was the rural areas that had suffered heavily then, as they were suffering now. Dave and his wife had plans of moving out of the city as soon as they could afford to buy a place. Dave realized ruefully that it was probably a good thing they had not been able to afford it before now.

Carl Martinelli had not been married. When Dave got back to the city, he would have to tell Carl's aged Italian parents about their son's death. He would stress that Carl had died trying to save a baby's life. At least he had not been killed by the humanoids, and it was still possible that his body might be brought home for a church burial, the kind of thing his parents would wish.

Dave reached down and switched on the car radio, at the same time glancing at the rifle beside him in the front seat. He had not tried the radio earlier, as if the decrepit condition of the car had satisfied his assumption that the radio could not possibly be still working while the rest of the vehicle had fallen to junk. But the radio *was* working, and an announcer's voice came on.

"...return to life and become carnal monsters, creatures that crave the flesh of the living in order to survive? Scientists have been examining the bodies of the living dead that have been immobilized by brain destruction. One theory at the moment seems to be this, and I quote: The dead cells of recent corpses seem to have been revitalized by some unknown type of malignancy. In other words, an unknown cancer, perhaps a virus, brings dead cells back to life. This is not a normal 'life,' but a malignant life-form that turns the human into a creature that is dead in most usual respects. Most scientists do claim it is something in the air, a virus born of pollution, an odd mixture of carcinogenic chemicals which attack cells that have recently died, causing them to be activated, bringing the dead back to a living death where nothing remains but an activated corpse driven by a craving for living flesh. It is as if cancer itself were destroying the species in the process. It has been discovered that 'death' or let's say 'immobilization' of the corpses can be achieved by destroying the brain. Once the brain has stopped functioning, all glandular and circulatory functions cease; at least the creature can be rendered immobile..."

Dave pulled the car into the gravel lot of the Log Cabin Gas Station, braked the car to a halt and turned the ignition off. The place had been looted. Locks were broken off two of the pumps, windows were smashed, the front entrance door was hanging open. Nobody was in sight. No attendant made his appearance and Dave expected none, though he had driven the car over an air-hose, causing the signal bell to ring twice.

After surveying the place from the car, Mr. Dorsey's rifle in hand, Dave got out and approached the building. He flattened himself against the wall and worked his way over to the front door. Not a thing stirred. The place had the feel of desolation. Dave nudged the door the rest of the way open with his foot and cautiously stepped inside. His eyes adjusted to the dim light; the only light inside the station building was the natural light from outside. The few shelves were overturned and half-empty; the cash register drawer open and containing only a few pennies. Most of whatever had been of value in the store was gone.

A click and a hum startled Dave. It was the hum of a refrigerator, just as he had been about to assume that there was no electric power in the place and if there was any milk it would be spoiled.

Dave looked around and found the refrigerator against a wall at the far end of a row of shelves. The shelves contained a few canned goods; other cans were strewn on the floor and Dave tripped over some of them. He opened the refrigerator, its light came on, and to his surprise he found it contained cartons of milk, orange juice, eggs and cheese, all labeled and priced for sale. Like many country stores catering to the emergency needs of out-of-the-way people, this place did not bother having a fancy display-type refrigeration case and made do with a used refrigerator instead. Dave thought himself very lucky. Whoever had raided the place had not emptied the refrigerator, probably not wanting to take items which would easily spoil.

Dave found shopping bags and loaded them with all the foodstuffs he could find, figuring to take the whole works to Mr. and Mrs. Dorsey. Then he began loading the bags into the car, working quickly and keeping a lookout for danger.

"Looks like he ain't going to make it, poor little fellow."

The baby was wrapped in a blanket and lying on the seat of an armchair, while Mr. and Mrs. Dorsey bent over it. Mrs. Dorsey gave up trying to get the infant to take just a bit of warm tea. She had the tea in a rippled bottle, the nipple wet with saliva from being refused again and again. She reached out with the hand which did not hold the bottle and pressed a palm gently against the baby's chest.

"He's still breathin'—I can feel it," Mrs. Dorsey said in a low whisper heard only by herself.

Mr. Dorsey called out to his son, who was standing hunch-shouldered so his eyes would be low enough to peer through a crack between two window boards. "Any sign of 'em?"

The boy shook his head in a perplexed sort of way, as though the question had stunned him into trying to think of an answer he could not possibly possess. He had a rifle in his hand, gripped by the barrel so that the butt dragged on the floor. "Nope," he said finally, after a length of time that almost took all the immediacy out of whatever the question had been.

Henry Dorsey took three quick steps toward his son and snatched the rifle out of the boy's hand before the boy was quick enough to realize what was happening. "On second thought," Dorsey said, "maybe ya better just sit down a while and give yer old man the gun before ya shoot somethin' else that ain't supposed to be shot."

"*Henry!* He stopped breathing!" Mrs. Dorsey had spun from the baby and had a shocked look on her face.

Mr. Dorsey stared at his wife and the baby from the center of the room. From outside came the sound of a car turning into the driveway.

Dorsey's son had his eyes to the crack between two of the window boards. "A car," he announced triumphantly, as though he had supplied important information.

"*Whose* car?" Dorsey said angrily, as he shoved his son away from the window. He peered out, his hands clenched on the rifle. It was Dave, opening the car door and pulling out some shopping bags full of groceries. Dorsey looked inquiringly at his wife, who had the baby in her arms. "I can't tell if he's breathin' a little bit or not. I don't think he is," she said in a tight, frightened voice, and began making rocking movements with her body, cradling the infant as if treating it normally would cause it to *be* normal.

Dave was pounding on the front door.

"Lay him down on the chair—maybe he's sleepin'," Mr. Dorsey said, implying that they could at least make it seem that way for Dave's benefit, and he looked his wife in the eyes until she got the point. She did as she was told. She pulled the baby's blanket up around his ears and sat on the edge of the chair to watch over him. In the semi-dark room, the scene did not seem alarming.

Dorsey undid the bolts on the door to let Dave in. The feeble-minded son had moved to the rocking chair in the corner of the room and was rocking squeakily back and forth, watching everybody.

"How's the baby?" Dave asked, setting down bags of groceries and rummaging for a carton of milk.

"Fine," Mrs. Dorsey said in a low voice. "I made some weak tea for him, like I said. He's asleep now."

"Think we should wake him to feed him?"

"Sure—bring the milk on in here and you can help me get it ready."

Carton in hand, Dave followed Mrs. Dorsey into the kitchen.

Henry Dorsey secured the door, then came over to where the baby lay and looked down at it. He bit his lip. His face was taut and his eyes had a faraway look. He was thinking that if the baby died, coupled with the accidental slaying of the State Trooper earlier, it might become necessary to kill Dave also. Dorsey was committed to the survival of himself and his family; if they were able to make it through okay, he did not want to stand trial later for manslaughter.

The baby stirred, letting out a tiny whimper. Dorsey looked at it, not knowing whether to be relieved or more frightened. It was clearly breathing now, though its breathing seemed labored. He was alarmed that the baby's breathing seemed to have stopped earlier. His wife was genuinely frightened that it was dead. Perhaps it was merely very sick and extremely weak from hunger; maybe now, with some warm milk and attention, it would make it through the crisis stage.

Dave and Mrs. Dorsey appeared with a bottle of warm milk. Dorsey turned away, presumably to check out the window while Dave and his wife tended to the baby. "He's breathin' weakly," Dorsey said, letting his wife know. Her eyes lit up.

Mrs. Dorsey held out the bottle. The baby took the nipple and began to suck hungrily. Dave smiled. The baby continued to suck greedily at the nipple. "We can't let him have too much at first," Mrs. Dorsey said, "or he'll get sick—poor little rascal." She did not look at Dave nor at her husband, but kept her eyes riveted on the bottle and its disappearing contents.

A gunshot rang out, shattering the stillness of the room.

Dorsey had fired from his post by the window. Dave ran to the other window and looked out. Outside in the lawn, three ghouls were standing under the overhanging branches of large maple trees. "I missed," Dorsey announced, and fired again after taking careful aim. One of the ghouls, hit in the shoulder, spun around and fell, then struggled to get up.

"Aim for the head—it's the only way to stop them," Dave said, wishing he himself had the rifle because Dorsey was obviously a lousy shot.

"Don't you think I *know* that?" Dorsey said, and fired again. The ghouls had advanced to within twenty feet of the porch steps, and at such close range Dorsey scored a hit, blasting brains and blood from the side of a ghoul's head.

Carrying another gun, Dorsey's son ran to the window where Dave stood looking out and Dave took it from him before he could protest. Dave poked the barrel through a hole in the glass, took aim and fired. His shot hit the second ghoul between the eyes, and the dead thing went down heavily, knocked back by the force of impact.

Dorsey kept firing at the third ghoul, but it retreated behind a tree, whether by accident or design the men didn't know. "Dammit!" Dorsey muttered, and in the absence of firing the two men had time to notice the acrid smell of burnt powder filling the room.

Deprived of the rifle which Dave had seized, Dorsey's son had gone to his rocking chair to sulk, and the chair was squeaking again as he rocked back and forth.

Dave kept his rifle poised, aiming at approximately the spot where the head of the third ghoul would appear if the creature stepped out from behind the tree. The head appeared, and Dave fired, scoring a hit. The thing made an odd groaning noise and keeled over head first, its legs supported grotesquely in midair by a low bush through which it had fallen.

"Hot damn!" Henry Dorsey said in his enthusiasm over the three kills.

Mrs. Dorsey had stopped feeding the baby and was cradling it in her arms. The noise had not caused it to start crying, and it seemed to be asleep. "Poor thing's too weak to be scared," she said to no one in particular.

"I hope there are no more of those things out there," Dave commented. He had retreated from the window after scanning the lawn and its environs carefully, and he still had his rifle in his hands.

"We got 'em all," Mr. Dorsey said, showing more exuberance than Dave felt the occasion called for, and Dave settled his eyes on the man in an attempt to calm him down.

Dorsey cleared his throat and looked at his wife.

The sound of the rocking chair kept up.

"You said the Kingsley estate is over the hill to the north," Dave said.

Dorsey sat in a chair, took the clip out of his rifle and began reloading it. "Can't miss it. Four miles beyond the golf course and the clubhouse. Just keep going straight. Say...ya don't figure on usin' my car, do ya?"

"I was hoping you'd lend it to me again," Dave said. "You've been so kind this far. The Kingsleys are in a lot of trouble. The gang of looters I mentioned is headed there, and they've got the two Miller girls with them. And Billy, Sue Ellen's boyfriend."

Mrs. Dorsey gasped. Henry let his breath out in a long, thoughtful sigh. "I guess I can let ya take the car," he said. "But gimme the rifle back. I only got two rifles—one for me and one for my son. I'll let ya have an ax and a knife."

Dave could not help thinking that Dorsey would do better not to ever let his son get his hands on a gun, but he figured he had best keep his mouth shut and accept whatever help the Dorseys were willing to give. He leaned the rifle against the wall by the door, not wanting to take personal responsibility for placing the weapon in the son's hands; whatever Dorsey did with it was his own business.

"You can leave the baby here," Mrs. Dorsey volunteered. "Reckon I can take care of it till you get back."

His rifle loaded, Mr. Dorsey hit the clip with the heel of his hand to make sure it was firmly seated. Then he chambered a round and clicked on the safety. "Like I said, I'll let ya have an ax and a knife— and the car. You leave the baby with us. We'll take care of it best we can." He was thinking that if Dave did not come back nobody would ever find out about the Trooper his son had killed, and it would be an easy matter to find some way of disposing of the baby.

21

Under a fusillade of gunfire, the remaining glass in the windows of the Miller farmhouse was being shattered to bits.

The barrage continued, the house surrounded by armed men firing away, concealed behind trees and shrubs. The men were members of Sheriff McClellan's posse. They had come up on the house in their search of the area, not knowing what they'd find, had heard noises and issued challenges. In reply they had received a burst of gunfire and had run for cover. One man had been hit in the arm and was being attended to by a medic.

From behind a tree, Sheriff McClellan cupped his hands around his mouth and yelled, "Come on out of there or we'll burn you out!" To emphasize the Sheriff's words, a few more shots rang out, peppering the house. The posse had it surrounded on all sides.

The Sheriff yelled again. "Hold your fire, men! Give 'em a chance to make their minds up!" He peeked around the side of his tree, aiming his own rifle at the front door of the house.

For a long moment, all was still. Then, from inside the house a voice called, "Hold your fire! Don't shoot!"

"Step on out with your hands high!" the Sheriff called.

He waited. There was the noise of the front door being unboarded, then the door swung open with a creaking sound and the leader of the gang of boys with bows and arrows stepped out, his bow slung over his shoulder and his hands held high above his head. Other boys followed, their hands held high also, having left their weapons inside the house.

McClellan lowered his rifle, knowing the rest of the posse would keep the boys covered, and stood with an exasperated look on his face. "Jesus Christ! *Kids*. What next? Step on over here, Robin Hood—okay men, frisk 'em and handcuff 'em."

The posse was made up of policemen and civilian volunteers. One of the men in uniform stepped up beside McClellan and said, "We better move through the house—see what else is in there."

The Sheriff nodded his head in approval, and the man whose suggestion it was rounded up a few other men and led them up the front steps and into the house, the men proceeding cautiously with their weapons ready.

Some of the posse members had shoved the gang of boys against the wall of the house and were pushing the boys around, searching and handcuffing them. McClellan watched this activity approvingly. Some of the boys looked scared or ready to cry, especially the younger ones, but the leader had kept his composure, a wry sarcastic look on his face threatening to erupt into a smirk. While he was being frisked, he eyed the Sheriff over his shoulder and spoke defiantly. "You can't arrest us. We didn't do nothin'. We saw this house, there were no *things* around, so we came in to hide."

McClellan took time to give the boy a hard look before answering. "Yeah? What were you doing in there?"

The boy spun around as his hands were being grabbed and roughly shackled by two posse members. "There's dead people in there, but you can't pin it on us. We didn't do it."

"Maybe you did and maybe you didn't," McClellan said, his voice even and noncommittal. "Right now we ain't got time to find out. But you're in plenty of hot water. It's for damn sure you were tryin' to *rob* this place."

"Rob a bunch of *dead* people?" The boy smirked, looking at McClellan as if the Sheriff were an idiot, almost snickering at the end of his question.

"Dead people have relatives sometimes," McClellan said. "Ever occur to you what's left in here belongs to *them*?"

One of the men who had gone in to check out the house burst through the doorway yelling, "Sheriff! Hey, Sheriff—there's a couple of dead girls upstairs—both with spikes in their heads. And I wouldn't swear to it, but it looks up there the way it looked after my wife had a baby." The man stopped in his tracks in front of McClellan, a perplexed look on his face as though he had said something incredible.

The Sheriff merely shrugged and shook his head. "Well, I guess any goddamn thing's possible," he mused aloud. "Come on, boys—let's finish up here and move on to the Kingsley estate."

One of the posse members finished shackling a boy and said, "Those rich bastards ought to be okay. They could afford a small army to protect their place."

"Just 'cause they could afford it don't mean they got it," McClellan said, and stuck a cigar between his lips and lit it. He took a long drag. He expected to meet up with emergency vehicles out where the dirt road joined the highway, then the posse would be transported to the Kingsley place.

22

Dave had found that Mr. Dorsey's old car shimmied uncontrol-lably if he tried to go faster than forty miles per hour. On the open highway it would have been preferable to go faster, but Dave had to content himself with the slower speed. This made him briefly aware of an irony: that he might fail to save the Miller girls or the Kings-ley family simply because of a decrepit old car that couldn't go fast enough. Dave floored the gas pedal angrily and watched the needle climb to fifty and past it. The shimmy did not subside, as will hap-pen sometimes, but merely got worse and worse. When Dave eased off the accelerator he had to wait through decreasing vibrations until the needle got down below forty again. He gritted his teeth against his impatience, and tried to think of what he would do once he got to where he was so eager to get.

Beside Dave on the front seat were the butcher knife and ax that Henry Dorsey had given him. He would have liked to have had a rifle, or at least a revolver. It was not going to be easy trying to cap-ture or kill three fully armed men. The best way would be to attempt to surprise and disarm one of them, then use a captured gun to take the other two.

Dave thought of the baby in the Dorseys' care. He supposed the baby would be all right. Mrs. Dorsey would take good care of it. She seemed to be the sanest one of the family. The old man was driven by fear and a single-minded determination to protect his own kin at whatever the cost to others, and the son was not worth thinking about except to watch out for the kinds of harm he could do by ac-cident. In normal times, Dave thought, the Dorseys would not be bad people. They probably wished only to stay by themselves most of their lives, tending their poor farm and eking out a living, at-taining the measure of dignity and self-respect that comes with be-ing self-sufficient. Under normal circumstances, they were probably kind and decent, if a bit hardened by the severity of their mode of existence. That hardness would help them survive the present emergency; so far they were doing okay, keeping themselves alive against odds that were truly frightening. It was more than a lot of people could do. But they had killed Martinelli, mostly as the result of panic and short-sightedness. His partner's death was pointless, meaningless; it should not have happened to Carl, especially after his having survived so much. His death seemed unreal and unbelievable, like most deaths, only more so because it was a death without a purpose.

The countryside was so bright and sunny, it was hard to believe this was not a normal day. The sun had completely burned off the early morning fog. It was almost noon. Remembering that there would be a Civil Defense broadcast on the hour, Dave switched on the car radio and turned the hum down so it would not be quite so disturbing; there would be nothing but a hum until the Civil Defense broadcast came on, as all regular programming had been discontinued. Outside of the subtly ominous buzz on the radio, a constant reminder to Dave of the sort of news he was waiting to hear, he could almost deceive himself into believing there was nothing much wrong, it *was* an ordinary sunny day and he was simply out for a quiet, leisurely drive in the country.

Suddenly he saw a corpse in the road and had to swerve to avoid running over it. In swerving the car, he caught a glimpse of its head and torso flattened by more than one set of tires. It was one of the humanoids struck by John Carter's truck in the early morning darkness eight or nine hours earlier. Since then, other vehicles had run over it, either not seeing it soon enough or deciding it wasn't worth avoiding. It was a grotesque bloody mess in the middle of the two-lane blacktop.

Braking fitfully as he came out of his swerving skid, Dave spotted a break in the metal guard rail on the right side of the road. He rammed the brakes on Dorsey's car to the floor, found that the brakes began to hold though it took a long time to stop, and pulled over to the side of the road to have a look. He armed himself with the ax and tucked the butcher knife under his belt. Then he got out of the car and approached the break in the guard rail, gaining a view of a rather steep embankment and a State patrol car smashed against a tree. He immediately recognized the patrol car that had once belonged to him and Carl; he confirmed it was the same car after reading the numbers on the license plate. There did not seem to be any movement or threat of danger in the immediate vicinity; nevertheless Dave kept his weapons ready as he worked his way down toward the wreckage.

He found Wade Connely dead in the car, and the body of a humanoid in the weeds nearby. Both Wade and the humanoid had had slugs blasted into their brains. Dave spent some time searching the surrounding brush for other bodies which might have been thrown clear of the wreckage. He did not find any traces of the Miller girls, though he searched carefully through the undergrowth, and he assumed that they had probably survived the accident. If they had not survived, Carter and Flack would have put bullets into their brains, as they had done to Wade Connely. Or would they? Dave silently thanked whoever had done it, and continued to wonder about the sisters. Perhaps the girls had not survived the accident and their bodies had been taken away by the other men.

Dave looked at Wade's mangled and mutilated body with a mixture of pity and disgust, the disgust fed by the knowledge that Wade had died wearing Carl's uniform. Reaching past the body, Dave took the car keys out of the ignition, searched the passenger area and the trunk of the car for any weapons that might have been left behind. As expected, there were no such weapons; Carter and Flack had been careful enough to clean everything out. Dave put the car keys in his pocket. One benefit of the accident, he realized, was that now he would not have to contend with Wade any longer, just Carter and Flack. His chances of taking them by surprise were increased.

With renewed strength brought on by a surge of hope, Dave got back into Henry Dorsey's old car. After a few tries, the engine turned over. Dave pulled out onto the highway, resolving to keep his eyes open for additional bodies in the middle of the road. He switched the radio back on, having turned it off before starting the car to give the ancient battery a better chance to do its job. Nothing but a low hum came from the radio. Dave looked at his watch. It was nearly twelve-thirty and he had missed the Civil Defense broadcast.

He kept the car at forty, driving down the road following Mr. Dorsey's directions. In three more miles, if Dorsey was right, he should be able to spot the country club and golf course.

23

Inside the luxurious mansion, three people lay bound and gagged in different areas of the elegant living room. Each had been tied to a large piece of furniture, additional insurance for their captors that they could not wriggle toward one another and try to undo each other's bonds. Roped to the heavy brocade-covered sofa was Gordon Kingsley, a highly successful executive in his early fifties, a large man, but paunchy due to too many business lunches and too few hours in the plush exercise room of the clubhouse he owned. From beneath bushy gray eyebrows, he tried to keep his eye on his wife and son.

Elvira Kingsley, a handsome woman a few years younger than her husband, lay tied to one of the legs of the grand piano. She had maintained her slim figure, and her hair was carefully dyed to a natural deep brown. Tied to an overstuffed easy chair was their son, Rodney, a sandy-haired boy of ten, nervous and high-strung. They were alone in the room, three trussed bodies scattered about on antique carpets, waiting.

The Kingsley family had felt relatively safe inside their mansion, because of extensive security measures which had always been present. The windows were protected by a grillwork of ornate wrought-iron, a feature incorporated into the original design of the building to discourage burglars or kidnapers. Mr. Kingsley had also had an elaborate and expensive alarm system installed that was hooked up to the Sheriff's office. The heavy oak doors were fitted with substantial locks, chains, and steel brackets and bars, the latter protection added in the beginning of the present emergency. Two armed guards with trained German shepherd dogs had afforded still additional protection, the dogs and men having been hired from a professional security agency to patrol the grounds and guard the house, day and night.

John Carter and Flack had driven the truck onto the grounds of the Kingsley estate. Just inside the entrance gate, they stopped the truck, leaving the Miller girls lying in the back, and got out. They began to walk toward the distant house. One of the two security guards saw the uniform and walked over, hoping for news of what was happening outside the estate. As soon as he came within range of the two men, he and the dog were shot, Carter and Flack killing with one bullet each. Then they ran back to the truck and sped down the tree-shaded road to the main house. Carter spotted the other guard and dog, and the grisly scene was played again. Taking advantage of the uniform, Carter hailed the man, and then he and Flack finished off both guard and dog. They arrived at the front door of the mansion and as soon as the maid had let in Trooper Carter and Deputy Flack and led them to Gordon Kingsley, they pulled their guns and demanded that everyone in the house be ordered into the living room. At gunpoint, the Kingsleys allowed themselves to be tied up, and had to watch as their maid and butler were shot. The two bodies were tossed on the lawn.

Now mother, father and son were bound and gagged in their own living room. From other parts of the house they could hear the sounds of Flack and Carter opening closets, going through drawers, looking for items of value. In the living room the TV was on, Carter and Flack having entered during the middle of a Civil Defense broadcast. With frightened eyes, the captives twisted their bodies to look at the television. On-screen was Reverend Michaels, explaining why he and his people believed the dead had to be spiked.

"God alone has the power over life and death. He has promised to call us all on Judgment Day. The rising of the dead prematurely is the work of Satan, defying the power of the Lord, punishing humanity for being weak and sinful. It is we who have failed God and have given the Devil this unholy power over Him. It is we who must repent and give power and glory to the Lord. We are part of His flesh, one with His body, and because we have been weak we have weakened Him..."

The broadcast continued, Reverend Michaels' words penetrating the hearts and minds of the prisoners on the floor, filling them with dread and fear of their impending fate.

Dave Benton turned off the engine to Henry Dorsey's car, got out, and closed the door gently. With each mile, he prayed the heap he was driving would last one more. But the battery seemed to be in good condition, and he hoped there was enough gas to get him out of here if he had to make a hasty exit. He could not count on being able to capture Carter's truck or commandeer one of Kingsley's fleet of cars, and this shuddering pile of ancient parts was all he had.

Dave looked around him. He was at the end of the long Kingsley driveway, about a quarter mile from the house. Armed with the knife and ax, it was his intention to work his way closer from here. He kept off the gravel driveway, walking in the shelter of the shadows from a row of evenly spaced maple trees. Two rows of trees ran the length of the driveway, keeping it in perpetual shade. Because of the curve of the driveway, Dave could see only a corner of Carter's truck, which was parked close to the house. The house looked quiet, and he could see no sign of Flack or Carter or the girls. Nobody seemed to be on guard outside. The two bandits must be pretty confident of themselves, he thought. Moving quickly and cautiously, keeping to cover where possible, Dave worked his way toward the mansion. He moved out of the trees and stepped behind a tall shrub, giving himself a better view of the expansive front lawn, meticulously landscaped and trimmed.

There were ghouls on the lawn, at least half a dozen of them, gathering together, meandering around in little groups, as if gaining courage to attack the house. Dave shrank back behind the shelter of his shrub, and a shudder went through his body. One of the ghouls appeared to have some sort of uniform on. Perhaps it was Carter; perhaps he had been killed in his attempt to gain access to the Kingsley grounds. But no—it was not a State Trooper uniform; it was more like the uniform of some type of security guard—and with a pang Dave realized that was probably what it was: a guard killed by Carter and Flack when they had attacked the house.

Dave heard footsteps on the gravel, and he spun around to see a humanoid crossing the driveway, moving painfully, headed his way. This humanoid was also dressed in the uniform of a security guard. The guard had been killed by a shotgun blast, part of his chest having been blown away along with the bottom part of his chin, so that the front of the uniform was a bloody mass of ragged cloth and blasted, riddled flesh. A fragment of jawbone with its lower teeth hung uselessly from a relatively intact upper jaw. Still the thing was driven by an urge for live human flesh and continued to come at Dave blindly, its face ghastly, bloodless and white, its eyes popped partway out of their sockets by the force of the shotgun blast that had made it one of the walking dead.

Terror filled every cell in Dave's body as he prepared to receive the force of the thing's attack, knowing he had to vanquish it somehow without calling attention to the struggle, without alerting either the other ghouls in the middle of the lawn or the men inside the Kingsley house. He had only seconds to steel himself as the dead creature moved slowly toward him, its lungs rasping and groaning eerily in painful accompaniment to its awkward movements. Dave stood his ground, forcing himself to wait until the thing was almost upon him, reaching out a bony hand to clutch him by the throat. Then Dave swung the ax as hard as he could and hit his target, cleaving through the dead skull. With a last groan and a splatter of brains, the dead thing went down with a heavy thud and did not move at all. The ax blow had been strong and true, destroying the brain centers activating the fiendish humanoid. Dave needed to look at it only a second to realize it would get up no more. Then he peered frantically out across the lawn, toward the spot where the group of humanoids had been. They were still there, and had not been alarmed. It took a lot of sound to stimulate their dead ears. Through his fright, Dave felt a tiny measure of relief. He hid behind a bush and he looked toward the house. Then he looked at his bloodied ax blade and knelt to wipe it off in the grass.

At that instant, with a shatter of glass, a rifle barrel was poked through a pane of glass in a downstairs window of the mansion, and the man behind the rifle began firing away. Flack had heard the sounds of Dave's struggles with the attacking ghoul, the groaning and the crash of metal on bone. Flack fired five or six rounds, peppering the party of ghouls in the lawn, but he didn't score any good hits. The ghouls were too far away. Flack got one in the chest, felling it dramatically enough so that it would have stayed down if it were human, but it merely rolled around and struggled to its feet and got up again. Flack quit firing. From behind his bush, Dave watched the rifle barrel being withdrawn from the window. He was pretty sure Flack hadn't seen him, and the noise just attracted him to a window where he noticed the things on the lawn.

Keeping to the shelter of the maple trees, Dave again began to work his way toward the house. When he had advanced about twenty yards further, a noise startled him and he stopped, rooted in his tracks, peering from behind the trunk of a tree.

The bars on the front door of the mansion were being undone. The door opened, and the Kingsley family hobbled out, bound and gagged, herded and prodded by Flack's rifle. A grin on his face, Flack stepped out onto the porch behind them. He had used the lengths of rope which previously tied them to pieces of furniture to tie them to each other, so that they could move only by lifting their legs and setting them down in unison. Flack laughed when the boy fell down and dragged his parents down with him. He prodded them with his rifle and waited while they all got to their feet. He herded them down off the porch and out into the middle of the lawn. Some distance away, a group of the dead things stood waiting.

"Come on," Flack said. "Step lively. We're all going for a nice little walk." The grin on his face grew more pronounced as he glanced around to make sure nothing was sneaking up on him.

Dave had to watch this hideous tableau, helpless to do anything to prevent it. He was too far away to make a rush for Flack; if he tried it Flack would merely shoot him down or else he would be jumped by the flesh-hungry ghouls. He knew Flack was going to kill the Kingsley family by feeding them to the ghouls, or else, he hoped, Flack was planning to force information out of the Kingsleys by just threatening them with that cruel fate. Either way, Dave could do nothing about it. He was too vulnerable, and would end up as zombie feed himself if he acted rashly. If he could not save the Kingsleys, maybe he could still rescue the Miller girls.

While Flack was preoccupied with his game of forcing the Kingsleys further out onto the lawn, Dave continued sneaking toward the house. When Flack came back to the porch, Dave wanted to be waiting. He made a break from behind a hedge after making sure that Flack was not watching, diving for safety behind the shrubs at the side of the porch, and looked up at the sound of Flack's insane laughter.

Flack had walked the Kingsleys far out onto the front lawn, within thirty feet of the group of flesh-eaters, and then had shoved the father to the ground, laughing as his body weight dragged his wife and son down with him. Bound and gagged, the family could not scream, could only scramble and struggle futilely as the ghouls advanced toward them. Flack backed away laughing, watching the ghouls close in.

In a matter of minutes, the Kingsleys were all dead, the flesh-eaters having converged upon them to rip and tear at the more vulnerable parts of their bodies—the soft flesh of necks, breasts, abdomens. Somehow the fact that there were no dying screams made the deaths more horrifying, thought Dave, as he watched from beside the porch. Flack backed up onto the porch steps, watching the ghouls fight over the newly dead flesh and the soft internal organs.

Flack did not see Dave coming. He had no time to think before his skull was split apart by a single blow from Dave's ax. Dave jumped back, splattered with Flack's blood, as the man fell without so much as a groan and tumbled down the porch steps, his rifle cracking against the pavement with a loud alarming sound. Dave was on Flack, sinking his ax into Flack's chest for good measure, the ax hewing through the bones of the sternum with a splintering noise that brought a gush of blood from punctured lungs. The second blow was unnecessary, the man dead instantly from the ax-stroke that had cleaved through his skull, but Dave needed to do something to let out, in a violent way, some of his anger and satisfy his fired-up thirst for revenge.

Dave snatched up Flack's rifle, worried that the gun might have been damaged upon striking the pavement. He worked the lever a couple of times and saw cartridges chambered and rejected—a good sign; the rifle was probably still working. The firing mechanism had, hopefully, remained intact.

Rifle ready, Dave mounted the porch steps and entered the house through the front door which Flack had unbarred. Flack's body remained at the foot of the porch steps, his chest cleaved through with Dave's ax, the blade still buried deep in his lungs, the ax handle sticking up in the air.

Dave found himself in a large foyer. To the right was the living room and directly ahead he saw a wooden banister and a long flight of curved, carpeted stairs. Dave heard noises from upstairs, the sounds of John Carter still going through dresser drawers, looting the master bedroom. "That you, Flack?" Carter called out. "Did you feed the zombies?"

Dave cupped his hand over his mouth and yelled off to one side, to disguise his voice, "Yeah! Everything's taken care of!" He clattered around, making a lot of noise on purpose while he re-barred the front door, hoping to lull Carter's suspicions by showing that, like Flack, he was not afraid to make noise. Then he advanced up the stairs, moving normally, knowing that Carter would hear his footsteps and think he was Flack.

In the master bedroom, John Carter had an opened suitcase spread out on the bed. The suitcase was half filled with jewelry, silverware, cash—whatever the room had contained that could be sold easily or turned over to a fence. Carter stood over the booty, eyeing it with a satisfied look. For a long moment, he did not even bother to look up when Dave Benton entered; then he looked and had a chance to register the surprise of recognizing Dave before Dave squeezed the trigger.

The loud report echoed in the room as Carter was blown back against a bedroom window, shattering the glass. The wrought-iron grillwork prevented Carter's body from falling through the window into the yard below. Dave fired again, the bullet ripping another hole in Carter's chest as he was going down, his body jerking with the force of the bullet's impact as still another shot was fired and the dead weight hit the floor. Dave worked the lever on Flack's rifle, ejecting a spent cartridge and chambering another round. He stepped over to Carter's motionless body, pointed the muzzle of the rifle at Carter's head, and squeezed the trigger. Another loud report crashed in the room as the bullet smacked into Carter's dead brain.

Dave cocked the rifle again and left the room, hurrying down the hall to still another bedroom. The door was half ajar. He kicked the door open and jumped back, half-expecting the report of a gun, but nothing came and Dave slowly entered the room. There were two four-poster beds, and on the beds were the two Miller girls, Ann and Sue Ellen, each tied and gagged, their bodies naked with their arms and legs spread-eagled and roped to the posts of the beds. They strained to look up at Dave, the fear in their faces softening when they realized he was neither Carter nor Flack. He bent over Sue Ellen first, because she was the closest one, and undid her gag. He told them who he was and, very briefly, what had happened. Before she could find words to speak he asked, "Anyone else in the house? Anyone besides Carter and Flack?"

"The Kingsleys...," Sue Ellen said. "The Kingsleys are prisoners downstairs."

"Anyone else?" Dave insisted. "Anyone who would be an enemy to us?"

Sue Ellen shook her head, perplexed and frightened. "No...no one. No one but Carter and Flack."

"They're dead," Dave said. "I killed them. The Kingsleys are dead, too. Where's Billy?"

Dave had his answer when Sue Ellen buried her face in her hands and began to cry. Still gagged, Ann continued to stare, her eyes filling with tears. As soon as she was untied she intended to ask about her sister Karen.

24

A convoy of trucks, ambulances and patrol cars brought Sheriff Conan McClellan and his men to the beginning of the private road that led from the edge of the highway through a stretch of woods to the Kingsley estate. The Sheriff climbed out of a patrol car and shouted a few orders while he waited for the men to form up. They intended to go the rest of the way on foot, checking out the care-taker's cottage en route to the mansion itself. The ambulances and patrol cars would remain on call in case they were needed. The trucks would proceed into town and refuel and load up with coffee and food for the tired and hungry men.

Overhead a helicopter circled, beating the air with metal wings, as it dipped and hovered, scanning the woods and meadows for signs of humanoids or people in need of help. One of the posse members had a walkie-talkie strapped on his back, by means of which McClellan and his men maintained contact with the helicopter and the patrol cars.

McClellan used a dirty, balled-up handkerchief to wipe sweat from his brow as he watched his men forming up in the middle of the road. The posse had been organized in a hurry, and many of its members were inexperienced and did not have the proper gear for living in the woods. In addition to the normally difficult problems of feeding and supplying a posse of forty or fifty men, there had been myriad pesky complaints common to novices such as poison ivy and blistered feet. Through it all, McClellan had alternately bullied and pampered the men, trying to keep them on the move in a disciplined fashion, combing the rural areas in search of those who might require aid or rescue.

The county had been divided into sectors, each sector to be pa-trolled by posse volunteers, policemen and National Guard troops. The objectives were to re-establish communications in areas where lines were down or power stations were out of commission; to bring safety and law and order to villages and larger communities, where order was threatened not only by marauding ghouls but by looters and rapists taking advantage of the chaos created by the emergency; and to send rescue parties out into rural or remote areas, where people could be trapped in their homes with no way of defending themselves adequately or calling for help.

McClellan's sector happened to be a particularly dangerous one, especially bothered by gangs of looters and hoodlums. He wondered if it were perhaps because of the unusual number of isolated and wealthy families, such as the Kingsleys. The county had once been a profitable coal mining area, and men had built fortunes from the mines as owners and overseers. These men had erected mansions and country clubs close to the source of their wealth, while around them, in contrast, clustered the poor of the mining towns—many of them now ghost towns—and the poor of the marginal farms, many still kept in operation by stubborn men like Henry Dorsey and Bert Miller. Gordon Kingsley had inherited wealth from the mines. McClellan's men were not overly anxious to help Kingsley or his family, the men feeling rightly or wrongly that they had been oppressed all their lives by toil in the Kingsley mines or factories, or by harsh dealings with Kingsley's banks and finance companies when the mines petered out and the county became poor. The men felt that Kingsley could afford his own protection and many resented being there and could not understand why they came to his land. Because Gordon Kingsley was so tight-fisted with a dollar, they muttered, other men—common men—had to risk their lives in his behalf. Because of these sentiments, McClellan, who knew his job was to protect everybody, wealthy or not, felt he had to drive the men a little harder and watch over them a little more carefully to make sure they continued to do a conscientious job.

The things they had found out at the Dorsey farmhouse, on their way to the main highway which would take them to the Kingsley estate, had helped spur on the men and forestall some of their grumbling and complaining. Henry Dorsey had refused to leave his isolated farmhouse for the protection of the city; he said he had done all right so far, by God, and would continue to fend for himself come hell or high water. He asked only for additional ammunition for his two rifles, after McClellan volunteered the information that the power lines would be fixed more than likely by the end of the day, and families such as the Dorseys would be able to communicate with firemen and police. McClellan said the emergency might be brought under control sooner than anybody originally expected, but it would be rough going for a couple more weeks. Dorsey said he would do okay for himself, and added that if everybody had continued to spike the dead as he had done to his own daughter, the thing wouldn't have happened in the first place. He then told about the State Trooper he had helped to go after the captured Miller girls. According to Dorsey, the Trooper was under the impression that the gang that had captured the girls was headed for the Kingsley estate. Dorsey did not mention the hand he and his son had taken in the other State Trooper's death; after all, if Dave was dead by now, nobody might ever find out. Carl Martinelli's body was no longer out on the lawn; apparently it had been carried off and devoured by a party of ghouls.

All during the discussion with the Sheriff, which took place in the Dorsey's boarded-up living room, Henry Dorsey refrained from mentioning anything about the baby his wife was watching upstairs in one of the bedrooms. The baby remained quiet, apparently sleeping, as it had done since having taken the little bit of milk. Mrs. Dorsey kept her eyes on the baby, made sure it stayed covered by its blanket, and thought she had never seen a baby look or behave so strangely. Still, the poor thing was lucky to be alive. Wasn't it? She shuddered and bit her lip against the frightening thought which forced its way into her confused mind and made her face tighten with nervousness and panic.

The information about the gang of looters and the captured girls pursued by the State Trooper, passed on by McClellan immediately to his tired and grumbling men, encouraged them to go on and to work harder. Now they realized it was not just the likes of Gordon Kingsley for whom they were working. They had a real mission ahead of them that they could believe in with more enthusiasm. Some of the men had been acquainted with Bert Miller and his daughters. Most of them did not care much for Bert while he was alive, but they respected him in death and sympathized with the girls as they would with anyone who was fatherless and homeless. It was easier for them to care about the Millers, being of their own class, than to care about Gordon Kingsley. If there had been a reward offered for saving Kingsley, it would have been a different matter.

Despite the extreme physical tiredness he felt, plus his exhausted emotions, Sheriff McClellan thought he could feel the emergency winding down. The ranks of the living dead were in a sense finite, replenished only by the newly dead who rose to take the place of those who were vanquished. Each humanoid shot down diminished the ranks by itself and its potential victims. The situation could be brought under control by making sure that all dead bodies were destroyed. When all the humanoids were "killed" there would be no more danger from them. They could not reproduce like humans; they were creatures of death, to be kept dead by destroying their brains. The procedure followed by McClellan's men was to avoid tangling with the flesh-eaters at close range and gunning them down at a distance. Then, by using meat hooks, they would drag the dead things to a pile, soak them with gasoline, and set fire to them. Anyone who had touched a meat hook, or anything suspected of being in contact with a ghoul, would wash his hands with plenty of soap and water and afterward in a strong solution of alcohol. So far these measures had seemed sufficient to prevent infection. They were the same measures followed once before, during the first outbreak of the disease which prevented total death and turned human beings against each other.

25

Flack could not hear his limbs being torn from his dead body. He could not hear bones and cartilage being twisted and broken and separated at the joints. He could not cry out when the ravenous ghouls ripped out his heart and lungs and kidneys and intestines, their task made easier by the ax that had cleaved through his torso, shattering the sternum.

The ghouls fought among themselves, clawed and struggled with each other for possession of the once living organs. Then, once Flack's body was completely destroyed, they went off, each to crouch alone with its meal, each aware of the presence of other hungry ghouls looking on, waiting for a chance to seize whatever organ or piece of the human body the lucky ones had managed to claim. The flesh-eaters were like dogs, dragging their bones off to a corner to chew and gnaw, while other dogs looked on.

Several of the ghouls, in search of a comfortable place to eat where they would not have to defend their meals from others, wandered back into the protection of the dark green woods surrounding the sculpted lawn of the Kingsley grounds. There they sat and ate, the sounds of teeth biting and ripping into dead human flesh and the rasping of the heavy breathing of dead lungs mingling with the chirping of birds and the rustling of wind through the leaves of trees in the hot, sunny afternoon.

From a window in the living room of the mansion, Dave Benton saw Flack's body being ripped apart. He watched the ghouls fighting over bits and chunks of Flack's corpse, and felt relieved when their struggle and their desire to sneak away with their prizes caused them to back off from their proximity to the front porch. Though Flack's fate was not undeserved, it sickened Dave to see it meted out. The result of the death of Flack and the death of the Kingsley family was that the ghouls had been temporarily satisfied in their craving for human flesh, and Dave felt that an escape from the house could be attempted. He had the keys to Carter's truck, which he had taken from the gang leader's pocket. He also had guns and ammunition.

Ann and Sue Ellen were still in a state of shock over their experiences of the past forty-eight hours. They had told Dave of the death of Billy, fed to the ghouls while Carter and Flack and Wade Connely made good their escape from the Miller farmhouse. Dave had tried to be as kind as possible in letting the girls know of the death of Karen and the birth of her baby, now being cared for by the Dorsey family.

The two sisters were sitting on a sofa in the Kingsley living room, not moving much or saying anything. The relief they felt at being rescued from Carter and Flack was muted by the emotion-shattering events of the past two days and their anxiety over what may be still to come. They had watched without speaking a Civil Defense broadcast which Dave had tuned in on the television. The commentator had made the point that teams of rescue workers were trying to get to those people trapped in remote areas. But the rescue efforts were proceeding slowly, hampered by the breakdown in law and order, and isolated people were warned not to count too heavily on being rescued; they were urged to make escape attempts if at all possible, and to try to get to emergency outposts or refugee centers. The commentator emphasized that those who did not get help or succeed in escaping stood a good chance of being eventually outnumbered and overrun by the marauding ghouls.

Dave had made up his mind to make a break from the Kingsley house. The ghouls were preoccupied with the remains of Flack and the Kingsley family. Dave reasoned that if he had driven to the estate without much trouble he should be able to escape from there. He could take the girls with him in Carter's truck, if they felt up to it, or he could go himself and bring help when he reached an emergency outpost. He had rifles and pistols and plenty of ammunition. He could leave weapons for the girls to defend themselves while he fought his way to safety. He felt the house was barricaded enough for the girls to remain safe inside.

When the TV broadcast was over, Dave turned the set off and confronted Ann and Sue Ellen. Patiently, in a lowered voice which he hoped sounded reasonable and kind, he went over the facts of their situation as he understood it. He explained that the phones were dead, possibly put out of commission by Carter and Flack or simply because so many lines were out everywhere. The two choices they had were to wait for rescue, which might never come, or to make a break for it. Dave said that one possibility was for him to try and make the escape alone, with the girls waiting for him at the house. If they felt up to it, he offered to take them with him, but wondered if that would not be more dangerous for them. He suggested that if he did go alone, and did not return in a reasonable amount of time, the girls should try and escape themselves in one of the Kingsley automobiles.

As Dave talked, he convinced himself that he should try to make it on his own, since if he did not succeed, Ann and Sue Ellen would still have a second chance. Someone might show up to rescue them, or, as they discussed, the girls could make their own run for safety. After some consideration, and perhaps a little unwitting prompting from Dave, the girls agreed to this strategy. Ann, more than Sue Ellen, seemed to have her wits about her. Dave found himself directing his comments mostly to her, in his efforts to impress upon the two sisters the measures they must take to keep the house secure in his absence and, in case his efforts met with doom, how they must go about trying to save themselves.

With Ann standing by with a loaded pistol at the unboarded door, Dave made a foray out to Carter's truck. He tested the keys in the ignition and checked the fuel gauge for a supply of gasoline. The tank was three-quarters full and the engine turned over easily and ran smoothly. The truck appeared to be in good condition, except for the battering it had taken in traversing rough terrain and thudding into and running over the humanoids that had chanced into its path. In the glove compartment Dave even found an owner's card, made out to John W. Carter. So, mused Dave, the truck had not been stolen; it had been Carter's legitimate property, and Carter had been his real name.

Having made sure that the truck would perform and that he would not get stuck inside it with a dead battery or empty fuel tank and an army of approaching ghouls, Dave turned the vehicle around and brought it close to the front porch of the house, where it would be handy for him to make his escape attempt. Then he went back into the house to complete his preparations. Ann and Sue Ellen watched while he loaded a rifle and revolver and checked the firing mechanism of each. He gave the girls a final briefing. Then Ann opened the front door for him, stood guard with the pistol he had given her while he got down off the porch and into the truck, and then she locked the door and barred it after he had gone. From the window she watched the pickup truck move at a rapid pace down the gravel driveway and out toward the dirt road. Across the yard, several ghouls started to move lethargically toward the truck as it gathered speed.

26

The helicopter hovered above the caretaker's cottage while a party of McClellan's men advanced. On his walkie-talkie, a posse member received word from a man on the helicopter crew that for the past five or ten minutes there had been no signs of movement in the immediate vicinity of the cottage. The foliage of the surrounding woods was thick, and it was impossible to see the ground from the air. If there were humanoids concealed among the trees, the men would have to go in with weapons and root them out.

On orders from a police sergeant, the men fanned out and approached the caretaker's cottage in the clear. There was no need to chance sending men into the trees and brush until an effort had been made to save whoever might still be in the cottage. Weapons ready and eyes peeled for possible danger, the men worked their way to about fifty yards from the cottage and took cover behind trees, hedges and stone fences.

The police sergeant shouted for anybody in the cottage to come out, emphasizing that he was a police officer and had come to provide help. As he could have predicted, his shouts got no response. The door to the cottage was wide open, the windows smashed in. The place had the feel of terror and death. Covered by the men who remained behind, a squad advanced and moved into the cottage. They found the signs of a terrific battle which had been waged between the people of the cottage and a party of attacking humanoids, a battle which the people had lost. There were half-eaten human remains in various parts of the house, as though the ghouls had gorged themselves and stopped, or maybe had been driven off.

McClellan arrived on the scene with the remainder of the posse, received a report which he accepted with resignation, with no outward show of emotion, and formed the men up to move on to the Kingsley mansion. The men continued to move on foot, spreading out to cover as much as possible of the terrain on both sides of the road, while ambulances and emergency vehicles followed at some distance to the rear on the dirt road. So far the men had not spotted any ghouls since disembarking from their trucks at the entrance to the Kingsley property, and this led them to expect trouble as they got closer to the mansion itself. They also knew, from McClellan's briefing, that they had to keep a sharp lookout for the gang of looters who had captured the Miller girls and were out to rob the Kingsleys or hold them for ransom. The tension among the men, especially the civilians, increased to a degree that was noticeable in the strain of their voices and the wariness of their movements as they advanced down the dirt road.

When Dave rounded a curve and saw the figure in the middle of the road, he stepped on the gas, hitting the man and knocking him into the air. Seeing the man frozen in his tracks with a drawn pistol just before the moment of impact, Dave had time to realize his mistake just as a shot rang out and a rifle bullet smashed into his brain. Then there was a barrage of shots as the truck was riddled, its glass shattered, Dave's body jerking and being pumped full of slugs. A bullet penetrated the fuel tank, the hit resulting in a tremendous fiery explosion, sending bits of metal flying through the ranks of the posse members still firing their weapons from where they had taken cover in the trees along the side of the road.

No one was hit by the shards from the truck.

Having been shocked into a cease-fire, the men stayed rooted in their positions for a long moment, as they watched the truck being consumed by fire. They did not doubt that they had killed one of the looters in the act of trying to make good his escape.

One of the men shouted for an ambulance as he knelt over the man who had been struck by the truck. The ambulance moved up slowly past the men who had to be told to clear out of the road. A couple of medics got out of the ambulance carrying a stretcher and some first aid equipment. The man who had been hit by the truck was not dead, but he was in shock, had suffered numerous bruises and lacerations, and his leg was broken. The attendants worked over the man, got him covered up and onto the stretcher and into the ambulance, which they proceeded to try to turn around in the road at a place where there was barely sufficient room to execute the maneuver.

McClellan swore under his breath as he watched the ambulance drive off, escorted by patrol cars in front and behind. For the sake of one badly wounded man, the supporting vehicles were now diminished by three. And who knew what was in store at the Kingsley place?

The Sheriff and some of the policemen in uniform got the rest of the men moved around the site of the burning truck so the march could be continued toward the main house. The man with the walkie-talkie had already put in a call for a tow truck to move the wreckage out of the middle of the road, so that other emergency vehicles would not be obstructed if they were needed.

McClellan did not know who had been killed in the burning truck, and he did not take it for granted that it had been one of the looters. He had asked for a description of the incident from several of the men who were close by, and nothing that they said totally erased the possibility that a mistake had been made as the result of spur-of-the-moment panic on the part of the truck driver and the edgy posse members. The Sheriff had seen worse things happen many times during his long career.

Just behind the spot where the truck was burning in the road, a police van pulled up and a group of policemen stood by while the driver of the van, also a policeman, came around to the rear of the vehicle and unlocked the doors. The van was full of police dogs, German shepherds, each dog trained and managed by one of the officers who now put the dogs on leashes and moved out to join the rest of the posse in their intensified advance.

In the distance could be heard the whir of the helicopter as it circled and hovered over the Kingsley mansion and the surrounding area, the men in the helicopter radioing reports to the men on the ground, telling them of the parties of ghouls dotting the grounds of the Kingsley estate. Finally the helicopter began to dip lower and to hover in places where men with rifles could fire at the ghouls from the safety of their whirring aircraft. They did not score too many hits in this way. Aiming for the head was difficult, and the sound of the helicopter tended to drive the humanoids back into the trees where it would be difficult for the men on foot to root them out and shoot them down. In a short while the tactic was abandoned, and the pilot took his machine higher to hover and circle while the men on the ground moved up.

Inside the house, Ann and Sue Ellen heard the helicopter in its maneuvers over the house and grounds. The sound of the machine frightened them at first, then gave them heart as they realized what it was. They were about to be rescued! Dave must have made good his escape. But then the helicopter went away, its whirring sound getting weaker and weaker until it could barely be heard. Ann Miller listened intently, watching from the windows until the roar of the helicopter's metal blades got stronger again. This time it seemed to be hovering right over the house.

"We've got to go outside," Ann said. "We can't take a chance on its going away again."

Sue Ellen did not reply, merely looked scared, as she kept her eyes riveted on the ceiling in a pose that seemed to say she could see the helicopter through the bricks and plaster of the house.

Ann knew Sue Ellen was terrified, and if anything were to be done she would have to do it herself. "I'll go out on the porch," she said. "I'll take the rifle. You stand watch by the door." She said these things looking at Sue Ellen, who did not look at her. Then she went back to the window, pulled back the heavy brocade curtain and looked out. The immediate area around the house seemed clear. But the helicopter had gone away again; it was hovering over a group of ghouls way out on the edge of the lawn. As Ann watched, men in the helicopter opened fire on the ghouls, hitting one and knocking it down while the rest retreated awkwardly and hid themselves in a clump of trees. The helicopter immediately rose in the air, and Ann expected it to go away, but instead it circled back toward the house where it hovered once more, directly overhead, the sound of the thing seeming to radiate straight down through the ceiling.

Ann whirled around and confronted her sister. "Sue Ellen—open the door! I'm going out!" She took her sister by the hand and led her to the door where they both began removing the bars.

The helicopter still kept hovering and circling over the house. Ann opened the door cautiously and stepped over the threshold, anxiously peering back to make sure that Sue Ellen stayed in the doorway with her pistol, keeping watch. Ann looked up, and moved to the edge of the porch. The helicopter made a wide circle, and Ann waved. To her surprise and delight the pilot dipped and waved back. Ann smiled and waved frantically. The pilot circled tightly and waved again. Convinced that the men in the helicopter knew she was a human being who needed help, Ann backed into the house and shut the door.

"They saw me," Ann cried. "We're going to be rescued for sure!" She hugged Sue Ellen, and they began to weep before they thought of securing the door. All they had to do was sit tight until their rescuers arrived.

"Ghouls! Ghouls—all over the place!" a voice yelled, and a bevy of gunshots split the air.

More men moved up, running and firing from behind trees.

The police dogs growled and strained at their leashes, hating the scent of the dead things.

The posse advanced in squads, firing repeatedly, felling the dead things with a hail of bullets.

Each time a ghoul fell, one of the men moved forward and hacked at it with a machete, until the head was severed from the body, making doubly sure the thing would not get up again.

Sheriff McClellan and his men had advanced to the lawn of the Kingsley mansion and were crouching and firing repeatedly, blasting down the dead creatures that surrounded the place.

"Shoot for the eyes, boys!" McClellan cried out. "Like I told you before—if you aim for the eyes you're gonna hit the head!" He aimed his own high-powered rifle and fired, and a dead thing fifty feet in front of him clutched at its face with a convulsive movement and toppled to the earth with a dull thud.

More gunshots rang out. And two more of the ghouls fell heavily to the ground.

"Get up here, boys!" McClellan yelled. "There's three more for the fire!"

The men with machetes moved up and, hacking quickly and furiously, severed the heads from the dead ghouls.

The flurry of gunfire was constant—*crack!*—*crack!*—*crack!*—as the posse surrounded the Kingsley house.

Then there was silence, as all the ghouls had apparently been felled, and the men's eyes scanned the house and its surrounding lawn, looking for a new target to gun down.

McClellan knew by means of a radio message from the men in the helicopter that at least one of the Miller girls was alive and well inside the Kingsley house. When he and his men had worked their way closer, he himself stepped up onto the front porch and rapped on the door—an action that struck him as a weirdly ordinary finale to the bizarre and unnerving events which had happened just before. He waited while the bars were removed and the door swung open slowly. Ann stood just inside the foyer, a shocked look on her face and a rifle in her hand.

McClellan did not jump back. The rifle was being clutched by its foregrip in a weak and inept way which told him that the numbed girl was certainly not going to use it in any dangerous way. When he took a step toward her, the rifle dropped to the floor, landing softly on the plush carpet, as the girl collapsed in his arms. There was another girl sitting quietly on the sofa, a pistol lying on the floor between her shoes.

In the surrounding woods, sporadic gunfire continued.

27

Escorted by an ambulance and two patrol cars full of armed men, Sheriff McClellan rode with Ann and Sue Ellen to the Dorsey farmhouse, where they expected to claim Karen's baby and take it in the ambulance to the nearest hospital.

They found the Dorsey place overrun, the family apparently the victims of a force of ghouls too numerous for them to overcome. The doors to the farmhouse were battered down, the windows broken in. There were no remains of the Dorseys. McClellan suspected that the family had been carried off and ripped apart elsewhere.

There were no ghouls around either. They must have done their damage and wandered off with their bellies full.

Pistols drawn, McClellan and two of his men entered the house. The place was quiet and still as death. The living room and kitchen had been wrecked in the final battle which had taken place. There were bloodstains, but no other signs of the ghoulish attack. McClellan began to wonder if, in those last moments, the family had panicked and run from the house. He mounted the stairs, followed by both of his men.

A bedroom door was half ajar. McClellan nudged the door open and pointed his pistol inside. He saw a tiny infant, alone by itself on the bed. The baby appeared to be asleep. The Sheriff gathered it up in its blanket and carried it downstairs to the patrol car which contained the Miller girls.

Ann and Sue Ellen smiled wanly as the Sheriff approached with the bundle in his arms. He smiled himself, as he bent and peeled the blanket from the baby's face. The two sisters began to cry. Ann took the baby from the Sheriff.

"We'll have him taken care of," McClellan said. "Or her, as the case may be. We'll get it a thorough checkup at the hospital and get the little rascal off on the right foot. If you don't feel able to take care of it, well, maybe me and the wife..."

"Oh, no!" Ann said. "We *want* the baby. It's all we have left of Karen. She'd *want* it that way."

She looked down at the baby and tried to smile but the smile didn't come. She wondered why the baby stared with its eyes so wide, so lusterless, so lacking the sparkle of new life. Yet it continued to breathe.